"Bob Proehl is one of those authors you can trust to guide you out of your comfort zone. *The Nobody People* is a gripping, haunting, and complex book, perfect for our times. It will take you on a warrior's journey. In fact, I'm reminded of something Gandalf said to Bilbo at the outset of *The Hobbit*: '... if you *do* [come back], you won't be the same.'"

—Michael Poore,
author of *Reincarnation Blues*

BY BOB PROEHL

A Hundred Thousand Worlds
The Nobody People

THE SOMEBODY PEOPLE

THE SOMEBODY PEOPLE

BOB PROEHL

NEW YORK

A Del Rey Trade Paperback Original

Copyright © 2020 by Bob Proehl

Published in the United States by Del Rey,
an imprint of Random House, a division of
Penguin Random House LLC, New York.

DEL REY is a registered trademark and the CIRCLE colophon is a trademark
of Penguin Random House LLC.

ISBN 978-1-524-79900-7
Ebook ISBN 978-1-5247-9899-4

Printed in the United States of America on acid-free paper

randomhousebooks.com

2 4 6 8 9 7 5 3 1

Book design by Edwin Vazquez

To those charged with fixing things we broke,
and those whose broken things we tried to fix

THE SOMEBODY PEOPLE

PROLOGUE
STARING AT THE SEA
1998

And in the red clouds rose a Wonder o'er
    the Atlantic sea—
Intense! naked! a Human fire fierce
    glowing, as the wedge
Of iron heated in the furnace; his terrible
    limbs were fire,
With myriads of Cloudy terrors banners
    dark, and towers
Surrounded.

—WILLIAM BLAKE,
America a Prophecy

A million tiny things add up to a death. Take away one, and life goes on. Laid out in perfect sequence, they lead to an end.

On Wednesday, two fifth-years at the Bishop Academy for the Arts turned in the same term paper, word for word. The teacher hauled them into Headmaster Kevin Bishop's office and left them to his judgment. Elton Daly claimed Marcine Walden psychically poached the paper from him, and Marcine insisted any theft was accidental. She was a dreamwalker, roaming the sleeping minds of students in the dorms while she slept. It was possible she *experienced* the paper while wandering through Elton's dream. She had no more control over it than any dreamer has over their own path. The way she saw it, *she* was the victim, subject to the nightmares and wet dreams of her fellow students, unable to dream for herself.

Kevin's cellphone came to life in his pocket like a lively cricket. He continued listening to the argument, tenting his fingers under his chin in a display of interest. The quickest thing would be to pry into their minds and confirm what he suspected. Marcine had easy smarts and a deep current of intellectual laziness. Elton excelled in all his academics but was failing Psychic Defense. *God help me, I know them all so well,* he thought. Rather than investigate and dole out punishment, he facilitated reconciliation. Marcine would rewrite her paper with Elton's help and would teach him to keep his mind shut.

As they left his office, Kevin caught a spark pass between them—not romantic but an understanding of mutual interest, the seed of community. He smiled at the small joys and miseries of his job.

His phone showed three missed calls from Laura at her house in eastern Maine. After the calls was a text from her cell:

> *been meaning to call u but worried im overreacting. have concenrs abt bobby and hoping u cd come up and talk 2 him.*

The message was no different from hundreds of others he received at the academy. Mothers and fathers sure their children were a danger to themselves or others. *Concerns.* They all had *concerns.* Kevin checked his calendar, then texted back:

> *So nice to hear from you! It's been too long. Busy with academy stuff until the end of the week, but I can take the early train up on Saturday and be there by afternoon. It will be good to see you and Tom and Bobby.*

Waiting for a response, Kevin went into the Hive to find Bobby and do a quick assessment. He could see the boy, a shimmer among a sea of twinkling lights. Nothing remarkable, which wasn't a surprise. Bishop had watched Laura closely growing up, but her ability hadn't been that impressive: some minor light manipulation. The man she ended up with, over Kevin's mild objections, was a low-level precognitive who made a living beating the stock market by seeing shifts a few seconds ahead. These things weren't genetic, but there were trends. When Laura called to tell Bishop she was pregnant after a long period of drifting among the communes and kibbutzes Resonants had built across the world, Kevin bought her a house on Oceanside Drive, near his own. The enclave in Maine was a yuppie iteration of hippie ideals, a nice place to settle into if you never wanted to feel alone. Kevin rarely made it to his own house there, but Laura and Tom had been over the moon and had lived there full-time since Bobby was born.

The shimmer of Bobby Foster's Hivebody solidified, and he looked at Kevin quizzically. He was tiny, but that didn't mean anything. Kevin had students who were physically hulking but manifested in the Hive as ninety-pound weaklings, Charles Atlas ads in reverse.

"Hello, Bobby," Kevin said. "Your mom tells me you've started to resonate. That's very exciting."

Bobby's expression didn't change. He'd never been a cheerful kid, sullen even on the Christmases when Kevin went out to visit, accepting expensive toys from "Grandpa Kevin" with politeness but no enthusiasm. His Hivebody dissipated like smoke.

Kevin came out of the Hive and checked his phone. There was a text from Laura: *thx.*

Delays and distractions piled up. A million tiny things. He'd forgotten a dance recital on Saturday and bumped his trip back to Sunday, when the first train out wasn't until nine, with a long gap between connections in Boston. The Boston-to-Ogunquit line juddered and start-stopped along ancient tracks, and one lurch spilled Kevin's lukewarm coffee down the front of his white shirt. By the time the train pulled into the Ogunquit station, Kevin was annoyed with the whole trip. He called a cab that took forever to show up because it was the off-season and there was only one cab in town. He texted Laura that he had to stop by his house to get cleaned up and he'd be there shortly.

Kevin's house was a bungalow with a sliver of beachfront. He hired people to keep the place up and tried not to think of them as "staff." The yard was trimmed and the house was spotless, with not a speck of dust on the collection of maritime kitsch that had come with the house. Upstairs, the dressers and closets were stocked with clothes. Kevin often thought of retreating to the beach house on a whim, no suitcases, but it never worked out. The clothes he kept there were castoffs from a former life, shed skins. He picked out a chambray dress shirt that was too sharp at the shoulders to be fashionable and snug around his paunch. He walked down Oceanside Drive toward Laura and Tom's place as the daylight sputtered out behind a row of new construction, houses built tall on the hill to afford the owners views of the water. Their long shadows crept over the street, over the smaller houses bought early and cheap, and onto the beach, inching toward the incoming tide.

Laura and Tom's house was bigger than Kevin's but modest: a family home on a piece of the beach that transitioned from rough sand to sharp rock, down from the breakwall that protected the nicer homes farther down the street. Their lawn was littered with Bobby's toys, sun-faded primary-colored hunks of plastic with edges rounded for safety, some of which Kevin remembered purchasing. From under a miniature picnic table near the side of the house, Kevin heard a mewling sound and went toward it. Squatting onto his haunches, he came eye to eye with Easter, the elderly and round-faced silver tabby he'd bought for Laura on her twenty-fourth birthday. The plump cat's hind legs had been replaced with the back end of a gray seagull. The thin bird legs couldn't support Easter's bulk. She dragged herself toward Kevin on her forelegs, webbed feet slapping uselessly on the wet grass. Kevin held out a hand to the cat, which bowed her head like a condemned man waiting for the mercy of the ax. He scratched under her jaw as dread stirred in his guts.

Kevin heard another noise from inside the house. It was wheezing and plaintive, not unlike Easter's pained cry. He pulled his hand back and headed toward the house, Easter trying futilely to follow, calling for him to come back.

Having come from his own house, Kevin was reminded by Laura and Tom's living room that there was a difference between a well-kept house and a lived-in home. Simple clutter, the echoes of use, imbued warmth to a space. Here it was augmented by the smell of nag champa burning and a Tori Amos album on the stereo. Laura had played it constantly in the months after her mother died, the dancing piano and lilting soprano drifting out of her dorm room whenever Kevin went to check on her. A year later, when she told him kindly but firmly that she was too old to stay at the school any longer and that it was time for her to be out from under his care, he played the same album to fill the absence in her wake. The songs came to hold conflicting emotions that were impossible for the words and music to bear. He hadn't listened to it in years, and hearing it now brought him back to the day she left. He stood in the doorway, momentarily lost, until he heard a whine of pain and fear from the kitchen.

The tile floor was scattered with shards of broken glass and a pool of red wine Kevin mistook for blood. Laura sat on the floor, leaning against the side of a counter. Her eyes were panicked, and her thin cry got louder when she saw him. Jutting out of her right side, where her arm ought to be, was the torso of Tom, his Patriots T-shirt seamed together with her blouse in a line that ran across his chest from one shoulder to the opposite armpit. Kevin closed his eyes and tried to mentally sort them back into their proper places. He tried to superimpose the image of the two of them from the most recent photo they had sent: Laura and Tom on some faraway beach with the sun setting behind them. Bobby had stayed with Tom's parents for a few days—"figured you had enough kids to deal with" the note from Laura said. He tried to restore them to the way they looked at their wedding, watching through tears as the closest thing Kevin would ever have to a daughter walked away from him again, this time toward another man. When he opened his eyes, they were still an inextricable tangle of parts. The fusion was inexact, failing to connect Tom's upper chest to a working set of lungs. His eyes bulged out of their sockets, and his lips had the blue tinge of a drowning victim. Laura clawed at the line where the two bodies rudely intersected as if she could separate herself from the dead weight of him.

"Room," Laura said, squeezing the word out from overtaxed lungs. She twitched her shoulder to point, and the motion shook the body melded to hers, Tom's head lolling sickly to the side.

Kevin reached into what was left of her mind. It was noise and horror, nothing coherent enough to be called a thought. *Laura, honey, it's me,* he told her. *I'm going to make it better. I'm going to make it stop hurting. Laura, it's me. It's Dad.* He could count on one hand the number of times either of them had used the term. Her wedding. The death of her mother. Once, when she was thirteen and he'd made a particularly atrocious pun and she let it slip.

And now.

He found a static place, the still center where a determined mechanism kept her shocked body alive despite itself. With less effort than snuffing a candle, Kevin shut the machine down. Laura's body went mercifully limp. He eased her eyelids shut and then her husband's.

I'm sorry, Mona, he thought. *I promised you I'd keep her safe. If I'd been a day sooner. An hour.* A million things had lined up in a sequence and brought him here. Kevin stood silently over the bodies, his eyes streaming tears but his body taut and still. His mind searched the house for an impossible presence, someone he knew couldn't be there but he nonetheless suspected. There was nothing.

"Sad old idiot," Kevin muttered to himself, his voice broken and hoarse. The Tori Amos album faded out, and Kevin heard the soft babble of a child, punctuated with the caws of a gull, coming from the hallway off the kitchen, the direction Laura had gestured. He heard the whir of the CD player as the disc returned to the beginning and started up again.

Bobby sat cross-legged on his bed, cooing baby talk to a seagull with the hindquarters of a silver tabby. Kevin's mind reeled at the implication: somewhere in this house was the rest of Tom's body, topped with Laura's missing arm.

Bobby's features favored his mother, delicate and girlish. They reminded Kevin of Laura's father, whose image Kevin had seen in Laura's face the day he went and got Laura to hide her from a man who never bothered to come looking. Laura had her father's beautiful face, which she'd passed undiluted to Bobby. Bobby's hand ran along the animal's back from feathers to fur. Its tail went up, erect and panicked. Bobby stopped talking and looked up when Kevin stepped into the room.

"You're not my real grandpa," he said.

"Have you been talking to your grandpa, Bobby?" Kevin asked slowly and quietly. "Has anyone other than me talked to you in the shimmering place? Someone named—"

"They called you here to take me away," Bobby said. "Because of what I did to Easter." He stroked the animal in his lap. "But she's better like this. See?" He held the animal up for Kevin's inspection, his little hands under its wings, which flapped in a sad attempt at escape. Bobby dropped the thing to the floor, where it landed with a thud. Its claws made skittering noises on the hard-wood.

"I don't want you here," Bobby said.

Kevin felt a pinch in his stomach. A cramp doubled him over. He jumped into Bobby's mind, looking for that still center, the static place he could shut down, or at least a memory he could exploit, a moment Bobby felt enough kindness or love toward Kevin to give him pause. He couldn't concentrate through the pain in his gut. Flailing, he found Bobby's ability instead and seized it. It was a writhing thing, hot with power but clumsy. Kevin tried to use it to undo whatever damage Bobby had done to his insides, but it was like molding raw meat with numb fingers. He managed to ease the pain before Bobby's ability wriggled away from his control.

Bright lights exploded behind Kevin's left eye as two blood vessels were soldered together. Kevin concentrated through it and gripped the boy's ability again. He extended it down into Bobby's chest; like slamming a door against a strong wind, he sealed the valves of Bobby's aorta and pulmonary artery shut. Bobby looked at him, surprised. His little hand clutched at his scrawny chest, and he fell off the bed. All Kevin could see were his sneakers twitching and spasming. The gull cat let out an inquisitive croak from the foot of the bed. Rubbing his stomach to ease the knot of phantom pain there, Kevin walked out of the room. He glanced at Laura's broken body for a moment as if he might have missed some detail and she could be hanging on to life, but he looked away and left the house.

The moon was low on the water, forming a figure eight with its own reflection. Easter dragged herself over and head-butted Kevin's ankle. *Why give the name to the head but not the tail?* Kevin thought. His mind swayed drunkenly with the thought, and he laughed, an unsteady hiccup. He bent down and picked her up, cradling her. Her weight was out of balance, top-heavy. He remembered her as a kitten, a puffball of claws and curiosity. She'd brought some piece of Laura back, something Kevin had worried was destroyed by her mother's death, and for that, he forgave the cat all the scratched furniture and pissed-in shoes.

Easter looked at him with the same pleading eyes as Laura. The minds of animals were alien things, and attempts to use his ability on them came with the danger of being lost within. Kevin petted Easter's neck. He took her head in one hand and braced her lopsided body under his other arm. He twisted, like taking a stuck lid off a jar. Easter shivered once and was still. Kevin rested her body on the damp grass and trudged out onto the beach. He sat down at the tide line, the waves flirting with his heels. Vision returned to his left eye, which was blurred with tears.

"No more," he whispered to himself. The surf swallowed the promise, as if the world didn't believe him. Kevin doubted the words himself. He'd said them before.

Behind him, he heard footsteps on the sand, the crunch of tiny shells crushed underfoot. He was sure it was Bobby, alive and coming for revenge. Laura and Tom, or Mona, or Raymond, or one of the countless other dead. *Whoever it is, they can have me,* he thought.

Kevin Bishop was done.

ONE

THE NEW WORLD

When you invent the ship, you also invent the shipwreck.

—Paul Virilio,
Politics of the Very Worst

VANTAGE

◇

Fahima Deeb looks out the window of the headmaster's quarters of the Bishop Academy onto the glittering and changed face of New York. The light in the mornings is pale and milky but illuminates a city warped from drab concrete into a science fiction dreamscape. The map of the city is altered: office buildings repurposed for housing or torn down to provide green space, sidewalks widened to shift dominance from cars to pedestrians. Looking up shows the biggest changes: well above the ground, the air is full of traffic. Bullet-shaped public transit craft piloted by telekinetics slice the air between spires of polished onyx that gleam in the dawn light, their architecture inspired by coral growth and the mycorrhizal root structures of fungi. She'd been concerned about the likelihood of collisions. People had enough trouble not smacking into one another with two vectors; introducing a third opened up the potential for an exponential increase in accidents. What she didn't account for was the amount of space. Every street in the city was a Grand Canyon. As long as the number of objects in the air didn't see a massive increase, there was space enough for all above the streets.

Fahima is not the first to adopt New York City as her home and alter it indelibly. She wonders if the ones who came before her felt they'd evolved the city into its final form. Her changes are more than cosmetic. The buildings are a sign of shifts beneath. Capitalism is an inefficient engine: so much waste for such a low yield. New York was built to fuel it with bodies, huddle around its meager light, suffer the punishing heat it gave off as by-product, and choke on its noxious exhaust. The city, the country, and the economy are machines constructed of obsolete components, with necessary inputs, outputs desired and undesired. But Fahima has improved it. She dreams in machines. She's inventing something better.

She looks down onto Lexington Avenue, where a film crew sets up lighting rigs and lays thick cable along the gutters. Trailers cordon off the block at either end. It shouldn't worry her: this is still New York. Occasional film crews are a mix of excitement, curiosity, and inconvenience she accepts as part and parcel of living here. But she's shaken. She picks up a Polaroid that's been sitting on her desk since she found it taped to the window last week with *5:45 A.M. Wednesday June 8th* written in black marker in the white space under the image. She holds it up, comparing it with the street below. It isn't a perfect match; she's twenty minutes late, and some things have moved, the light shifting with the speed it does in the early morning. But the angle is right and the parked cars are the same, the lighting rigs and the trailers that weren't there yesterday but are here today. The photograph was taken from her apartment window this morning and stuck to the glass a week before it was taken.

Fahima dresses and starts the coffee. There's a collective that grows strains of Ethiopian Yirgacheffe out in Nyack, creating microclimates to mimic its home, adjusting chemicals in the soil. People swear by it. There's plastic in the palate, a burnt rubber taste as if the plants are rebelling, aware they've been displaced. Fahima gets Sumatran coffee in the Bed-Stuy black markets. It's an indulgence, a confession that capitalism has perks for those in the ruling class. For all her egalitarian plans, Fahima lives in a tower.

She looks into the guest bedroom where Sarah Davenport sleeps. Some days she doesn't wake up at all. Others she screams in the middle of the night because she doesn't know where she is. People with small children talk about how beautiful and peaceful they look when they're asleep, but Sarah's rest is fitful, if prolonged. She mutters names without context, twitches like she's being hit. Fahima quietly closes the door.

She sips her coffee as her mind rattles through lists of the people she's about to meet. Omar gave her dossiers and a cheat sheet with names spelled phonetically, position, country of origin, and predilections. Eito Higashi, Japan's minister of economy. Two daughters, a dog, a list of proclivities Fahima hadn't known there were names for. Malik Antoun, low-level Saudi prince and avid horse breeder with a penchant for alcohol while abroad. Niklas Babisch, former German ambassador to the United States, now the *Großonkel* of the New Left in the Bundestag. On paper, Babisch is Fahima's greatest ally out of the dozen in the group. He'll be a pain in the ass.

All men, powerful but not too powerful. Each one has a reason for being here that avoids the perception his country is reopening diplomatic relations with the United States. Everything is run through the Bishop Foundation, orchestrated by its executive director, Fahima Deeb. Last night she dreamed Kevin Bishop came back from the dead and saved her from having to go through with this.

She goes over the dossiers, comparing her incorrect and incomplete recollections with the facts as written, then puts them in her bag. She tucks the photo in as well, quickly, like she's trying to pull a sleight of hand on herself. She picks out a hijab Ruth bought her in Chicago, a piece of shimmering blue cloth with whorls of deep green that coalesce into a map of the earth, spin like a globe, then sublimate back into abstraction, repeating on a hypnotic loop. Fahima thinks it's on the nose. Ruth reminded her these are government employees and the most obvious symbolism might fly over their heads. Fahima arranges the hijab perfectly, tucking in errant strands of hair, then clasps it with a gold pin in the shape of a handshake. *I might as well wear a fucking tie-dye and beads,* she thinks as she steps out her front door.

Omar Wright waits for her in the hall. His tan Yves Saint Laurent suit offsets his dark skin. Omar perpetually informs Fahima and anyone else who'll listen about the brands of his suits and has tried to encourage Fahima to be *less schlubby* for big events, going as far as to pick out her outfit for this evening. Between Omar and Ruth, she feels like a doll being dressed by enthusiastic children: Muslim Barbie.

"Oh, hi," Omar says, as if surprised to see her. Omar's official title has never been decided. He calls himself her majordomo, but refuses to tell her what that means. He takes the edge of her hijab between his index and middle fingers and lifts it to assess. He gives a slight shrug. "Sort of on the nose," he says.

"Ruth," says Fahima.

"Sweet kid," Omar says. He shimmers and divides into two identical copies of himself, each in the same Yves Saint Laurent suit. They face each other, then launch into a game of rock paper scissors that takes five rounds before one of them loses. The winner gives a triumphant *hmmph* and proceeds into Fahima's apartment.

"Should it bother me that I get the loser every morning?" she asks.

Omar shakes his head. "Watching Ms. Davenport's a cushy job," he says. "Chances are she'll sleep all day and he'll sit around watching porn."

"I was better off not knowing that," says Fahima.

"You asked," Omar says as he steps into the elevator.

When they redesigned the building to accommodate the new floors above the thirteenth, Fahima decided on a maglev shaft. The ride is fast and smooth, and unlike an Einstein-Rosen bridge up the building's spine, there's no risk of rending space-time, which is a plus.

A pack of students load in with them, conversing in the stage voices of teenagers, asserting their place in the world by sheer force of volume. Below the thirteenth, the students own the building. Fahima insisted on it. What goes on above the old headmaster's quarters, in the new floors obsidianists built after the Armistice, might be antithetical to everything Bishop believed in, but the original building Kevin bought and loved remains a school.

"I'm telling you, I could see her down there," says one of the kids.

"Bullshit," another retorts.

"You have, like, a passing interest in her," says the first. "I'm a superfan who happens to have telescopic vision. I'm a student of her work, and I am telling you I can identify Leida LaPlante by the top of her head from eight stories up."

"We're all sorry your ability is basically *doesn't need binoculars*."

"Five bucks says Harris used his ability to look down her shirt and jerk off."

"No one is going to take that bet."

"Fuck every one of you and I'm telling you it's her."

"Who's she even playing?"

"I heard she's playing Ji Yeon Kim."

"They got a white lady to play Ji Yeon Kim?"

"Not a white lady. Leida Fucking LaPlante."

"It's some bullshit."

The doors slide open at the fifth-floor cafeteria with a *ding,* a digital approximation of the physical bells once installed on every floor. *We should have left them,* Fahima thinks, the tinny facsimile in her ears. *We should have kept one real thing.*

"You ready for this?" Omar asks once they're alone.

"Not remotely," says Fahima.

The elevator hits the ground floor and bounces. One more thing she keeps meaning to fix.

The Bishop lobby is slipping into slow decline. Flakes of gilding peel off the columns, and tile floors are scuffed to the texture of pumice. A senior art sculpture old enough it took damage in the siege sits in the center of the lobby, waiting for a student to announce their brilliance by replacing it with their own work. Building resources are unlimited, but new floors would erase desire paths worn into the tile by decades of rushing students, and Fahima won't let it happen.

"Good morning, Dr. Deeb," says Shen. He's the only person who attaches the proper title to her name, and she's endlessly grateful. "Big day all around."

Like the lobby, Shen is getting old. In his case, it's physical degradation related to his ability. Shifting sizes ravages his joints and connective tissue, but Fahima's afraid metal hips and knees wouldn't shift along with the rest of his body. Resonant-specific medicine is an infant field. He's useless as a security guard; he moves with leaden slowness. Fahima can't bring herself to replace him for the same reason she hasn't had the lobby redone. There are so few remnants of the old Bishop. So much has been changed and written over.

"Where do I take a dozen international diplomats with various dietary exclusions for breakfast in this city?" Fahima asks Shen.

His brow crinkles. "Breakfast's tough," he says. "Foundation's dime?" Fahima nods. "Norma's at the Parker on 56th and Sixth. It's not what it used to be, but they can cook an egg."

Shen's understanding of the changes in the city is unique. For him, the displacement of millions of non-Resonants from the city primarily resulted in a restaurant holocaust, with hundreds of the city's finest chefs shunted off to the Wastes or, at best, the Bronx. Where Fahima built a miracle of urban planning, Shen sees an apocalypse for takeout options.

"Make a reservation," Fahima says to Omar. She's already lost the name of the restaurant in a tide of names, titles, hobbies and interests, lactose intolerances, gluten allergies, and religious restrictions.

"Don't worry, Dr. Deeb," Shen says. "They're only people."

There is a way they've taken to talking about the world outside that catches Fahima's ear strangely. The implied sentence is *They're only people, not like us.* It's the product of a war won, a verbal expression of the policy of "separation as protection" that followed. It's also the seed of an ugly form of racism, one today's meeting, along with the government's discussions of reunification, might stamp out. Equality was built into Kevin Bishop's teaching, and it was the first thing discarded when the situation came to open blows. Shen is one of the kindest people she knows, but he looks down on *common humans* with bemused contempt, as if they're children. Because of this, he thinks today's stakes are low. Assuming a group is weak blinds you to its strengths.

Once they're through the revolving doors, Omar doubles again so he can stand on either side of Fahima, guiding her through the scrum of people out front. Lexington Avenue is drenched in lights. Fahima turns back to look at the Bishop building. Lit up as it is, something about its appearance that's been teasing at the edge of her brain finally comes to her. With the black glass stripped off the lower floors of the edifice, all the floors that still hold classrooms and dorms, and the new upper floors that housed Black Rose Faction offices and Patrick's quarters, all reinforced with black glass, the spire that was once the Bishop Academy looks like a match stood on end.

Racks of kliegs are aimed at the building, and cameramen hover above, checking shots. The street is snaked with electrical cords and blocked off at either end by trailers. Tanks and Joint Light Tactical Vehicles are parked with their fronts oriented to the academy's entrance. Trucks full of weapons sit ready, and men in Homeland Security uniforms make small talk while sipping coffee or sit awaiting the application of makeup. Fahima's knees buckle with a sense of déjà vu. Seven years ago, she looked down on the same vehicles, the same men, from the window of the headmaster's quarters with Sarah Davenport and contemplated the war that was about to happen. Obsidianist shapers had to carve out the space for windows again after the Armistice, pulling the black glass carapace back like curtains of opalescent tar. It was a sign to the students and to the rest of the city: *Bishop no longer needs its defenses. Bishop is safe.* But when Fahima looks up at the building, those holes have been filled in, completing the feeling that she's returned to the beginning and will have to fight the war all over again.

"What is all this?" she asks.

The Omar on her left smiles at her indulgently. "Do you not look at the permits you sign off on?" he says.

"They're shooting the last night of the siege," Right Omar says.

"But it's daytime."

"They fix it in post."

Fahima turns back, watching through the glass as dozens of people work to re-create a moment of Fahima's life, a place where her narrative intersected with a narrative large enough, important enough to be considered history.

"Are any of those people famous?" she asks.

"You really are out of touch, boss," says Left Omar.

"If any of them are famous, get them to the thing tonight," she says. "All the famous ones."

"On it," says Left Omar. He blocks a floating coil of cables from smacking Fahima in the head as they turn off Lexington and head toward the N station at 59th.

When the end comes and someone asks Fahima, *What achievement would you like to be remembered for?* she will say this:

I fixed the New York City subway system.

Sleek maglev trains serpentine through pristine tunnels, piloted by telekinetics who can stop on a dime or ease to a gentle halt as they slide silently into a station. At hub points around the city, metalurges divine the location of each train and relay the information to Hiveweb operators, omnipaths embedded in slabs of black glass like Han Solo in carbonite. They're human Internet servers, bridging the Hive and the actual world to form a communication network that spans the city, accessible by touching the veins of black glass that thread through the architecture and sidewalks. The operators redirect pilots to points of building congestion. Stations are spotless, temples of gleaming tile. Voiders move through the city like coprophages, sending the trash of 20 million inhabitants into the null. Do some of the stops smell like urine? Yes, some of the stops smell like urine. Fahima is working on it.

Above, the city creeps skyward. With no room to expand out, New York grows up. Six buildings in Manhattan are taller than the

Burj Khalifa. Rich emirates try to snatch up as many obsidianists as they can get their hands on. Fahima's impressed by how many pass on offers abroad to complete the work that needs doing here. Between black glass and other makers, they can build at next to no material cost. New construction is mostly residential, as are the towers that used to house trading firms and banks. The financial sector of the economy has been nationalized, run by a corps of precogs. They take up little space. Wall Street is all low-income housing. Fahima hasn't eliminated capitalism, but she's expelled its worst practitioners. She has spiteful dreams of investment bankers in the Wastes struggling to convince anyone they have useful skills. Between the new residential units and the ones vacated on Exodus Day, there are enough apartments in New York for anyone who wants one. Waitresses can afford one-bedrooms, and bike couriers live in Battery Park. Universal housing within the city is the next step, but for now, no one sleeps on the streets in the five boroughs.

Upstate, useless suburbs have been plowed under for farmland. Westchester County is a massive agrarian commune, the weather regulated by a team of pressure manipulators. Produce pours into the city's new farmer's markets. No one has to go hungry.

Schools across the city are palaces, and the teachers want for nothing. The Bishop Foundation runs most directly, but there are others. Real arts schools, like the one the Bishop Academy used to masquerade as. Conservative prep schools that teach kids how to suppress their abilities. And the Black Rose Faction training schools, which take a mix of the martially inclined and the problem kids from other schools. Those Fahima tries not to think about.

In hospitals and clinics, healers and menders work like sleepless saints toward Fahima's ultimate goal for New York: no more dying. First in the city, then the country, then the world.

After a quick transfer, they get off near the Museum of Natural

History and walk along Central Park West. They pass one of the few buildings in the city left at its original height, now dwarfed at a mere fifty-eight stories. Fahima had paid it special attention, leaving its garish exterior like a blemish on the face of the city but gutting the interior and throwing the stock of the gift shop on a bonfire. They melted down the ridiculous gold embellishments throughout the huge upper apartments and sold them off to create a resource center for immigrant Resonants. Before the war, she'd cross the street to avoid falling in its shadow; now she smiles every time she goes by it.

One of the Omars points to the sky over the park at what looks to be a translucent cloud. "We're late," he says, and the three of them pick up their pace, falling just short of a jog.

Ruth Hammond refers to it as the Craft, but everyone else who works for Bishop calls it the Amoeba. It becomes bullet-shaped speeding through the air, but no one except Ruth ever sees it like that. They see it the way it is now, a translucent blob wavering like a soap bubble, hovering over the lake in Central Park. It holds Ruth and twelve worried diplomats like fruit floating in a Jell-O mold. As it descends, it casts thirteen shadows on the grass, surrounded by a vague ring. Its shape becomes more definite, flattening on the bottom until it looks like a proper UFO, an upended pie plate. It lands silently, each bureaucrat's feet gently set on the ground, before retracting like a tablecloth yanked back by a magician and disappearing somewhere inside Ruth.

"Gentlemen," says Ruth Hammond. "Welcome to New York."

Fahima walks up to Ruth and kisses her on the cheek. Ruth grabs Fahima's hip and holds her close for a beat before letting her go. Ruth's hair smells like ozone and rain.

"What time you make?" Fahima asks when she's back at arm's length.

"From London in a half hour," Ruth says.

"They puke?"

"Not a one."

"Good girl," says Fahima. She's aware of her habit of infantilizing Ruth to keep her at a distance. Awareness doesn't stop her from doing it. Fahima turns to the assembled bureaucrats, who wobble on shaky legs. If Fahima had her way, they'd stay punch-drunk and susceptible the entire visit. There was talk of putting the psychic whammy on the lot of them and skipping the show, but Fahima decided that determining the global future that way was morally unacceptable. Plus, with Kevin Bishop dead and Sarah Davenport broken, no one on the Bishop staff had the psychic chops to pull it off.

Omar distributes universal translators the size of jelly beans. The British representative attempts to shove his in his ear, and Omar explains via gesture that they're to be swallowed. Fahima allows a minute for the gel caps to dissolve, releasing floods of nanites. *Tiny sexy genius machines*, Alyssa used to call them. Fahima's mind drifts through Alyssa's nicknames for Fahima's inventions, the small of Alyssa's back and how the smell of hospital disinfectants on her skin drove Fahima wild, the series of body-blow accusations Alyssa landed in their last fight, leaving Fahima too stunned to cry until Alyssa was out the door and out of her life. She tugs at the hanging edge of her hijab, pulling her head a tick to the right and returning to the moment she's in.

"Gentlemen, I hope you had an amazing flight," she says. "In case Ms. Hammond didn't tell you, you were traveling at ten times the speed of sound in a craft that requires no fuel other than a hearty breakfast for the pilot." She winks at Ruth and immediately understands it as a mistake. "Which, incidentally, is our first stop."

Omar motions for them to follow, and eleven of them fall in line. He's singular, presenting as a perfectly average personal assistant. Fahima finds it's best not to show them any abilities that raise serious existential questions like *What does identity mean when you can spread your consciousness over several bodies?* Abilities like Omar's have been fodder for late-night stoned conversations at Bishop since the academy opened its doors. At this stage, it's easier to keep the metaphysics out of it.

As Fahima hoped, one of the diplomats points to the spectacle at the bottom of the hill, his mouth gawping like a fish's. She notes the anchor-shaped mole on his cheek, flips through her mental Rolodex, and determines that it's Eito Higashi, the Japanese minister of economy, who's holding his translator pill pinched between his thumb and forefinger. He repeats the same phrase over and over. Fahima doesn't speak Japanese, but *what the fuck is that?* is universal even without tiny sexy genius machines to translate it. She takes his hand and lifts it slightly toward his mouth, then mimes putting a pill into her own mouth and swallowing. Higashi repeats whatever he's saying.

"I call it the Glitch," says Fahima. "I like giving things capitalized common nouns for names. It makes me feel like I'm in a science fiction story." Behind her, a Yemeni boy sits in the grass. He grins as his eyes follow the parabola of an invisible object above him. On the crest of the hill, three men unshoulder bulky weapons and take aim at the spot the boy is watching. A fourth man points to the invisible object, raises his hand and clenches it into a fist, and points again. An ignorant seagull repeats a half circle of flight, jumping back to her origin point each time she reaches the end of her arc. After two seconds, they reset and repeat. They've been doing this for seven years.

Once there was a boy in the air, the focus of everyone's attention. The boy is gone, and there's this tableau locked in a looping piece of time. "It's a reminder that our potential is also a threat when used improperly. When used in fear or anger." It's a message, landing them here. *Be fucking afraid of us. Be amazed but also pants-shittingly afraid. Notice I said* when *and not* if.

She's glad Bishop isn't here to see her do this. He thought they could win hearts and minds by cleaning up oil spills and curing cancer. He thought they'd get power through democratic channels and the moral arc of history. She wonders if he'd be proud of where they are or horrified how they got here.

DESTROY EVERYTHING YOU TOUCH

◇

The light from Jonathan's chest glows like a warm coal through his silk sheets. Carrie is impressed by his commitment to terrible aesthetics. Of course he has silk sheets. His wardrobe of Paisley print shirts and vintage bell-bottom jeans complements an apartment decorated with bead curtains and beanbag chairs. It would be funnier if she wasn't sleeping with him.

He wakes as she's dressing. She pulls on jeans crisp with yesterday's sweat, dusty from her run out to the Wastes. Last night she came directly from the road, a twelve-hour drive in a truck with a busted AC. She skipped her apartment, stopping only to pick up the bottle of whiskey that's now on the nightstand, a swig of it left in the bottom so Carrie can claim they didn't finish it all in one night. In a dreamy mumble, he asks her to stay. He promises coffee. This is becoming routine, which makes it worse.

"I've got that thing with Bryce this morning," she says.

"Show and tell?" he says, tugging down on one of her belt loops. She swats his hand away, sure to make it clear it's not a flirtatious swipe. "I don't go on shift until seven," he says. "You could stop by beforehand."

"I have dinner plans," she says.

"You could bring him dinner now, and he wouldn't know the difference," Jonathan says. "He's got no idea what time it is down there."

"Don't talk about him," Carrie says, turning away, looking at Jonathan over her shoulder.

Jonathan puts up his hands. "I wasn't saying anything bad."

"Don't talk about him at all," Carrie says. What she means is *don't talk*. She wishes she could keep Jonathan in one room and Miquel in another, her life compartmentalized and discreet. *This room is for touching. This room is for talking. This room is mine.* Physically, she has all three. She wants to build up the walls in her head, to slam and lock the doors between.

Jonathan's Marlboros, Bic, and Moleskine float across the room. He never refers to cigarettes, pens, or notebooks, calling each by its proper brand name and accepting no substitutes. He haunts street markets for artifacts of the old world. "I had a line come to me in a dream," he says. The pen uncaps itself. A cigarette jumps out of the pack and into the corner of his mouth, where it hangs unlit. If he ever tries to read her one of his poems, this thing is over.

"I'm working till close if you want to come by after," he says. His cigarette bobs like a conductor's baton. He stares hard at the page like the line from his dream is written behind it. The good parts of their routine are the ones that don't involve speaking. Letting herself in with the key under the mat. Finding him already in bed, reading, or asleep, or waiting. He's made a commitment to her. The key under the mat implies fidelity, no one else in his bed. It's her or nothing, for now.

"Maybe," she says. She leaves without saying goodbye, easing the apartment door shut so she doesn't wake Mrs. Ogilve next door, who isn't a Resonant but seems to have superhuman hearing. There's an *R* spray-painted on Jonathan's door in hunter orange, the third time it's happened since he and Carrie started sleeping together. This one's been here a few weeks, and Jonathan seems resigned to leaving it alone. People in Pilsen don't hide their dislike of Resonants. As someone with an ability that's visibly apparent, Jonathan's an easy mark. No amount of helping Mrs. Ogilve bring her groceries up will endear him to the neighborhood. Carrie asked him once why he put up with it, and he quoted her his current rent.

The neighborhood bustles with life; it provides everything to its residents. North of Roosevelt Avenue, it's risky for non-Resonants to walk around without papers to prove they've got a reason to be there. Within this handful of blocks, they can leave the house without documents, pick up a six-pack or tamales, and not worry.

The man working at La Catrina passes for friendly as he fixes Carrie a café con leche and fills a paper bag with churros. He used to own the building; now he rents from a Resonant who bought it cheap after the Armistice and hasn't been south of Roosevelt since. Chicago is the only integrated city left, an exception carved out in the Armistice, but it has its own dividing lines, some unspoken and some written into law. Non-Resonants are allowed to stay, but they're second-class citizens, without property rights. They're tenants in their own homes, employees of businesses that had been in their families for generations. They could stay, but Carrie didn't understand why any would want to.

Carrie fishes for her wallet, but the man waves her away.

"The suit paid for you," he says, gesturing with his chin. Carrie spins in time to catch the back of someone walking out. The sharp lines of a dark blue suit stand out among the soft curves of the other clients' attire. Carrie stuffs a bill into the tip jar without checking the denomination and tries to catch her benefactor. She runs into an abuela waiting in line who gives her a look that says she knows what Carrie is. She can tell from the way Carrie moves through the world as if she belongs in it. Non-Resonants don't walk that way anymore even in their own neighborhoods. Carrie eyes the dark spot of coffee spilled on her wrist, and an irrational anger moves across her mind like a cloud of heat. The abuela sees the change in Carrie's face, flinches, and steps aside.

"Sorry," Carrie says, lightly patting the old woman's shoulder. She leaves the café and checks her corners, looking for the dark blue suit. She spots him about to turn onto Sangamon. Before taking off in pursuit, she checks the other direction. A man wearing the same suit takes the left onto South Carpenter. Carrie freezes, unsure what to do. Both suits are out of sight. Carrie convinces herself she didn't see what she saw and that it doesn't matter anyway. Some idiot trying to pay it forward, screwing up the natural cadence of her day with a kindness unasked for. She follows the suit that headed toward Sangamon Avenue, but only because it's the way she was going.

At Halsted and 16th, carrying the still-warm paper bag of churros, she waits for the number 50 bus. It's right on time, gliding up to the curb a foot off the ground. On the side there's an ad for Hayden Cohen's new album. Hayden has spent the last year touring Europe as a cultural ambassador, assuring other countries that what's left of the United States isn't a feudal state. Carrie hasn't talked to them in months.

She gives a halfhearted smile to the operator, who doesn't return it. He's a college-age kid, hasn't been working more than a year. Older operators, magnetics and telekinetics, banter with passengers while they maneuver their buses. It takes all this kid's concentration to keep his afloat. Out the window, she sees the suit standing on the sidewalk. The bus windows are tinted, but he waves as if he sees her, a dainty twiddling of his fingers that's the physical equivalent of *toodle-oo*. The bus pulls away from the curb, and he's gone. Carrie moves to the back of the bus, which is full of janitors and maids, dishwashers and busboys headed into the city for work. Some of them were doctors, professors, and middle managers, but they take whatever jobs they can find.

Carrie feels the anger that flashed at the woman in the café, but unfocused. Something in her wants to jump off the bus, to get herself away from these people. She tells herself it's shame. At Bishop they talked like they were morally evolved. They saw enough oppression and rejected it outright. It took work to put hurt aside. The last seven years had shown Resonants willing to recycle old scripts, roles reversed, lines read more emphatically this time, delivered with the vitriol that comes from knowing the feel of the boot heel on your neck.

"It isn't natural," Bryce said to her once. "All the shit we've done to regular people and we're okay with it? How do you have it done to you and then you turn around and do the same shit back? Something in us got twisted up. Something went rotten."

Carrie puts her earbuds in. She spins the click wheel on her ancient iPod, searching for something calming or distracting. She starts a Joanna Newsom album, but the waterfalls of harp make her edgy and impatient. With nothing but dead air in her ears, she sticks her nose into the bag of churros, inhaling the deep earthy smell of cinnamon. The bag is Swiss-cheesed with transparent spots of grease. She watches the city change as the bus moves uptown. They're renovating the university. Obsidianists cover red brick with dull black glass. Makers coax it up from the ground, gnarly and branching like coral. Shapers work in teams of two, melting it down into balls and flattening it into sheets. A lot of Pulsers turned out to be obsidianists, an ability that didn't exist before the Pulse. It's a point of pride, a retort to older Resonants who say that Pulsers aren't *real* Resonants. *We even discriminate among ourselves,* Carrie thinks. The black glass is a symbol of progress, of possibility in the new world. Carrie can't stand the sight of it here or in the Hive, where it pops up in formations like scrub grass, some as tall as she is. Everyone she knows stays out of the Hive. Everyone she likes, at least. The people who spend time there have something different about them. A mean edge.

Carrie gets off at Hyde Park. The school isn't far from the university, a beat-up brick building at Cottage Grove and 55th. The Bishop Foundation took over the schools in Chicago after the first Bishop school, the megachurch on North Avenue, was repurposed as a training academy for the Black Rose Faction. This one is unique among all the schools in the city. The Unity School is the only integrated high school left in America. Carrie scans the temporary security card Bryce gave her and enters. It's before first period, and kids loiter in the halls. A handful are visibly Resonant; Carrie sees a girl with a row of four bright blue eyes and a boy whose body is a rapidly spinning sandstorm below the neck. With many, there's no way to tell. They interact as equals. She assumes the normal striations of high school social life are at work, with kids glomming on to their own kind, but the groups seem to be mixed. It doesn't prove her cynicism unfounded, but it impresses her. Maybe kindness and tolerance increase from one generation to the next. There may be hope even if that hope excludes Carrie, who's fought so hard for it.

"You're late," Bryce says as he emerges from the principal's office.

"I brought churros," she says.

Bryce grabs one from the bag. "You get these around here?" he asks, knowing exactly where she got them.

"A place," says Carrie.

"Uh huh," Bryce says. He hugs her, his skin rasping against her cheek. Carrie thinks of her closest friends as a star inscribed in a pentagon: five points connected by ten lines. The time in Topaz Lake bonds Carrie, Hayden, Miquel, and Bryce, leaving Waylon on the outside, constantly aware that he dodged captivity. In the months that followed, her friends dropped away one by one: Miquel left behind when they escaped, Bryce returning to Chicago instead of fighting with them to attack the camps, Hayden going back to normal life after they finally returned to liberate Topaz. The thrum of pride and shame over everything they did is strongest between Carrie and Hayden, but she feels it with Bryce, too. A signal passed back and forth, an undersong to every word and gesture that says *You're okay. We made it, and all of that is over, and you're okay.*

"You're going to shadow me for the day," he says.

"Is that supposed to be a joke?"

"Was it funny?" he says. "Come on. I'll give you the tour."

There isn't much to tour. There's nothing novel or revolutionary about the place itself. It feels prewar, the way Carrie remembers the school she went to before Bishop. What's remarkable about the Unity School is how unremarkable the students seem.

"They wanted to call it the Kevin Bishop Unity School," Bryce explains as they walk the halls. "But I wasn't having it. I mean, yes, the man was a saint or what all. But if Kevin Bishop wanted a unity school, he could've built one. You can talk about protecting us from them or teaching us to protect ourselves. But at the end of the day, you have to look at the fact that we went to a segregationist school."

"That's an interesting way of looking at it," Carrie says.

One of the female teachers coos "Good morning, Principal Thomas," batting her eyelashes before fixing Carrie with a back-off glare. It's all Carrie can do to keep from laughing. When Bryce started out at Bishop, a towering sixteen-year-old, he was the hottest commodity in the school's sexual economy. Girls were shattered when he came out. It's funny how within a school patterns repeat infinitely, the same dramas played out forever and always for the first time.

"What we're doing here is something completely different. Completely new," Bryce says. "We're saying to these kids, *be kids. Don't be baseliner kids, don't be Resonant kids. Be kids.*"

"How is this not an *all lives matter* thing?"

"Because we got ours," Bryce says. "That *all lives matter I don't see color* noise was white people asking people to get over stuff that wasn't over." There's a hesitation in his voice every place he wants to use the word *shit,* a tiny hitch as he searches for something G-rated. "This is us, and we won the war. Now we decide who we're going to be. If we choose to be like them, the whole thing repeats. We stay locked in this forever, hating on and beating the stuffing out of each other until there's nobody left."

"Sign me up for the newsletter," she says. "Put me down for a donation. Why am I here?"

"I'm offering you a job," says Bryce.

"I have a job," she says. "I work for your husband."

Bryce leans in as a passel of students runs by. "I want to offer you a job where you don't have to carry a knife," he says.

Carrie's hand moves reflexively to the small of her back, finding the bone handle of the knife holstered there.

"You think I'd come into a high school unarmed?" she says with a forced grin.

"Waylon told me what happened in Vegas," Bryce says.

"I haven't even told him what happened," says Carrie.

"He knew the minute you got back into town," Bryce says. "He said you were freaked out. Said he could've seen you from the air."

"He's being a drama queen," Carrie says. Her reports on her

sorties to the Wastes usually amount to *I'm back, aren't I?* Three days' drive from Vegas hadn't dulled the buzz of adrenaline in her blood. She hadn't talked to Jonathan about it because that would be outside the boundaries of their arrangement. Miquel would make too much of it, more than Waylon apparently had. She wishes she could talk to Hayden about it. Hayden would see the joke in it.

"We worry about you," Bryce says. Carrie never gets tired of Bryce or Waylon referring to their couplehood as *we.*

"Don't," says Carrie, but it sounds unconvincing even to herself. She won't admit it, but she never tires of their parental concern for her either.

"You can do some good here," he says. "I need a psychic defense teacher. You were always good at that white flame thing."

She smirks with pride. "That's hippie meditation stuff," she says. She'd been the top of their class in psychic defense at Bishop, which was like winning an award for most emotionally unavailable. Still, top of her class.

"Come on part-time," Bryce says. "As a mentor."

"I am terrible with kids," Carrie says.

"Spend the day and think about it," he says.

Carrie wraps her arm around his waist. It barely half circles him. "I am going to spend the day here because my friend has built something amazing and I want to see it," she says. "But that's all. Understand?"

"Yes, ma'am," says Bryce.

"Don't say that," Carrie says. "It makes me feel old."

A girl flies down the hall, fists forward like a cartoon superhero. A small boy rides on her back, whooping with joy.

"Look around," Bryce says. "We're ancient."

Happy hour at Vibration is slow, and Waylon's behind the bar, prepping for Jonathan to come on later. Electrics who spend the night sitting on conductive chairs generating clean power for the city work their way through the happy hour special. They smell like ozone and sweat. A quartet of off-duty bus drivers sits in a corner booth with two stringers from the *Trib*. Voiders, fat on the trash they consume, toast call girls and rent boys who need a solid buzz before they hit the streets for the evening.

"He's been asking about you," Waylon says before Carrie can sit down.

"What did you say?"

"I said you were late," says Waylon. "That you'd be here when you could."

"You want a churro?" Carrie asks. "They're cold."

Waylon reaches across the bar, then draws his hand back and rests it on his burgeoning gut. He hasn't been idle, but he's grown soft. He's the man in the chair, the spider who can wait on prey. Waylon's earned the right to get thick in the middle, and Carrie's happy he's content. He sleeps assured he's doing enough good, unhaunted by anything outside of his sphere. He hands her back the bag unopened. "Go see your man."

Carrie heads for the kitchen, where Carlton is doing dinner prep. Unlit joint hanging out of the corner of his mouth, he takes a potato out of the burlap sack, tosses it into the air, and juliennes it with the bright red monofilaments that extend from his fingertips. The slices fall into a ten-gallon bucket with a wet thud. Carrie lets herself into the walk-in cooler, pulling the door tightly shut behind her so Carlton won't scream at her on the way out. She pushes aside a cart of lemons and limes Waylon gets from a thermic farmer in eastern Ohio, then pushes the back wall till it clicks and pops open, revealing the stairs to the basement. Carrie takes a deep breath before she descends. She tries to scrub all thoughts of

Jonathan out of her head. She imagines her mind is a cool white flame.

At the bottom, everything glows green. Inhibitor tech has been illegal since the Armistice. Practically all the extant machines were turned over and destroyed. The lights are such a heavy electrical draw, Carrie couldn't get away with setting one up in the apartment. It would be a red flag on the city power grid, like when cops used to find meth labs because of microwave ovens. The club has excuses for massive electrical draw. Waylon hired contractors he trusted to build the room. It's got a twin bed, a two-range stove, and a makeshift inhibitor made from plans they found online. Carrie offers to bring pictures and posters, single-purpose kitchen gadgets. Miquel insists he has everything he needs.

The buzz of the lights makes Carrie feel like her transgressions are written on her skin. Miquel huddles under a blanket, watching a black-and-white movie. He has an infinite supply, from classics to trash, and watches them constantly, reveling in the emotional responses they evoke. He keeps journals of the synesthetic effects of each one. Carrie reads them while he sleeps: "*Casablanca:* cool crimson cube with pocks on the surface like old concrete. *Harold and Maude:* cat with thick brown fur, sleeping. *The Matrix:* spikes of yellow and blue."

He turns to Carrie as she comes in, smiling although his face is wet with tears. On the screen, Montgomery Clift clutches Elizabeth Taylor like a life preserver. Miquel takes two fingers and wipes his eye. He holds them up like he's pledging an oath, fingertips shiny in the dull green light of the inhibitor.

"Look," he says. "All mine."

She hunkers down, holds his sleeved wrist lightly, and kisses the tears. He winces as her lips touch him and pulls his hand back like he's been burned. The inhibitor does a decent job, but when he touches someone skin to skin, their emotions blare at him like a trumpet. Miquel got broken at Topaz Lake. It took weeks for his ability to function, and when it did, it was like a thousand radios tuned to different stations with the volume cranked. A lot of people exposed to the inhibitors long-term had trouble afterward. There were discussion groups in the Hive, real life-support groups in church basements all over the city. Most people got better within the first year. Miquel didn't. The inhibitor didn't shut him off, which would have been easier. Carrie hoped recovery was something they could do together. They had scars coming out of the war, but taking care of Miquel was the priority; anything she might have shared would burden him. If he got better, he'd know what was going on with her. If he wasn't broken, she wouldn't have to say.

"I brought you churros," she says.

"From La Catrina?" he asks. "That sounds amazing." The first time she brought them, he asked where they came from. Carrie lied about making a run down to Pilsen to deliver crates of fresh produce. She added details about scurvy outbreaks, embellishing until the lie was improbably ornate. Miquel said they were great and encouraged her to pick up more whenever she could. She was sure he knew and was giving her his blessing. Every time she brings them, his gratitude stings.

"*From Here to Eternity*?" she asks, pointing at the screen.

"*A Place in the Sun*," says Miquel. "*Eternity* is Clift and Donna Reed."

"But it's sad," Carrie says, sitting next to him. She takes one of the cold churros from the bag.

"Movie sad is good," he says. "Movie sad is dark blue, but soft like fabric."

"What's real sad?" Carrie asks.

"Same color," Miquel says through a mouthful of churro. "Slick like a raincoat."

He leans into her. The blanket forms a border between them, and she kisses Miquel's shoulder through it.

"Every time you leave me for a minute, it's like goodbye," he says. "I like to believe it means you can't live without me."

The words startle her. It's rare that he talks about emotions as analogous to other emotions, the way a normal person would. She smiles sadly. "I always come back," she says.

"It's from the movie," says Miquel, pointing at the screen. "Taylor says it to Clift near the end."

"I *can't* live without you," she says. She trails her fingers near his cheek, not touching. She imagines they brush his stubble, enough contact for an electrical charge to jump between them, but she's swiping air.

After *A Place in the Sun* ends in a swell of violins, they watch two Marx Brothers movies. Carrie sits on the couch, and Miquel sits on the floor at her feet. He makes them a salad with vegetables he grabbed out of the walk-in cooler. "Don't tell Carlton," he says, winking. She knows he goes upstairs sometimes. Waylon finds Miquel in the club chatting with strangers. Miquel swears he can manage it in short bursts, but he sounds like an alcoholic saying one drink won't be the end of the world. He binges on emotions. He looks in from the outside, and before he knows it, he can't differentiate other people's feelings from his own. He's inhabited by them, experiencing them without the coping mechanisms people build for themselves. Someone's decade-old grief at the loss of their father hits Miquel as if he's just gotten the call from the hospital. A buried grudge against a friend erupts as fighting rage. Once, he convinced Carrie he could handle a "date." Carrie got dressed up and met him at the bar. Two drinks in, it was going well. It felt normal. While Carrie was in the ladies' room Miquel followed another woman out of the bar with her boyfriend. "But I love her," Miquel told Waylon, joyful tears welling in his eyes as

Waylon dragged him back into the club past a stunned and confused Carrie. Carrie didn't visit for a few days after that.

While Carrie washes the dishes, he recites lines back at the screen.

He says, "I've had a perfectly wonderful evening, but this wasn't it."

He says, "You canna fool a me. There ain't no sanity clause."

She imagines versions of them in black and white, speaking in movie quotes. She'd be bumbling Cary Grant to his cool Hepburn. He'd be Bacall to her Bogie. He's more fluent, quicker on the draw. She'd be Margaret Dumont to his Groucho Marx.

Carrie nods off halfway through *A Day at the Races,* and Miquel shakes her awake.

"Your dreams are purple liquid," he says. "Children's cough syrup." His face looks stricken, and Carrie tries to remember what she was dreaming about. When her dreams seep into his head, it's time for her to go. She puts her hands on his shoulders, leans down, and kisses the center of his chest through his shirt.

ROOSEVELT ISLAND/PARK SLOPE

◇

Officially, it's the Roosevelt Island Research Facility. In four years working there, Clay Weaver has never heard anyone call it that. On his paychecks, he's listed as "Operator, Remote Site Five." The site numbering developed during the war centered on the Bishop Academy in Midtown as Site Zero, an origin point. Their Fort Sumter. Clay didn't buy into the mythology of the war, but the structure of thinking about places as strategic points never left him. He can list remote sites up into the midtwenties like some fucked-up nursery rhyme: *One for the Chicago school, two for LA. Three for the Houston school the feds blew away. Four is the Phoenix, lost in the collapse. Five is the island where Fahima builds traps.*

The people who commute here daily call it the Ruse, the sound falling away at the end as if they're talking about medieval Russians: *Rus.* Clay likes it because it sounds like wind racing across the East River from the Lower East Side. He waits in line with the rest of the employees at the checkpoint on Vernon and 36th, sipping coffee he polluted with too much milk and sugar to cover up the bitterness. He sees Thao Bui, one of the other operators, and two shapers who work in the physical plant on the west shore. One's Wesley and one's William, but his brain refuses to track which is which. No one talks outside the checkpoint. Everywhere that isn't on the island is an unsecure environment. It's never been clear to Clay who might be listening, but no one talks.

A Faction agent with a dead expression Hivescans Clay. It's never the same one two days in a row, or it's the same one every day. They're fungible. The Faction runs the checkpoints and polices the borders, but they aren't permitted on the island. Clay thanks the agent, who doesn't respond, and crams onto the maglev that ferries the employees across the East River. As soon as the doors shut, chatter picks up, the silent train serving as the Ruse's watercooler. Employees group by type rather than assigned project, techs with techs and heads with heads. There are only a handful of operators like Clay, and they tend to be left out of light morning conversations. Clay is eavesdropping on a discussion of the latest Hayden Cohen album when he's gripped by the shoulders from behind and given a vigorous shake.

"There he is," says Thao, delivering what he considers a massage. "How are you feeling today, Mr. Weaver? Ready to change the world?"

"Hey, Thao," Clay says.

"Can I tell you I feel amazing?" Thao says. "I am going to bury the needle today. Omars are going to be like *what the fuck?*" He sustains the last word like an opera singer holding a high note. Clay cranes his neck to see the expression on Thao's face. Sometimes his enthusiasm is so overpitched, Clay's convinced it's an act. He waits for a knowing wink from behind the mask, but Thao is all mask.

"That's awesome, man," says Clay. He assumes a boxer's stance and feints a jab to Thao's middle. "Get in there and knock it down."

"I'm going to kill it all day," Thao says. Clay winces at his choice of words, and Thao catches it. His rubbing turns into a two-handed pat, which is no more relaxing. "You know what I mean." He gets a faraway look that for most people would mean they've vacated their bodies and dropped into the Hive. For Thao it means he's having a thought. "They should find a way to like combine our abilities," he says. "Like my power and your restraint or whatever. I'm the gas and you're the brake, and then you slam on both at once and—" Thao does a chef's kiss gesture that, combined with his failure to understand how cars work, might warrant a chef's kiss gesture for idiocy.

"You should tell the Omars, man," says Clay.

"I'm going to take it right to Miz Deeb," Thao says. "She'll be like, *Thao, you have saved us all.*" He delivers this with his hands clasped under his jaw, eyelashes fluttering.

"Go see her first thing, man," Clay says, "or I'm going to steal your idea."

"You wouldn't even."

"No, man," says Clay, tossing back the last dregs of his coffee. "It's all yours."

Clay and Thao disembark at the lab bays of Project Tuning Fork. Thao fist-bumps Clay as he peels off for Beta Bay. Clay trudges down the line toward Theta. The bays and their operators are arranged in order of how promising they are, with Alpha Bay currently vacant and waiting for the operator-device combination that can replicate the Pulse at its original scale but without the lethal side effects most of the operators produce. They call the empty bay the Throne, although there's no device in it. The closest it came to occupancy was three years ago, when Ollie Carson's numbers indicated he could hit a 70 percent activation rate over a ten-mile radius. Before Ollie and his device could assume the Throne, Cedric Joyner—head of the department and serious creep—took Ollie to Indianapolis for an unauthorized test run. It ended with half the city activated and the other half dead, Ollie catatonic, and Joyner fired, exiled to the Wastes. Everyone on Project Tuning Fork assumed they were finished, but another operator who was nowhere near as talented as Ollie came in and took over as head of Tuning Fork, and the work continued.

Clay nods to Roxane and Marlon in Gamma and Delta. He notes that Zinzi's been jumped up to Epsilon from Eta, and Lauren in Zeta is still out sick. Another week and Clay will get bumped up into the vacant lab bay, but for now he's at home in Theta. Omars Eleven and Six greet him with their standard grunts of *here we are again*. Fahima makes the Omars on the Ruse wear numbers on their lapels, like the citizens of the Village in *The Prisoner.* Clay is secretly thrilled that he gets to work with Number Six. On his first day here, when Fahima was giving him the tour, Clay did a passable rendition of Patrick McGoohan's *I am not a number, I'm a human being* speech that left everyone but Fahima confused. She doesn't come around the labs much lately, but since that day, Clay's sure he's her secret favorite.

"You boys have anything new for me today?" Clay asks.

"You have anything new for *us*?" says Omar Eleven. His voice drips with snark.

"Yeah, I developed radical new abilities this morning over breakfast," Clay says. "I think it's going to really blow your skirt up."

Omar Eleven rolls his eyes and turns back to his console. "Fahima was in tweaking the Chair last night," says Omar Six. "So who knows, maybe today's the day it all clicks."

"Let's make some magic," Clay says. He opens the door to the entry room, where his suit hangs like a discarded skin. He wonders if they clean it every night or if there are a couple they rotate through. Mostly he doesn't think about it. Thao imagines himself a science hero, but for Clay this is a job no different from the one he had before the war. Ramifications are above his pay grade, the practicalities of laundering the suits below it. From nine to five, it's him and the Chair and nothing else. He strips and pulls on the suit. Part of the reason Thao thinks so highly of himself is that they dress operators up like comic book superheroes. Bright colored spandex hugs every line of Clay's softening physique like an editor circling typos in red ink. He opens the inner door with a hiss of released air and steps into the bright lights.

Clay circles the Chair like a dancer sizing up his partner. He looks for anything different, a new blinky light. He'd notice any change; Clay and the Chair know each other intimately. They have a sense of each other's limits and possibilities. They work as much against each other as in collaboration, each trying to overcome a lack in the other. Unable to spot Fahima's latest tweak, Clay sits down and attaches sensors to the suit.

"There's a connection between the Hive and time," Fahima explained to Clay when he was hired. "The first Pulse was the result of a decent device combined with an extraordinary operator." She didn't give the operator's name, but Emmeline Hirsch is a legend on the Ruse. She hadn't died causing the Pulse, but if she hadn't expended so much energy creating a hundred million new Resonants, she could have won the fight at the Bishop Academy on her own instead of eating a bullet. As combinations of new devices and operators fail from Beta to Omega, they harbor secret hopes for the second coming of Emmeline Hirsch, emerging from the gray water of the East River, the solution to all equations.

The idea is to create a fracture in the Hive by using time as a wedge. Done right, the Source the Hive links them all to will come pouring through into the real world, replicating the Pulse, creating new Resonants en masse. On a good day, Clay pokes pinholes through the Hive, letting energy dribble through. He can spread

Resonance at the rate someone can hand out flyers for bus tours on a street corner. They're aiming at something bigger.

Omar Six's voice comes through the tinny speakers that hang above the Chair. "You ready to fire up?"

Clay smiles. Omar Six feigns enthusiasm at the beginning and end of the day. In between, he shares Omar Eleven's boredom with their constant failure.

"Ready as I'm getting," says Clay. He feels the buzz as the Chair comes to life. It searches for his ability, zeroing in on the parahippocampal gyrus, the magical spot in his brain. Clay pushes against the Chair's prodding, expanding the buzz outward. A translucent bubble forms around him and the Chair, a membrane where regular time meets the faster, more fluid time Clay's ability produces. In the lab window, the Omars check the readouts, moving as if suspended in a viscous liquid. He wonders if the Omars know how much longer the days are for him inside the bubble. He wonders if Fahima has considered that his ability ages him faster than it does them during the day, like the stationary sibling in Einstein's twin paradox. He wonders if any of them care that every day he shows up to work, he's dying a little faster.

Before the war, Clay worked on the sales team of a publishing house. He's familiar with the concept of a work bar, a place where people convene after clocking out to prolong the workday by having a beer or two and complaining about the eight hours that came before. The alternative was to carry the work home and dream about the numbers or the fall frontlist. They pay for your days, and they get your nights for free.

The Ruse modified this concept by placing the New Deal on the island, within the security checkpoint. They didn't want packs of Ruse employees out in the wilds of Midtown, getting drunk among the civilian population. Because it's right next to the mag-lev heading out, a stop at the New Deal at the end of the day is socially obligatory, if not compulsory. Clay tries to sneak out, but Roxane and Marlon spot him through the window. When he shrugs and gestures to a nonexistent watch, they beckon him over, and he capitulates.

The New Deal aspires to the aesthetics of the cookie-cutter spots he used to find in suburban malls. The drink prices are subsidized, but beyond that there's not much to recommend it. High trebly classic rock punctures conversation, but tomorrow it might be AM gold ballads floating at the edge of audibility. Heads huddle around a corner booth, spouting ideas for alchemical machines that convert base matter into weird drugs. A cluster of Omars chat among themselves at the bar, raising the eternal question of how individuated they are. Marlon complains about his assigned Omars, and Roxane laments the lack of lumbar support in her Chair. Clay settles in with a beer that disappears faster than he intended and feels pinned when Thao shows up with another.

"You see the match last night?" Thao asks.

"Missed it," says Clay. Thao's a huge fan of Hiveball, a confusing, violent hybrid of jai alai and football with rules constructed by someone who thought Quidditch was too simple. Clay prefers football matches from an underground European league that allows Resonants to play. It's glacially slow, but Clay understands the predictable movement of the ball even as players disappear or dart across the pitch at impossible speeds. They play in the middle of the night under the blue patina of sodium arc lights. Bootleg footage shows up on the Internet a week after the matches, and Clay stays up to watch them at the same time they're played so he can feel exhausted with the players.

"I thought Krieger was going to get killed," says Thao. "Like as in literally killed." Clay's lack of interest in the sport never dissuades Thao from talking about it. "Chicago fucking sucks. You know their goalkeep's a Damp?"

"That's a shitty word," Marlon says.

Thao ignores him. "Like yes, we get it. Your town is this pinnacle of integration or whatever. Can't I watch a game without it being all politics? Everything else in my life is political. Can I have one thing?"

"Work's not political," Clay says.

Cheeks chipmunked with cheap beer, Thao shakes his head and swallows. "Work's political as fuck," he says. "If it wasn't, we'd be working for Cedric and this shit would be done."

"Cedric was a monster," Marlon says.

"And a creep," Roxane adds. "Wasn't bad enough having him stare down my shirt, I had to feel his grubby brain slinking around my thoughts."

"But he had vision," Thao says.

"So did Hitler," says Marlon.

Thao rolls his eyes. "Hitler Hitler Hitler," he singsongs.

"Seriously?" says Roxane.

"Cedric understood there's such a thing as collateral damage," Thao says. "Can't make an omelet and shit." He slaps Clay on the arm. "You were in the war; you get it."

"I was in communications," Clay says. He takes a quick swig of beer and looks away.

"I thought you were in the shit."

"I was a glorified mailman."

"Were *you* in the shit?" Roxane asks Thao.

"Dude, I was fifteen," says Thao. "But I would have been. I'm saying if it wasn't for politics, me and every operator from Zeta up would be out on our European tour."

"You think 'we shouldn't kill baseliners' is a political position?" Clay asks.

"I'm saying thinking it matters is a political position."

Loosened by two beers, Clay is ready to wade into the argument. He's prepared to let loose on Thao and end the détente of their work friendship in the service of shutting down one more bit of ignorance in the world. As he draws a deep breath, he feels an insistent tug at the back of his head in the aching spot where his ability resides. He raises one finger, about to ignore the tug and continue schooling Thao, but thinks better of it.

"Excuse me," he says. He leans back in his chair and drops into the Hive, letting his body go limp. He's old enough to remember when answering your phone in public was a dick move. Now he abandons his body in midconversation to take a call.

His Hivebody manifests, leaving trails like in an acid trip. Dominic is waiting, his Hivebody brilliant in sparkling facets, like his real body. He's as beautiful as he was when they met and doesn't seem to have aged in the years since. His posture radiates impatience.

"Where are you?" he says.

"I'm having one at the New Deal," says Clay. "It was a whole day."

"It's a whole day for *you*." Dom turns his head and mutters this as if he's speaking to an invisible audience, then turns back to Clay. "You know I have the thing tonight."

"Shit," says Clay. The gala Dom has been planning for months, the only thing he's talked about this week. "Yes, I know. I forgot."

"And there's the thing at Rai's school. Did you remember *that*?"

"I slipped," he says. It's a loaded word between them, and Clay shouldn't use it as a shield. It's out before he thinks it.

Dom flinches, then lays a glittering hand on Clay's shoulder. "Honey, I need you not to slip today." This is the part when Clay gets issued his orders. Dom is the organized one, the planner. Clay is the one who does as he's told. "I'm at the site," says Dom. "It starts in an hour. Can you head right to the school?"

"I'm on the next train," Clay says.

"You're not all sweaty?" Dom asks. What he means is a combination of *do you smell like beer?* and *do you smell working class?* The answer is *yes* to both.

"I'll throw some deodorant on and I'm good," he says.

"Honey, then you're going to smell like sweat and deodorant."

"I can be a little smelly or a whole lot late," Clay says.

Dom closes his eyes and takes a deep breath, something he does when he's accepting things in the world that he can't change. Many of those are things about Clay. "I love you, and I appreciate you're going to this for us," he says.

"I love you, and you're going to be the prettiest one at the ball," Clay says. Dom kisses him on the cheek. In the Hive's absence of feeling, Clay has the memory of the sensation of diamond brushing against his stubble.

"I'll bring you some strawberry cake or something," says Dom, a botched lyric from a Bjork song. When they were dating, Clay tried to get Dominic into things Clay considered cool. Strange bits of that time stud the strata of their relationship. Even if Dom doesn't remember why, he promises to bring Clay strawberry cake from every event he organizes.

Dom's Hivebody fractals and fades. Clay comes out of the Hive, aware of the closeness of Thao's face. Thao's poised with a Sharpie to draw a mustache on Clay like some frat boy prank. Clay grabs his wrist, squeezes it hard. The Sharpie drops to the floor. For a second Thao gets a glimpse of the monster Clay used to be. Thao's ability flares up, slowing time around them, but he's panicked and clumsy. Clay's ability sloughs it off. They stalemate and release. Clay slams Thao's wrist on the table, clanking empty glassware.

"Fucking idiot," he mutters, letting go of the arm. Thao rubs his wrist and gives Clay a toss of his head to indicate they're cool. Marlon and Roxane shake their heads, but Clay knows he's shown them something he shouldn't have.

"I gotta go," he says, making a point of not including Thao in the goodbye. "Kid stuff."

"We'll see you tomorrow," Marlon says. Roxane doesn't say anything. Clay picks up his bag and walks out of the bar as a drum counts in the beginning of another song.

Berkeley Carroll is arguably the best private school in Brooklyn, particularly if the parent of a Berkeley Carroll student is doing the arguing. Clay knows because he looked into it; before the war, he and Dom weren't anxious Brooklyn parents mapping out cost-benefit analyses of every educational outlet in the borough. If they made the choice back then, Berkeley Carroll wouldn't have been on the table. The tuition was higher than Clay's salary, and between that and Dom's event planning start-up, they were scraping to make rent.

After the war, the Bishop Foundation poured massive resources into education. Berkeley Carroll is among the city's best, though not by so stark a margin, and comparable options brought the price down from the stratosphere. It would have been out of their budget, but *arrangements had been made.* This is one of Dominic's favorite things to get to say, offhandedly, as if the influence he's expended is drawn from an infinite wellspring of clout. When they were dating, it was such an established Dominicism their friends adopted it to announce they'd saved seats at a movie or picked up beer on their way over. Like so many things about Dom, Clay loved it on the days he loved it and seethed at the sound of it on days when anything Dom did was too much, too him.

On the subject of Berkeley Carroll, Clay was torn. He wanted the best for Rai. He wished the best wasn't so stereotypically bougie. Every time life required him to step into the hallowed halls of Berkeley Carroll, he worried he'd be told to use the back entrance or greeted with "What are *you* doing here?" He feared the day he'd commit some faux pas in front of Rai and his friends, prompting his son to hide his eyes in disgust, or explain to his chums that they mustn't blame his father for being a bit *low;* he hadn't come up with the same opportunities they had. They're irrational fears, as Dom never gets tired of telling him, but irrational fears are the most persistent. Taking a glass of champagne off a tray, Clay would be more comfortable taking the tray, serving the elite the way he did back at his college catering job, and smoking with the cooks at the end of the shift.

A bell tinkles, and the parents file into the auditorium and take their seats. As far as he can tell, Clay's the only one here on his own. Berkeley Carroll attracts superparents who move heaven and earth to attend parents' nights and school plays. Not the kind who hustle their asses out of a bar to get there on time. On the stage, the boys and girls of Berkeley Carroll line up on risers, standing as still as wax figures. Rai is in the top row, tall for his age, staring determinedly at a spot on the back wall of the auditorium. Clay stands up and waves, trying to avoid being the hokey parent by being a parody of the hokey parent. Rai's mouth twists into a knot that's a smile and a scowl combined. It's an expression he inherited from his mother.

Maaya and Koyo Taneda, Rai's birth parents, were part of Clay's Bloom during the war. Each group of five was organized on the basis of compatible ability sets; Clay's time dilation allowed Maaya to launch rocks the size of beach balls at the government troops as if she'd shot them out of a gun. Rai was six when his parents joined up, and they talked about him all the time. During the calm between fights, Koyo constructed a hard-light projection of Rai and set it toddling around their encampments. Stationed a few blocks from the Houston school, Maaya held Clay's hand in both of hers and asked him to take care of Rai if anything happened to her and Koyo. Clay laughed. Their Bloom had the highest success rate in the Faction. They were untouchable. It was an easy, inconsequential promise to make.

They made it to the second floor before they realized the school was rigged. An inhibitor surged once like a flashbulb, wiping out all of their abilities. The little voice that buzzed in their heads was silent for what seemed like the first time in months, but by then they could predict orders before they came in. Rather than abort, as they should have, they continued, as they imagined they would have been ordered to. The psychics said students were locked in their dorms on the upper floors. When the bombs started going off, he lost track of the rest of his Bloom as he weaved his way through blast and shrapnel. He saw Koyo fall through a tile floor as it melted under his feet, and watched Jorge vaporized as he opened a classroom door. Maaya's body he found later, crisped. He never found out what happened to the Kid. Only a handful of Faction made it out of the school, and none of the students or faculty inside survived. Clay saw a chance to walk away and took it, wandering across the wreckage of the school rather than back to the medical tent. He left the fight a father, although the reality of that wouldn't settle in until he'd suffered little Rai's sobs and fists at the news that his parents were dead, until the survivor guilt subsided and the monotony of raising a boy, the repetition and the act of it, worked like a trellis for the real feeling to cling to and grow on.

Clay gives Rai a double thumbs-up. Rai rolls his eyes in a way unique to teenagers expressing loving exasperation and embarrassment with their parents. The headmaster, a posh skeleton of a man whose name Clay forgets, takes to the podium in front of a wall of stoic-faced students. He welcomes everyone to parents' night and produces a stack of index cards from the inside pocket of his suit coat.

"The question is, how best to live in the world?" he proclaims. Heads in the crowd bob as if they had been, moments before, pondering this exact problem. "But then, when was this not the question?" This gets a polite chuckle from the crowd before the headmaster's face returns to its serious mien and everyone hushes up. "While others look to what has changed, here at Berkeley Carroll we look deeper, into what remains. So much is different than it was when you or I last stepped into a classroom. In this brave new world, there are still truths. And there is, still, Truth." He says this so it's understood to have a capital *T*, and the audience nods to show they've received the message. "I like to think that if you were to take one of the young men or women of this school and place them at any point in time, they would possess not only the skills to thrive but the wisdom to live a life both upstanding and wondrous."

The word, delivered with swooping rapture, elicits the polite rendition of thunderous applause, fingertips rapidly tapping the meat of hands wrapped around the stems of champagne flutes. The woman next to him clinks her glass against Clay's in what can only be a toast to themselves as paragons of parenting. The gentle chime of crystal on crystal throughout the room is as loud as the preceding applause.

As the clapping fades, a single male alto voice hangs high in the room on one sustained note. Clay finds the sound of young boys singing unsettling, ghostly. Another voice joins him a step lower, followed by a third on the same note. The sopranos come in on a cascading series of eighth notes, grouped in fours. The tenors, Rai included, take the vocal line, lyrics about coming home to an empty apartment, words Clay has loved since he was Rai's age, too young to understand their meaning. He looks around to see if any of the other parents recognize the song, but he's apparently the only Duran Duran fan in the audience.

"Easily the best power ballad of the nineties," he told Rai when he played "Ordinary World" for him last month. In typical Rai fashion, he described the song he wanted but not what he needed it for. *Power ballad* wasn't a phrase in Rai's vocabulary, so it took a while before they hit on songs that met his criteria.

"Is there anything more . . . modern?" Rai asked.

On the couch, Dom busted out laughing. "That song's older than we are," he said.

Grumbling for show, Clay played more recent songs, songs he and Dom danced to when they were dating and still went out dancing. "All My Friends" by LCD Soundsystem was too long and rhythm driven. "Maps" by the Yeah Yeah Yeahs was too romantic. Clay played songs he'd loved in college. Lorde's "Green Light," Carly Rae Jepsen's "Run Away with Me." Both too dancy. He thought about songs the Kid used to play as they traveled from one battle to the next. She had an old-school iPod full of new music, songs that sounded like folk standards run through a wood chipper and reassembled, singers whose voices bypassed the rational brain and played the listener's emotions like a harp. It had been easy to forget that culture was still happening. People were making art and singing songs and fucking and going to work while other people got ready to kill one another. All those songs got lost, swallowed up in the war.

When Rai failed to find the perfect song for his obscure purposes, Clay let his annoyance flare up. "Do some pop song," he said. Rai, not so much wounded as trying to keep Clay happy, asked him to "play the nineties one again." Clay watched as the song sunk in, as Rai's mind moved past the specifics of the verses into the plaintive sense of being permanently lost that rang through the chorus.

"Yes," Rai said. "That."

The student's a cappella rendition swells to its ending; harmonies thread together and peel off one by one until the alto is alone in the room. Then nothing. Clay doesn't give a fuck about decorum. He gets to his feet, unabashedly whooping and cheering, clapping as if he's trying to smash the champagne flute between his hands. People throw side eye his way, but Rai looks directly at him, so proud of himself, and so grateful to see that pride reflected in his dad's face.

The parents are herded back into the lobby, where each is handed an individualized schedule, a minute-by-minute agenda for their evening at Berkeley Carroll. Clay reads down the list of Rai's teachers, whom he'll be meeting in ten-minute snippets to review Rai's progress. He exchanges his empty glass for a full one. A better class of parent could manage this without being seen.

The conferences confirm what Clay already knows about his son. Rai is sweet and adept, impossible not to like. Unlike Clay or Dom, he excels at most things he tries, if without the commitment or engagement his teachers might like. Each teacher wants Rai to select their subject area as his lifelong passion. "I believe he could . . ." followed by some astounding and imminently possible feat of academic prowess Rai might accomplish.

Lightly buzzed, glazed over from the assault of effusive praise, Clay knocks on the door of Rai's psychic defense instructor, Mr. Castillo, his last meeting of the evening. Dominic had singled him out to Clay at parent orientation, tugging at Clay's belt loop and pointing from the hip. "Your type," he said. It might be true; Castillo's the waifish, nerdy kind of man Clay chased before he and Dominic got together. Clay resented Dominic pointing it out and took a determined dislike to Castillo. Clay and Dom had never been a couple who called attention to outside objects for the other to desire. Dominic started doing it after he *slipped,* before Clay found out about it. It went away for a while as they worked things out in the wake, figuring how and if to move forward. It resurfaced when Dominic was explicitly forgiven, at which point the implication was clearer. Dominic wanted Clay to stray once so they'd be even. He wanted it to happen so he could forgive it. It was typical of Dominic to fail to understand that their relationship was not a mechanism made of inputs and outputs, scales in need of balance. He could construct events with dozens of moving parts, vast orreries of social interactions, but he understood the heart as a machine of ventricles and atria working in perfect rhythm rather than as its true shape, a mess of frayed and sparking wires tangled in inextricable knots.

What made it worse was that the introduction of forgiveness put infidelity on the table for Clay in a way that was counter to who he wanted to be as a partner. As he sits across the desk from Mr. Castillo, his mind strays a moment down that path. *I'm allowed one,* he thinks. *I'm* owed *one. One slip.* Like an extra arcade token in his pocket, the idea hums with possibility.

"Mr. Weaver?" says Castillo, returning Clay to the room, the correct path.

"Sorry."

"Sorry, no," Castillo says, flustered. "I was saying this is probably the most *practical* class Rai will take. It's a life skills issue rather than something academic. Not to say it isn't important, but it's not as if he's going to pursue a career."

"Right," says Clay. He thinks of boys like Castillo he dated in college, how their sweet self-effacement rankled after a while, set him up to be swept away by Dominic's swagger and assuredness.

"That said, Rai is doing well for someone in his position."

"In his position?"

"Pre-Resonant," says Castillo.

"He's young for his grade," Clay says. "His father, his biological father, was a late bloomer too. Nearly sixteen."

"Is his biological father . . . in the picture?"

It could be a come-on line. It's hard to read through Castillo's general sense of discomfort.

"He died in the war," Clay says. "Dominic and I adopted Rai when he was seven."

Castillo nods, and Clay searches his expression for a trace of disappointment. "They start younger than we did, mostly. We, I mean, are you a—"

"Pulser," Clay says. "You?"

Castillo shakes his head. "I was a student at the Bishop Academy when the Pulse hit. I wasn't there for any of what happened. They evacuated us before things started. I spent most of the war hiding in Chicago."

"That was a good place to be," says Clay.

Castillo shakes his head to clear it, but he's flustered. "There are always a couple, though, who haven't resonated yet. External defense is more meditative, but for Hivecraft, we have the option of more of a theoretical curriculum." He laughs. "It's like watching *Enter the Dragon* instead of taking a karate class."

"Boards don't hit back," says Clay.

Castillo smiles warmly at him. "Exactly."

Your type, Clay thinks.

"Rai has the knowledge," Castillo says. "When he reaches the point where application is an issue. I mean, there are concerns, of course."

"Of course."

A gentle bell rings, signaling the end of their session. Clay stands up and extends his hand across the desk. "Thank you, Mr.

Castillo," he says. "I'm sure Rai will be ready when the time comes, and he'll have you to thank."

Castillo takes his hand, shakes it, and holds it a beat too long. He looks Clay directly in the eye. "Mr. Weaver, would you like to grab a quick drink?"

"I've got to get Rai home."

"There are things I still want to talk to you about," he blurts out. "They really don't give us much time here."

Clay thinks about how much time he could give them. He could envelop them in a bubble where seconds last hours.

"Please," says Castillo. Something in his voice is unambiguously not flirting. Clay can't tell what it is, but he knows what it isn't.

"Rai can get home on his own," he says reluctantly. "Not like he hasn't before."

"There's a place on Flatbush," says Castillo. "Sharlene's, not the 333. The whole Berkeley Carroll staff will be at 333 in twenty minutes."

"Sharlene's on Flatbush. In, what, half an hour?"

"Perfect," says Castillo. "Thank you."

The handshake, held limply in the air through this exchange, finally breaks, and Castillo dashes out of the room, leaving Clay alone among the desks and framed motivational posters.

In the gym, the students divide neatly along gender lines. The boys play basketball with shirtsleeves rolled up, ties loosened. The girls choreograph dance routines to a Hayden Cohen song. Each group studiously avoids checking to see if the other is paying attention. Rai passes the ball when he sees Clay and jogs over, sweaty dark bangs falling into his eyes.

"What'd you think?" he asks.

"You guys sounded great," Clay says, pulling Rai under one arm for the closest thing to a hug the boy will allow in public.

"I did the arrangement," he says. "Ms. Zimmerman helped, but it was mostly me."

"It was amazing," Clay says as they exit the gym. In the hallway, parents schmooze, in no rush to retrieve their children. For some people, kids are the least interesting thing about being a parent.

"We ready to go?" Rai asks.

"I was wondering if you could get home on your own," Clay says. "One of your teachers wants to talk to me."

"Which one?"

"Don't worry about it."

"Nothing good comes out of you talking to my teachers," Rai says.

"I'll be home in an hour," Clay says. "I'm sure he wants to tell me how as a Berkeley Carroll man, there are certain expectations."

"Fundamental truths," Rai says in a snooty imitation of the headmaster.

"Eternal ideals," says Clay, his impression not as spot-on as Rai's. Probably every kid at the school does a killer version of their headmaster. "Go home, throw a pizza in the oven. I'll be home before the cheese melts."

Rai grunts. "Can I order one?"

"Preheat the oven," Clay says. "Wait till it dings. Throw it in. This is well within the skill set of a Berkeley Carroll man."

"Be back before it gets cold," Rai says, pointing at Clay to hold him to his word. Clay nods, and Rai joins a pack of kids who've grown impatient with their chattering parents and decided to make a break for it on their own.

GALA

They expect it, so it happens. Fahima would prefer a massive soiree she doesn't have to attend. Omar took on the planning but refused to strike Fahima's name from the guest list. It's held at the Edison Ballroom on 47th, a large space renovated before the war to look like an early twenty-first-century vision of thirties Deco. Dull orange ghost lights haunt the crystal chandeliers, swooping down to the parquet dance floor to twirl and minuet among the guests before returning to the air. Flowing silver sculptures writhe and twist to catch pale illumination, chrome flowers bending toward the sun. The artist is in attendance; Isidra Gonzalez's work is displayed in European galleries that are willing to ignore the embargo in the name of the *avant*.

Omar has gathered a few Resonants with celebrity status abroad. Sanford Vang, a model with glistening blue scales who relocated to London because the Brits can't get enough of him and because, according to Omar, he's burned his way through everyone fuckable in New York. Marcine Walden, a film director working with images lifted from people's dreams. Aaron Faber, a lithic and stand-up comedian whose deep self-loathing makes his blatantly anti-Resonant routines a favorite of foreign audiences who like their bigotry served under a cover of ironic deniability. As asked, a few of the actors filming out front of the school that morning are here in costume. The actress playing Ji Yeon Kim wears a punk T-shirt with the band logo shiny and new, carefully cut to expose a hint of the bottom of her breasts, and purposefully small jean shorts. A young black girl who is supposed to be Emmeline Hirsch, her face streaked with bloody makeup and dust, sips a Shirley Temple through a straw.

Fahima forgets about the public narrative around Emmeline's death. It can be hard to keep her lies straight. She worries she'll run into her own doppelgänger, but Fahima was kept out of the story of the Battle of Bishop Academy. It made it easier for her to assume her current role if she was seen as unsullied by the war.

When Fahima sees the real Ji Yeon Kim, she experiences a vertigo not unlike what she experiences when she turns away from one Omar to find another behind her. Fahima can't help but remember Ji Yeon as the kid from the Revere standoff, clad in vintage T-shirts and worn-out Converse, razor haircut and litany of revolutionary rhetoric. Ji Yeon's fashion aesthetic has changed from riot grrrl to corporate terrorist. She looks like the person they send in to coolly and silently pick the carcass of an acquired company for assets before the employees know it's been sold, but her bangs are still razor cut across her forehead. Behind her, three members of her Bloom try to pull off the same look, but their dark suits and skinny ties make them look like a self-serious indie rock band.

"Aren't you short one?" Fahima asks.

Ji Yeon smiles. "We're here as guests," she says.

"But this is your Bloom," says Fahima, gesturing at the man whose arms look like skewers, the girl hovering a foot above the dance floor, the hulking woman whose massive black suit forms a backdrop for the rest. "Are they the only friends you have?"

"I have friends everywhere," says Ji Yeon.

"And your other guy, he didn't get invited?" Fahima says. "That's got to be bad for team morale."

"Busy with other things," Ji Yeon says. "Maybe he'll come by later."

Not in the mood to spar with Ji Yeon, Fahima says, "Be seeing you," makes an okay sign with her fingers, looks through the circle at all four of them, and flicks her hand downward before walking away.

She finds Niklas Babisch, former German ambassador, on one of the balconies, drinking a beer and watching the crowd move on the dance floor like protozoa on a slide. He fled the embassy with his family when the war broke out, and his expression has vacillated between wistful and angry all day.

"Are you impressed?" she asks as she sidles up to him on the railing.

"How could I fail to be impressed, Doctor?" he says. "You have made here a city of wonders." His translator renders his English with a light remnant of his accent, which makes him sound like a Bond villain. She wants to give him a cat to stroke.

"It's the beginning," says Fahima. "We're planning the overhaul of five more cities in the next—"

"I've read the brochures," he says. "And I have seen your miracles. I'm more curious about the things we haven't seen."

"If there's an infrastructure project you'd like to—"

"Tell me about the riots," he says. "Near here. In the Bronx."

The Omars took bets among themselves about whether someone would ask. Fahima hoped they wouldn't but was prepared. From the generating station they toured in Astoria, they could see the smoke rising across the East River. The wind coming in from the north carried the chants and occasionally the screams, although they were usually hidden behind the high whine of the power inverters that changed the direct current the dayshifters generated into usable alternating current.

"There are protests," she says. "That's all."

"I'm told there are water shortages," says Babisch. "Cuts to electrical services. People without food."

"Everyone there has the opportunity to leave."

"To go where?"

"West," says Fahima.

"The area you call the Wastes?" He overpronounces the word, or the nanites overrender it.

"We don't—"

"I've heard it called that," he says. Fahima is done with his cutting her off. She's used to being allowed to finish her thoughts. "Let's call it as you say. These people have options, yes? They can leave, or they can stay here and what? Be liquidated?"

"Nothing is happening to them," says Fahima.

"Nothing is happening *for* them," Babisch says. "On this side of the river, you have everything. There, they wait to die."

"Baseliners liquidated four camps," says Fahima. "In the first days of the war. Before you could even call it a war. Alta Mons. Half Moon. Holiday Home. Topaz Lake. They blew up a school full of kids in Houston and sucked all of Phoenix into a black hole fucking around with things that weren't theirs to fuck around with. We are working on forgiveness, but some of us are not there yet."

"And you?" Babisch asks.

"I'm tired of people dying," Fahima says.

Babisch mulls this a moment, then nods. "This is a good answer, Miss Deeb."

"You're very informed," she says. It's as much a lament as it is a compliment. "Most people here don't even know about the riots."

"Even a tight lid releases a bit of steam," Babisch says. His eyes never leave the dance floor.

"Who's been in contact with you?"

"Zealots," he says. He searches for a word. Fahima can hear the translator nanites in his bloodstream struggling. "*Verwandtschaft.* Family?"

"Kindred," says Fahima. The Kindred Network was a right-wing news conglomerate that quietly funded militia-run camps in the days before the war. It persisted as a fraternal organization, a bigoted boys club. Fahima keeps tabs on the cell in the Bronx, but they're mostly harmless, if awful. There's money backing them, but their goals beyond being a mutual aid society aren't clear. She's not thrilled to hear they're playing politics abroad.

"They offer us information in hopes we'll send military aid to take the country back for *real* humans," Babisch says. "They speak of the brotherhood of man."

"Are you sending them aid?"

Babisch shakes his head. "I know a Nazi when I hear one."

"Are you talking about me or them?"

He gives her a weak smile. "I did not like the situation in your Bronx, Miss Deeb," he says. "I do not like that you allow this to happen in your backyard. It makes me question either your intentions or your capacity."

"Why did you come?" Fahima snaps. She should be better at this. She *has* been better at this, but she's done this dance too many times to care about the steps. Anger flickers in her, and Babisch senses it, wincing like he's about to be struck. She smiles, draining the accusation from his question.

Confident the ground is safe, Babisch proceeds. "I don't want my country to be made obsolete," he says. "Or to become a colony ruled over by—"

"No one's colonizing anyone," Fahima says, waving this away with annoyance.

"You brought us here to make an offer," he says. "Make it."

Fahima nods. "Seven years ago, we engineered an event that's been commonly referred to as the Pulse." The first little lie. Non-Resonants are uneasy knowing the Pulse had been created by one person. Any Resonant will tell you Emmeline Hirsch caused the Pulse and, weakened from the effort, was killed in the first outbreak of combat at the Bishop Academy. Publicly, especially abroad, the Pulse was a project carried out by a team of Resonant scientists led by Fahima. The implication of plurality helps normalize the fantastic. "This event actualized the potential Resonance of a significant portion of the population of—"

"Significant but not all," says Babisch.

"Not all," Fahima says.

"What happened to those who were not actualized?"

"Nothing happened to them," Fahima says. "The event occurred. Some changed. For others, nothing happened."

"Like the people in your Bronx," he says. "Or in the *Wests*." His pronunciation lands exactly middistance between *west* and *Wastes* in a way Fahima is convinced he's practiced.

"That is a simplification of a complicated political—"

"There was a war, and they lost," Babisch says.

"There were political conditions particular to America at the time that led to hostilities," says Fahima. "Conditions you don't have at home."

"Yet," Babisch says. He's afraid Fahima's selling him the same war that split America. There are days she doesn't think about the war despite the dead, despite Denver and Boston gone, miles of the California coast dropped into the ocean. It's her job to deal with the result, the half of the country that belongs to Resonants and the disenfranchised enclaves that refuse to move or be moved. The war was a readjustment, the balancing of a scale that had drifted out of true.

"The terms of the Armistice reflected resentments born out of the action of the previous government," she says.

"You're very good at this, Dr. Deeb," Babisch says. "I might imagine talking around uncomfortable truths is your superpower."

Fahima grits her teeth. "We don't use the term *superpower*."

"*Fähigkeit.*" The nanites inside him hum. "Ability, is that right?" says Babisch. "Some of the words in our languages are close but inexact. My assistant wrote me up a style sheet for this conversation, but I only skimmed it. *Ability* is the preferred term?" She never gets used to the way the humans from the old world talk to her, the way they make her feel *less than*. It feels like setting the clocks back seven years. "May I ask what your ability is?"

"Your assistant should have told you it's rude to ask."

"Then may I be rude?"

They always ask. With fascination, with horror, or with the condescension Babisch is showing her, the high hand of demanding that an off-duty magician do a parlor trick. They always ask, as if they don't believe you are what you say you are.

"I make impossible things," she says. "I invent miracle machines." *But do you?* asks a nagging voice that sounds like Alyssa's. *How long's it been since your last miracle? How's your latest dream machine coming along, Fahima?*

Babisch rolls his eyes theatrically. "So you're very smart," he says.

"About some things," says Fahima. "Less so about others. Can I continue?" Babisch nods. "We believed the Pulse was a unique event. But we've been able to duplicate it." Another lie. The tech isn't there yet. Fahima's selling notions, setting up buyers, when she should be in the lab, making the thing work.

"How many of these men have already agreed to your terms?" he asks.

"I'm not at liberty to say," Fahima says.

"I suppose I'll find out soon."

Fahima gives the barest hint of a shrug.

"Your *method* doesn't work on everyone," he says.

"We estimate a two-thirds effective rate."

"And the rest of us are left behind?"

"The rest are exactly who they were before. Nothing changes."

Babisch smacks his hand on the railing. "*Everything* changes," he hisses.

That's the fucking point, Fahima thinks.

"You're thinking at an individual level," she says. "I'm asking you to think at the level of nation. How would *Germany* be affected? How could *Germany* be helped?"

"Has America been *helped*?"

"You've seen New York," Fahima says. "It's the dream of what a city can be. Our other cities aren't far behind." Another lie. No place else has received Fahima's direct attention the way New York has. They've gotten the scraps, the bits that are easily replicable. "I'm not talking only in terms of technology. The impact on race relations, on economics and class, has been revolutionary."

"For your people," Babisch says.

"We're working to share what we have," Fahima says. "Admitting mistakes, we are expanding our positive impact."

"You knew my answer when you mailed me my ticket to your magical kingdom," Babisch says. "You need to see it on our faces, don't you? I wager every one of us looks the same when we submit. *Yes, dear overlord, we want the gifts you offer. We need them lest we become a backwater of mere humans.*" He swigs the rest of his beer and twirls the bottle by the neck. "Germany will take the deluxe package, please. Will that be cash on delivery or is there an installment plan?"

Babisch is right: There is a look they all get. It's the hopeless eyes of someone in the moment they act on a horrible decision they've already made. And it's the same every time.

Fahima takes a delicate sip of her drink. "Consider it a gift."

PARK SLOPE

◇

Sharlene's on Flatbush would be the perfect bar at which to begin a lazy affair. Dominic walked Clay through every detail of his dalliance like a proper lapsed Catholic. He had to carry on in dives in the Lower East Side for fear of running into anyone they knew. The inconvenience of hiding was the cost of cheating first. Sharlene's is blocks from their apartment, a hangout of their friends and acquaintances, and Clay sits at the bar, waiting for a man who is not his date but could be. *I'm allowed one,* he thinks.

Transplanted from the harsh fluorescents of the Berkeley Carroll classrooms to the buttery yellow light of Sharlene's, the draw of Castillo's Victorian pallor is gone. It lets Clay focus, and as Castillo bumps and squeezes his way across the crowded room, Clay tries to suss out what was behind the invitation, the thing that wasn't sexual but had the desperation and want Clay associates with his earliest closeted trysts.

"Thank you again," Castillo says as he sits down. "Can I get you a— Oh. You have."

"Can I buy you one?"

"Please," says Castillo. "I'll have"—he glances uneasily at Clay's whiskey—"one of those. Sure." Clay summons the bartender. When the drink arrives, Castillo takes a gulp and winces at the burn of it going down. He recovers and lays his hands delicately on the bar between them. "So, for one thing, you're right: Rai is young for his class. And everyone is different. At first I wasn't worried about him. Also, I'm new here. I don't have a lot of context. But he's such a good kid. And I'm worried."

"Mr. Castillo—" Clay says. He stops short of putting his hands over Castillo's.

"Nick."

"Nick," Clay repeats. "If there's something you dug out of Rai's head during a lesson, that's none of my business. Kids keep secrets. When I was his age, I had a real whopper." He smiles knowingly at Castillo, who looks back at him blankly. *Maybe I was way off,* he thinks. *Am I so old and off the market I can't even spot anymore?*

"This isn't a secret," says Castillo. "Rai doesn't know. Or he does. I don't know. I shouldn't have done it."

"Nick," says Clay. This time he does put his hand over Castillo's. It's shaking.

"I did a sounding," Castillo says. "A deep Hivescan. Even with nascents, there's something you can pick up. Some people say even as babies you can tell. But by Rai's age there's something there. Except with Rai, there isn't."

It's Clay's turn to stare blankly while Castillo pushes the implication of what he's said. "His parents were both Resonants," Clay says. "They led a support group in Crown Heights. They were some of the first I met."

"I don't think that matters."

"He's young," says Clay. "In another year, he'll be—"

"In a year they'll sound him," Castillo says. "The beginning of second year in the upper school, all the students who haven't resonated get brought in and sounded by the Faction. They claim it's because it can shake things loose. I don't think it does. I think they want to weed out anyone who isn't."

"What do they do if someone isn't?" Clay asks. He can't bring himself to form the question around Rai, to ask what happens if *Rai* isn't.

"I don't know," Castillo says. "I've been trying to ask, quietly. Theoretically. But everyone shrugs. I don't think it happens often. But something must happen. They wouldn't do it if they weren't going to do anything about it."

"Have you told anyone?"

"I wouldn't do that," Castillo says emphatically. "I'm supposed to. I'm a mandatory reporter. I could lose my job. But without knowing what would happen, I couldn't tell anyone." He puts his elbows on the bar and rests his head awkwardly in his hands. "I didn't know what to do." The bar's not the right height for this gesture of defeat. Castillo raises his head and shoves his hands in his pockets. Clay wants to comfort him even though he knows it's a bad urge. His discomfort with other people's pain, even if they deserve it, is what made him so quick to forgive Dominic. "I thought if you knew, you'd have better options," says Castillo. "Or some options at least. Because if the Faction knows, then whatever happens is going to happen." He sniffles, lifts his drink, and takes the daintiest sip. "I was thinking Chicago."

"We have lives here," says Clay. "We can't up and go."

"You can make a choice," Castillo says. "Right now, you can choose." He looks across the bar at the group that just entered. "Shit," he says. "My coworkers. I have to go. Thank you for the drink. I'm sorry."

Castillo stands and turns his back on Clay, giving a wave to the rest of the Berkeley Carroll staff gathering to discuss the insufferability of the parents of Brooklyn's elite. This is their work bar. *We pay them for their days, and they talk shit about us as soon as they're off the clock*, Clay thinks. *As it should be.* He watches them for a second, then turns to his empty glass. He looks at Castillo's glass, mostly full, and slides it over in front of himself.

THIEVES LIKE US

◇

Carrie leans her back against the bar, watching how the kids dance. She and Miquel and Hayden and Jonathan used to dance with abandon, thrilled with the irrelevance of an old world aging away around them. They wriggled and writhed like they were sloughing off old skin, molting into something new. There's a mean side to the way the kids at Vibration dance, a razor edge in the music the DJ plays. Songs aren't given space to finish; there's no time. At the end of things, everything has to collapse. Songs and bodies crash into one another. They intersect at wrong angles. They create something static, a supersolid, striving toward a moment that can pass through a singularity and survive.

Bryce, rum and Coke in his massive bark-covered hand, smiles at her as he makes his way over. If Bryce is here, it's a Friday. He doesn't drink on weeknights; it would mean having less than his best self to give to his students in the morning. Carrie needs these markers to keep the days from bleeding into one another.

"How's the patient?" he asks.

"Don't call him that," says Carrie.

Bryce huffs apologetically. He's circumspect when talking about Miquel, but the liquor's loosened him. "How's Miquel?"

Carrie raises a finger to signal Jonathan for a beer, careful not to give him the eye contact he wants. Jonathan stands at the edge of Carrie's peripheral vision, the light in his chest pulsating out of sync with the beat of the music. He grins at her, waiting for some acknowledgment, then heads off when it's clear none is coming.

"He's a mess," Carrie says. "Sometimes when he gets better, it makes it that much clearer how bad off he is."

Bryce nods and stares into the throng. "You choose to be a caretaker," he says.

"What's that?" Carrie asks. She lost track of him for a second, trying to parse the transition from a danceable Lorde song to a minor-key dirge off Hayden's second album. The bodies on the dance floor sway like seaweed, a tidal rhythm.

"You fall for someone," says Bryce. "It's a blind fall. You realize he's someone you have to care for. It'll never balance out. Never pay back. And you choose."

Carrie wonders how much this is true and how much Bryce is projecting his experience onto hers. Bryce and Waylon balance each other out, with each fixing the other's flaws. Before Carrie and Miquel got together, their friends knew they would. *Fuck him already,* Hayden said at least once every party they ever went to, sometimes encouraging and sometimes bored with what Hayden called *the will-they-won't-they sitcom bullshit.* Carrie moved toward Miquel like an object rolling downhill. When he was in Topaz and she was out in the world, the distance between them, the unlikelihood she'd see him again, allowed her to look at their history. Her love for Miquel was shaped by everything around it, negative space bordered by expectations she dutifully inhabited. It didn't make their relationship any less valid.

The day they liberated Topaz Lake, Carrie and Hayden wrenched open the sealed metal door to the fallout shelter under the community center to find Miquel and a dozen children, huddled and starved, the last ones alive. Clothes soaked in someone else's blood, Carrie saw Miquel and felt absolved of everything she'd done, every faithless thought she'd harbored. She was so cleansed, she was surprised to see the blood was still there. She didn't register the horror on Miquel's face at the sight of it. As his ability came back like a bone badly set, it was clear she hadn't saved him, only moved him from one basement to another. But she treasured the time when they were pulling each other out of the dark. It was the wedding album they didn't have; she took the moment out now and then, along with a handful of others, to draw the energy she needed to move forward with him. Their relationship was a charm bracelet, baubles strung together on a barely visible chain.

"Miquel got broken," Carrie says. "It wasn't his fault."

"It's never their fault," Bryce says.

"You should talk," says Carrie, swigging her beer.

Bryce shrugs like a breeze through bare branches. "I went in eyes open," he says. A smile tugs the corner of his mouth upward. "Waylon's the same pain in the ass he was at Bishop."

"Worse," says Carrie. As if summoned, Waylon sits down on the stool next to Bryce.

"Creeper at table five's asking about you," Waylon tells Carrie. He nods his head at a corner booth. There's a man in a sharp suit sitting alone, sipping whiskey, watching the dancers with a smirk so overly prurient that Carrie goes translucent to prevent him from taking her in with his voracious gaze. It's the suit from the coffee shop. He stands out here as much as he did in Pilsen, put together in a way no one in Chicago bothers with anymore. His jacket, sharp at the corners, traces the lines of a body at home in the gym. His tie is tight at his Adam's apple this late in the evening, rather than tugged out like a hanged man loosening the noose. There's control in how he carries himself; he moves like an actor in a play.

"Fuck, you want to hand me to the filth?" says Carrie.

"I don't think he's Faction," says Waylon.

"He's something no good," Bryce says. "What do you read off him?"

"Nothing," Waylon says. "He's white flame–trained."

"That's not possible," says Bryce.

"I'm telling you he is."

"Too young," Carrie says. "Younger kids were image aversion–trained." Image aversion technique involved remembering the worst thing you'd ever experienced and throwing it at anyone trying to read you. Students who'd gone through real trauma were the best at it; Hayden could chase anyone but Sarah Davenport, their teacher, out of their head within a minute. Some people never needed to learn anything else. For the rest, it was a gross-out contest, useful for deflecting a psychic invader into a fit of giggles. It was easier than white flame but easier to break through.

"Say I'm not here," Carrie says. She spins on her stool and slumps toward the bar.

"He said he's got a job for you," says Waylon.

"It's a fucking trap," Carrie says.

"I'll watch your back," Waylon says.

"You already gave me up."

"*I'll* watch your back," Bryce says, crossing his arms over his chest and drawing up to his full height. The suit, who's been watching them this whole time, appraises Bryce and smiles approvingly.

"He asked about you is all," says Waylon. "I've got nothing for you the next two weeks. I thought you could use work."

"I told you I was offering her a job," Bryce says.

"You told me she wouldn't take it."

"Not if you're lining up side work for her."

"I didn't line it up," Waylon says. "Guy came in, asked for her. I said sometimes she's here."

Carrie raps her knuckles on the bar. "Sold. Me. Out."

"You going to talk to him?" Bryce asks.

Carrie eyes both of them warily. "You two are not my friends," she says. She grabs her beer and crosses the room to the stranger's table. The bar is filling in, and she weaves clumsily between bodies to make her way. The kids don't have this problem; they move through crowds like water running through gravel. *There should have been a time I felt at home here,* she thinks. *There should have been years without this taken away from me. Who would I have been without the war?*

An exiting dancer bumps her shoulder so hard Carrie nearly drops her beer. She braces herself on the edge of the suit's table. Regaining composure, she slides into the chair across from him. He waits a beat before he looks up, fixing her with the same lecherous leer he affords the dance floor.

"Miss Norris," he says, standing and extending his hand.

"Mystery Date," Carrie says, nodding to dismiss the proffered hand.

The stranger smiles, shrugs, and sits back down. "Can I buy you a drink?"

She holds up her half-empty beer. "One of these," she says. "You can talk until I finish it."

"That's fair."

"I drink fast."

He calls a server over and orders. He gives her a smile and calls her "hon," but it's not with the prurient condescension of some patrons. There's something sweet and sad, Southern manners shielding a need to connect. It doesn't mean his attention isn't about sex, but there's a human sentiment behind it. "You come highly recommended," he says to Carrie.

"If I had clients, they'd be smart enough not to recommend me to strangers."

He makes a small shrug of apology. "You have a reputation."

"That's a liability."

"It's a good reputation," he says. The server puts a beer in front of Carrie, and the suit nods in thanks.

Carrie leans in. "I don't like you," she says. "You give off— I hate to use the word *vibe*."

"I'm not Faction," he says.

"It's a vibe, though," Carrie continues. "An impression that says whatever this person wants, I should do the opposite."

The suit nods. He's letting her blow off steam, waiting her out. On the dance floor, a girl made of smoke wends around her partner, wisps of her drifting out of his collar and the cuffs of his sleeves. A dancer hovers above the crowd, contorting her body into impossible shapes. She stays out of reach as people stretch hands upward, mesmerized, to touch her. At the far corner, a man who looks like the suit grinds with a burly Voider who was here when Carrie first came in.

"My employer wants something brought back from out west," the suit says, drawing her attention back before she can register what she saw. He holds Carrie's gaze but then gets distracted by a thin wisp of a boy who wanders sweat-soaked off the dance floor.

"Who's your employer?" Carrie asks.

The suit's eyes follow the boy all the way to the bar, then return to Carrie. "I'm not at liberty to say."

"I've got no patience for cloak-and-dagger shit."

"You're in the wrong line of work."

"What's my line of work?"

"You get people and things to the places they can do the most good," says the suit. It's a generous description. It would be more accurate to say Carrie gets people and things to where they're worth the most; not all her jobs are altruistic. Systems of value have shifted so much that when Carrie steps across certain lines, mundane objects become magical, base metals turn to gold. Every little town where she drops a parcel of medical supplies or fresh citrus, she thinks of as nothing. When she leaves Vegas with pockets full, knowing the luxury goods she smuggled in will be auctioned off to the bourgie and desperate, she reminds herself the money buys those medical supplies and citrus. The journey isn't important, and neither is the destination, which leaves the constancy of motion. "My employer left something in a place it's not helping anyone. They want you to go retrieve it."

"What's the payment?" she asks.

"My employer will help solve your problem."

"Right now my problem is answers on a postcard."

"We're asking for trust," says the suit.

"You're in the wrong fucking town," Carrie says. She's been thinking this herself, wondering if the flare-ups of anger and disgust she feels mean she's not cut out to live in an integrated city. Anywhere else might be easier, if she didn't have Miquel to worry about.

"I like it here," says the suit. "It feels real."

An obviously underage boy who seemed to be swaying along with the music lurches past their table, cheeks distended and palm pressed to his lips in the universal medical sign for *about to puke*. "Yeah, it's very atmospheric."

"Do this for us and my employer can fix him," says the suit, finishing off his drink and fishing out his wallet. Carrie's eyes flash toward the doors to the kitchen, sure she'll see a Bloom with Miquel in cuffs. It's her biggest fear, bigger than being caught: descending the stairs to find him gone, having him used as leverage against her. It scares her because it would be effective. She'd give them everything.

"We want to help," the suit says, as if he knows what she's imagined. He reaches across the table to touch her hand, then thinks better of it and pulls back. "We're the good guys."

"You don't come off like a good guy."

"I'm a charming rogue. A lot of people like me." When the server comes over, the suit points to Carrie's beer and hands the server a couple more bills.

"Why not get in touch with me through the Hive?" Carrie asks.

"We don't use the Hive," says the suit, looking around nervously. It's the first time his cool breaks. It makes her trust him more. Anyone who knows to be wary of the Hive has one thing right. He reaches into the inner pocket of his jacket and takes out an old flip phone, a beetle shell of brushed metal with what looks like a nub of ivory for an antenna. He places it on the table between them, and Carrie makes no move to pick it up.

"Is your employer's office in the nineties?" Carrie asks. "There isn't a live cell tower on the continent."

"This one works everywhere," the suit says. "My employer will call you."

"What is it I'd be retrieving?" Carrie asks.

"A weapon," says the suit with forced nonchalance. "You'll know it when you see it."

"You don't know," Carrie says.

"My employer likes information compartmentalized," he says, his jaw tight.

"Burns your toast, doesn't it?"

The suit shrugs. The lines of his shoulders shift angles as if on hinges. "More I know, the easier my job is," he says.

"Then why didn't you ask?"

"No one said a job's supposed to be easy." He asked and didn't get an answer, and this is the first time he's found himself on the outside. He gazes at the dance floor, looking wistfully the way you do at people who are having more fun than you are. While he isn't watching, Carrie snatches up the phone and pockets it.

"It's bullshit," Carrie says. "He can't be fixed."

"My employer says when you find the weapon, you'll understand."

"What if I don't answer when your employer calls?"

"They call me and I find someone else," he says. "I figured start with the best and work down."

Carrie grins despite herself. "See, right there I almost liked you."

"This DJ's good," says the suit. He leans back, nodding his head steadily to a beat that flutters and jerks like an erratic heart. "Music scene sucks in New York right now. Half nostalgia, half futurism. As if there's a future." He lifts himself out of his chair. "I'm going to go dance." He holds out his hand, palm up, an inversion of the proffered handshake that started their meeting. "Want to come? I bet you had some moves back in your day." Carrie doesn't know whether to be flattered or insulted. Before she decides, the server passes between them to deliver Carrie's beer, and the suit fades into the crowd. Carrie takes her drink back to the bar, where Jonathan's been leaning, watching the conversation.

"Who's that?" he asks.

"Nobody," Carrie says. "Potential client."

"He's cute," says Jonathan. "Young."

"Sure," Carrie says, not listening. She pulls out her wallet. "Can you close me out? I should get home."

Jonathan folds both his hands over hers. "You know your money's no good here."

"Thanks," Carrie says, thinking how much she prefers knowing the cost of things.

"You going home or are you going downstairs?" Jonathan asks. The question catches Carrie off guard. It's pitched as casual curiosity, but there's an accusatory note.

"I'm going home," she says.

"You could go to my place," Jonathan says. "Maybe Waylon will let me—"

"Not tonight," Carrie says more forcefully.

Jonathan grabs her forearm lightly, only enough to stop her. "I know our thing is casual and I fully understand my place and all," he says. "But picking up guys in here while I'm working is . . . it's not cool by me."

Carrie looks at his hand on her arm, feels a gentle but present telekinetic push on her hip back toward him. She wants to pull out her knife and plunge it into Jonathan's wrist, piercing the divot where the arm bones meet the carpals and pinning his hand to the bar.

She yanks her arm away from his loose grip.

"Fuck off, Jonathan," she says, the swearing a poor substitute for stabbing. "I'm going home."

BLAST

◇

Fahima isn't *into* music. She doesn't need it the way Alyssa did, constantly humming or whistling, filling the pleasant unsilence of cooking or a long drive with endless albums. She doesn't use it as a component of her identity the way some of the Bishop kids do, conceptualizing themselves as punks or B-girls, mall Goths and hard-core kids. As she listens to Hayden Cohen play songs on acoustic guitar, the world falls away and Fahima understands how music becomes your life.

Dominic, the event planner, taps her on the shoulder, and she crashes back into normal life. Background and foreground shift, and the music is only a hum in her ears, not a hook in her heart.

"Is everything exceeding expectations?" he asks.

"No, Dominic," she says, smiling at him. "Because I know all your events will be perfect."

"Nothing's perfect when there are people involved," he says. "One of the servers found your British friend passed out in the bathroom."

Fahima smirks. The British delegate had cried when he agreed, and although she's ashamed about it, she counted it as a victory. The United Kingdom had been staunch opponents of any recognition of the new government. "Where is he now?"

"We have a room upstairs for situations like this," Dom says. "He's been temporarily disappeared."

"See what I mean?" she says. "Perfect."

Dom takes a tiny bow. "Are you speaking after the music?" he asks. "I can have the DJ start up immediately after, or you could say a few words."

"I've said everything I need to," she says. It isn't precisely true, but she's said everything she's going to. Every delegate has gotten their tailored sales pitch, and now they're trying to lose themselves in the performance, to forget the ultimatum on the table. Fahima tries to find her way back into the music, but the door is closed and she's stuck in her own head.

She sneaks into the kitchen, hoping some of the hors d'oeuvres are still warm. She'd watched longingly as trays buzzed by her while she talked up the delegates. Some of them grabbed crab cakes and puff pastries and chewed on them as Fahima talked, although most didn't have the stomach. The kitchen is empty, the staff spirited away to alcoves and corners where they can watch Hayden play without being seen. Ruth is plucking items from a tray and looks up when Fahima comes in.

"Hey, you," she says. "I was making you a plate. I figured you might not have eaten."

"I'm good," Fahima says. Ruth looks crestfallen, and Fahima wonders why she tries not to accept kindnesses from Ruth. She's never liked being taken care of; she used to hide minor illnesses from Alyssa for fear she'd be treated like a patient. It's the burden of having someone care for you, the weight of their help and the way it pulls you toward them. Ruth puts the half-filled plate on the counter and smiles to show it's no big deal. Fahima slides the plate toward herself and eats two canapés and a baby carrot, enough to indicate gratitude but make it clear the gesture wasn't necessary.

Omar enters holding three drinks. He proffers a martini to Fahima like a boy offering a flower to his crush, and against her better judgment, she takes it. He hands one of two bright purple cocktails to Ruth and keeps the other for himself.

"Enjoying the party, boss?"

"Please kill me," Fahima says.

"You should win an Oscar," he says. *"I'm tired of people dying."* He clasps his hands, his voice cartoonishly earnest. *"Won't you help me protect . . . life?"*

"Stop talking," Fahima says, sipping her drink.

"She did not say that," says Ruth.

"I'm paraphrasing slightly," he says. He sits next to Fahima on the edge of the counter, and Ruth takes a spot on the other side. For a second, it feels like she's with Sarah and Patrick. The relationships she formed when young locked in patterns she goes back to.

"So the kraut's an asshole," says Omar.

"He's scared," Fahima says. "The future is always scary when you're an old white man."

"They're not all old," Omar says. "Curious; what is the policy on sleeping with the delegates?"

"The policy is don't."

"What is the policy on activities that are not technically fucking but might be, say, in the realm of sexual activity."

"Keep it in your pants for one night," says Ruth.

"You should talk," he says. "The Spanish ambassador has been eyeing me like I'm a snack is all I'm saying. If there's any doubt of him being on board, I could help seal the deal."

"Everyone's on board," Fahima says. "The only problem is we don't have a boat."

"You'll figure it out," Ruth says.

"So if they're already in the bag, there's no real harm."

"Go ahead and fuck him," Fahima says. Her eyes dart to Ruth's, and she feels a hot flush in her cheeks. "Duplicate yourself into dozens, make an orgy of it. We can celebrate."

Omar extends his glass to cheers. "We did good, right, boss?" It's an honest question, exactingly phrased. Omar doesn't mince words. He doesn't want to know if they did *well,* if they've been successful. He wants to know if what they've done this evening is for the best. If it's *good.*

"We did good," Fahima says, clinking her glass against his, then Ruth's. It says something about the work they're doing that everyone Fahima works with has to ask if what they're doing is right. She's not sure getting consent from governments on behalf of the people they represent or rule is better than setting off a global Pulse without asking. Her pitch reeks of old world diplomacy. *What would it mean for Germany?* She speaks to them in the language of nations when what she wants is to end nations. Some of them know that. Some see the threat she offers them, the promise of an empowered populace. Guaranteed revolution. They'd take it for themselves and keep it from their people. She'll work around them. She'll find ways to build the devices in secret, near villages, far from palaces. Fahima knows exactly the shape of the world to come. No masters. All gods.

Ruth puts her head on Fahima's shoulder and holds it there for a second before applause starts in the ballroom. "Oh, the music!" she says, rushing out. She turns back, grabs Fahima's empty hand, and gives a tug. "Don't let me forget, I got you a present," she adds before disappearing through the doors.

"I bet she did," Omar says. Fahima swats at him.

"I've got to shut that down," she says.

"What you need is to consider what she wants and what you

want and see if there's some hot little area that overlaps," says Omar.

"Why are these things so much easier for you young people?"

"'You young people'?" he says. "You sound fucking ancient. It's not easier for us. We do the work rather than sweat over our baggage."

"I don't have baggage," says Fahima. "And I'm only thirty-nine."

"You carry the whole world around," he says. He kisses her on the cheek. "The world's going to rise or fall without you. Tell yourself that every now and then." He leaves, letting stray notes through the door as it swings open, then shut.

After the performance, Hayden is surrounded by half the delegation. Whenever Fahima thinks about Hayden, she remembers telling Avi Hirsch that what Resonants needed was a celebrity best friend in the public eye. Hayden hit that mark perfectly, if too late. Their star rose before fighting broke out, but they'd spent a year in the camp at Topaz Lake as conflicts rose to a boil outside. Now they're one of the safe ones, a Resonant who can move through the world without being perceived as a threat.

"It was so *intimate*," the Belgian delegate says.

Hayden waves this off. "Intimacy's easy in a small room," they say. "The challenge is being intimate with a whole stadium of folks at the same time."

No one laughs—the translator nanites can't cope with double entendre. One more thing to work on.

"Excuse me," Fahima says. "I need to borrow Hayden a minute."

"Of course," Hayden says. They hold out their hand so Fahima can extract them. "I'll be right back," they assure the group. "And I want to hear more about the value-added tax as soon as I do." They let Fahima guide them out of the circle and into the narrow hallway that leads to the bathrooms.

"Thank God," Hayden says. "They were boring the shit out of me. How did you find such a collection of drab little men?"

"Drab little men run the world," Fahima says. "For the moment." She pulls up her sleeve, revealing a thin bracelet set with a single pearl. Fahima pinches the pearl, and the noise of the party grows faint and fuzzy. "Baffler," she says, as if Hayden will know what this means. "Act as if we're having a normal conversation."

"I don't remember what normal conversations look like," Hayden says.

"Every thirty seconds or so laugh like I've made a joke," Fahima says. Hayden breaks out a stage laugh, and Fahima rolls her eyes. "You haven't reported in," she says. "I thought you were dead."

"My phone was confiscated in Moscow," Hayden says. "I bricked it before I handed it over and told them it was a memento of simpler times."

"They bought that?"

"The Russians aren't buying anything," Hayden says. "At least not from us."

"Who are they talking to?"

"They've talked to everyone here," Hayden says. "The quiet line is anyone who signs on with you catches hell from them."

"What's their play?"

Hayden shakes their head. "All I can tell you is there were Americans at the after-party," they say. "They didn't come up and introduce themselves, but they wanted me to know they were there. They wanted to be seen cozying up to the Russian bigwigs."

"The *Russians* are signed on," Fahima says, incredulous. "They didn't send a delegate because the agreement's already gone through."

"They didn't send a delegate," Hayden says. "And an agreement's a piece of paper."

"Anything else?" Fahima asks.

"I need a new phone," says Hayden.

"When do you head west?"

"Tomorrow," they say. "Hoping to see some friends in Chicago before I cross over."

"I'll get one to you," Fahima says. "Be careful out there. I know there's talk about reconciliation, but don't forget they hate us."

"That's the name of my next album," says Hayden. "Anyway, I'm always careful." They down the rest of their drink and turn to leave. "By the way," they say, "the Japanese delegate isn't Eito Higashi."

Fahima looks out at the dance floor, where Higashi stands apart from the other delegates, eyeing the kitchen door. "How do you know?"

"He hasn't spent the evening staring at my ass," says Hayden. "I met him in Tokyo. He was . . . affectionate. He hasn't so much as said hello."

"Maybe he's shy."

"He's a fake," Hayden says. "You get the difference between seeing something and knowing something?"

"Let's say yes."

"You look at him and you won't see him, but you know it's him."

"Psychic?" Fahima asks.

Hayden nods. Fahima glances at Ji Yeon and her Bloom that is missing one member. Maybe he's here after all.

"Faction?"

They shrug. "Racist as fuck pretending to be Asian, though." They take a deep breath as if drawing their star persona back into their body. It works. Hayden looks taller, more full and complete, as they rejoin the crowd. Fahima clicks the baffler off, and the noise of the party floods in. She follows Hayden at a distance, then wanders the floor. One loop of the room is enough to tell Fahima no one here wants to talk to her. Most actively avoid her eyes. This is a funeral for the old world, and Fahima's the one who's killed it.

She passes by Eito Higashi and sizes him up, which causes a tiny headache in the spot between her eyes. It's like what Hayden described: she can see it's not him but knows it is. There's a compulsion to move along that starts in Fahima's feet before it registers in her head.

Fucking psychics, she thinks. She makes a mental note to find out what's happened to Eito Higashi but worries her memory of him will be gone by tomorrow.

On the edge of the dance floor, a waiter sets down his full tray of champagne flutes, which topple like bowling pins, spilling champagne onto the parquet. He approaches a knot of bureaucrats conversing among themselves, their backs to him. He catches Fahima's attention because he's moving slowly across the empty floor. His lips are moving, but she can't make out what he's saying. She grabs Dominic, who's futzing with the lighting. "Who vetted the servers?" she says.

Dominic looks at her, dumbfounded by the question. The waiter reaches into his pocket and comes out with something the size of a roll of quarters. His voice builds to a shout that barely rises above the sound of the DJ. "They who collaborate with devils will be treated as devils," he says. "We true kindred will defend our own even unto death."

Fahima's eye catches Eito Higashi, whose lips move along with the waiter's. Ji Yeon yells something, and the hulking girl from her Bloom is across the dance floor faster than anyone that big should be able to move.

"Down!" she shouts as she throws her body at the waiter and

the waiter's body is engulfed in flames. Dominic steps between Fahima and the bomber, transforming his body to crystal. Shrapnel strikes him with a tinkling sound like glass breaking. Fahima doesn't register the sound of the blast, only the ringing afterward. She watches over Dominic's shoulder as the agent's body expands outward, shielding the visiting dignitaries. Chaos erupts on the floor as the charred remains of the waiter and the Faction agent's body fall away from each other like dance partners bowing at the end of a waltz. Omar doubles and doubles again, dispatching duplicates to rush the dignitaries to safety.

Fahima spots Ruth, her eyes welling with tears that won't fall, mouth moving like a fish. Fahima grabs her by the shoulders. "Are you hurt?" she says as slowly and loudly as she can.

"I don't know what happened," Ruth says. "I was dancing. I was—" Her voice is husky, her throat singed by a breath of smoke. Fahima presses her keys into Ruth's hand.

"Go to my apartment," she says. "Wait for me. Stay safe until we know what this is."

Hearing without comprehending, Ruth nods and walks out of the building like a wind-up doll set on its course. With one less thing to worry about, Fahima scans the scene. She grabs an Omar by the sleeve of his perfect suit. She doesn't know which one he is, but it doesn't matter. She points to the agent's corpse at the center of the varnished dance floor.

"Get everybody out, including *them*," she says, her eyes on Ji Yeon and her diminished Bloom. "Then disappear that body. Whatever happens, do not lose it." Omar nods. Copies of him check the delegates for injuries while one coterie of Omars ushers Ji Yeon and the others out the main exit and another picks up the Faction agent's body and leaves through the kitchen.

SAID YOUR NAME IN AN EMPTY ROOM

◇

A Bloom of Faction agents loiters on the corner across from the bar, failing to look casual. You can spot a Bloom because together they look like a public service ad for cultural diversity in the workplace. There'll be a Mohawked punker and a businessman and a soccer mom; there'll be a flannel-clad hipster sharing a cigarette with a woman on her way to a cocktail party, a homeless man chatting intently with an academic. You see all five together only when they want to be seen, and the spot across from Vibration is a regular observation post. The Faction gives zero fucks about Waylon's side business with Hong, but it's important he know they know.

Carrie feels the urge to walk up to them and confess, although she doesn't know what she'd be confessing. Since they oversaw the evacuations after the Armistice, the role and mandate of the Faction have been ill defined. Somewhere between a police force and a domestic KGB. By merely being there, they inspire a sense of guilt. Carrie's sure she's not alone in feeling this. She walks by the

Bloom without making eye contact, her arm held across her stomach, left hand resting on the phone in her right pocket.

On the corner of North and Ashland, an old man sings a Simon and Garfunkel song out of both of his faces, harmonizing perfectly as he accompanies himself on guitar. The sound echoes in the chasm of the empty block. He's past her apartment, but Carrie walks over and throws a five in his hat. He nods appreciatively without breaking off the song.

Carrie grabs the mail and climbs the stairs, the high harmony line following her like a frail ghost. She drops everything on the counter and tosses junk mail in the trash, amazed that junk mail persists as a thing. Shuffled in with the flyers for the Church of Resonant Truth and the Unity Council meeting is an envelope addressed to Carrie and Miquel in calligraphic script. There's no note, just two tickets to Hayden's concert at Symphony Center next week. Better seats than the one Carrie bought for herself. Carrie lets herself imagine going with Miquel. A date. A small, normal thing completely out of their reach.

Last time they talked, Carrie tried to give Hayden the impression things with Miquel were not that bad, getting better. She knows it isn't the intent, but the tickets feel like a challenge to that, Hayden's way of saying *prove it.* She puts them back in the envelope and puts her hand in her pocket, feeling the warm metal of the flip phone. Something hums in her head like a stereo left on in a silent room. It's not a message or a transmission, not someone trying to contact her through the Hive, but an aggregate of feelings, shame mixed with a righteous anger, and it's in her head without being of her head. She braces herself on the counter. *My mind is a cool white flame,* she thinks. She visualizes emptiness, processes and flows, until the hum fades. It's been so long since it's caught her alone, she's forgotten the gut-sick feeling when it's gone.

She opens the window, hoping the busker on the corner is loud enough for his song to find its way in, but there're only the low sounds of the city going to sleep. She thinks about putting on a record to fill the space, but the weight of choosing one is too much to bear.

She goes to the fridge to get herself a beer she doesn't need. As she bends and reaches in, she's eye level with a Polaroid pinned to the freezer by a souvenir magnet from Navy Pier. It's the only item on the front of the fridge, and it wasn't there when she left the apartment a week ago. She snatches the beer, closes the fridge, and pulls the photo from under the magnet. She sets the beer on the counter unopened and examines the picture. It's her and Hayden, huddled into the frame with two kids Carrie doesn't know, a boy and a girl younger than any of the students she met this morning. They're all smiling, and if Carrie's smile is less energetic, it matches the overall weariness on her face. A scar she doesn't have runs from the center of her forehead to below her left cheekbone, a livid lightning bolt. She looks at the kids. A memory for faces is critical in Carrie's work. Spotting a newcomer to a settlement where you've felt safe can keep you clear of trouble. There's something familiar about the kids, like aspects of her face in a black-and-white of some long-dead great-aunt. Carrie doesn't like the way the picture makes her feel, vertiginous, as if she might topple into it and keep falling forever.

In her pocket, the phone buzzes, pulling her out of the picture. Dizzy, drunk, hopeless, Carrie answers.

PROSPECT HEIGHTS

◇

When Clay gets home, Rai is sitting at the kitchen counter, the contents of his backpack splayed across its surface as if he's autopsying it.

"Hey, Dad," Rai says. He's looking at a photo, a Polaroid like the ones that had a hipster revival before the war. Clay can't remember if he or Dom ever bought one, but if they hadn't, one of Rai's friends' parents had.

"You eat?" Clay asks.

Rai tilts his head at the stove, where one slice of a frozen pizza sits, tide pools of grease congealing on its surface. Clay crosses the kitchen, gripping Rai's shoulder and using it as a pivot. He glances at the photo quickly so Rai doesn't catch him at it. It's a selfie, Rai and a girl Clay doesn't recognize, although she must have been in the gym this evening, playing at the game of flirting by completely ignoring that the whole school seemed engaged in it. *That settles one question,* Dom would say if he saw it. If it were any day but today, Clay would laugh.

He eats the lukewarm pizza without a plate or paper towel, something he does only when Dom's out of the house.

"Your teachers all think you're great," Clay says, his mouth full.

"They like me because I'm not a rich shit," says Rai. "I'm a breath of fresh, lower-middle-class air."

"Watch your language," Clay says. Rai smirks. "Anyway, we're *middle*-middle class."

"Everyone I go to school with has two houses," Rai says. He puts the photo in the front pocket of his backpack. "We have heaters that sound like a bad drum solo. I feel like that's not middle-middle."

"We're in a good neighborhood," Clay says. He sounds like his dad, who slowly moved the family out of public housing into a cookie-cutter suburb and thought of that as his crowning achievement.

"Did they make you talk to everybody?" Rai asks.

"It was like speed dating," Clay says.

"Gross."

"Mr. Castillo's intense."

"Castillo's creepy," Rai says. "It's not his fault, I guess. It's his job to get into our heads and shit."

"Language."

"But it feels rapey," Rai continues. "And he looks you right in the eye. I hate that."

"Yes, human contact is to be avoided at all costs," Clay says. He's making a good show of everything being perfectly normal. He's pretending to put it out of his head. Nothing will get decided tonight; there's no rush.

"What did he want to talk to you about?"

"Psychic defense," Clay says. His voice sounds false.

Rai nods. "He's always like *this is the most vital skill you will ever learn.*"

"It's an adult thing," Clay says. "You convince yourself your job is the most important thing in the whole world. Then you have to convince everyone else."

"You don't do that."

"My job is self-evidently the most important thing in the whole world," Clay says, "plus I'm not allowed to talk about it." When Rai was younger, he used to ask Clay about himself all the time, badgering him with questions Clay would put off by saying he couldn't or didn't want to talk about it. He assumed it was the way kids were, until he mentioned it to friends. They said their kids had solipsistic lacks of interest in their parents' lives. Clay also assumed Rai's curiosity would persist and he could answer Rai's questions when they were both ready. Whether he grew out of the phase or grew tired of being put off, Rai stopped asking, even when Clay floated hints or telegraphed that he was open, finally, to being asked.

"So nothing bad?" Rai says.

"Nothing bad," Clay says.

Dominic's keys jangle, ineffective and clumsy, in the lock.

"Dad Number Two," says Clay.

"I thought you were Dad Number Two."

"I am clearly Dad Number One."

As soon as Clay sees Dominic, he knows something's wrong. He has a haunted stare that barely takes Clay and Rai in.

"Dad?" says Rai. His son's voice snaps Dom out of the trance he's in. He goes to Rai and hugs him, which reminds Clay he forgot to do that when he came in. It used to be the first thing whenever he walked in the door. Little gestures, tiny attachments that wither over time.

"I'm okay," Dom says, his voice muffled by Rai's shoulder. "I was near the blast, but I was crystal and I was okay."

"Dom, what are you talking about?" Clay asks.

"Do we have anything to drink?" Dom asks. They don't usually keep liquor in the house, but there's a bottle of rum someone brought for Christmas in the back of a cupboard. Clay pauses to remember where it is, then digs it out, puts ice in two glasses, and pours. "There was a bomb at the gala," Dominic says. "One of the servers blew themselves up a couple feet from the delegates."

"Holy shit," says Rai.

Eyes wide, Clay pats Dominic down, looking for injuries, for bloodstains hidden by the darkness of his suit. It's an old habit kicking in, and he notices Rai watching him, fascinated but also scared.

"I'm okay," Dom says, swatting his hands away. "My ears are ringing, but I'm okay."

"Was anyone—"

"A Faction agent stopped him," Dom says. "Jumped on the bomb."

"Who attacks a gala full of . . . whoever?" Rai asks.

"It was fucking Damps," says Dominic, too loud. "It's like the war is still going on. There could be one of them left and they'd try to kill us. Swatting at us with a stick like a cornered animal."

"Honey, calm down," Clay says.

"*You're* telling *me* this?" Dominic says. His eyes are frantic. Clay wants to check his temperature. He tries to remember the signs of shock. "How calm were you after Denver? Did you cool out after Damps killed Maaya and Koyo?" Rai flinches at the mention of his biological parents. "Fuck calm, okay? Fuck. Calm."

"Hey, buddy," Clay says to Rai. "Why don't you go hang out in your room for a bit? Give Dad some space."

Rai glares at him. He's teetering between being a child and being a teenager, and there are only so many more times he'll let himself be dismissed like this.

Doesn't matter for shit now.

His displeasure registered, Rai retreats down the hall. Clay puts his arm around Dom, tentatively at first and then firmly, as if trying to hold him down. He wants to say *You shouldn't talk like that in front of Rai,* but he can't. Not without explaining it all. Dom's shoulders shake with rage and fear. He didn't go through what Clay did in the war. Dom's part in things was the one Clay publicly claims: a communications job, a cog in a machine that moved people toward their deaths without getting itself bloodied. Dom's not inured to horrors. The world can still touch him.

Clay will have to carry this thing with Rai a while longer. A day or two until things go back to normal. Until he has to shatter everything anew.

INQUIRY

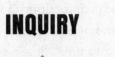

Propped against the wall in the hallway between the elevator and Fahima's front door, Ruth drinks red wine from the bottle. Fahima's keys rest in her palm.

"What took you so long?" she says, smiling nervously. *She's so young*, Fahima thinks, situating Ruth on the other side of an indeterminate age divide, in the land of the still sexually viable. It's toxic; we form attractions at a certain age, and some part stays there, pining not for people younger than us but for a younger version of ourselves that could keep up with them.

"Cleaning up," Fahima says. "I'm sorry."

Ruth hands Fahima her keys and holds up the half-empty bottle. "I started without you," she says. She hoists herself up from the floor and steps aside for Fahima to let them in. Her confidence is attractive. Fahima unlocks the door.

"You could have waited inside," she says.

"I didn't want to go in without you," Ruth says. "Is everyone okay?" She wanders around the room, running fingers over surfaces like she's reading Braille. She drops onto the couch without being asked.

"A couple delegates got their suits singed, but they're tucked away for the night," Fahima says. Ruth looks at her expectantly, and Fahima realizes she's forgotten to perform the normal human response to this situation. "Are you okay?" she asks.

"I'm fine," Ruth says, forgiving the lag. "I feel wired, like I won't be able to sleep." She grabs her bag. "I almost forgot. I got you a present while I was in London." She extracts a bottle of gin by the neck and hands it to Fahima. "Is it a good one?" she asks. "The man in the shop said it was the best."

Fahima appraises the bottle. There are new distilleries in Brooklyn hustling to fill the export gap. They have fake future names: Gyn. Jyoonper. Intoxant. *In the future, we will only use the last quarter of the alphabet,* Fahima thinks. They all err on the side of too big: like their names, they lack the stately calm of dry British gin. It's a problem when you remake the world. In the rush toward the new, everyone wants to abandon everything, even things that were perfectly good.

"It's lovely," Fahima says. "I haven't had this in years. Would you like some?"

"I'm good," Ruth says. Fahima goes about the stage business of fixing herself a drink at the Deco liquor cabinet with Kevin Bishop's chrome shaker and crystal martini glasses. She sits on the couch next to Ruth, who clinks her bottle against Fahima's glass. "I'm glad you're here," she says. They've tap-danced around getting together for months, held back by Fahima's shyness and worry about being seen in public with an employee. Telling her to come here advanced things more than Fahima's ready for. Ruth, for her part, seems prepared. Fahima takes a big gulp of her drink.

"You've got all night," Ruth says. She rests her fingertip on the base of Fahima's glass. "Pace yourself." A tiny laugh escapes her throat, and Fahima sees Ruth is as nervous and unsure as she is. She's converting adrenaline into something else, covering shyness with an attempt at sultriness. It's the shyness underneath that's the draw, heady enough that Fahima tries to shut it down.

"Ruth," she says in the unmistakable tone of an adult speaking to a child. Ruth curls her legs up under her and juts out her lower lip in a pout.

"I can go if you want," she says.

"I don't want you to go," Fahima says. "I like spending time with you."

"Then spend time," Ruth says. She makes it sound so simple. The benefits are obvious, and what could be the harm? Hasn't Fahima earned a little comfort for how far she's made it, how much she's done? Where is it written that she has to lose everything all the time?

"I just got out of a long-term relationship," she says. It's a line from a bad soap opera. Some sentences feel false even when they're true.

"I've known you five years, and you've been single that whole time," Ruth says.

"I haven't," says Fahima. "I am now. But I wasn't."

"So why did I never meet her?" Ruth asks. "It was a her?"

"It was," Fahima says. "She was. She didn't come around."

"Who ended it?" Ruth asks. She seems determined to logic Fahima into bed. Fahima isn't beyond convincing.

"She did," Fahima says.

"She thought you worked too much," says Ruth.

"Good guess."

"How long ago?"

"Three years," Fahima says.

"Three years?" Ruth repeats. Pulsers think in apocalyptic time. History is stupid and meaningless; the past has no fucking point.

There is no time available; there is all the time in the world. The idea of mourning a relationship for three years is ancient, out with hair shirts and self-flagellation.

"We went through some serious shit together," Fahima says, trying to translate her feelings into the foreign language of youth.

"Were you married?"

"Muslims don't believe in gay marriage," Fahima says.

"They don't believe in gay *anything*. Or drinking booze," she adds, tapping her fingernail against Fahima's martini glass.

"Marriage I was willing to abstain from," Fahima says.

"She dumped you because you wouldn't marry her?"

"There were other concerns."

Ruth crawls nimbly across the couch. She leans on the armrest, looking up at Fahima. "I don't want to marry you."

"Ruth," Fahima says. This time she doesn't know how it sounds, only that it doesn't come out the way she wants it to. One word, a name, a field across which meaning can be disputed.

Ruth puts her hand on Fahima's wrist, and Fahima's head goes light. For a moment she thinks she might be fainting like a heroine in an old-time novel. She feels the downward yank on her consciousness of someone pulling her against her will, submerging her into the Hive.

Fahima comes here so rarely that she's shocked at what it's turned into. It looks like the root structure of some vast plant grown upward from the ground, each branch cast in black bone, knobby and knuckled, jointed and forked like a cast of fulgurite in sand. The sky, which Fahima remembers as shimmering like pale pearls, is the purplish yellow of a half-healed bruise. The Hive bustles with people chatting, oblivious to the horror around them. Maybe they see it differently, she thinks. Before her mind can swirl into the eddy of freshman-year epistemology, a dark canopy arches over her and closes her off from the rest of the Hive. She's confronted by Ji Yeon Kim, her Hivebody spiked with spines. Her Bloom, short one, stands behind her. A mousy-looking Babbitt of a man has replaced the girl who stopped the bomber. He looks nervously at Fahima, then away.

"Miss Deeb," Ji Yeon says. "I hope you weren't hurt."

"I'm sorry about your friend," Fahima says.

Ji Yeon's Hivebody ripples, a wave passing over it. When it's gone, what's left behind is softer.

"Heidi was nice. We aren't all, but she was nice." The ripple shivers up her Hivebody, starting from the ground and rising to the top of her head. *How much of you is still in there?* Fahima wonders. "But you," says Ji Yeon. "You weren't hurt?"

"I'm fine," Fahima says. "Don't let me take up your time."

"You're a major asset," Ji Yeon says. "I wanted to be sure you were secured."

"I feel all warm and fuzzy."

Ji Yeon flashes toward Fahima, her body traversing the space between them all at once. "I have never understood why he doesn't keep you on a leash," she says. Her face is close enough that if there were breath in the Hive, Fahima would feel Ji Yeon's on her cheek.

"Because I'm not his fucking pet," Fahima says.

Ji Yeon smiles. "It's not as bad as you imagine." She makes a sweeping gesture that takes in the whole of the Hive. "It's like this all the time," she says. "Constant connectivity."

Fahima pulls away from her. "I treasure my alone time."

Ji Yeon shrugs. "Who vetted the waitstaff?" she asks.

"Dominic Pastorius," Fahima says. "He's beyond reproach. Fought in the war."

Ji Yeon laughs. "A lot of people 'fought in the war,'" she says, throwing air quotes around the words. "*You* 'fought in the war' from your lab. Any reason to think he might be sympathetic?"

"To whom?"

"To Damps," says Ji Yeon, spitting out the word. "Like the one who wandered into your dance party wearing a catering uniform and a bomb."

"Dom had nothing to do with this," Fahima says.

"We'll talk to him."

"The bomber was Kindred," says Fahima. It's a mistake to volunteer information.

"We assumed," says Ji Yeon.

"I'm telling you," Fahima says. "He was spouting off before he—" She mimes an explosion with her hands. "Real cult stuff. Not like you hear locally."

"We're shaking some trees in the Bronx."

"He didn't sound like them," Fahima says. "Those guys are a frat. They're a boys club. This was something else."

"We'll look into it."

"I'm trying to help."

"Of course," says Ji Yeon. "There was one more thing. We got a head count on the delegates afterward. We came up one short."

"I can send the dossiers over," Fahima says. "Although I don't think the safety of the lesser duke of Luxembourg is a problem for the Faction."

"Your delegates would be so much meat if Heidi hadn't stepped in," says Ji Yeon. "That makes it a Faction problem."

"I'll send Omar up with everything we have first thing in the morning."

Ji Yeon smiles the way Fahima imagines call center employees used to, her face twisted to wring a drop of pleasantry out of her words. "That would be really great, Miss Deeb," she says. "Thanks so much."

Ji Yeon nods to her lackeys, and the gang of them disappear soundlessly from the Hive. A pressure lifts from Fahima, and she flies upward, back into her body, gasping like she's been let up for air.

"Where were you?" Ruth asks, kneeling next to Fahima, lying on the couch.

"I'm okay," Fahima says. "You should go."

"You were in the Hive," Ruth says.

"I'll talk to you tomorrow and we can—"

"You told us never to use the Hive."

Fahima kisses her on the mouth. It's a cruel, manipulative thing to do, but it's shorthand for every contradictory thing she needs to communicate. *I want you. Please go.*

"You should go," Fahima says. "There are things I need to do right away."

Ruth kisses her again, and all the panic and shock Fahima's body is holding floods her brain, drowning out the voice that wants to tell Ruth to leave.

I CAN'T FEEL AT HOME IN THIS WORLD

◇

Hong Wu refers to his role in the world as criminally subsidized altruism. "Like Robin Hood, but drug stuff," he says. He produces and sells massive quantities of recreational drugs, alchemically synthesizing them on demand with his ability. They range from classics like cocaine and ecstasy to bespoke highs custom made for rich clients. Rez, which briefly simulates Resonant abilities in people without them, is still a brisk business in Chicago and out in the Wastes. Carrie handles some of the distribution, and her head spins when she tries to imagine how much money Waylon and Hong make.

Hong lives above the auto garage in Cicero that belonged to his father, although he now owns the entire block. He also owns and maintains a fleet of vehicles, mostly trucks, that ferry needed goods to the Wastes, and employs a dozen drivers to make the trips. Some do milk runs, there-and-backs to settlements over the border. A couple, like Carrie, specialize in longer jaunts, carrying contraband farther west. Those runs risk arrest by the Faction, piracy by the natives, or worse on runs that skirt the West Coast territories.

She finds Hong helping a pair of runners load a white cube van. Most people go out with a partner. Carrie's not much for company. Hong passes a crate to a runner in the back of the van. Hong's dark hair is shot through with wires of gray and his eyes have dark pouches, but he hasn't lost the paranoid energy he radiated when Carrie first met him. When he sees her, he calls someone over to take his place. "Walk with me," he says to Carrie. He puts an arm around her shoulders, pulling her conspiratorially close. "Let me ask you. Last trip, did you see anything weird out there?"

Carrie pauses to consider, then bursts out laughing. "You're going to have to be more specific."

"Drug use," he says. "Huge, weird drug use."

"I'm not hanging around and partying with these people," she says. "If I lived out there, I'd be high all the time."

"I had a ton of Rez go missing last week," he says. "A literal ton."

"Stolen?"

"Not from what I can tell," Hong says. "No signs of a break-in. And I have this feeling like I sold it all, but I don't remember selling it all. And I definitely don't have a new ton of money socked away. Look at my eye." He pulls down the lower lid of his right eye, exposing the pink underside and a bloodshot cornea. "See anything?"

There's a myth that people co-opted by the Faction have black floaters in the whites of their eyes, telltale spots. Carrie's spent time at the mirror examining her own eyes.

"There's nothing," she says.

He nods, convinced but not calmed. "I heard they got around that," he says. "Bleach in the suspension fluid." Carrie marvels at the way Hong's paranoia turns the absence of positive evidence into positive evidence. "What are you doing here?" he asks. "Waylon said you're out of rotation for a bit."

"Off-the-books job," she says. "What do you have for me?"

He gives her the keys to a beat-up green Kia Sportage. "Gutsy," he says, kicking the tires. "But she won't carry much. How light?"

Carrie shrugs. "I'll know when I get there, apparently."

"Sounds like a trap," Hong says.

"That's what I said."

"You hear about New York last night?" Hong asks. Carrie shakes her head. "Suicide bomber blew himself up at some foundation thing. It's in the *Trib.*" He hands Carrie a copy of the morning paper, words underlined, circled in pen, connected by sweeping lines like a map of the way Hong sees the world. The picture on the front page shows a ballroom with a scorched circle in the center of its dance floor. Carrie recognizes Hayden in the huddle of the crowd in the background, their face poised as if they know someone's taking a picture.

"Anybody hurt?" she asks, trying to keep the concern out of her voice.

"The bomber and somebody who jumped him," Hong says. "It shows the natives are restless. I'm only sending out milk runs the next couple days."

"This is a milk run," Carrie says. "Out and back in a day, maybe two."

Hong shrugs, knowing better than to argue with her. "Be gentle with my car," he says. "They're like my children." He tells her this every time but never complains when the cars come back dented, shot up, gouged, half dead.

She nods to him and settles into the driver's seat. Carrie plugs her aging iPod into the auxiliary jack. When she was a kid, before she went to Bishop, she used to listen to the college radio station out of Evanston in the car. The signal barely stretched to Deerfield. She had to lean toward the dashboard for hints of what strange bands the college kids were listening to. Her mother never tolerated it; she'd switch to the easy listening station and push Carrie back into her seat. Her father didn't mind or at least didn't complain. Carrie misses the way you surrendered yourself to the whim of invisible signals. That's gone now. She clicks on Neil Young's *On the Beach* and leaves the city behind.

The interstates around Chicago are still in decent shape, even to the west of the city. Concerned citizens and hobbyists do voluntary upkeep, filling potholes with black glass and voiding trash. It creates the illusion that the real world persists beyond the boundary, and for most Resonants working roads still exist as far west as they're ever likely to go. The guitar line and harmonica whine of the album's last track die in the speakers as the sign for the Deerfield exit looms. Once she's off the exit ramp, there's no guessing what condition the streets will be in. The Kia crawls pass the VILLAGE OF DEERFIELD sign, its paint chipped and faded, the stag that once emerged from the center of the letters beheaded when someone cracked the wooden crest of the sign in half.

When people talk about the war, they talk as if it happened everywhere at once. Some call it "the Uprising," a guaranteed sign someone is bullshit. Hayden calls it the outbreak, saying that if anyone wrote a history book about the war, the maps would look like epidemic spread maps from a plague movie. Then they said no one would write a history of the war because history is over. As much as all this was true, there were places unscathed by fighting, places with zero strategic importance. Deerfield was like that. Any Resonant who lived there when the fighting jumped off went elsewhere to join it; everyone else stayed and kept their head down.

There was no physical damage except for the decay of the last seven years. As she drives through the center of town, half the shops in the redbrick strip malls look as if they're closed for a holiday, although dust cakes the windows, obscuring the insides, and a few pieces of plate glass have been shattered by the village's notoriously harsh winters. *They think they have it rough in Chicago,* her uncle Jim used to say about Deerfield weather, shaking his head and leaving the rest implied. Uncle Jim joined up with one of the Kindred Network's do-it-yourself militias during the war and died in the early days of fighting.

The tiny parks on corners that used to be vacant lots, bought up under eminent domain as part of the New Deerfield revival the village was attempting when Carrie moved away, flourished in the absence of residents: verdant grass rises to waist height, and the root systems of trees buckle the nearest sidewalks. Carrie thinks about the fairy tale of Briar Rose, a whole city asleep, waiting for a princess at its center to wake. She can imagine Deerfield's residents rising from slumber and emerging from their front doors to greet the new day, but every house here is empty.

Carrie was here the day Deerfield was "evacuated," a trite euphemism that made it sound as if it was in the best interest of those it was done to. Watching the war play out on television, the people here weren't ready when the peace came crashing in. Unlike in bigger cities, this evacuation was quiet and quick. A psychic message broadcast over the width and breadth of the village: *You have an hour. Take what you can carry.* Within fifteen minutes, the queue of cars headed out to the 94 West on-ramp was backed up past Wilmot and Waukegan. Evacuation rolled west like a wave after the Armistice, so maybe people were ready for it. Or maybe they'd given up months before and prepared themselves to submit to anything that came.

The stereo hisses dead air as she pilots the Kia along the narrow suburban streets to her parents' house. She made this trip a dozen times when she and Miquel lived together, never as many times as her mother said she'd have liked but as many as Carrie's family could handle. When she was in Topaz, she wondered if her parents were relieved not to have to endure their visits, if the soft forgetting that settled in after she left for Bishop returned over time. Carrie pulls into the driveway behind her brother's Honda Fit, all four of its tires deflated. They took the station wagon when they left, loaded with the oddest assortment of ostensible necessities: grocery bags of canned goods and a shoebox full of extension cords. Passports and birth certificates issued by a government that no longer existed. The manila folder with her mother's unpaid medical bills and insurance claims, because her father had his own war and wasn't ready to give up even after the enemy was gone. They packed as if they were coming back, as if they were going on the camping trip her parents used to threaten Carrie and Brian with. The station wagon was the last out of town that night; in Carrie's memory, its taillights pulling onto the on-ramp were the punctuation mark at the end of Deerfield.

The door is unlocked, and the air inside tastes as if it hasn't moved since that day. She's glad the house hasn't been reclaimed by nature. One broken window could be a seed that grew an abandoned house into a terrarium, letting in birds and squirrels, pet cats left to go feral, and endless armies of bugs. The Norris house is silent and feels like it's settling into itself, prepared to collapse into nothing. There's the echo of a bad smell, a trace of something gone to rot in a cupboard or the defunct fridge, but her father was thorough cleaning the place before they left, as if readying it for new owners who never took occupancy.

Carrie walks through the house, trying to connect to something in it. Every time she came back, she felt more like a guest. When she and Miquel came for dinner, her father invited them to stay the night, and Carrie politely declined. It was an imposition on a place that was no longer hers, and sleeping in a guest room in the house where she'd grown up was less appealing than the ride back, even after a few glasses of wine.

People look back at their childhood homes with nostalgia, filtering out anything bad that happened there to create a place that felt safe, that felt like home. For Carrie, the most vivid memories of this house are the ones at the end of her time in it, when her ability manifested and she haunted rooms, overlooked by the rest of her family. She remembers sitting at the kitchen counter doing homework as her mother readied dinner. Her mother crashed into her full bore, as if she weren't there, and stood staring through Carrie until Carrie came into focus for her. Her terse *didn't see you there* was an early sign something was wrong; she wasn't imagining she'd become invisible to the people around her. Coming before she understood what she was, the moment was one of panic, a dream in which she shrank away into nothing.

A flush of that panic hits her as she walks through the kitchen, like passing through a patch of cold water in a swimming pool. Carrie forgets why she came; she stands in the kitchen, searching the closed cupboard doors for a sign. On the fridge, her father stuck a calendar of her mother's chemo appointments for April, seven years ago. Carrie walks over to it, thinking back to the evacuation and landing her finger on the date. She counts the chemo sessions that would have come afterward.

She goes upstairs to her parents' bedroom, a sanctum sanctorum she and Brian were never allowed in. Finding the door ajar makes Carrie uneasy. She imagines her mother dead in the king-size bed, rotted to a skeleton but recognizably her mother. She imagines a creature hunched over her mother and feeding, and that creature is herself.

She opens the door, and the room is empty, the air more stagnant than in the rest of the house. The room is sparsely furnished: the bed, her mother's vanity, and the small bookshelf her father used as a nightstand. Carrie picks a couple of books off the shelf, John Le Carré and James Clavell, ones she knows her father read and reread. She takes the picture on the vanity of her parents on their wedding day, an old photo that had begun to yellow even when Carrie was a kid. She considers her mother's jewelry but can't tell what's valuable and what's cheap. She doesn't remember her mother wearing any of it, so nothing has sentimental value. She picks up a necklace, a gold filigree flower with an opal set in its center, and holds it in front of her, letting the pendant rest below her throat, but it feels childish and idiotic, and she drops the necklace as if it's burning, letting it land on the carpet with a dull thud. She leaves the room without bothering to pick it up.

She goes into what used to be her room, ceded to Brian when she left for Bishop. She wouldn't know what to take; anything that was hers had been moved piecemeal from here to her apartment, more tiny erasures of her time in the house. Her toe kicks the controller of Brian's Xbox, which had been left on the carpet as if he'd been playing it when the evacuation notice blared into his head. Carrie picks it up and sets it on the unmade bed along with the rest of what she's gathered. She kneels in front of the television and pulls the game system off the shelf where it sits until the wires tug taut. Reaching blindly around the back, she detaches each one from its source, finishing by pulling the plug out from a breaker strip. The wires dangle like lifeless tentacles.

On a shelf above Brian's bed, there's an old Polaroid Sun 660. When she was nine, Carrie went around "framing shots" in the square created by her thumbs and index fingers, whispering *click* when she had it perfect. In a rare moment of attention to his daughter's interests, Carrie's father bought her the Polaroid and a stack of film cartridges, which he repeatedly pointed out were not cheap. The intervention of an actual camera revealed that Carrie had no eye for photography, and she retired the camera before using up all of the initial film, but she loved the bulky weight of the Sun 660. She hefts it in her hand, even puts the strap around her neck, before stopping herself, feeling as silly as she had with the necklace.

She tears open the packaging of the last cartridge and rips through the foil. She pushes the latch forward to open the film door and slides the cartridge into the camera, then clicks it shut. Carrie likes the mechanics of things: the click of her iPod's wheel that she can feel in the pad of her thumb, a car's engine coming to life, the power of it vibrating through her foot and becoming part of her. She puts the camera in the box along with the Xbox and exits the house.

She tries to pull the door shut behind her by hooking her foot around the edge of it, but it thuds weakly against the frame and swings back open. She stops and turns, then decides to leave it. She imagines wildlife waiting in the bushes to take possession. *Let them have it,* she thinks. She puts the things she's gathered into the Kia's trunk and slams it shut. She starts the car, selecting an upbeat pop album that is the exact opposite of her mood, one she knows she'll turn off after two or three songs, and continues west.

PROSPECT HEIGHTS

◇

Once Rai has left for school, Clay tries to get Dominic to skip work the next day. Dom isn't having it. "They're all going to be freaked out," he says.

"Tell them all to stay home," Clay says.

"We've got a wrap party for that war movie at the end of the week," he says, packing his bag.

"That's the end of the week," says Clay. "It'll wait."

Dominic pauses where he's standing, takes a deep breath, and gives Clay his *you just don't get it* face. "If they stay home today, they won't come in tomorrow," he says. "They'll sit in their apartments thinking about what happened and about how easily it could happen again. You can't stop after something like this or you never start again."

Clay knows Dom's right but doesn't want to say it, so he kisses him goodbye twice on the way out the door. Alone in the apartment, Clay thinks of how easy it would have been to stop Dom long enough to tell him about Rai. It's always easy once it becomes impossible.

In the shower, he takes stock of himself for the first time that day. He has a bit of a hangover: his mouth is cottony, and he can feel the shape of his brain inside his skull, glowing with a dull pain. He dry swallows two aspirins and brushes his teeth, wandering out of the bathroom with a towel wrapped around his waist.

There's a woman in their living room, looking at the pictures on the wall, mostly Rai's school photos. Something in her stick-up-the-ass posture telegraphs to Clay that she's Faction. "What the fuck?" Clay says through a mouthful of toothpaste. He slows time around him in order to make a better assessment of the situation. He could be out of the room in less than a heartbeat, could even take the time to go get dressed before he rabbits, but if he runs from his own apartment, where can he run to? The other option is to take her out, but that's a hornet's nest he won't poke unless he knows he needs to. He lets time come back to its normal speed.

"Sorry to let myself in, Mr. Pastorius," she says. "I had some questions for you about the incident last night."

Relieved that whatever the woman is there for, she's not there for him or for Rai, Clay goes to the kitchen sink and spits, setting his toothbrush down on the stove. "I'm not Mr. Pastorius," he says. He wipes his mouth with a dish towel. "I'm his husband. Dom's at work."

"My apologies," she says. "I thought after what happened, he'd take some time."

"That's what I said, too."

She pulls a notepad out of the air in front of her and passes it to Clay. "Would you mind writing down the address where he works?" she says. Clay takes it and does as she asks without hesitation. The best way to get through a casual encounter with a Faction agent is total compliance. "Thank you," she says, folding the notepad and disappearing it with a gesture too fast for Clay's mind to register fully. "Since I have you here, may I ask you a few questions about your husband?"

"I'll tell you what I can," he says. "But Dom doesn't tell me a lot about his business."

"Of course," she says. "Work-life separation is important, I hear. This is more personal, so maybe you can help."

"Shoot," says Clay, trying not to sound reluctant. Faction agents have a way of making people feel like they have something to hide even when they don't.

"Does Mr. Pastorius have any friends in the baseliner communities? Maybe acquaintances in the Bronx?"

Clay shakes his head. "I don't want to sound racist or anything," he says. "We don't have anything in common with those kinds of people. I mean, what would we even talk to them about?"

"Do either of you have family that went west?"

"Dom and I are both only children," Clay says. "And our parents, mine and his, all passed away before . . ." He waves his hand in a slow-motion version of the way she'd disappeared the notebook. "All this."

"Thank you," she says. "We're looking at all possibilities with an incident like this."

"I completely understand," Clay says. "I—" He's about to say *used to be one of you* but catches himself. Faction might have a way of making everyone feel guilty, but with Clay it's more pronounced. He deserted, after all. He never violated a law or broke a promise, but he left. He figures someday there'll be a reckoning for that. "I'm glad no one got hurt," he says.

"We lost a good agent," she says. "Died protecting Damps from Damps. Someone's going to settle up that bill."

Clay opens the door for her, gripping his towel with one hand. "I hope you find whoever did this," he says.

She stops in the doorway and shakes her head. "There's no who to something like this," she says. "It's all of them. It's how they are."

KLATCH

◇

Waking up next to someone changes the shape of the day. When Fahima reemerges into consciousness in contact with another body, it orients her attention to the world around her rather than inward. It precludes that first moment of self-examination and assessment. *I am here, in this body. Am I all right?* Asking the question introduces the possibility of a negative answer, the idea that she's not all right. There have been many mornings when Fahima's lain in bed tangled in the sticky threads of this thought. *Am I okay? Do I even know what it might mean to be not okay? Have I gone too far to see the way back?*

To wake to another set of questions, to start the morning with an external crisis, a concrete problem to be solved, has a relief to it. She feels Ruth's arm around her waist and is forced to recall the night before. She creates a plan to extricate herself from the arm. These are things she's good at, tasks suited for her particular skill set. Self-psychoanalysis not so much. Any mental apparatus she constructed for it was nothing but an intricate, redundant set of grinding gears.

She gingerly lifts Ruth's limp wrist, but Ruth is so nearly awake that even this stirs her. She pulls Fahima closer in. It's a shock, as it had been last night when Ruth finally and definitively leaned across the gap between them and kissed her. Fahima is so good at making decisions and acting on them when the choice involves assessment of known facts, but she's in awe of people who act in the face of unknown emotional variables. For a second she feels trapped. Then she lets all of that go, sinks into the body next to hers, and falls back to sleep.

The second time, she wakes to the high whine of coffee grinding in the kitchen. She pulls on a robe, noting she's missed Fajr. The operating system of her mind plays its error alert, the sound of Fahima's mother sucking her teeth. She thinks of something Ruth said last night after the initial kiss, when Fahima was unsure. "Let this happen," she said, pleading. What Fahima heard, how her mind translated the words, was *Let yourself have this.* They were two different sentiments, but they were connected. Both were about permission and surrender that wasn't native to Fahima.

Drawn by the promise of coffee, Fahima doesn't notice that the pile of blankets next to her in the bed still includes Ruth. She opens the bedroom door and sees Patrick Davenport in her kitchen, measuring out coffee spoons with a shaky hand. Sarah sits bolt upright at one end of the couch, staring blankly forward. Fahima closes the door behind her, wishing she could lock it from the outside, and Patrick turns at the sound.

"Fahima," he says. "Thank goodness you're all right."

Patrick Davenport does not look well. His skin is pale, which is understandable because he rarely leaves his office at the top of the Bishop building, much less the building itself. But it isn't the pallor that makes him look ill; it's the way the skin hangs off him.

He looks deflated, like something's drained away his insides, and the fluidity his ability once gave his body has slumped into a boneless droop that turns all the straight lines into bowed umbras. His attention flits around the room as if there's a fly circling his head. When he smiles at Fahima, one corner of his mouth doesn't join in the act and he has to shove it upward with the palm of his hand, which pushes the whole side of his face out of place, giving his right eye a look of surprise.

The kettle whistles on the stove behind him, and he turns to get it, twisting at the waist like a hunk of taffy. "I hope you don't mind I let myself in," he says. "I heard what happened." This is obvious bullshit. Nothing happens that Patrick doesn't know about. His waist untorques; his face molds itself into a perfect imitation of concern. "Are you all right?"

"Super," says Fahima. She stays in the doorway, blocking it and pulling the knob to hold it shut.

"Patrick's here," Sarah tells Fahima brightly. She pauses, her whole body frozen, unsure what to do next, what she did a second ago.

Patrick pours two cups of coffee. One of his arms extends across the room to give Fahima hers. "You still take it black?" he asks. He walks over to Sarah, his arm distended between his torso and Fahima like a clothesline. Fahima takes the cup from him with both hands, and the arm retracts. He arranges Sarah's hands into a bowl shape in her lap and puts the coffee cup into it.

"Terrible stuff," he says. "I know we approach these issues from opposite sides"—he touches his index fingers to each other, and when he pulls them apart, the tips stick, stretching like two pieces of chewed gum a second before separating—"but a thing like this is on both of us really. A security failure and a failure to . . ." He puts a hand out toward Fahima, spinning it at the wrist as he searches for a word. "To try to make everyone happy."

"I don't feel responsible for what happened last night," Fahima says, thinking about the man who wasn't Eito Higashi and the way his lips moved in sync with the bomber's.

"That's because you're not," Patrick says. "Any more than I am. It seems so preventable, though."

The doorknob twists in Fahima's hand, and there's a tug too strong for her to pull against without spilling hot coffee on herself. Ruth pulls the door open wearing a med school T-shirt Alyssa left behind. "Hey, boss," Ruth says, wiping sleep from her eyes. "I was wondering if you wanted to—"

She stops, looking at the full room.

"Hey there," Patrick says cheerily. "I'm sorry, I didn't know you had a guest." He moves from Sarah's side back to the kitchen like paint being tossed out of a bucket, re-forming behind the counter. "How do you take your coffee?"

"To go," says Fahima. "Ruth, you should get going."

"Don't be silly," Patrick says, pouring another cup. "Fahima, introduce us." It's a request, not a demand. It's always requests with Patrick. If he demanded anything from her, Fahima would tell him to fuck right off, but his requests seem impossible to deny.

"Ruth, this is my roommate, Sarah Davenport," Fahima says, gesturing to Sarah on the couch. "And this was her brother, Patrick."

Patrick's smile tightens for a second, baring teeth.

"I'm Sarah," Sarah says, less to Ruth than to herself. Patrick's hand stretches across the room for Ruth to shake, which she does warily.

"Fahima and I go way back," Patrick says. "We went to school together in the Dark Ages."

"Ruth should really get going."

"Were you there last night, too?" Patrick asks with feigned concern. "You weren't hurt at all, were you?"

"Sugar but no cream," Ruth blurts out. She blinks rapidly, trying to absorb and assess what's going on.

"Of course," Patrick says. "I almost forgot. Fahima, where do you keep the sugar?"

"I don't have any," Fahima says.

"Black's fine," says Ruth. "I'm fine."

"Fahima, I don't want to be indelicate," Patrick says. "But what is Ruth's level of clearance?"

"I'm just the—"

"She's not attached to Tuning Fork if that's what you want to talk about," Fahima says. "If that's what this is, she has to go."

Patrick sucks a long hissing sound between his back teeth. "I'm afraid it is."

"Give us a minute," Fahima says.

"Of course," Patrick says. Fahima leads Ruth back into the bedroom.

"What the fuck?" Ruth says. "I thought Sarah Davenport was dead. They taught us she—"

"She's not; she's just not in great shape," says Fahima.

"And no one's seen Patrick Davenport, like, ever."

"Now you have," Fahima says. "Which is not a great thing." While Ruth hurriedly dresses, Fahima opens the drawer of the nightstand, which pulls out only halfway. Fahima jimmies the back panel, and it opens. A collection of old flip phones spills out, each one with a white nub of Hivestuff for an antenna. Ghost phones. She removes one, then packs the rest behind the panel, clicks it into place, and shuts the drawer. She presses the phone into Ruth's palm.

"Hopefully this will never ring," she says. "If it does, it'll be me. When that happens, I need you to do exactly what I tell you."

"What if I need to call you?" Ruth says.

"Emergencies only," Fahima says. "This will always find me, but there might be consequences."

"Why are they here?" Ruth asks.

"We used to be friends," Fahima says. "All of us." Ruth is fully dressed, the phone secreted somewhere on her person. Fahima opens the bedroom door and pilots Ruth through the living room to the front door. She pushes her out and shuts it behind her.

"No kiss?" Patrick says.

"Fuck off," says Fahima, picking up her coffee and taking a sip. "This is terrible," she adds. "You have to let it steep. You were always impatient."

"I know what you're hinting at when you refer to me in the past tense," he says. "But it's me, Fahima. I'm different, but we're all different. Everything's changed."

"What do you want?" Fahima asks.

"About last night," he says.

"Other than the bombing, how was the party?" says Fahima. Patrick smiles, and Fahima feels the same urge. There's a relaxation that comes from being around someone you've known forever. Too often when talking to him, she's drawn into it and has to remind herself it isn't entirely Patrick in there. Or at least, he's not alone. "No surprises," she says. "Green lights across the board."

"What coverage does that give us?"

"Most of Europe," Fahima says. "Africa with a couple of holdouts. Southeast Asia. Saudi Arabia, but not much traction in the Middle East."

"But nothing from Russia or China?"

Fahima decides to keep her suspicions about Russia to herself. "I hear the Chinese are working on a device of their own."

"Have they had any luck?"

"They don't have me," Fahima says.

Patrick smiles. "And where are we in terms of research?"

"We're around the same numbers," says Fahima. "Affected range tops out at three miles. Within affected range, 50 percent actualized, 50 percent dead. Give or take, depending."

Patrick nods as if she hasn't said the devices would have a fatality rate in the billions. "It's a shame we don't have access to Emmeline Hirsch."

"Access to her?" says Fahima. "She's dead. She died in the riot."

Patrick looks at her, surprised, and for a second Fahima is sure he knows.

"You never call it that," he says.

"She died the day the war started," she says. "Better?" Neither of these is how she thinks about that day. For Fahima, it will always be *the day Patrick and I took over Bishop*.

He laughs. It's an unpleasant strained sound. A burp of air squeezed out of a bubble. "I have to say, eliminating nonactualized humans *would* simplify things."

"I had someone who worked for me who thought that way," Fahima says. "I had his ass arrested."

"I know," says Patrick. "It was my people who took him. I'm suggesting you should be open to outside viewpoints."

"We don't turn the devices on until I fix the numbers," she says. "That was our agreement. I have enough on my conscience."

"I wouldn't ask you to. I keep count of the dead, too," he says. "But sometimes what seems like a bug turns out to be a feature. Didn't you tell me that once?"

"I told *Patrick* that," she says.

"It's still me, Fahima," he says. "The person you went to school with. Your friend. I'm not a monster."

"Not yet," Fahima says quietly. But she has reports of villages in the Wastes wiped out by Faction squads, of plans to nullify the Chicago Accords if there's any threat of an uprising. Things the Patrick she knew never would have done. He smiles. It's supposed to look kind, but he misses the mark, extending the corners of his mouth too far into a pained rictus.

"Sorry about the coffee," he says, walking casually over to Sarah and kissing her on the cheek. Her hand goes to the spot he kissed a second afterward, wondering what the lingering moisture is from. "And the interruption. I was worried about you. I'm glad you weren't hurt." Fahima is terrified that he's about to hug her, an outcome that would be awful enough if it were Patrick Davenport she was speaking to. Instead, he makes a bow and leaves the room.

"Fahima, Patrick's here," says Sarah.

BADLANDS AIN'T TREATIN' US GOOD

◇

Two fliers double helix overhead, then circle back and buzz so close to the Kia's roof that Carrie can hear them laughing over the stereo. The Armistice says no Resonants between the boundary and the West Coast territories, but kids come out here all the time to fuck around, sometimes worse. When they do, they stay near the interstates to avoid getting lost, even fliers.

Spooked, Carrie takes the next exit and from there on keeps to winding roads and crumbling asphalt. The tiny car rattles like a mechanical bull underneath her, jostling at every pebble and divot. Her ass is numb by the time she gets to Sioux City. Two years ago, this was one of the stable cities. Ten thousand people lived here, safe beyond the boundary. The ones who understood the terms of the Armistice had an advantage. They bought houses in second-rate cities out west before property values skyrocketed. They rented vans or drove with whatever they could load into their cars without Faction agents looming over them in a forced evacuation. Accepting the horror of their situation gave them an edge. Some people settled on the western bank of the Mississippi, like dogs at a screen door, waiting to be let back in. They caught another kicking when the border was pushed back. Others went farther west, knowing it bought them more time. They'd never be at peace, but they could approximate it for a while, maybe until they died. Everything between the big rivers is subject to evacuation with no notice. Most of Sioux City's residents packed up and kept going west. The people here are stragglers and risk takers, willing to stay until they're rousted rather than move on now.

Carrie's learned it's possible to autopsy a city once it's died. She can see the eventual cause of death and the marks of the sickness that came before. She maps the history of the city's body over time. None of her theories about particular towns and cities can be confirmed. She's become a storyteller for dead cities, eulogizing them without any facts. Sioux City, she assesses, hit its heyday in the mid-1980s: the architecture of the center downtown is hack postmodernism, a hodgepodge of styles mashed together in a way that felt fresh and new for three minutes but now shows branded scars: empty Pizza Huts and abandoned Blockbuster Videos. Sioux City was half empty before the war, but there are patches where life has pushed back up from fallow ground. A block of coffee shops and bars and pizza places where young people who had money but lacked the drive to leave had tried to make the place livable. Some look open; people out front of a coffee shop smoke the herbal cigarettes popular and easy to get out in the Wastes if you didn't live near one of the new tobacco farms, or have a line on cigarettes snuck over from the Carolinas. They're tight sticks of mullein, mint, and sage that smell lovely but are harsh on the throat. Carrie makes a habit of bringing proper cigarettes, less for barter than as a handshake, a way to establish trust.

The smokers stare at the Kia as it passes. They don't see many cars out here because most of the gasoline denatured years ago.

She's well enough known here, her presence associated with the things she brings. She's not welcome, but she's tolerated.

When she makes delivery runs, she stays with Peter Massey, a single dad with a four-bedroom he's been living in for years. Peter was a literature professor in Boston. His wife died in the evacuation. A lot of American academics found jobs in Europe after the Armistice, but now it's impossible. Peter does some tutoring and takes in boarders. Every time she stays here, Carrie tries to pay and Peter refuses. Carrie leaves money with Reuben, who's twelve and reliable about sneaking the money into his father's wallet.

"We weren't expecting you," Peter calls from the doorway, Reuben shielded behind him.

"I'm on a quick errand," Carrie says, shouting through the rolled down window. "If you've got room for the night."

"We've always got room for you," Peter says. His eyes flick toward downtown. "How about you park out back?"

Carrie pulls the car around the house. She's startled by a horse batting its nose against the back window of the garage. She peers in at it, shielding her eyes from the light, but the horse has lost interest in her.

"I was about to get dinner started," Peter says when she comes around front. "Hope you're hungry."

He cooks them potatoes and chewy greens from the garden and so much garlic Carrie coughs on the first bite and eagerly bolts down the rest. An old floor fan wired to stolen solar panels takes the teeth out of the heat. Peter couldn't garden or build worth a shit before—he taught himself, to keep him and Reuben alive. "One of the things about being a parent," he told Carrie, "is that you're never allowed to die."

The horses are a new addition since the last time she came through, bought from a hostler in Ames. Reuben's been learning to ride.

"Hustle's my favorite, but Wendigo is a jerk," he says. Great clumps of greens are wedged between his teeth. "He tossed me the other day, and I got this." He pulls back his blond bangs to show a short, angry gash.

"I almost told him that was the end of horseback riding," Peter says.

"Dad," Reuben says, embarrassed.

"I figured it's a good idea to be ready to make a quick getaway. Off into the sunset, like in the movies." Peter smiles as if this is a joke, and Carrie forces herself to return his smile. "You're traveling light," he says to change the subject.

"I'll be back through again soon," Carrie says. "We've got some water filters they need out in North Platte."

Reuben and Peter both stare down at their plates.

"North Platte's gone," Reuben says. Carrie doesn't know what to do with this information. She doesn't know where to put it because it doesn't make any sense.

"They went west?" she asks.

"They're gone," Peter says. He lowers his voice as if he can prevent Reuben from hearing. "Culled. Faction."

Carrie has heard the word *cull* used before in reference to disappearances. It's a myth, a phantom. Three people strike out on their own and are never heard from: culled by the Black Rose Faction. A family in a farm at the outer edge of a settlement gets sick and dies before the one doctor in town gets to them: poisoned by the Faction as part of a program of genocidal culling. It gives meaning to meaningless deaths, but it makes no sense even on a small scale, much less a whole settlement. Especially not now, when the Bishop Foundation is in diplomatic talks with the Europeans. They wouldn't commit genocide back home while playing nice abroad. Peter's face brightens into a mask of optimism. He stands up with his hands clasped, chipper as a television house-wife. "We've got cherries for dessert," he says.

The cherries are bitter and underripe, and afterward Carrie feigns exhaustion and retires to a room upstairs. She lies on the twin bed, paging through one of her dad's Le Carré novels with a plot she can't make sense of, listening to A Tribe Called Quest with one earbud in. Peter knocks almost inaudibly on the door. When she opens it, he's standing behind Reuben, presenting the boy like an offering. Carrie imagines the man Peter must have been, so different from the mousy thing he is now.

"Roo's been having headaches," he says. "I know sometimes that can be a sign."

"It could be a lot of things, Peter," she says.

"But it might."

"I didn't resonate till I was fourteen," Carrie says.

"I heard in Boulder they're screening kids," he says. "They're taking them back."

"There's nothing definitive," Carrie says. "People back east, some of them are still angry."

"But if he has powers, he's one of you," Peter says, shaking the boy for emphasis. "They'd take him in. They'd take him back."

It would be easy enough to check. It wouldn't be a hundred percent—sometimes a kid's potential wasn't apparent to an amateur like Carrie and it took a deeper scan called a sounding to be sure—but if there was a glimmer there, she'd probably be able to sense it. The problem that confronts Carrie is no news is good news. If she tells the kid he's a Resonant, she's driving a wedge between him and his father, one she's experienced. If she tells him he isn't, she's damning him to spend the rest of his life here or somewhere worse. She has no interest in delivering either message.

"You have to wait," Carrie says. "You have to wait to see what happens with him and what happens with the law." She puts her hand on Reuben's flushed cheek. "For now, the best thing he can do is work on his horseback riding." Relieved, Reuben runs out of the room, but his father stays. Carrie looks at him sadly. She's subjected to these conversations everywhere she goes, a parade of children offered up for inspection. She'd love to find one she could bring back with her. The new government is good at getting things built but bad at creating policy. The Path to Return has been in talks for two years. It would grant citizenship to any Resonant born in the Wastes. The name has a feudal air, the sense of a ruling class reaching down and plucking an occasional peasant out of the shit.

"Even if he was," she says, then pauses. "If they took him back, it'd be just him. They'd take him from you."

"They'd get him out of *here*," Peter says through clenched teeth. "There's nothing here. I've tried to get him papers to get out of the country, but the people on the West Coast, they want so much money that I—"

"Don't deal with anyone on the West Coast," Carrie says. She's heard horror stories about people trying to get off the continent from ports in Seattle and Vancouver, sympathetic Resonants who will teleport you across the ocean for a price. The better ones are scams, the worst are traps. There's a slave trade all up and down the coast, baseliners who show up attempting to buy their way out and end up in situations unimaginably worse. "Keep him here," she says. "Keep him safe. That's what a parent does."

Peter's face twitches and twists. She can see him swallowing something he wants to say, but he turns to go instead. The door is nearly closed when he comes back in; whatever he tried to swallow has come back up, burning his throat. "A parent doesn't just keep their kid *safe*," he says. "They do what's *best* for their kid, even if it fucking hurts. You take care of your kin." The word is hot and mean, the sound of a stick breaking over a knee. Maybe it's only a word, but Peter knows the significance of that word out here. He chose it for her. Regret mixes with the heaviness of travel, the pull of the bed behind her, and Carrie mutters "I'm sorry" as she closes the door on him.

"We used to have more options than *safe*," she hears him say in the hallway before he leaves. She expects the words to follow her down into sleep, but she's out in minutes and sleeps dreamlessly.

RENDEZVOUS

◇

"**W**hy don't you have Ruth fly you?" Omar asks. "Did you two have a fight?"

"We did not have a fight," Fahima says. She doesn't know whether Ruth told him or whether he had a copy listening at the door, but Omar knew immediately that things had turned physical between her and Ruth. He isn't shy teasing her about it either; one of the downsides of his unclear job title is that he never treats Fahima much like a boss. "Descending on them in a magical bubble wouldn't send the message I'm looking for."

"Fair enough," he says. "Be careful with her, though. She adores you."

I adore her, too, Fahima nearly blurts out. But the word isn't right; it has a hint of idolatry. "I'll be careful," she says.

"Speaking of careful, I would like to restate how much I hate this thing today," Omar says.

"Your concerns have been noted."

"My concerns have been summarily ignored," Omar says, cramming into the same wedge of the revolving door as Fahima so he can continue to gripe. "Why not have him come here?"

"He'd be out of his mind to come here right now," Fahima says.

"You're a high-value asset," Omar says as he opens the car door for her. "You don't put a high-value asset into a nonsecure environment."

Fahima glares at him. "Where do you get any of those words?"

Omar shrugs. "I'm seeing a boy who's way into spy movies."

"We need to get past spy talk and have a conversation with these people," Fahima says.

"With all due respect, boss," Omar says, "maybe we don't."

After the Armistice, when the Bronx established itself as a refuge community, the decision was made to separate it from Manhattan as much as possible. The little bridges that spanned the Harlem River were closed off or destroyed, although the Washington Bridge to the north and the RFK Bridge that crossed Randall's Island, which had been converted into a training facility for the Black Rose Faction, were still in use. It was an impractical, spiteful thing to do, but spite drove a lot of policy in the first weeks and months. It made getting into Manhattan from the north impossible without routing through Jersey and cut off commuter towns like New Rochelle and Norwalk. Separation was key to the peace.

One of the Omars drives them over the RFK, across a barren stretch of fields fenced off on both sides with trespassing warnings posted regularly. Fahima mentally tags him as "Front Seat Omar," willfully ignoring that this makes the Omar sitting next to her "Backseat Omar," an appellation that has seedy implications. Front Seat Omar eases them into the snake's nest of off-ramps and roundabouts where traffic from Queens and Manhattan once converged and takes the exit north toward the Bronx. Before the bridge over Bronx Kill, they're stopped at a checkpoint. No cars ahead of them, no cars behind. No cars through the southbound lane. A solitary Faction agent sits at a lonely little booth at the edge of a body of water Fahima could swim across if she was determined.

Fahima flashes her credentials. "Reason for entry?" the agent asks. He's a portly white man in his late fifties with a thick Brooklyn accent and a beard that glows with nebulous lights, a helpful reminder that not every member of the Faction is master race material.

"We're with the Bishop Foundation," she says, showing her ID. "It's sensitive."

The agent rolls his eyes. "*Sensitive* reason for entry?"

"I can't discuss—"

"I need something to put on the paperwork," he says, clearly bored.

"We set up sewage treatment in Morrisania a few months back," Front Seat Omar says. "A charity thing."

"I didn't hear about that," the agent says.

"We didn't make it a big deal."

"What's it got to do with today?"

"See this?" says Front Seat Omar, pointing to an inch-long scab across the high crest of his cheek that Fahima missed earlier. She looks at the Omar next to her and sees that he has the same scab. "I got sliced when one of these motherfuckers blew himself up at a party last night," Front Seat Omar says. "We're here to shut it down. Let these fucks drown in their own shit."

The agent gives the smallest chuckle, nods, and waves them through. As they cross the bridge, Backseat Omar keeps his eyes on the water, out the window.

"That was convincing," Fahima says.

"You have to speak to them in their own language," he says. But he doesn't turn to look at her, and his finger traces the scab on his cheek. Fahima can't help but wonder if he believes what he said.

It's not as if she's never thought the same thing. *They tried so hard to kill us. They hate us so much. Why is it on us to keep them alive?*

American ruin porn was an established visual genre even before the war. Tourists came to see the empty factories and abandoned housing developments of Detroit the way they snapped infinite selfies in front of the Colosseum and the Parthenon. Something about standing in the ashes of empire appeals cross-culturally. The truth of occupied ruins bears little resemblance to the photogenic face tourists seek out. It's not an echo of empire but an indictment of it. As the car moves through the Bronx, Fahima is confronted with the flip side of everything she's achieved. She doesn't want to believe that for some to live in a utopia, others must suffer in a dystopia, but she can't argue with the streets around her. People slumped against buildings, passed out drunk or dead. Dogs fight over pieces of trash that hold a whiff of food. An empty bottle smashes on the roof of the car, raining glass into their path. It's an obvious target because none of the other cars here run. Both Omars crane their necks to see where the bottle came from and if there are others coming. They can't spot any source, as if the streets chucked the bottle as a form of welcome. Dogs look up at the sound, then return to their scraps.

Front Seat Omar pulls the car over in front of what used to be a butcher's shop. The window is covered over in brown paper, but a decal depicts a pink pig grinning as he raises a carving knife to slice into a piece of ham on the bone.

"I'm going in with you," Omar says. "Like sixteen of me."

"We told him I'd be alone," Fahima says. "I've got a panic button. You can come flooding in by the dozen if I give you the sign."

"Panic button won't help if he shoots you in the head," says Backseat Omar.

"They won't kill me," Fahima says. "I'm a high-value asset." If it goes south, it's much more likely they'll take her as a hostage than off her on the spot. She steps out of the car and does a quick scan of nearby rooftops. She doesn't see snipers, but that doesn't mean they aren't there. She grips the handle of the front door, thinking that any resistance might be a sign it's rigged. She won't be able to tell without pulling. When she yanks the door open, she isn't blown back into the street. So that's good. Fahima gives Omar a quick nod, then steps in.

The room is candlelit, almost romantic. The power's out more often than it's on in the Bronx, but it's morning and the room would get ample light if they took the paper off the windows. The object is to keep this meeting secret, but half the Bronx watched Fahima come in. Surrounded by candles, flanked by what look to be lumberjack backup singers, Gavin Olsen, leader of the Bronx cell of the Kindred Network, looks like a hipster wizard or some demonic bartender. He has a full beard and a mustache twisted and waxed until it extends to arrow-sharp points at either end. His skinny tie and suspenders stand out like a shiny new penny among the roughshod denizens of the Bronx.

"I thought we said alone," Fahima says, gesturing at his entourage.

"I didn't mean I'd be alone," Olsen says. "I wouldn't risk being alone with one of you."

"I was thinking the same thing," Fahima says.

"We're no threat to you," Olsen says. "Please, sit."

Gavin Olsen was an inevitable side effect of the policies of the Armistice. He was a wounded ally. He had been a professional influencer, one of those people who mastered social media before anyone else had ideas about what it was for. He was one of the first to come out in support of Resonants' rights, immediately after they'd gone public. As tensions escalated, he wrote articles for a number of outlets against the rising tide of xenophobia and encouraged his followers to calm the fuck down and accept Resonants for who they were. Only half the general public ever favored policies like internment or worse. Most were indifferent, and some, like Olsen, were actively against it.

Reading over his pieces in retrospect, Fahima could see a change after the Pulse and the realization that he hadn't been one of the chosen. Once fighting broke out, people quickly chose sides. The bulk of them sided with the government. How could they not? The prevailing narrative was that Resonants were the aggressors. But there were still people rooting for the Resonants to win. The Armistice threw them out along with everyone else. The sting was brutal, and some, thus betrayed, joined anti-Resonant groups like the Kindred Network. Olsen rose quickly through the ranks, using the same skills that had made him a social media guru to create real life networks in the enclave the Bronx became.

"You know we met once," he says. "It was after Kevin Bishop's speech at Columbia. This would have been, what, eight years ago? Different world."

"I'm sorry, I don't remember," Fahima says. "That was a tough day."

"It's difficult to imagine what you mean when you say *tough day*," Olsen says. He turns to the men behind him. "Mark, you had any tough days lately?"

"My mom died of a staph infection last year," says one of the lumberjacks stoically. "Treatable, but they couldn't get the antibiotics. Those were tough days."

"Died of a staph infection across the river from the greatest city in the Western world," Olsen says, shaking his head. "That *does* sound tough. But I'm sorry, we were talking about *your* tough day."

"You know what I'm here to talk about," Fahima says.

"You didn't need to come all this way," says Olsen. "We didn't do it. The Kindred Network didn't bomb your party."

"I needed to hear you say it," Fahima says.

"To see if I was lying?" Fahima nods. "And can you tell? Is that one of your abilities now? Maybe you should have brought a psychic."

"I believe you," she says. "You know anything about it?"

"We're an island out here," he says, chuckling at his half-assed joke.

"You're not in touch with anyone out west?"

"Via what?" Olsen asks. "Smoke signal? Pony fucking Express?"

One of the lumberjacks nudges him in the shoulder, a motion Fahima isn't supposed to see but does. Olsen's brow knits, considering something. "There've been people coming in," he says. "A handful. I don't know how they get here. They don't show up at meetings, but they've approached our people. They promote a more . . . zealous vision of what our organization should be."

"Have they made inroads here?"

"I wouldn't know if they had," Olsen says. "Our people are freethinkers, not some sort of Hive mind." He smirks, pleased with himself.

"We can't have the Faction coming in here," Fahima says. "You understand that?"

"Because it'd be bad for you?" Olsen says. "Think how bad it'd be for us."

"So keep your people quiet," Fahima says. "Calm them the fuck down."

"They aren't *mine*," Olsen says. "The network's a support structure. Like one of those groups you join when your pet dies and you can't cope. We're helping people through it."

"By encouraging them to riot?"

"They don't need encouragement," he says. "The riots are about material conditions. The riots are slaves asking for better treatment from their masters. Nothing more. The network aids with less material issues. We help people come to grips with the fact that we're the last generation of humanity."

"I don't even know what that means."

"The fuck you don't," says one of the lumberjacks.

Olsen holds up his hand for silence and lets them all sit in the quiet for a beat. "Our children are being born like you," he says. "Every child who's hit their teens since the Pulse has resonated. All of them. We won't know for another couple years, but most of us believe that children conceived after the Pulse will be Resonants as well. Our own children won't be like us. That's the theory. It was enough for me to get myself snipped, if you know what I mean."

"That is way outside the scope of this meeting," Fahima says.

"You came here to accuse us of an act of hatred, and I am telling you we aren't angry anymore. None of us have the energy to be angry. We are grieving. We are grieving our own deaths. We don't have it in us anymore to give a single fuck about any of you. And I don't delude myself that it will matter. I don't think for a second it will stop you and yours from using this attack as an excuse to wipe us out. Because you have the time and the energy to hate us. You have that luxury, among so many others. I envy you your hate."

Fahima stands up, and all four of the lumberjacks twitch. She holds up her hands. "Thank you for your time," she says. "I've got some people coming in tomorrow. Healers. They'll be at Temple Emanuel near St. Mary's Park all day."

"No one goes near the park," says Olsen. "The Faction holds most of the South Bronx."

"They'll pull back for the day," Fahima says. "Tell everyone it's safe."

"Thank you, master," Olsen says, bowing his head. "Much obliged."

ROOSEVELT ISLAND

◇

Clay stops to rest, and time around him reintegrates with its normal flow. The air in Lab Bay Theta is warm and thick, and condensation fogs the observation window. That never happens when the Omars are working. There must be something they do to balance the heat generated by Clay's exertions, the friction between time inside his bubble and outside of it. Dominic says the membrane is like a push of hot air moving constantly outward from Clay's body, trying to keep the rest of the world at bay.

He strips off his spandex down to his boxer briefs. He grabs a towel and wipes sweat from his forehead and chest, then uses it to get rid of some of the fog from the window. The lab is shut down for the night. He asked Omar Six to fudge his clearance, claiming he had ideas he wanted to try out, ways to shape his affective field so it interacted with the Chair differently. It was bullshit; he had no more ideas today than he'd had when Fahima hired him. Omar Six grumbled how exciting it would be to come in and find heaps of data already waiting for him, what a pleasure to start every day behind, but he adjusted the clearance so Clay could come and go as he pleased. Being the only one on the island reminded him of the book he read to Rai in which two kids ran away to the Metropolitan Museum of Art and hid out at night. Quotidian spaces become wild when abandoned. Every child knows this. As an adult, Clay forgot. He imagines mischief he could get up to when he hears a door clicking shut. Someone emerges from a janitor's closet and walks toward the unused Alpha Bay.

Clay puts on his shirt, pulls on his jeans, and pads out of Theta barefoot, easing the door shut behind him so he doesn't alert the other person to his presence. The intruder hunches over the terminal, hunting and pecking at keys, a hijab obscuring her face.

"Working late, Ms. Deeb?" he asks loudly. Fahima startles, her hand going to her hip like a gunslinger.

"Fucking hell, Clay," she says. "You're not supposed to be in here."

"No one's supposed to be in here," Clay says.

"Yeah, but I'm the boss of here, so I get to be here whenever I want."

"Omar changed my clearance," Clay says.

"Six?" Fahima asks. Clay nods. "He's my least favorite." She shuts off the terminal before Clay can see what's on the screen and eases herself into the chair. "So what's got you here in the middle of the night?"

"Honestly?" Clay says. He pulls up a chair next to her. "I didn't want to be at home."

"Wife mad at you about something?" Fahima asks.

"Not any more than he usually is," Clay says. Fahima holds up a hand to apologize for not knowing. It's funny that he knows she's queer but she didn't know it about him. He's had bosses invested in the personal lives of their employees and others who saw the people who worked for them as appendages. He imagined Fahima in the first camp, although she's never given him reason to think so. Their brief but chummy conversations on her visits to the Ruse had the contours of a friendship but none of the substance.

"My ex and I both had work. Too much, constantly," Fahima says. Because they aren't exactly friends, the quiet, darkened lab becomes a confessional. "It was an understanding. We never needed to sneak away or make up an excuse. We had work as a legitimate excuse, and we took it when we needed to. Until we didn't. Maybe we wouldn't have lasted as long if we hadn't had it the whole time. Maybe we would have lasted forever."

"I have something I'm not telling him," Clay says. It's an opportunity to voice the thing fit to burst out of him. "And I should."

Fahima nods. "Does he know what you do here?"

Clay shrugs. "He knows I do research. He thinks I'm some kind of a scientist, which is hilarious. I was an English major. I can't bring myself to tell him I'm a lab rat."

"That's not true," Fahima says. "That's not what any of you are. You're the operators. You make the Chairs work."

"We don't, though," Clay says. "How long now and none of us can make them work?"

"That's on me," Fahima says. "It's not you that's wrong. It's the machines."

"Bullshit," Clay says. "You made it work at least once." She smiles. "Can I ask you something?"

"Shoot."

"If it works again, will it do anything for people who didn't get it the first time?"

Fahima shakes her head. "There are people who won't be affected no matter what."

"Not everybody's special."

"Not everybody's a Resonant," Fahima corrects. "It's not a sin, being normal."

"Go tell that to folks in the Bronx," Clay says. "Nothing we do's going to make things any better for them."

"We can make things more comfortable. Easier," Fahima says defensively.

"Easier and more comfortable is what you say to your parents when you put them in a home."

Fahima flinches as if Clay has hit a nerve. "Some days I wish I could turn everybody on," she says. "Others I wish I could turn everybody off. Mostly I want things to be nicer for all of us."

Clay hesitates. He's ready to tell her about Rai. Whatever else Fahima is, she's a problem solver. She'll look at the situation coolly, without the emotional baggage Clay brings to it. Without a heart in the way. She could fix it, fix *Rai*. Make the whole thing go away.

But it's not only what Fahima is, it's who she is. She's an authority, the head of the Bishop Foundation, which is the smiling face that masks the Black Rose Faction. You don't get to the big chair by breaking rules on behalf of the hired help. She'd be obliged to run Rai's case up the chain, hand him over to the Faction for the exact test looming in their future.

"I'm going to get back to it," he says, jerking his thumb toward Theta Bay.

"You should go home," Fahima says. "The Chair'll be there in the morning."

He shakes his head. "I'm in it now," he says. "Wouldn't get to sleep anyway."

"Maybe we could take a look together," Fahima says. "Tweak the Chair. Save the world."

Clay smiles. After some time together, it'll be safe to share his situation with her. "I've got nothing else going," he says.

Fahima rises from the seat, rubbing her hands together eagerly. Clay wonders how much of this she gets to do now that she's effectively running the entire country. "So let me ask you," she says.

He hears the sound of a phone buzzing in her pocket, a sound that feels outdated, like a dial-up modem or the scratch of a needle on a record label. "Shit," Fahima says, looking at the screen of an old-school flip phone. It's quaint seeing one again; in the postwar rush to restore infrastructure, cell networks were written off as unnecessary. The Hive already connected everyone instantly, and so there was no reason to risk colony collapse in the country's bee population for the sake of sending a text. He's about to poke fun at her, but her face is serious. "I've got to take this."

"Saving the world's got to wait?" Clay asks.

Fahima nods absently, staring at the phone. "Have Six send me your data tomorrow," she says. "I'll take a closer look at what you're putting out."

"I'm going to have it all worked out by tomorrow," Clay says, trying to get a laugh. Already on the phone, Fahima nods and gives him a dismissive wave as she makes her way back around the circle of lab bays. Clay turns and looks into Alpha Bay, where the Throne sits, permanently empty. He knows it isn't true, but there's part of him that's convinced if only he were better, stronger, more adept, he could fix Rai and put all these fears to rest.

MAINLY JESUS AND MY HOT ROD

◇

Carrie wanted to be on the road before dawn, but her clock is off, and she wakes to late-morning light coming through the curtains. She leaves some bills under the pillow and gathers her things, hoping to leave without another conversation. When the front door creaks open, Peter calls to her from the kitchen.

"Hey, sleepyhead. I'm making breakfast."

Carrie shuts the door and slinks back into the house.

"I made coffee," he says. "Chicory, mostly. Tricks my brain into believing there's caffeine."

Carrie accepts a mug of steaming brown liquid that resembles coffee in appearance only.

"I can't eat," she says. "I have to hit the road."

"I'm sorry about what I said last night," Peter says, flipping an egg. "It wasn't fair to you. You're one of the good ones."

Carrie thinks about all the ways *one of the good ones* has been used. The guards in Topaz Lake used to say that about Miquel even as they explained tragic accidents that befell Resonants who weren't *good ones*. She thanks Peter and passes on breakfast, resolving never to stay here again, to throw herself on the riskier and more public mercies of the Hotel Irma downtown. Peter piles eggs on Reuben's plate and carries her bag out to the car. She sits in the driver's seat exhausted again, as if all of last night's sleep has drained from her.

"You should come out around Thanksgiving," he says, leaning on the edge of the open window. "Terry down the road's been raising turkeys. I've got dibs on one of them. It doesn't have to be the exact day. I'm sure you've got family back east."

She looks up at the house and sees Reuben watching her from the porch. "I'll see what I can do," she says, and rolls up the window. She gives a wave and turns the keys. The engine struggles once, twice, and a third time. On the fourth it catches, but Peter's already tapping on the glass.

"That doesn't sound good," he says.

"I'm thinking of trading it in," she says with a forced smile. "Is there a Lexus dealership around here?"

His laugh is as fake as her smile. "There's a shop out by the highway," he says. "I don't know if the guy's any good." He gestures to the garage that once housed cars but now stables the horses. "You should have him take a look. You don't want to die out there."

She knows he means she doesn't want the car to die out there, and she corrects it in her head. Peter writes down the address for her, and she thanks him as she pulls out of the driveway. Reuben rushes down to the end of the drive to wave to her as she heads off.

The edge of Sioux City is a tangible border. The city has no suburbs, not even the encampments that orbit the larger settlements. Beyond a radius, the city drops off into nothing and the plains open up like a sea. The front of the mechanic's shop doesn't fill Carrie with confidence; it's a tin-roof shack with a cinder-block office attached. Neither does its proximity to the city. She considers driving past, chancing that it was only a hitch that caused the engine to sputter. But if the car dies in the middle of nowhere, she's dead with it. She pulls the Kia into the driveway, startled by the sound of the service bell as it rolls over the warning tube.

An ancient-looking man emerges from the office, hunched over so severely that Carrie wants to slip a cane under his hand to support him. She turns off the car and gets out, but he barely looks at her, moving slowly and directly toward the car.

"This little gook piece of shit giving you trouble?" he asks.

Carrie is taken aback by the sound of a racial slur she hasn't heard since her grandfather passed away. She recovers and explains the problem she had starting the Kia that morning.

"Alternator most likely," he says. "Did it sound like this?" The old man does a shockingly accurate imitation of her car, with a deep warble in the back of his throat and a precisely modulated raspberry blown through his thin lips.

"That's it," Carrie says. The old man nods, rests his hands on the edge of the hood, ignoring the heat it gives off, and points with his wattled chin for Carrie to pop the hood latch. When the hood's up, the old man sucks in a deep breath through his nose.

"Smell that?" he says. Carrie sniffs the air but registers nothing. "Like a burnt fuse," he says. "Alternator, like I said. I got one around that'll work." He sizes her up with his gimlet-ringed eyes. "Cost ya," he adds.

What he means is he knows what Carrie is and he's going to gouge her for the work. She can't begrudge people out here their acts of rebellion, but she worries he's going to fuck her on the work as well. She hopes there's a mechanics' code of ethics to prevent him from fixing the Kia enough that it gets her out of town but dies on the plains.

"Whatever it costs to get it right," she says.

The old man nods again. He lifts one hand, a talon twisted by arthritis, and points to a folding chair next to the office, sitting in full sun by a bin of food scraps.

"Have a seat," he says. "Take me about an hour. Ain't as quick as I used to be."

Carrie eases herself onto the hot metal seat. She puts in her headphones and cues up a playlist full of rockabilly and country. She puts her sunglasses on and leans her head back, soaking in the music, the sun, the stench of the scrap pile. Terrible material circumstances can be endured, even enjoyed. There's a moment when everything is so awful it obliterates her, frees her from the burden of self. Skin baking and nostrils full of stink, Carrie is present, without history, a thing enduring this situation second by second and nothing more.

The screech of tires pierces through a Johnny Cash song. A pickup truck, the kind you buy when you don't need a truck but want to be the kind of guy that drives one, all noise and no real guts, pulls in behind the Kia, leaving two crescent moon skid marks behind. Work boots emerge from the driver and passenger sides, and men continue to pile out of the truck's cab like clowns out of a Volkswagen.

At final count, there's a half dozen. They stand out front of the tin-roof garage, watching Carrie. They aren't the finest specimens of humanity. An image flashes in her head, a short movie in fast forward in which she kills all six before the first one hits the ground clawing at his slit throat. Sometimes she feels violence like a pleading thing inside her, asking to be let out. She stands and steps out to talk to them, swaggering on road-weary legs; one hand rests on the handle of her knife, and the other is out, showing them her empty palm.

"I'm passing through," she says. "Should be out of here within the hour."

"This man is our kindred," says one of the men, weak-chinned and scrawny. He shapes the word *kindred* with his lips as if what these men are is a secret and he's gifting her a hint. "Any harm done unto him is as harm done unto us."

"I'm not doing unto anyone," says Carrie. "Just conducting a bit of good old American commerce." She slides her hand down and takes her wallet out of her back pocket. She holds it up by the corner, both hands in the air but ready to drop the wallet and grab for the knife. If they're going to have a go at her, they might as well get it over with.

"This isn't America," says the man. Everything pauses. These men are acting out a scene they saw in a movie. The mechanic slams the Kia's hood, shattering the mise en scène they're trying to build. The tension breaks, and all attention shifts to the old man, who hocks a thick loogie onto the broken asphalt.

"Girl's right," he says. "Money's money, and I've got bills same as you. Head back into town and don't be getting yourselves into my business."

The men haven't planned this encounter past the issuing of vague threats and look relieved. They sulk back to their truck, cramming in so tight that Carrie wonders if they have to sit on one another's laps. The truck roars to life and kicks up a cloud of dust as it leaves.

"Fuckin' crackers," the old man mutters. Carrie is comforted that his use of epithets is so multivalent. "Make it so a man can't make a living." He points to the car. "You're all set there, miss. I wouldn't take it far if I was you, but I don't imagine you've got much choice. Thing is built cheap and once it starts coming apart . . ." He shakes his head grimly, issuing a terminal diagnosis.

Carrie thanks him, pays him what he asks, and continues west, happy to have Sioux City in her rearview. She enters the expanse of the plains listening to Nick Cave singing about murder and feeling blessedly tethered to nothing, unmoored from the world.

PROSPECT HEIGHTS

◇

Clay makes it through most of the day at work. In the middle of the afternoon he's struck by a splitting headache, a pain that radiates out from the center of his head. He pulls his ability back, listening to the mechanisms in the Chair wind down.

"You guys mind if I call if for the day?" he yells up to the booth.

"Please!" says Omar Eleven over the speakers. "Six and I are going to be here all night processing this shit."

"Fahima says send the data to her," Clay says.

Both of the Omars stop what they're doing. They talk to each other without activating the intercom for a minute, then press the button to speak to Clay. "You saw her?" Omar Six asks.

"I'm fucking with you," Clay says. He worries he's done something wrong, betrayed Fahima's trust, although the Omars are all devoted to her.

Clay takes the subway home. At the other end of the car, two teenagers, overdressed for the weather in thick parkas with faux fur–edged hoods, shadowbox with their abilities. One feints at the other with a fist lit up by electric sparks. His friend bobs, weaves away, then lands a punch to his padded gut. The high chemical smell of burnt Gore-Tex floods the car as the electrical boy curses his friend for ruining his coat, and then they're at it again, fiercer this time with less feint and more fury. A broadly missed uppercut opens the fiery boy up for a shock to the kidneys that staggers him back into the seats. He huffs and comes up grinning maniacally, licking the coppery taste of electrocution off his teeth.

It could easily spill over into true violence. Part of Clay wishes it would, and recognizing the bloodlust in himself, he feels sick to his stomach. He wants the boys to stop. He wants to get off the train, but he worries if he moves, they'll see him. The train stops at DeKalb and a Bloom of Faction agents get on. No one he recognizes. They group around one of the poles, doing that thing Faction Blooms sometimes do where they look as if they're miming a conversation without moving their mouths. They pay no attention to Clay or the boys, but the fighting stops and the boys return to their seats, folding their hands in their laps as if chastised.

Clay has the feeling he's been caught doing something bad, as if the Faction saw the flash of blood hunger flare up in him. There are no laws against casual cruelty, and nowhere is it written that anyone should strive to do no harm. A society is a system of trade-offs, sacrifices and benefits, limits in exchange for protections. Look at the choices made and read a culture's priorities. Since the war, freedom is the thing most highly prized. Some might argue it's equality, but equality is a place to start from. Beyond equality is the promise of infinite freedom. Do what thou wilt shall be the whole of the law. When a society creates open space within itself, a level field, there's the risk it'll become an arena. A place of battle, free of restraint.

One Faction agent flicks his gaze at Clay, noticing him for the first time. Clay feels seen with a brutal intensity. He feels it as a weight on his skin, a pressure in his stomach, and a chill in his skull. They give the impression they know everything already. In Faction interrogations, there's no need to compel confession. People's guts come pouring out because they assume it's already too late. Clay imagines that when this Bloom gets off the train, they'll dispatch another to Clay's house to pick up Rai and send him out into the Wastes. It's already happening; he's sure of it. He betrayed his son, he betrayed Dom. He broke his family apart without so much as a thought.

The next time the doors open, he hurries off, a fifteen-minute walk from their apartment. He's certain he'll come home to a door off its hinges, Dominic in the living room in tears, Rai's room tossed. A hurricane of bedsheets and books with an emptiness at its center where Rai should be. But he arrives to find the door locked. Dom is in the living room, watching reruns of some sitcom. He looks startled when Clay comes in, then relieved.

"You're back," he says, muting the television.

"I should have called," Clay says. "I was trying something new with the Chair, and I got caught up."

"All night?" Dom says.

"Yeah," says Clay. There's a conversation Dom's trying to prize out of him, but Clay isn't having it. "Listen, I'm exhausted."

"I bet."

"Something you want to say?" Clay asks. Clay's not an idiot; he knows he's upset about keeping Rai's secret and he's letting it out as anger at Dom. But knowing's not the same as stopping. Dom turns his attention back to the television, watching it with the sound off. "I'm going to crash out, but I was hoping you and I could make some time to talk."

This gets Dom's full attention, which is not what Clay wanted. *We need to talk* is a phrase that can't help but set off alarm bells in a relationship even when it means only what it means.

"Are you leaving me?" Dom says. It's a telling phrasing. *Leaving me* rather than *leaving us*. Dom says Clay would never think of leaving because of Rai. Being parents together is different from being married. The latter isn't a bigger deal than dating. There's documentation, legal and financial knots that bind, but nothing that couldn't be coolly severed. All that ends when you become a parent. There's no Solomonic swipe to divide a child evenly. When they adopted Rai, sureness descended on their relationship. Underneath was Dominic's fear that one day Clay would take Rai and go.

"Nothing like that," Clay says. "There are things we need to discuss. If we don't carve out the time, we never find it."

"If there's something bad, don't make me wait for it," says Dom.

"It's nothing bad," Clay says. "I want some of your time. And I can't right now. I'm tired, and I have a headache. I'll take a day off. You take a day off. We'll go out for lunch and talk. It'll be like a date. It'll be nice."

"Okay," Dominic says, not in the least mollified. He turns the volume back up. On the way to the bedroom, Clay touches him on the shoulder and there's the tiniest flinch, like a petulant child refusing comfort.

NO CHURCH IN THE WILD

$\diamondsuit$

Supplies run from Chicago to Boulder weekly, if not more often. Mostly medicine, sometimes electronics and food. It's the easiest of the longer runs. The Faction turns a blind eye. Picking off smugglers with a truckload of Rez is one thing, but it would be bad press to starve an entire city. Carrie never makes the run, but she knows the locations and shibboleths.

Boulder is walled off like a medieval keep, quarried stone and mortar sanded smooth as glass. *They could have built more housing,* Carrie thinks. *Solar panels and hospitals. They could have saved more people. Instead they made this to keep people out.* She can't deny it's effective. Las Vegas doesn't have a wall. Its dense city center metastasizes into tent cities that snake across the desert. Its Wild West ethics appeal to people haunted by cowboy dreams and Mad Max fantasies. You're more likely to get rolled for your shoes than you are to find an apartment with the doors still on. Boulder has laws and regulations, a gated community at the end of the world. You can raise a family here, provided you can get in.

Carrie drives past the city, parking the Kia in foothills three miles out. She pockets her iPod and crams the things she took from her old house into a tote bag to hike the two hours back the way she came. From the east, the wall is a sheer face looking out on miles of crater where Denver used to be. To the west, the wall is dug into the contours of the wooded landscape. The lip is level, but the base runs a jagged line along the ground. There's a dry culvert set into the hillside that runners use for entry. It's not big enough to drive the Kia in, much less the trucks used on runs. In the normal course of things, a team helps runners unload. She enters the culvert alone with the dim glow of her iPod to guide her. Ten yards in, there's a thick metal grate crusted with rust and filth. On one side are shiny new hinges, and on the other a keypad lock. Carrie enters the code, and it swings outward.

The light behind her condenses to a point before any light emerges in front. Feeling her way along the edges, she moves in darkness. *Maybe this is faith,* she thinks. *Groping in the dark toward a light you're not sure is there.* A beam of bright yellow shoots out of the black at her, a flashlight in an unsteady hand, bucking and shimmering in the confines of the space.

"Who's that?" calls a woman's voice.

"Blackwell," Carrie answers. She has a set of nicknames she uses on runs. When she delivers food, she's Cicely Tyson, after the chicken company. If her truck's full of electronics and computer parts, she goes by Fiona Apple. On medical supply runs, her pseudonym is the decidedly less funny Liz Blackwell, the first woman to receive an MD in the States.

"You new?" calls the voice. "It's supposed to be Rosie."

"First time on this route," says Carrie.

"You have antibiotics?"

"I'm not on a run," says Carrie. "I just need help."

"Don't we all," says the voice. The woman holds the flashlight like a kid telling a ghost story. Her features cast strange shadows upward.

"I'm picking up something for someone back east," Carrie says. "Sentimental value. If I can get a place to stay for the night, I'll be out of here tomorrow. I'll owe you a favor."

"I don't need favors. I need drugs," she says. "Tetracycline, erythromycin. We've had an outbreak of typhus."

"They haven't sent you drugs?" Carrie asks.

"Thousands of people," she says. "Drugs come in and they're gone." She snaps her fingers; the small sound echoes in the dark.

"I can't piss antibiotics," Carrie yells. Her voice caroms off the pipe. She takes a deep breath. "I will do my best to help you, but I need you to help me first."

"You don't have to scream about it," the woman says. "Come on, then." Even though the pipe is level, Carrie can't shake the feeling she's descending into storybook depths. Dante's Hell and Carroll's Wonderland. The mines of Khazad-dûm and the city of the Silurians.

A dim light appears. "Thank God," mutters Carrie. Her steps pick up from the slog of the last ten minutes. The light feels breathable, pouring into her through her eyes. The culvert ends in a small water treatment plant. Sodium arc lights burn bright white. A chlorine smell hangs above the fug of moldering concrete. Boulder doesn't treat its sewage anymore. It dumps its shit in Boulder Creek to the south, millions of gallons' worth. They don't put sentries on the southern wall; the smell is defense enough. This *fuck wherever our shit lands* psychology is the same one that built the wall and arms the sentries. *We take care of our own,* the city says. *Everyone else can get fucked.*

"You're a nurse?" Carrie asks.

"I'm a doctor," the woman says. "My name's Alyssa."

"Why are you hiding in a pipe?"

"I get pinged when someone opens the gate," Alyssa says, pulling up the edge of her shirt to reveal a clunky beeper. "I assumed you were bringing drugs."

"I'll get word back," says Carrie. "A friend of mine *can* piss antibiotics. He'll churn out tetracycline for you faster than we can carry it here." When she says it, she means it, but there's no way of getting word to Hong except through the Hive, and Hong avoids the Hive even more studiously than Carrie does.

"You have a first name?" Alyssa asks.

"Liz," says Carrie.

"Short for Elizabeth?"

"Yeah."

"So you're Elizabeth Blackwell?" Carrie nods. "Sure, whatever," says Alyssa. "We've all got trust issues."

As they emerge from the facility, the sun is setting and the city is winding down for the evening. The part of town they're in reminds Carrie of a nicer, richer Deerfield: long rows of ranch houses, evenly spaced. A garbage crew makes its way down the street on foot, pulling a wheeled trash barge. The men who grab bags from the curb have to work fast; if the barge stops, it'll take the whole team to get it rolling again. The pullers cheer the grabbers on like high school coaches. Out front of one house, a man digs up the dry dead grass of his lawn, piling sheets of sod in the driveway.

"Not enough water for green grass, not enough wood for picket fences," Alyssa says. Other lawns are covered in slate or gravel.

As the buildings get taller and the city becomes less suburban, vendors take down their displays and roll carts off their corners. Fruits and vegetables. Mass-market paperbacks and iPhone chargers. Batteries of every size and voltage, some of them clearly homemade. Sweaters and scarfs that look unsellable in the morning's rising heat. Carrie remembers summer trips to buy winter coats. *Everything's cheaper when nobody needs it,* her mom said.

Alyssa walks a few steps ahead of Carrie like a tour guide. "You mind me asking what you're here for?"

"Yes," says Carrie. They continue in silence for few more blocks. "You mind me asking where we're headed?"

"All the way to the top," says Alyssa. She points ahead to a building that looks like a modern iteration of an Aztec ruin. "You've got a date with city hall."

Carrie stops, and her hand finds the knife handle at her back. Alyssa turns to her, frowning. "The mayor asked to meet with any couriers that come through," she explains. "You're nobody's enemy here."

"I'm not here as a courier," Carrie says. "This is a private job, and I've been asked to be discreet."

"*I've* been asked to bring any couriers to her honor the mayor," says Alyssa. "And since she sets my hospital's budget, if she wants you dropped off on the steps wrapped in ribbons, that's what I'm going to do." Carrie doesn't move. She has the address for the pickup, but she won't know how to find it on her own. She hoped Alyssa was someone she could trust, but now she's considering bolting. Alyssa sighs and takes a step toward her. "The mayor's a sweet old hippie lady. You'll love her."

Carrie wants nothing more than something to eat, a bed to crash in, and a clear path out of town. This job feels cursed, not the trap she suspected but bad from the jump, and her best course might be to bail entirely. She musters the energy for one more hurdle.

A woman who is unmistakably the sweet old hippie lady Alyssa described stands on the steps of the city hall, perfectly framed by the building itself. She's plump with a small cloud of gray hair, wearing a faded floral print dress, and she comes down the stairs with her arms open, ready for a hug. Before Carrie knows it, she's engulfed in flesh and homemade perfume.

"It is *so* good to finally *meet* one of you," the mayor says into the top of Carrie's head. She frees Carrie from her embrace but holds her by the shoulders to inspect her. "I am fully aware of how dependent our city has been on the efforts of you and those *like* you, and it just breaks my *heart* that I have never had the opportunity to thank a single *one* of you until now. But all of that is about to change."

"Mayor Cummings," says Alyssa, "this is Liz Blackwell." Alyssa's tone communicates to Carrie that she knows the name's a fake without arousing suspicion in the mayor.

"Please, call me Pam," she says. "Everyone calls me Mayor Pam."

"Pleasure to meet you, Mayor Pam," Carrie says quietly.

"The *pleasure* is all *mine.*"

Alyssa gets a distracted look on her face, like she's forgotten something critically important, and in the pause while she tries to come up with an excuse, Carrie hears the buzz of a cellphone on vibrate. She wonders if Boulder's managed to get a cell network up and running, along with the physical phone grid. "Excuse me, Pam," Alyssa says, "There's something at the hospital I have to get back to. Liz. I hope to see you again soon. With drugs." She turns away, fishing in her pocket as she goes.

"This is *such* an *exciting* time for us," says the mayor, pulling Carrie toward city hall by the elbow. A tall, thin man descends the steps toward them. His smile is too sweet for Carrie's taste, and his shirt, a Hawaiian number with winged hot dogs dotting it, is the kind Carrie's mother might have disparagingly referred to as *fun.* "Do you know Mr. Joyner from the Bishop Foundation?"

The man extends his hand, hanging it in the air like a dead fish.

Carrie wants to explain that not all Resonants know one another, but instead she smiles politely and shakes his hand, repulsed by its clamminess. "Cedric," he says. "Nice to meet you Miss—"

"Liz," says Carrie. His name rings familiar, but a warmth pulses through his hand and the memory is gone before she can retrieve it.

"You're in from Chicago, yes?" he asks.

"I'm not sure I want to say."

"Oh, there's no need for *that* now," says Mayor Pam, fluttering her hands like she's drying them off. "That's what Cedric is *here* for. We've made wonderful progress together. A sort of détente. It's starting here, but I can't help but think bigger things are yet to come." She looks expectantly at Cedric, who raises his eyebrows to indicate that all things are possible. "But you must be *starving*, Liz, driving all that *way*," she says to Carrie. "There's a wonderful place right near here; we'll get you something to eat."

Carrie allows herself to be pulled along, one arm hooked into the mayor's elbow, the other hand resting lightly on her knife.

POSTMORTEM

◇

For all Fahima's effort, people still die in New York. The murder rate has crept upward. Some people attribute it to how easy it is for Resonants to murder one another. As bigots love pointing out, some Resonants are human weapons. It wasn't difficult to murder someone before; people managed without abilities for thousands of years. Fahima wasn't naïve enough to think improved economic conditions would eliminate violence, but she expected a drop in the murder rate when people had the things they needed. New Yorkers find reasons to kill one another with depressing regularity. Fahima has theories about the uptick in violence, one of which she's pursuing in the office of the medical examiner on East 26th Street.

In the lobby, a receptionist with shaggy fur regards Fahima with one dark marble of an eye.

"Can I help you, miss?" she asks.

Fahima is not cut out for detective work. Her spit feels syrupy in her mouth. She's closer than she's ever been to an answer, and her nerves are kicking in. She wants to pet the receptionist's fur to see if it's soft or bristly. She roots in her pocket. Her arm slides deeper and deeper in until it feels like she could grab her ankle. She comes up with a high-level Bishop Foundation ID she printed up that morning. She displays it to the receptionist, who is unimpressed. "I'm here to see Archie Gibbons," she says.

"Archie's in the basement," says the receptionist. "Take the stairs at the end of the hall. Keep going down till you abandon all hope."

Fahima mumbles thanks and rushes out of the lobby. The fluorescents in the stairwell flicker violently, a paparazzi worth of flashbulbs. She can hear them struggling to hold on, asking her for relief. There are times she wishes she'd worked harder at Bishop to develop this side of her ability, but when machines speak to her now, it's a garble, ramblings in a language she used to understand. If she could calm them down, she'd be less likely to miss a step and tumble to an ironic death outside the door of a morgue. She grips the railing and eases her way down.

"Mr. Gibbons?" Fahima says as she comes to the bottom of the stairs. "A friend of yours sent me. A couple friends."

Archie Gibbons stands up at his desk, almost dropping his sandwich. He's in his fifties, with a physique Fahima associates with grandfathers: stocky without being fat, sturdiness covering up whatever health-related time bomb ticks inside him. He has an old Brooklyn face, round and rosy. He wipes greasy hands on his apron. Given the state of the apron, this can't make them any cleaner.

"You're Omar's friend?" he says quietly. Fahima nods. Archie shakes her hand but stops in midpump. "You're not one of them, right?"

"Faction?" Fahima asks.

Archie nods. "You have to tell me if you are. Otherwise it's entrapment."

"No, it's not," says Fahima. "And no, I'm not." There's a comforting myth about the Faction that they're bound by laws restricting the actions of the police. They're restricted only by what they can do and what they're willing to do. "That bear lady upstairs doesn't like me," Fahima says. It's not okay to refer to Resonants with permanent physical manifestations like that, but Fahima is too exhausted to be a decent person. She's happy Archie doesn't judge her for it but judges him a little for his failure to do so. *We all have to get better,* she thinks.

"Ulrich doesn't like anybody," says Archie. "People whose looks changed after the Pulse are bitter as shit about it. I sympathize. I mean, her husband walked out on her right off. Took the kids. But it's not my fault the lady's got paws."

"You've got a body?" Fahima asks.

"Yah," Archie says, thick Brooklyn accent coming to the fore. He leads Fahima through the office and into the morgue, talking the entire time.

"I'm a Pulser myself," he says. "I was with the police department, in evidence. One day I pick up a stapler, and it's like I can see everyone that's ever touched it. I'm telemetric, is the word." Since the Pulse, there's more vocabulary around abilities. Groupings are like guilds or castes. Thermics and lithics. Empathics and readers. Physicals and ethereals. "Working with bodies is easier. Organic matter doesn't carry the same charge as objects. I can be up to my elbows in someone's stomach cavity and get nothing." He smiles, a piece of lettuce screaming green at Fahima from between his front teeth. "It's a relief."

The wall of silver doors makes Fahima think of library card catalogs. Relics from before the new world arrived. Archie opens one of the doors and slides the drawer out. The body under the

sheet consists of the tattered remains of a young woman. The fluorescents make her skin pale as fish belly. She's smaller than when
Fahima saw her at the party and looks distended, her features not
right, her torso flattened, and her arms and legs uneven. Her entire
body is badly burned.

"Meet Heidi Pryzborowski," Archie says.

"No one else knows she's here?" Fahima asks.

"Omar," says Archie. "He and my son are kind of a thing."
Omar, you beautiful slut, Fahima thinks. "I didn't approve at first.
But Archie Junior's happy, which is new. Anyway, I told Omar if I
could ever help."

"You have," says Fahima. "This is very helpful."

"You want me to stick around?"

"I'm good," Fahima says. Archie shrugs and returns to his sandwich as Fahima takes a slow lap around the body. It's easy to forget
to sympathize with members of the Black Rose Faction. A lot of
them volunteer. Maybe Heidi had signed up enthusiastically, yip-
ping hooray for fascism as she handed over her better self. But
maybe she was pressed into service against her will. Some Faction
recruits are "reformed" criminals and dissidents. Fahima whispers
the dua for the dead girl, however she got here.

"O Allah, forgive Heidi Pryzborowski," she says. "And elevate
her station among those who are guided. Send her along the path
of those who came before and forgive us and her, O Lord of the
Worlds. Enlarge for her her grave and shed light upon her in it."
She hates how robotic the dua has come to sound, how casual she's
become about speaking it over the bodies of people younger than
her, people she feels charged to protect.

She pulls out her phone. Like the ghost phone she made to talk
to Ruth, this one communicates across an impermeable boundary
dividing a country from the straggling remnants of what it used to
be. There's no enforced policy of noncommunication, but from a

practical stance, it's difficult to talk with anyone in the Wastes. Her ghost phone network, a collection of jagged lines and winding paths, grew exponentially every day, as networks are prone to do. After a few rings, Alyssa's annoyed voice answers.

"I'm right in the middle of something, hon," she says. The endearment is a reflex. Alyssa will drop it once the shock wears off.

"Hey, Lys, how've you been?" Fahima says, attempting to sound light. They've spoken only a few times since the breakup; Alyssa accepted the phone as a condition of the end of things. Fahima imagined she'd throw it into the Colorado River at her first opportunity, so it was a surprise the first time Alyssa called. It set the tone for every call that came afterward. Alyssa barked out some demand, something the hospital needed or something she left in the apartment in Brooklyn. Fahima promised she'd take care of it, then Alyssa hung up. Every time. There's no catching up or checking in, and this is the first time Fahima is the one to initiate contact. It's the first time she needs something from Alyssa rather than the other way around, and it isn't a dynamic she loves.

Alyssa gives a deep sigh. "We've been having rolling blackouts for about a week," she says. "Last night someone broke in and stole our month's supply of painkillers. This morning the whole hospital was at a dull moan."

"I can make some calls."

"We have our sources," Alyssa says. "None of us are out here waiting for your help." It has a toothless snap to it, more venom than Alyssa intended. "Sorry. What do you need?"

"I need your help."

"Of course you do," Alyssa says.

"If I needed to extract a person's parahippocampal gyrus, how would I do that?"

There's a pause. "You want me to walk you through brain surgery."

"The patient is already dead," Fahima says.

"That makes things easier," Alyssa says. "Take a bone saw and pop the top off."

"The top of the saw?"

"The top of the head."

Fahima looks at the trays and racks full of horrifying tools. One terrifying silver thing calls out to her. *Here I am.* It looks like a wheel of sharpened teeth balanced on the tip of a spindle. Fahima pulls the trigger, and the toothed wheel spins with a high, vicious whine. Fahima grins, forgetting for a moment what she's about to do, lost in the noise of a powerful machine.

"Are you doing this right now?" Alyssa asks.

"That's why I called," Fahima says. She wedges the phone between her shoulder and her ear. She pinches Heidi's cheeks and turns her head from one side to the other. "How much should come off?"

"Parahippocampal gyrus is fairly low in the brain," Alyssa says. "I'd say slice above the eyebrows, then dig down through the middle."

"Reach in and dig?"

"This is one of those times when not knowing what you're trying to do makes it impossible to help you," Alyssa says.

"I can't tell you that."

"Oh, good, it's Fahima's greatest hits," she says. "Do *I can't keep you safe.* That one's my favorite."

Fahima doesn't want to fight with her, but if she wanted to avoid it, she shouldn't have called. Too late for that now. "I'm sorry, Alyssa."

"Yeah, I like that one, too, but you can't dance to it."

"Are you doing all right? Is there anything you need?"

"You want me to tell you it's not that bad out here. I can't do that. It's that bad. Good luck with your skull." The line goes dead. Fahima puts the phone down among the sharp and awful things.

With the whirring discus of the bone saw, she cuts off the crown of the dead woman's skull, slices the brain like a ham, and digs down with gloved fingers, rooting until she feels something alive, squirming. Coiled around Heidi's parahippocampal gyrus, a little black worm wriggles and twitches even after its host has expired. It responds to Fahima's touch, curling around her fingers like she's its new host. It's the length of a finger, and it has the same flat matte darkness as the black flowers that grow in the Hive. She drops it into a jar of embalming fluid and holds it up to the light.

"Hello, little fucker."

EAT THE RICH

◇

Carrie wonders if Boulder was always a gated community. You don't have to build a wall to keep people out. If you're clever, you make it so there's no place for them inside.

There were kids at Bishop who came from money. Darren and Lynette Helms invited everyone out to parties at their parents' beach house in Oyster Bay. Carrie went to a few of them with Hayden and Miquel and Waylon and later with Bryce, but it was clear the invites weren't meant for them. The parties weren't to share what the Helmses had; they were to show it off and call attention to the fact that life would never be like this for Carrie or her friends. Some kids arrived at the parties and felt at home, stripping down to designer bathing suits and jumping into the pool. The enthusiasm that had built up on the drive out was quashed as soon as Carrie got there. She sulked in corners drinking lukewarm vodka and juice out of Solo cups because she couldn't imagine joining the others in grabbing champagne out of the ice-filled tub, shooting the cork into the air, and stumbling around with the bottleneck gripped in her fist. She felt like she was on the opposite side of a piece of glass, a zoo exhibit none of the rich kids bothered to look at.

Dinner with Mayor Pam and Cedric Joyner evokes the same feeling of falling into a world where she doesn't belong. The menu items are unintelligible, and, taking pity on her, Cedric orders for the table. Plates arrive in front of her with items she has no idea how to eat, and Cedric provides gentle correction, suggesting a spoon where Carrie has chosen a fork, modeling the way certain things are scooped up to the mouth with the fingers. She doesn't enjoy anything she eats, too aware of all the mores she's breaking, every little thing she's doing wrong. The waitstaff stands nearby, smirking. It's the same as it was with the mechanic: her ability gains her nothing here; all the power is theirs.

"It's been the most *remarkable* breakthrough," says Mayor Pam as she slurps down something gooey and uncooked with the consistency of raw egg. "More than we'd let ourselves hope for. We hadn't *hoped*."

"We must always have hope," says Cedric, skewering a paper-thin piece of pink meat and popping it into the back of his teeth.

"It seemed to me it was a *problem* built into the *system*," Mayor Pam says. "A contradiction at the heart of the Armistice. Because what was the dividing line between us? Was it the arbitrary boundary? Or was it Resonance itself?"

"It was both," Cedric says. "Therein the contradiction."

"And so it was a *surprise* when the Bishop Foundation sent Mr. Joyner to extend a sort of olive branch."

"An opening gambit," Cedric says.

"A Path to *Return,*" Mayor Pam adds.

"None of that's been approved," Carrie says. "It's a figment. A proposal."

"Proposal, exactly," Cedric says, pointing his two-tined skewer at Carrie in a way that makes her feel like it's destined for her eyeball. "Consider that word a minute. When you propose marriage, it's not a public event. It's between two parties. Same here."

"So what's the proposal?" Carrie asks, sipping her wine.

Mayor Pam looks at her quizzically, as if the details have suddenly escaped her. Cedric puts a hand on her arm.

"It's all very complicated," he says. "But essentially, we've set up a screening facility for local youth and teens to see if they have Resonance. Those who do, we repatriate."

"Exactly," says the mayor, confidence returning to her face. "These young people are given a *chance* to live up to their potential."

"And what about the rest of you?"

"We're *fine* here," says the mayor. "And the Bishop Foundation has promised us a steady flow of certain supplies."

"Items they previously had to purchase through your black market networks," Cedric says, his eyes following the arrival of a new plate and avoiding Carrie's.

"That's not an *accusation*," Mayor Pam assures her. "We appreciate the work you've done."

"So does the Bishop Foundation," says Cedric. "But it's no longer necessary. At least not here. When you get back, you can tell your friends that Boulder no longer needs anything. All is being provided for them."

"Like what?" Carrie asks.

Various utensils stop in midair, and again the mayor looks as if she's forgotten what she came into the room for.

"Whatever they need," Cedric says. "Think of it as a grand experiment. First here and then across the rest of the Wastes."

Mayor Pam looks at him, shocked to hear the word come out of his mouth. Everyone out here knows what this part of the country is called back east, but they refer to themselves as the West or they still think of it as America. Cedric's hand falls over Mayor Pam's. His index finger raises slightly and makes a tiny circle in the air. Her indignant expression disappears, replaced by a bright smile.

"We could be one *nation* again," she says. "Your famous singer, Hailey Cohen, will be here next week with her unity concert under joint approval from my government and yours. Isn't that *amazing*?"

"Hayden," Carrie says. "And it's *their* unity concert."

"Whose?"

"Hayden's," says Carrie. "They use neutral pronouns."

"How *neat*!" Mayor Pam says, barely restraining herself from clapping her hands. "But *theirs* is exactly the message we're looking for right now. All of us together again. Different but united."

"Separate but equal," Carrie mutters.

"I think that's a very cynical way of looking at things, *Liz,*" Cedric says. "Aren't you from Chicago? A great experiment of its own?"

"I'm sorry," Carrie says. "I'm just . . . road tired, you know?"

"We have a room ready for you," says Mayor Pam.

"Are you staying long, Liz?" Cedric asks.

"I'm not," she says. "It's funny, the thing is, I'm not on a courier run. Or I am, but not in the way we're talking about. Somebody paid me to come get something he left here. A family heirloom. He went away to fight and never made it back here. I wouldn't normally take a job like that, but we all have to work, right?"

"We do," says Cedric. "But work should be rewarding. I make a point never to do a job purely for the money."

"That's a good policy," says Carrie. "But sometimes you have to put food on the table." She spreads her hands to indicate the ridiculous variety in front of them.

"I'm sorry you won't be staying with us longer," says the mayor. "You said this was your first run. Is it?"

"First time here, yes," says Carrie. "But like I said, not a run. Small private job. Picking up a bowling trophy or something for some rich"—she almost says *idiot*—"person."

"Do you have the address?" Mayor Pam asks. "I could have someone escort you."

Carrie bites her lip and sighs. "I haven't been entirely honest," she says. "The thing I'm picking up? It's not a bowling trophy. It's a porn collection. Weird fetish stuff. And the person I'm working for?" She looks at Cedric. "It's a name you'd know. Big Bishop Foundation higher-up. A job like this, part of what they pay for is discretion."

Cedric grins. "Everyone's entitled to their little kinks," he says.

"I'm good with a map," Carrie says. "I'm assuming the street names are all the same."

Mayor Pam chuckles. "*Nothing's* changed here, Liz," she says. "The things that have, we've worked very hard to change them *back*."

"We'll get there," Cedric says, patting her hand. "The Path to Return; the very phrase means so many things."

"*So* many," says Mayor Pam absently, staring into Cedric's eyes. Carrie wonders if they're fucking. She wonders what Cedric's ability is and how often he's used it on Mayor Pam.

"You should write down the address where Liz will be staying," Cedric says.

"Of course," says Mayor Pam, jotting it on a beverage napkin.

"Maybe we could provide a safe for your room," Cedric suggests. "In the interest of discretion."

"You've both done so much already," Carrie says. "I think the traditional brown paper bag will be enough to keep prying eyes away." This gets both of them laughing, loud overdone laughter older people use to show they're comfortable with things like pornography. Feeling marginally safe, Carrie barehands a crab puff, tosses it in her mouth, and washes it down with a gulp of wine.

Working streetlights give the impression that everything is fine. The horror movie cliché of the sputtering light gets its power from the comfort functioning infrastructure gives. Boulder is working. Boulder is fine.

Carrie makes her way through an open-air mall that's lit up like daylight, strings of high-watt bulbs hung between lampposts like garlands. In front of restaurants and bars, middle-aged couples chat drunkenly and clink glasses together. She never imagined any place in the Wastes could feel so normal.

Carrie spots the couple and immediately makes herself invisible. To anyone else, they look like a pair on a bad date, but Carrie's known them for years. Martin Scholl was a student with her at Bishop, one of the fliers who helped catch the shooter on Public Day. He'd been working with the National Parks Service but signed on with the Faction after fighting broke out at Bishop. Thandi Nneka's a shapeshifter who did relief work for most of the war, running into war zones after the fighting had moved elsewhere. The bombing of the Houston school had been the last straw, and she joined the Faction for the tail end of the war.

They sit not talking, not touching their drinks. Martin's gotten soft, with a hipster beard and a paunch. Thandi makes herself look older than she is to fit in with the middle-aged crowd. They're watching people with more attention than the activity requires. The fact they're relaxed makes Carrie more nervous than she'd be if they were actively looking for her. *They're stationed here,* she thinks. *They're guarding something.* And if there're two, there are three more nearby.

Carrie pushes herself deeper down, below her passive state, under slippiness, into a place where she turns away people's attention. Miquel called it her "homeless leper" state. She holds it together as she comes to the end of the pedestrian mall and turns onto 13th Street and the address the voice on the phone gave her to memorize two days ago, the only time they spoke.

Boulder reestablished itself as a tourist spot after the war. People who couldn't afford to live there might manage a short stay, a chance to remind themselves what life used to be like. The hotels thrive, and the Boulderado, a 1950s relic that had been struggling before the war, was a wild success because of the way its nostalgia skipped over the war and the years leading up to it, which now seemed tainted. It suggests an era not only before people knew about Resonants but before they existed.

Carrie follows an elderly couple into the Boulderado, ducking into a coat room and scanning the lobby. She marks security cameras in each corner, swiveling to cover the full room. She skirts around the edges of the lobby toward the elevators, out of sight of at least two of the cameras.

She steps into an elevator behind three middle-aged ladies too absorbed in themselves to notice her even if she was visible. She rides up to the fifteenth floor with them, then back down to the eleventh. The hallway is empty, no cameras, and Carrie comes back up to visibility. Plush carpet muffling her footsteps, she walks to room 1107.

Carrie raps her knuckles on the door, which is different from the others on this floor: dark carved wood rather than painted metal. She's certain this has all been a joke and the other three members of the Bloom are waiting behind the door, the couple from the restaurant on the way up in the elevator behind her.

The dead bolt clacks. With a protest from the hinges, the door swings open. A black woman in her sixties stands in the doorway.

She wears a loose sweater, and she smiles. Carrie knows she knows the woman but can't place her. She's from too long ago, another life. Behind the woman, at a table with three chessboards, there's a girl at the end of her teens with dark skin, bright blue eyes, and tight spirals of hair that fall around her face like a fountain of sparks. The older woman smiles at Carrie, then turns to the girl.

"Look, Emmeline," Kimani Moore says. "We have a guest."

THE LOVE SONG OF KEVIN BISHOP

A CRITICAL ASSEMBLY

1940–1945

This is Eternal Death, and this the torment long foretold!

—WILLIAM BLAKE,
America a Prophecy

The first time Kevin Bishop met Raymond Glover was in April 1940 on the train from Albany to Santa Fe. A second-year grad student in the physics department at Columbia, Kevin had been approached by a man in a dark suit in a bar on the East Side that was not generally patronized by men in dark suits. It was a bar Kevin frequented hoping to be approached, only to go home drunk and bitter no one but the bartender had said a word to him. He'd wonder later if the man chose to approach him there to imply a threat of revelation in his offer to join the war effort—visiting, much less frequenting, an establishment like that would violate the university's code of conduct—but he didn't think about it at the time. He wanted to join. He was susceptible to the promise of combating evil with science, but the true appeal lay in the rumors of what the work would encompass. No one was talking, but the silence had its own shape, and the list of scientists who had up and left tenured positions, disappearing overnight, suggested something of grandeur. The man in the suit wiped off the bar in front of him with a handkerchief before deigning to touch it and spun lines to Kevin about honor and country, but he knew to promise Kevin the outermost boundaries of science. A week later Kevin was on a late-night bus to Albany to take the train west from there the next morning. The man said not to go directly. Even in the bustle and thrum of Penn Station, his exit might be noted.

The slim envelope the man gave him for expenses didn't contain enough cash for a berth, and the first night Kevin slept in his seat. The strain on his back woke him eventually, and he moved to the observation car, hoping for an open bench. He passed through the club car, which was empty save for a young man who raised a glass of whiskey at him and nodded as if they were regular commuters on this line, used to seeing each other every day. Kevin passed him without comment and sprawled out on the hard bench of the observation car, tucking his wallet down the front of his pants for safety. The next morning, he woke to the sounds of enthusiastic children yelping at the view of the plains, city kids with cramped concepts of space calling for their parents to come see the vast expanse of nothing.

In his suitcase, he had papers and journals: Fermi on the Chicago Pile-1, Bethe on experimental nuclear dynamics. It seemed risky to bring them out, as if he'd be revealing his identity. He dug in his bag for something less conspicuous and found a yellowing copy of *Zeitschrift für Physik* with an old paper by Leo Szilard about Maxwell's demon. It was one of Szilard's first publications, written in German, which could raise suspicions, albeit the wrong ones. Fishing out his glasses and keeping the journal in his lap to obscure the title, he started in. He slogged through what he could of the article, interspersed with abortive attempts to nap. Time took on a static quality, one he'd think about for years afterward. The end point of his trip was set, the course inevitable. The train ride felt like something that already had happened or was always already happening. He was between New York and Santa Fe, a point strung out into a line so that the Kevin Bishop in Buffalo, in Cleveland and Chicago and Kansas City, had a form of existence, too, a ghost of him that was yet to come and already was. It was comforting and unsettling at once.

That night, back pain once again drove him out of his seat, wading through the sea of snoring, drooling humanity to find six feet of horizontal space. In the club car, the same handsome man raised another glass of whiskey, contributing to Kevin's sense that time wasn't behaving as it should. The population of the train had turned over almost completely at Chicago, and Kevin was surprised to see him. He went to pass through toward the observation car, but the man grabbed his bare wrist.

"Do you buy what he's selling?" he asked.

Kevin stopped, his sport coat tucked under his arm. He looked at the man blankly.

"*Kaufst du was er verkauft?*" the man said, his German crisp and academic. "Figuring the spent entropy of the demon into the system. The effort to do the information collection and sorting. Do you think it outsmarts Maxwell?"

"I'm not sure I care," Kevin said. "It's a game."

"There is no demon, there are no chambers," the man said. "A very Eastern approach. I don't think Siz would approve. He takes his thought experiments seriously. I heard after he read Schrödinger's paper, he was spotted luring stray cats in Hell's Kitchen."

"I took a class with him last year," Kevin said. "He's very practically minded. Nuts and bolts stuff."

"Who has time for thought experiments while the world burns?" the man said. He stood up, dauntingly tall, and summoned the sleepy bartender. "What's your poison?" he asked Kevin.

"Gin and soda," Kevin said. The man looked at him as if he'd farted in church. He reached across the bar and stopped the bartender from picking up the soda siphon.

"Give my friend a respectable drink," he said. "A gin martini, vermouth from a fresh bottle if you have one. And another scotch for me." The bartender obliged, and the man insisted Kevin take the chair next to him. Intrigued in equal parts by the man's breezy mention of a mind like Szilard and the stark silent-film-star lines of the man's face, Kevin obliged as well.

"If you studied with Siz, you must be at Columbia," the man said, clinking his glass against Kevin's and sloshing a drop of gin onto the table. Kevin nodded and worried the surface of his drink with the speared olives. "Princeton, myself," the man said. "I imagine we're headed to the same place."

The man who recruited Kevin had been clear that he was to speak to no one about where he was going. *They might be German,* he'd said. *They might be one of ours. Either one may kill you if they know what you are.*

"I'm on sabbatical, is all," Kevin said, avoiding the man's avid gaze.

He threw Kevin a quick wink. "Me, too," he said. "Constitutional in the desert. Doctors say it'll be good for my lungs."

"Dry air," Kevin said.

"I think it's a problem of time," the man said after a pause. Kevin looked at him, confused. "The demon. Entropy increases as time moves forward, yes. But it decreases as time moves backward."

"Time doesn't move backward," Kevin said.

"I'm not convinced it moves at all," the man said. "Like you said, there is no demon, there are no chambers."

"I didn't say that," Kevin said.

The man waved this off. "It's information," he said. "It exists in a permanent state. You can roll it backward and forward in your mind like a kid moving a toy train back and forth on a track. The system contains all of it. The chaos at the beginning, the neatly sorted molecules at the end. The demon reporting for work in the morning, eager to get down to the business of organization, the demon clocking out at night, eyes bleary from tracking the speed of molecules, shoulder stiff from opening and shutting the door. All of it always happening."

This idea hewed so close to the thoughts Kevin had been having earlier that it seemed he might have fallen into a dream in which he talked himself through the puzzle his brain had banged up against all day. The train lurched, spilling gin onto Kevin's pants. The handsome man was up with a handkerchief immediately, dabbing at the spot.

"You don't look like you're going to make it all the way west," he said.

"I couldn't spring for a berth," Kevin said. "I've been sleeping sitting up the last two nights."

The man fished a key out of the inner pocket of his jacket. "Go get some kip," he said. "Push the clothes and such off to the floor and take a rest."

The key glinted wondrously in the dim light of the club car, promising rest. "I couldn't," Kevin said.

"I'm not using it anyway," he said. "Can't sleep. I'm like a kid on Christmas Eve."

"I normally wouldn't," Kevin said.

"I don't think normal is an issue for you and me," he said. He grabbed Kevin's hand in a full, hearty shake, the key pressing into his palm. "Raymond Glover," he said. "Maybe we'll run into each other out there in the desert. In the dry air."

"Bishop," Kevin said. "Kevin." His brain swam with gin and exhaustion and something more significant and impairing than both.

Raymond Glover didn't join Kevin that night, but the next, knocking gently on the door of the berth. Raymond had given him the key and with it the power to say no but must have known he wouldn't. He had to be read as straight so he didn't get the shit kicked out of him, but he had to be legible as gay if he didn't want to be irrevocably alone. Kevin tried to send signals while also not sending them. Misreading signals could get his teeth kicked in. It was a dance. Those who knew the steps did better for themselves than more attractive or charming men who couldn't communicate who they were or recognize their own.

Kevin was surprised how easily Raymond knew what he was and responded to it. When Kevin woke with Raymond crammed into the small cot next to him, he attributed it to echolocation on Raymond's part. Raymond believed he deserved to be loved and assumed Kevin would love him. Working off a lifetime of evidence, Kevin was convinced he couldn't be loved and was fundamentally unworthy of affection, and his attempts to passively solicit it, sitting by himself in bars or staring at his reflection in Third Avenue shop windows late at night, had been doomed by his own conviction that they were doomed. The dreamlike quality of the trip became amplified, losing its form in Raymond's arms. Distance was a ticking clock as their destination approached and with it the end of the affair. The thing Kevin wanted was approaching, and it would destroy this thing he'd barely dared to want.

They elected to report a day late. There wasn't much negotiation; neither had been explicit about why he was in New Mexico. The train got in late, and they took adjoining rooms at the Hotel St. Francis. The next morning he watched the clock over Raymond's

shoulder as checkout time slipped by, followed by his appointment time. Late that afternoon while Raymond showered, Kevin
called the number the man in the suit had given him.

"I'm sorry I missed it," he said. "The train was delayed out of
Chicago and just now got in."

"That's funny," said the woman on the other end. "We had a
whole crew come in fine on the train from last night." Kevin
hemmed and hawed, and the woman chuckled. "It's fine, Mr.
Bishop," she said. "Perfectly normal to get cold feet. You're not our
first late arrival. A little advice, though?"

"Please," he said.

"A bad truth serves better than a good lie in this man's army."

"I'm not in the army," Kevin said.

"Mr. Bishop, you are deeper in it than the boys in the trenches,"
she said. "You'll do well to remember that. Be sure you're here tomorrow, bright and early." She clicked off, and he heard the last
drips of water falling in the bathroom.

Keeping up appearances, they said their goodbyes in the room,
making love one last time. Raymond swore he heard cleaners making their rounds in the hallways and bit down on Kevin's hand as
he came. Kevin left first and was settling his bill when Raymond
came down. They didn't acknowledge each other in the lobby, or
out front as the valet summoned Raymond a cab, which he didn't
offer to share. Kevin asked directions. The valet rolled his eyes
when he saw the address.

"East Palace is three blocks over," he said, throwing his arm in
the direction Raymond's cab had gone. "If you hurry, you can
catch the last guy's tail."

The city moved through the cool damp morning with a gold
rush hustle that reminded Kevin of New York. If he didn't look up

and see the borders of Santa Fe, where it dropped off into the void of the desert, he might feel at home. Without the forward momentum of the train or the drunken buzz of Raymond's skin against his he thought about turning back. He couldn't go back to Columbia. His academic life would be over, and it was not impossible he'd be arrested for desertion.

The sense that he was nearing something historic was terrifying and reinforced things Raymond had suggested about the future as something that already existed, a space he could move away from or toward. Santa Fe seemed like a way to hover in the orbit of that future without toppling into it. Before he could make a decision, he was out front of the office at 109 East Palace Avenue, Raymond grinning broadly at him from the doorway.

"I guess we can drop the pretense," he said. He held the door, and Kevin stepped inside.

They were told they should never call it Los Alamos. It was Site Y, or Project Y, or the Hill. For the sake of any written correspondence with outsiders, of which the less the better, it was Post Office Box 39 in Santa Fe. *Greetings from Box 39,* WAC girls wrote on postcards to boyfriends back east, blank on one side and black with redactions on the other.

They were briefed on security by a dull lieutenant droning about the city, the project, all the things they weren't allowed to say and who they weren't allowed to say them to. Information radiated outward in dissipating concentric circles, and they were the bright burning light at the center. Robert Serber, not anyone interesting or famous, not Oppenheimer or Fermi, caught them up on the state of the project. There are men who can make the thrilling drab, and Serber was among them. Kevin would come to appreciate his ability to render complex concepts into plain language, but the orientation lecture nearly put him to sleep.

He was assigned to work on the gun assembly, nicknamed Little Boy. It was the less elegant road to chain reaction: the "bang two rocks together" approach. They would fire two pieces of fissionable material at each other and hope that they would not simply explode but keep exploding. Raymond was on Fat Man, or the implosion assembly: a meticulously machined metal sphere around a fissionable core. The plates had to match up perfectly and fire off within milliseconds of one another to have a prayer of working. "Even if we get the science," Raymond said, "we'll never crack the engineering." He called it the Triple F: *Fussy Fat Fuck*.

Being assigned to separate projects meant they saw each other only in passing as they rushed from lab to lab within Tech Area. They timed the beginning of their days so they'd meet at the checkpoint each morning. They talked dirty in code as the MPs inspected their clearance. Raymond would mention how he hoped to inspect Kevin's shaft if he could fit it in. Kevin told him he'd been thinking about him the previous evening when he had a predetonation mishap. Puerile but sustaining. It turned out a lifetime of saying without saying had prepared Kevin for top-secret military work. Proper nouns vanished behind their vague code names. He never thought the word *bomb,* only *Gadget*. Los Alamos became the Hill. Fucking Raymond became *fusion,* both the euphemistic and actual meanings theoretical.

The labs ran twenty-four hours with a constant population of sleepers in the paper-walled dorms. There was no time or space to be together, but the Hill wasn't without social functions. There were movies and civic events. Oppenheimer hosted scientists at his house for chamber music and stiff drinks. It was Oppenheimer who taught Kevin to mix a martini, treating the components as if they were volatile. There was the canteen, which devolved over the course of each evening from a cafeteria to a rathskeller, its culture and appearance shaped by the transported Brits and their need for something approximating a proper pub. They imported dartboards and sabotaged the coolers so the beer was flat and tepid to their liking. The social world of the Hill was very public and very straight.

Raymond met Mona while playing errand boy for Szilard, running the day's computations across campus to the barracks where the women worked. Mona Dawson, one of the girls in the "steno pool," took pity on two boys in love. The steno girls were human computers: they crunched the numbers Fermi and Szilard threw off as intellectual by-product, the way a lightbulb emits heat. Mona and her ilk spent their days hunched over sheets of calculations but in the evenings devoted whole hallways of the women's dormitories to parties. Some were coed; most were exclusively for the calculators. Mona, sensing something about Raymond, invited him to one of the girls-only gatherings in a way that wasn't accusatory or threatening. She told him he could bring a friend. He brought Kevin.

Mona held court at the dormitory parties whether they were coed or just the girls. At twenty-five, she had lived everywhere and done everything. A cocktail sloshed in her hand as she flitted about the room playing matchmaker, pairing girls with boys and girls with girls. Nothing made her happier than uniting two closeted Sapphics, and the night she led Raymond and Kevin upstairs from the revels and handed them the key to her room, she crowed, "I love *love*!" before carefully shutting the door on them.

It became routine, and routines were dangerous. It allowed Kevin the comfort of forgetting he wasn't normal or entitled to normal things. He was so tired of carrying his fear around, he set it down at the first opportunity and neglected to cloak himself in it when he went back out into the world, where it was necessary that he not be seen.

It was high summer, and in the summer the girls got drunk fast, guzzling gin like water. Sweat-drenched, Raymond and Kevin came downstairs after midnight to find a tableau of passed-out women strewn dramatically about the room's sofas and armchairs like an audition for fainting Southern belles. They tiptoed through the minefield of bodies to the front door and emerged into the cool of the evening holding hands—such a small thing, the barest sign of affection.

"Bishop," called a voice from across the yard. His hand reflexively pulled away from Raymond's and shoved itself into his pocket. It was Todd Harris, one of Kevin's colleagues from Little Boy. Harris was a Harvard grad with the ingenuity of a stump. Rumor had it Oppenheimer wanted him out because he was an embarrassment to the Crimson, but Groves didn't want any scientists spit back into the real world for fear they'd be snatched up by the Germans. Harris stayed on, getting more and more bitter because of his failure to contribute. Kevin was the next one from the bottom of the ladder on Little Boy, and Harris's enmity for him was special.

"What the hell are you doing out at this hour?" he asked.

"I could ask you the same thing," Kevin said, trying to echo his standoffishness. Raymond, drunk, stood too close, his chest brushing the back of Kevin's shoulder. It would have been better if they'd run into a guard. They would be assessed a demerit—an empty mark on their records came with being found out after hours—but there would have been no consequence. The way they stood together told Harris everything he needed to know.

"Fermi was running tests in C lab," Harris said. "He asked *me* to help." He said this with smug pride, as if they didn't know Fermi was in the habit of recruiting the Hill's most expendable to stand near the C lab tests to see if they'd get ill from the radiation.

"Some of the girls needed tending to," Raymond said, pressing up against Kevin. "They asked us to help."

"What would *girls* want with a flower like you?"

"A scorpion," Kevin said. "In the shower. You know how women are about—"

"You two make me sick," Harris said. "Say what you want about Hitler, but he's got the good sense not to let fairies into the German army."

"What's his policy on idiots?" Raymond asked. "Is he as open to them as Uncle Sam is?"

Harris went through Kevin to get to Raymond, shoving Kevin aside with one arm and throwing his punch with the other. Kevin heard the crack as Raymond's nose shattered and blood arced through the air, landing in dark black drops on the dirt path.

"Don't be out after dark again, little flower," Harris said. He spit on the back of Raymond's head as Raymond pulled himself up out of the dirt.

"We should report him," Kevin said.

"We're not in a position to without giving ourselves away," Raymond said. "Fermi's experiments have probably sterilized him. The next generation won't have to deal with little Harrises running around."

They went back to the women's dorm, where bodies rose from the dead. Mona patched Raymond up, knocking his nose back into shape with a shove as brutal as Harris's punch.

"You need a disguise is what you need," she said.

"Tomorrow it'll look like he's wearing a mask," Kevin said, tenderly tracing the beginning of a shiner under Raymond's right eye.

"I'll be the Lone Ranger," Raymond said.

"You need a girlfriend," she said.

"That is the last thing I need."

But Kevin got what she meant. He'd kept himself secret long enough to know how. People might have doubts about him, but their uncertainty wouldn't be more than an itch at the back of their brains. Raymond presented himself as different. Even if you didn't guess exactly what it was, you could tell there was something worth fearing or hating in him. Something that needed to be covered up.

That night, at Kevin's insistence, Raymond Glover and Mona Dawson became a couple.

Mona wanted Kevin to find a girl for himself. "Four is a better number," she insisted. But none of the girls she threw at him stuck. Whatever flicker and spark sexual interest generates, he couldn't fake it, and the girls he met at the dormitory parties were unwilling to live without it.

After a month, Mona and Raymond applied for and got an apartment together in H Lot, which neatly solved the issue of Raymond and Kevin being together. The story was that Kevin suffered from misophonia, unable to sleep in the tumult of the dorms, so Raymond and Mona offered him permanent residence on their couch. In truth, the couch was Mona's and the bed belonged to Raymond and Kevin. But the apartment was all of theirs. They hosted parties for sympathetic girls and their unwitting boyfriends. Raymond cooked and Kevin mixed drinks while Mona took the stage. Once the last guest was seen out the door, Raymond and Kevin would kiss Mona good night and go to bed. It was an amazing year, a lesson for Kevin that normal was a term that encompassed many things and that he was as deserving of them as anyone.

As part of the Fat Man team, Raymond was cleared to watch Trinity with the elite in the observation tower near Alamogordo. Kevin and the rest of Team Little Boy were left to sulk around the campus. Raymond declined, and they made a picnic of it, the three of them. They requisitioned a car and drove south through a downpour to Tularosa, a few miles northeast of the test site in Alamogordo. They brought gin, vermouth and ice, summer sausage and Ritz crackers, and Kevin mixed martinis in the car as they waited for the rain to let up. It relented before dawn, and they relocated to a ridge that looked out across what seemed like all of New Mexico. Like all of the earth.

Repeat a word over and over again and it loses all meaning. The same happens with a name or an image stared at too long. Kevin saw the mushroom cloud so many times in the years afterward —in memory, in nightmare—it meant nothing to him. The first time it was terrifying: a pillar of fire like something out of the Bible. A new sun.

The cloud hung in the air, the image hung on his retinas, and Kevin felt as if something reached through the heart of the blast, through his forehead between the eyebrows, and gave the lightest tap to a spot in the center of his brain. The initial sensation was one of connection, as if time split open and allowed him inside, except there was no inside or outside. He could perceive everything that was or would be, but he could see it from a hill in Tularosa, in the shadow cast by Trinity. This perception faded, and he had the sense a bell inside him had been rung and continued to reverberate in his skull. It twinkled with a song, its melody faint and indeterminate. In its undertone, he could hear Mona's mind screaming at the horror of what she saw. When he looked over at her, she wore a tight smile, as she did when a romantic pairing she'd put together seemed to be hitting it off. She sipped her drink, never taking her eyes off the site of the blast, but her mind was a slurry of random words and emotional aggregates. Kevin would come to understand this was due to his inexperience with other people's thoughts, which were largely incoherent, a torrent they winnowed into speech, panning a river for words the way a miner pans for gold.

He heard Raymond's mind, a clear and noble tenor. *Beautiful,* it said. *My God, it's so beautiful.*

What have we done? Kevin wondered, putting the thought out into the same space, the chamber into which Raymond and Mona's minds had "spoken."

Only Raymond turned toward him. Mona stared at the ghost of the blast.

We won the war, Raymond's thoughts said.

"Show's over, darling. Should we head back for some sleep?" Raymond asked Mona.

She nodded dumbly and collected herself. "Of course," she said. "It'll be all basking in glory for you boys tomorrow while the girls and I sift the ashes." Her mind thrummed with a low refrain of *no no no no* as she gathered up their meager picnic and loaded it back into the car.

There was an inkling in Kevin's mind of how he had changed in the wake of the blast. It was as scary as the bomb itself: newness come into the world. But there was comfort, too. Raymond was with him, and he was not alone.

The question Kevin came back to was: *Why him?* It was an attempt to attribute will to something that had none, but it was a natural impulse even for an atheist like Kevin. People wanted order; they saw the complex ways natural systems interacted and assumed history had a similar design element.

His first assumption was that whatever it was chose him in

order to lift him up, to give strength to something weak. It spoke to the way he thought of himself at the time. He saw his sexuality as a flaw, if not an illness. Choosing him, the universe compensated for something it had failed to give him.

As he came to terms with who and what he was and watched whatever Resonance was moving through the world and making its choices, he came around to the opposite way of thinking. It found those who made themselves strong, whose differences and preexisting otherness tempered something inside them—a wire in the blood along which a unique strength was conducted through the body, latent but ready to be called upon. Maybe it was none of that. Kevin might have turned the echoing boom of expanding superheated air in the lightning's wake to the sound of angels' trumpets. He might have been mythmaking to help himself sleep.

The day after Trinity, neither Raymond nor Kevin got out of bed. Mona, who was back to work on an hour's sleep, attributed it to the gin. The truth was that their abilities had set upon them, after only a glimmer the night before. But as with gin, sometimes a little is preferable to too much. In full bloom, Kevin's ability was a blazing brightness upon his senses. He experienced everything seen, thought, smelled, or touched by anyone on the Hill on a day when emotions were already extreme. The girls were working: there was data to be analyzed, adjustments to be made before the sun they created in the desert could descend upon a populated city. He was with Mona and the girls as they calculated the bomb's payload, then recalculated when the men said the numbers were four times what anyone expected and must be wrong. He was in the map room with Groves as he drew circles around Japanese cities, estimating how much of each one would be destroyed by what they'd built. He suffered in bed with a hundred hangovers. He was both halves of nihilistic couplings in the barracks and dorms, pairs of people barely attracted to one another but needing assurance their skins had not been made monstrous. He wept in twenty rooms at once, and in three rooms he sat staring, beyond tears, hefting a bottle of sleeping pills, a razor, and a service weapon, contemplating the obliteration of himself.

On a calm spring day in a sparsely crowded park, this multiplicity of senses would have been maddening, but on that day, in that place, he was lucky he survived. He was blessed that in the next room Raymond suffered under the same onslaught of sensation. Their minds found each other, two notes played on separate instruments. Harmonics are a matter of math, of agreeable simple ratios. Raymond and Kevin resonated with each other, amplifying each other's note so that it could pierce everything else.

Language was insufficient to describe what they had become. It shunted everything down the path of a single sense. When Raymond and Kevin decided to call it resonating, it was because the language around sound had roots in science and math, whereas vision was tainted by poetics. They could think about it in terms of ratios and harmonics. It was limiting and excluded parts of their experience. It imposed the interaction of sound and space, the idea of lag time, on what was instantaneous. It cut out the heart. But it gave them somewhere to begin.

In the absence of anything but estimates, they assumed they'd killed everyone. Hence the party.

Fermi proposed it in his odd English. His sentences spiraled upward like citrus twists dropped into poisoned drinks, giving the impression he might be joking, or the option to claim he had been. At the test site, he took cash bets from terrified NCOs as to whether the Gadget would ignite the oxygen in the atmosphere, incinerating all life on earth.

The party was a victory dance and a wake for uncountable

strangers. Its motives and goals were inscrutable, and it surged with nervous energy, the men jittery drunk, sweating in the dry oven heat of New Mexico in August. The nights were supposed to be cooler. Some nights, Kevin could even sleep. But that night, the sun's departure gave no relief. Hadn't they created a new sun? Maybe Fermi would win his bet and the world would end in flames, gradually rather than all at once. He was smart not to put a time limit on the wager.

"What's impressive is how unimpressive they really were," Feynman said to anyone who'd listen. Fermi no one could read; Feynman they could read all too well. Feynman would have fired off the Gadget even if he *knew* it would light up the atmosphere. He was obsessed with the limits of the possible. "You think about the firebombings in Germany? You know a firestorm pulls air *into* itself? Imagine you see the bombs land and start hoofing it the other way and you're yanked backward the way you came. A hungry ghost. At least our girls kick you the fuck out. Numbers-wise, the real killers are the pencil pushers at DOD tallying lives up on a ledger. When the books are written, we'll be the monsters because our girls did it all in one go."

It reminded Kevin of what he'd heard Bainbridge muttered to Oppenheimer at the test site. Opje had spouted poetry. "Now I am become death," he said, staring into the blazing star where the Gadget had been. "Destroyer of worlds." The men in the bunker looked at him blankly and looked away, but Bainbridge held his gaze.

"Now we are all sons of bitches," he said, translating Opje's nonsense into English. Kevin had spent the last month trying to place himself between those two statements, trying to decide what he was now. He listened to Feynman prattle, amazed the man's thoughts matched up exactly with what he said. Another terrifying thing about Feynman, one Kevin had learned only since the test: he was absolutely honest, always.

Raymond and Mona sat down next to him at the high bistro table in the corner. It had been *their table* since Raymond and Mona had become a public thing. That word again: *become*.

"To butchery," Raymond said, lifting his drink.

Mona slapped him on the arm and set her vodka soda down.

"To genocide," Kevin said, clinking his martini glass against Raymond's whiskey.

"To the end of it," said Mona, not wanting to feel left out. Their glasses rattled together like links in a chain. Under the table, Raymond ran a finger over the knuckle of Kevin's hand, then rested it on his knee. He'd been offered a job at Cal Berkeley, and he and Mona had discussed marriage as the logical evolution of their disguise.

I worry she's in love with me, he buzzed to Kevin through their connection. Theirs was a clear channel, but Kevin had begun to hear other buzzings—not the din of people's thoughts but a resonance that told him there were more like them out there.

Don't worry, Raymond; you're an unlovable monster, Kevin told him. Raymond grinned and projected lewd pictures into Kevin's mind as Mona went on about where the various girls were ending up.

Toward the end of the night, Todd Harris stumbled over to them, carrying two pints of beer. He held one out to Raymond, who looked at it like Harris had offered him a dead rat.

"I wanted to say no hard feelings," Harris slurred. His eyes were watery, and a goofy grin spread from one ear to the opposite one. "For what happened between us last summer. No hard feelings."

Raymond smiled quizzically, like he couldn't remember the incident Harris was referencing. Then he buzzed into Harris's head, loud enough so that Kevin heard.

Smash that pint glass into your face.

Harris cocked his head at Raymond, quizzical.

Your right hand.

Still smiling, Harris extended his right arm and brought the pint glass hurtling toward the middle of his face. It shattered, embedding chunks of glass in his cheek and shredded lips. The other beer dropped to the ground, and Harris wailed like an injured animal. He fell to his knees, pressing his hands to his face, which drove the glass shards deeper, eliciting another scream.

Mona looked at Raymond, and in that moment Kevin thought she knew. There was a horror on her face like on the ridge at Tularosa as the bomb ripped into the world. Kevin was about to go into her thoughts, to calm her, but then she went off as if a switch had been flipped inside her. Her face went calm even as Harris writhed on the ground. Raymond suppressed a grin.

"Jesus, what the fuck happened?" Feynman asked, standing in the pool of blood and beer foaming on the floor.

"He said he couldn't stand what we'd done," Mona said, her voice flat. "He said he kept thinking of all those dead Jap babies, and then he smashed that pint glass into his face."

As she spoke, Kevin could hear the words buzzing from Raymond to her, like an echo that came before the noise it mimicked.

TWO

BEYOND THE BOUNDARY

I hear my being dance from ear to ear.
I wake to sleep, and take my waking slow.
—THEODORE ROETHKE,
"The Waking"

ON LIVING

◇

The war functioned strangely. There was no front, no place it was happening. It sprang up here, then there, the way mushrooms on opposite edges of a forest are part of the same organism, linked underground. Fighting in New York, in Los Angeles and Boston and Denver; it was all part of the same war. No place was safe.

Sometimes they were nowhere for days. They stockpiled supplies and came apart from the whole world. Those were bad days. Emmeline thought about that song with the astronaut floating in a tin can that her father liked. She'd lose all orientation, even up and down. The air aged. She breathed oxygen she'd breathed already, like sucking the last drops of juice from a squeezed orange. She pleaded with Kimani to anchor them somewhere, to open the door.

They spent a year in Paris, where the risks of staying outweighed the risks of leaving. It was a good year. Emmeline was thirteen, exploring the city on her own like an urchin in *Les Misérables,* which she and Kimani read together every night. Kimani anchored them in the fourth arrondissement on the third floor above a boulangerie, the two of them in her little room. Emmeline walked out the door in the morning with no plan and no map for the day. She came back at dusk bearing fresh bread and a bundle of new French phrases, smelling like cigarettes and petrichor. The shop around the block let her buy wine if she said it was for *ma mère,* and Kimani sipped red as they decoded *Le Monde* to learn how the war was going. It was as close as it came to touching them: traces of newsprint on Emmeline's fingertips.

In French, *surrendered* is *s'est rendu.* As in *Le gouvernement Américain s'est rendu.*

They watched peace unfold, watched America separate out like milk curdling into its ugly component parts. Emmeline didn't know who they were hiding from and thought they'd be able to go back. They didn't, month after month. People lost their homes and were sent west. European and Asian countries cut ties and recalled ambassadors. Emmeline and Kimani made slow progress through a massive French novel. Emmeline thought they stayed because they were safe in Paris. Why would they want to leave?

The day she saw Black Rose Faction agents on the plaza at the Centre Pompidou, she knew why they were there. She'd read about them, the elite troops of the war, now functioning as "peacekeepers." *Gestapo,* Kimani said the first time she saw a press photo of a full Garden, twenty-five Blooms of five Faction agents apiece, each agent with the same dead-eyed stare. She came home and cried into Kimani's shoulder. They left that night. The night before, Kimani had read the chapter about Cosette joining the convent school. It was titled "Cemeteries Take What Is Given Them." Emmeline stayed up drawing a picture of Valjean in the coffin. In the drawing, he looked like her father.

They never finished the book. Emmeline couldn't stand to think about Paris once she'd left it.

Boulder was nice at first. They lived in a hotel in the middle of a city that functioned the way it had before the war. Kimani pushed her limits and expanded their room until it was an entire apartment. Emmeline had her own space for the first time since she had moved out of her parents' house and into a shared room in the Bishop dorms. It was difficult for Kimani to maintain it. She got tired more quickly. They stopped reading together at night, and Emmeline spent more time alone. She didn't mind. She was a teenager and wanted to be alone, or thought that was what she was supposed to want. Sometimes she missed the closeness of sharing one room with Kimani, falling asleep on the couch with the sound of Kimani's sleeping breath nearby.

Feeling safe was complicated. She had to be aware of a threat first. She couldn't think of herself as safe without the perception of danger. When Emmeline was little, she had an imaginary friend who visited her when things got bad. The first time it happened was when she burned herself with the water on the stove while her father made dinner. The memory was nebulous, but someone was there immediately, before her father registered the clatter of the pot on the linoleum. Her friend calmed her with a smile and a finger to her lips.

Subsequent visits were similar; her friend showed up to chat, to tell Emmeline it would all be all right. It hadn't happened since her first time in the Hive, when she got caught, caged in a box of black bone. Her friend broke her out. There were times she felt paralyzed, waiting for her friend to show up and tell her what to do.

In Boulder, nothing changed. Emmeline couldn't remember a time previous when nothing changed. She took a job cleaning rooms at the hotel part-time. They didn't need the money, but it gave her a way to structure her time. The girls she worked with needed the money badly, and she felt she was taking money that should have been theirs. If there had been a way to sign her paychecks over to the other girls, divvy it up among them, she would have. She felt apart from them. For them this was permanent; for her it wasn't. She didn't know what the exit would be or when it would come, but this wasn't her life, even as one year bled into the next.

Kimani tried to make it feel permanent. "A girl your age needs her ground," she said. They found ground in Boulder, and Kimani held Emmeline's feet to it, ballast to keep her from floating away. Kimani watched the door, waiting for a knock, good or bad. One day, Emmeline saw a couple checking in and knew they were with the Black Rose Faction. As soon as they were out of sight, she went and told Kimani.

"Just two?" she said.

"I only saw two."

"Where there's two, there's five," she said. "We need to head out."

"No," she said. She was tired of running. It wasn't that she wanted to stay in Boulder, but she didn't want to leave anywhere anymore. "It's a coincidence," she said. "They're tourists, slumming in the Wastes. They're not here for us."

Emmeline had seen Resonants in the hotel before. It was unusual but not unheard of. Something in them called to something dormant in her, and she knew them for what they were. Faction agents were a different situation. Emmeline pleaded with Kimani, insisting that they could get out in a snap. In a week, she said, they'd be gone and everything would be back to normal.

Kimani relented, but only if Emmeline took a few days off from work. They holed up in the room as if there were a hurricane in the hall. The lack of windows, which never bothered Emmeline when she knew she could open a door, shrank the room until it felt like the days they'd been physically disconnected from everything, drifting in Hivespace.

It was their fourth night in what Emmeline started calling the Bunker. They were playing chess in the living room. Kimani made Emmeline play on three boards at once. "You and I have to think like that," she said. "Keep all the wheels turning in our heads." She beat Emmeline more often than she lost, but that night Emmeline had Kimani in mate on two boards when someone knocked on the door. It was the first time it had ever happened, and the sound, strange and new, startled and thrilled Emmeline.

They never did get to finish that game.

"Can I get you a beer or something?" Kimani says. "We don't have much, but there's a couple beers from a local place that aren't half bad."

"We should get moving," Carrie says.

Emmeline tries to find something recognizable in her face, the girl she met her first day at Bishop, the one who was kind to her and, more important to Emmeline that day, was kind to her father. It's like excavating ruins. There's so much piled on top of that girl, but everything since then took on the shape of that foundation.

"Emmeline, go to your room and pack up some of your things," Kimani says.

"Why?" asks Emmeline. "The room's coming with us."

"Emmeline, go pack your things," she repeats. It isn't a voice Emmeline has heard her use, but it's one she knows. It's the voice of a mother who will not be debated with. Emmeline has thought of Kimani as her mother before, a notion that was fleeting and guilty. It's a betrayal of her real mother, and when the thought pops into her head, she quashes it. There were times, curled up next to Kimani reading a book or watching her smile as she ate, when the feeling welled up in Emmeline's body, unasked for and unexpected. She let herself float in the sensation of love for and from a mother. Having felt that, she's afraid of angering Kimani. As ordered, she goes to her room. She scurries, hiding from that look.

"You go help her," Kimani says to Carrie. "I need a minute."

The walls of Emmeline's room are papered in drawings, photo-realistic sketches. Her dad at the stove, stirring a pot with a wooden spoon, looking over his shoulder at the viewer with a tender smile. Her mom in a ratty bathrobe, hair up in a wrap, reading a paper-back novel. Little Emmeline clutching a stuffed sheep, flanked by her parents. Emmeline spinning like a top in the center of a flock of geese. The Bishop Academy seen from Lexington Avenue, the newly added floors perched on top like a raven on a fence post.

"Can I ask you something?" Carrie says, examining the drawings as Emmeline pulls them off the walls and stuffs them into a folder.

"Sure," Emmeline says.

"Why did you stay here? There's no one like us in Boulder."

"I'm not *like us,*" Emmeline says, twirling a thick silver bracelet around her right wrist. "I haven't been *like us* for a long time." She takes a drawing of her parents out of Carrie's hands and puts it in the folder, then puts the folder in her rucksack.

"Kimani could have gotten you out of here anytime," Carrie says. "She could have opened a door, and you could have walked out to anywhere."

"She didn't," Emmeline says. She looks at Carrie, who looks horrified. She's finding out Emmeline has lived this way for years. There's no way to communicate across that, so Emmeline shrugs and continues packing. Kimani waits for them in the living room.

Emmeline can see she's been crying; her eyes are red-rimmed and puffy.

"I think it's best we get out of here quick, Ms. Moore," Carrie says.

"You don't have to call her that," Emmeline says. "We're not at school."

"Stop now," says Kimani. "It's nice having someone address me with respect for a change." She smiles at Emmeline to let her know this is meant as playful, but Emmeline slumps petulantly under the weight of her rucksack all the same.

"You can take us to my apartment in Chicago," Carrie says, "while I—"

Kimani smiles and shakes her head. "If I move, they'll see me," she says.

"You're not coming?" Emmeline says.

"Emmy, how do you think they've been finding us?" Kimani asks. "Every time I move, I throw up a firework for them."

Kimani had talked around her refusal to use her abilities so often that her logic was carved out for Emmeline in negative space. "There are predators who can't see you unless you move," Kimani said. "You could be right in front of them, and as long as you keep still, they walk right past you." She answered questions sideways like that. It cut down on the number Emmeline asked. There's knowledge Emmeline won't let herself absorb, to keep herself safe. Kimani was the closest thing she's had to a parent for years, and Emmeline let herself consider the absence of her biological parents without imagining separation from her adoptive one.

"But they haven't found us," Emmeline says. Her lip trembles.

"Is it Faction that's after you?" Carrie says. "I saw two agents on my way here."

"They're on vacation or something," Emmeline insists.

"They wouldn't come here if they weren't looking for something," says Kimani.

"Where there's two, there's five," Carrie says, and Emmeline flinches at the echo of what Kimani had said earlier.

"Shut up!" Emmeline says, her voice just short of a shout.

"I'll find you," Kimani says. "When it's safe."

"This is bullshit," says Emmeline. "I'm not leaving with *her*." She jerks her thumb at Carrie.

"I have a car parked a little ways out of the city," Carrie says. "It's a hike, especially in the dark, but it'll get us far enough from here that we can figure something out."

"That's your plan?" Emmeline asks. "Drive us to the middle of nowhere and *figure something out*?"

"My plan is to get you where you need to be," says Carrie.

"I don't need to be anywhere," Emmeline says. "I can stay right here. Everything is fine."

"We talked about this," says Kimani. "You knew today was going to come."

"I thought you'd go with me," Emmeline says. "You never said—"

"You're right, I didn't," Kimani says. "I didn't want to think about it either. Now here we are."

"I can give you a couple minutes," Carrie says.

"You can fuck off and leave us alone," says Emmeline. Kimani puts a silencing hand on her shoulder.

"A couple minutes," she says. Carrie steps out into the hall and shuts the door.

Kimani stands in front of Emmeline. They're nearly the same height, Emmeline edging her out slightly. Kimani takes Emmeline's right hand in her left. She taps the bracelet. "There's another thing we haven't talked about," she says.

"I'm not taking it off," Emmeline says.

"At some point you're going to have to," Kimani says. "You decide when that is. Not that girl in the hallway. Not anybody else. You'll know when you're ready."

"I'm not going to," Emmeline says.

Kimani nods, understanding that the point is not worth arguing. "If you do," she says, "you're going to feel the pull back into the Hive. Like you did that first time. Do you remember?"

Emmeline nods, thinking of hands that reached up from the ground and held her down, thinking of an obsidian cage.

"Honey, you cannot go in there," Kimani says. "If you do, they'll see you, so go only if you are absolutely desperate. If there is no other choice, you go in there and you call for me and I will come gather you up."

She pulls Emmeline in and holds on to her desperately, the way you grip something you're about to lose.

I'LL FALL WITH YOUR KNIFE

◇

The girl doesn't say a word as they make their way out of town, but at least she isn't crying anymore. Carrie's not sure how she'll comfort Emmeline, and she wishes she'd been informed that the weapon she was picking up was a teenager. Hidden by Carrie's ability, they leave the hotel and head back to the culvert Carrie used to enter the city. They don't see the Faction agents Carrie spotted on the commons, but that doesn't mean they're gone. Carrie would feel better if she could see them. Knowing where they are means they aren't coming up behind.

Emmeline enters the water treatment facility with no complaint but balks when it's time to descend into the pipe.

"That's a sewer," she says, the first words she's spoken since they left Kimani's room.

"It's not a *live* sewer," Carrie says. "If it was a live sewer, you'd know all about it." She makes her way down the ladder without looking back. The implication is clear: *I'm going, so you can either come with me or take your shitty chances here.* When Carrie's reached the bottom and Emmeline has yet to begin her climb down, Carrie thinks she may have miscalculated and sent the girl running back to Kimani. One leg extends over the edge above, a sneaker pads onto the ladder rung, and Carrie marks this in her head as the beginning of the journey.

When Emmeline gets to the bottom, Carrie cautions her to stay close and lights their way with the iPod, an artifact Emmeline seems not to recognize. The walk through the dark is easier knowing how long it will take. With the moon high and full, light spills into the far end of the tunnel after a few minutes' walk.

Carrie motions for Emmeline to wait and steps out of the culvert, invisible. She scans the top of the wall for lookouts. Seeing none, she signals for Emmeline to join her. The girl doesn't move. She stands in the open mouth of the culvert, dwarfed by her rucksack, the wall, and the full moon suspended above them like a searchlight.

"Come on," Carrie says. "Car's south of here, an hour or two's hike."

"It's dark," Emmeline says, as if Carrie doesn't notice. She talks like a teenager even though she's spent most of her teenage years in isolation. How does that happen? Quirks and habits of being an American teenager genetically encoded, like oncogenes waiting for a trigger, and the trigger is time. Carrie thinks of her brother at this age, before he and her father left Deerfield and came west. The way he stated the obvious as if she was unaware of it and refuted the obvious if she stated it. He needed to be the sole arbiter of reality. Carrie smiles at Emmeline.

"Moon's full," Carrie says, pointing up. "There's plenty of light. Too much."

With a huff, Emmeline comes out of the culvert and follows Carrie, back to being silent. Carrie hides them both with her ability, which isn't easy. Emmeline keeps lagging behind, falling outside the umbra of Carrie's invisibility so Carrie needs to let her catch up. She considers asking Emmeline to walk out front, but if she lets Emmeline set their pace, they'll never get to the car. When they're far enough that Carrie can look back and not see the wall, she relaxes. They're translucent, ghosts in the woods. Carrie whistles "Moonlight Mile" by the Rolling Stones, flat and tuneless.

"My *dad* liked that song," Emmeline says. It's the cruelest thing a kid can say to someone who thinks of themselves as young. It knocks Carrie back a generation, into the kingdom of the obsolete and uncool. "How much farther are we going?" Emmeline asks.

"Till we get there," says Carrie.

"Jesus, you are totally a dad," Emmeline says.

Carrie looks back at her and wonders how Kimani handled her for so long. A stranger could mistake Kimani and Emmeline for mother and daughter, but the bond between them was different. They hadn't chosen each other any more than a parent chooses their child, but they came to each other at a point in their lives when they understood what they needed and what they were able to give. The last time Carrie saw her mother, she was in a hospital bed. Carrie looked down at her, thinking, *We never got it right, you and I.*

Emmeline huffs and grunts, an unnecessary show of travail. *She's lost her mother, too,* Carrie thinks. She resolves to be gentler, knowing this won't last through more than one angry question or smarmy remark.

Unlike coming through the culvert, the walk back to the car is out of proportion with the walk to it. Doubt tickles the back of Carrie's neck, a nagging sense she's lost her way. Nothing is familiar, even things she noted on the way into Boulder.

"It's big out here," Emmeline says. Her voice is a shock in the white noise of night sounds. "In town all you can see is mountains on either side. Like you're in a bowl."

Carrie doesn't respond, checking the bark of a tree for a chalk mark she's sure she left.

"I remember you from Bishop," Emmeline says.

Carrie keeps searching, running her finger along pieces of bark. "I remember you, too," she says.

"You were gone before the fight," Emmeline says.

"I was in one of the camps," Carrie says. "Were you there?"

"I got sent away before it happened," Emmeline says. "I feel like that's the last thing I remember from the real world."

Carrie spots the chalk mark on a tree, and it looks nothing like she remembered it. The car is hidden in underbrush nearby, bits of blue peeking out from the green.

"Finally," Emmeline says. They throw their packs into the trunk and get in, but when Carrie tries the keys, the Kia sputters and dies. She keeps trying, but the engine sounds are weaker each time. Cursing, she gets out of the car and paces an angry circle around it.

"Let me try," Emmeline says, hanging off the open passenger side door.

"It doesn't matter who tries," Carrie snaps. "The car is fucking dead." She hurls the keys into a copse of paper birch. Each tree looks like Bryce, arms crossed, chiding her. *What're you going to do now, kid?*

"You kind of suck at this," Emmeline says. Carrie ignores her and pops the hood. She looks for obvious signs of tampering: a cut hose or a wire pulled out of its proper place. That there aren't any doesn't mean anything. Carrie knows ways to kill a car without leaving a trace. It's as likely the Kia died a natural death, and either way where they're at is more important than how they came to be there.

"We should sleep," Carrie says. "There's a clear patch we passed a little ways back."

"And then what?" Emmeline says.

"Then we go back," Carrie says. "But let's get something to eat in us and at least a half night's sleep."

The terrain is rocky and the tree cover isn't as heavy as Carrie might like, but she can't push the girl any further. She watches Emmeline eat granola bars while she checks the blade tucked in the back of her belt and the other at her ankle.

"Your nose," Emmeline says, pointing.

Carrie's hand goes to her nostril and comes away bloody. "It's nothing."

"It's fucking blood," says Emmeline.

"It happens," Carrie says. "Don't worry about it."

"Does it hurt?" Emmeline asks.

"Fuck yes," says Carrie.

Emmeline pauses, about to say something sympathetic. Instead, she chucks her apple core up and into the woods. Carrie winces at the noise it makes falling through the branches and crashing to earth. Emmeline curls up like a cat and falls asleep on the rocky bed of stones and roots.

Carrie cleans the blood from her nose with the hem of her black shirt. She thinks of how few changes of clothes she has and decides it would be best if one of her three shirts wasn't crusted with blood. She remembers a creek farther back. Pausing to be sure the girl's asleep, she heads through the woods.

She hears someone moving, coming from the east, the way they came. It could be a coincidence. There aren't many recreational hikers in this forest, especially at night. She centers her ability, making herself entirely invisible. Even the sounds she makes are imperceptible. She barely exists. It hurts, an all-body ache along with the dull throb in her brain.

Carrie moves toward the sound, taking a wide circle away from their makeshift camp. In a clearing, she sees Martin Scholl hovering a few inches above a crag that gives him the advantage of higher ground. His toes point downward, his legs trailing.

Her ability negates the need for stealth. The spy Miquel imagined she'd grow up to be would sneak behind Martin and press herself against his back with her blade at his throat. Carrie doesn't need to do any of that. She pulls the knife out of her belt, holding it so the blade rests against her forearm. She sprints across the open space of the clearing. The moon is ahead of her, but she casts no shadow. The night is dead quiet, but her feet make no sound in the dry, crisp grass. Standing in front of Martin, her eyes at the level of his knees, she stabs her knife into his foot, sliding it smoothly through the flesh between the slotted bones. Martin yelps and crashes onto the ground, falling splayed at Carrie's feet. He clutches his foot and wails like a cat in heat as he rolls on the ground. Still invisible, she straddles him and cuts his throat. His cries drown in red gurgling noises. As the blood hits her, hot and coppery, it disappears like drops of water on a hot skillet.

"Fuck," Carrie says. "Fuck, I'm sorry, fuck." Behind the apology, an unpleasant thrill seethes, an affirmation of every ugly urge that's welled up in her since she left fighting behind. It fills her lungs like a former smoker's first drag in years. The guilt and the rush crash together in the pit of her stomach, and Carrie doubles over, retching up all the culinary oddities she forced down at the restaurant.

As she collects herself, she hears a voice calling Martin's name. She wipes the blade on Martin's sleeve, leaving a red slash. Out of habit and instinct, Carrie hides behind the rock to wait for her.

Thandi enters the clearing, wearing her own face, younger than Carrie. She was a Pulser and a pacifist who took to the violence of the Faction's work with zeal once she let herself go. She sees Martin's body and rushes to it, lifting an arm to check for a pulse and then dropping it dispassionately. "I can *feel* you, bitch," she says loudly, as if Carrie's in the trees somewhere. "I know you think you're the ultimate ninja badass because you killed Marty, but here's the news. Marty got winded opening a bag of chips. You're not half as hard as you think you are. You never were."

She steps around the rock to where Carrie can see her. She looks like Carrie seen through a smeared lens: her shoulder-length brown hair, Carrie's mother's nose that doesn't match up with Carrie's cheekbones. Carrie's drawn to her, like noticing something off about her reflection and leaning in to examine it. They approach each other around the crag, Thandi who looks like Carrie and Carrie who doesn't look like anything.

"I'm going to kill the kid while wearing your face," Thandi says. She's shouting; she can't see Carrie right in front of her own face. "Her last thought's going to be like *Why are you doing this? I trusted you!*" Carrie's closer, but Thandi's features are blurred, her imitation of Carrie out of focus. Carrie comes near enough to touch her, to lay a hand on her own face. She squints, trying to make Thandi's imitation of her face distinct. She presses the knife in below Thandi's sternum and shoves it up.

Thandi's rendition of Carrie registers the shock of the wound, then flutters like a swarm of moths and resettles into the girl's real face. *She was prettier than me,* Carrie thinks fleetingly, the shallowness of the thought more striking to her than its content. Thandi's hands go to the handle of the knife, wrapping around it as if she's cradling a tiny animal to her chest. As she slumps to the ground, Carrie eases back up into the visible world, bringing all the blood with her.

ON REENTRY

◇

When she wakes, Emmeline's body feels less rested than disjointed and bruised. Sleep was a bad idea; it made things worse.

"Why'd you change your shirt?" she asks Carrie. The other one had the name of a band Emmeline had at least heard of.

"Black gets too hot in the sun," Carrie says, checking their bags to be sure they aren't leaving anything behind.

"This shirt's black, too," Emmeline says. Carrie ignores her, slinging her sack over her shoulder like she's Santa Claus and starting toward the city.

Sneaking back into Boulder as the sun comes up draws a line under what a bad plan all this is. What's worse is that Carrie won't let Emmeline go home.

"We can stay with Kimani until you figure out what the fuck you're doing," Emmeline says. "Which could be forever." She's flirting with the edge of Carrie's patience; her mood is worse coming back than it was going out, which Emmeline wouldn't have thought possible. She wants to pick a fight. If she can get Carrie to hate her, maybe Carrie will let her go.

"She won't be there," Carrie says, talking down to Emmeline like she's some idiot kid. "Kimani said they see her when she moves. If she wants to keep you safe, the best thing she can do is jump out of here and hope they follow her. The door won't be where it was."

It's not a theory Emmeline can discount, so she shuts up and lets Carrie lead her through downtown. Passersby look right through them, and a few times Emmeline has to jump to get out of someone's way. There's no thrill to being invisible, no promise of mischief. It makes Emmeline feel less connected to the world, not much of a change from how she already feels. They end up at Avista Adventist Hospital, which looks like a modern airport grafted onto a 1970s office building.

"Let's find someplace to put you," Carrie says.

"I'll stay with you," says Emmeline.

Carrie grips her temples. "I need to go in there and be seen," she says. "I can't hide you while I do that. I need a break." She tells Emmeline to hide behind a medical waste dumpster while she goes in. After what seems like an hour inhaling the smell of shit and blood and rot, Carrie comes back with another white lady, this one a few years older than Carrie but not as old as Kimani. She introduces herself as Alyssa. "This is my sister, Esther," Carrie says. Emmeline starts to correct her, but Carrie gives her a glare that shuts her up.

"You two are sisters?" Alyssa asks.

"Half sisters," Emmeline says. "Different dads."

"Sure, great," Alyssa says. Carrie extends her ability to cover all three, and Alyssa gasps as everything around them takes on the opalescent quality it does when you're looking out from inside invisibility.

"Stay quiet," Carrie says.

Their path takes them back the way they came, but when Emmeline asks where Alyssa is taking them, Carrie shushes her. Frustratingly, Emmeline's response at being shushed is to silently seethe at Carrie, which gives Carrie what she wants anyway. They end up at a hospice facility downtown, a modest brick building with only a small sign to mark it. Malcolm, the nurse who runs the facility, buzzes them in when he sees Alyssa but stops when Carrie fades herself and Emmeline back up into visibility.

"This is a sacred space," he says.

"You're empty," says Alyssa. "It's a few nights."

"I don't want *them* in here," he says. He must have been in college when the war started. He probably imagined a whole life that never happened and thought its loss entitled him to bitterness, as if it hadn't happened to everyone else.

"*They* are the ones supplying us with antibiotics and painkillers," Alyssa says. "They are half the reason your hospice isn't full up with the dying, and I'm the other half." She gives him a shove to the side, and Emmeline falls slightly in love.

Carrie takes a room, and Emmeline takes the one next door to it. The walls are decorated with a pantheon of religious icons. White Jesus and Black Jesus. Buddha and Ganesh. Beautiful scrolls of Arabic script. There's a peace about the room, a deep calm that makes Emmeline think of her mother. She imagines hundreds of souls leaving the world from this room, wearing away at the border between here and whatever's next the way drops of water erode a rock over a thousand years. It's a beautiful idea constructed of things Emmeline can't bring herself to believe.

Alyssa makes a call from the phone at the nurse's desk. Emmeline watches through the doorway, mesmerized. It's been years since she's seen anyone use a landline outside of the old movies Kimani likes. When she's done, Alyssa convenes them in Emmeline's room.

"I'm working on getting you a car," Alyssa says, sitting in the armchair next to the bed. "Might take a day or two. The bus lines run on the electric grid. There aren't many working cars in town, much less gasoline. We could get you an electric. How far are you headed?"

Emmeline looks at Carrie, hoping to get some glimmer of a plan.

"Far," Carrie says.

"The settlement in Wichita's within range of a charge if their grid is up and running," she says.

"It's got to be gas," Carrie says. "Lots of it."

"I've got folks on it," says Alyssa. "They'll call me as soon as they've got anything."

"Thank you," says Carrie.

"Don't thank me," Alyssa says. "Get your friends back east to send me a shit-ton of antibiotics. Or a shit-ton of morphine. If I can't help people live, I'll help them die."

She leaves them alone in the relative silence of the hospice. "So you're like a drug runner?" Emmeline asks.

"I get things where they're needed," Carrie says.

"And I'm one of those things?"

"There is a whole lot going on here, and the bulk of it is none of my business," says Carrie. "Someone is paying me to come get you and take you somewhere, and that is the job. You are the job. It's a shitty state of affairs, but that's where we're at."

"I don't get to know where we're going?"

"You were at Bishop, right?"

Emmeline nods.

"How far'd you get? What year?"

"Fourth," says Emmeline.

"Did you train with Sarah?" Carrie asks. "How to keep people out of your head?"

"I was signed up for it the year after," Emmeline says. She can remember all the classes she was registered for her next year at Bishop, the ones that never came. Psychic Defense with Sarah. The Ethical Community with Lesa Ferreira. Ability Theory with Fahima Deeb.

"Your psychic defense probably sucks," Carrie says. "That's nothing personal. It's a training thing; it doesn't come naturally. I have to figure anything I tell you, a psychic could read off your head like a billboard. We have to keep information compartmentalized."

"It's funny how you sound like you're good at planning and everything but we're stuck here where we started with no way out and people hunting us," Emmeline says.

"It's a rough start," Carrie says. "I've had worse jobs."

The part of Emmeline that thrilled when Kimani opened up a book to read to her, that hungers for stories, wants to hear all about those jobs gone bad. The rest of her takes offense at being reduced to nothing but a job and shuts down.

"I'm going to sleep," she says.

"It's three in the afternoon," Carrie says.

"What else am I supposed to do in a hospice?" Emmeline asks. "It's sleep or die."

Carrie leaves her alone and turns out the light on her way out. In the gray-lit room, Emmeline takes her sketchbook out of her rucksack, along with a small purse of mechanical pencils she stole from a papeterie in Paris. She sketches Kimani's face, noting that the details—the lines around her eyes, the odd angle of her front teeth—are fading from her mind.

A SONG IN WHICH TO WEEP

◇

"This is bullshit," says Emmeline. "At least I was stuck inside a *house*. Now I'm stuck in an empty hospital, and I can't even go outside." She sits on Carrie's bed, next to the bag of things Carrie took from her parents' house. Malcolm begrudgingly agreed to wash their clothes, so Emmeline wears a billowing hospital frock over a pair of shorts. It keeps slipping off her shoulder. Carrie has trouble fixing Emmeline's size in her mind. As she holds a mental picture of her from Bishop next to the reality of this young woman, Carrie's first thought is a parental *how big Emmeline's gotten*. When she compares Emmeline to the size of the real world, she looks too small, insufficient to whatever task Carrie's employer has in mind.

It's been three days. Alyssa found a car but not enough gas. A couple people around the city refine denatured gas in their basements, like distilling booze. The output is minimal, unreliable, and expensive. Alyssa has an order standing for forty gallons, enough to get them at least back to Sioux City, if not clear across Iowa.

With every refiner she knows devoting their full output to Carrie, it'll be another day at least. Emmeline's climbing the walls. She digs into the bag next to her, coming up with the Polaroid camera. She lifts it to her eye so it obscures most of her small face and trains it on Carrie.

"I've never seen one of these," she says.

Carrie reaches for the camera. "Don't click it," she says. "The film's—" She was about to say *not cheap,* the words her father spoke every time she took a shot, but before she can, Emmeline snaps a picture. The afterimage of the flash dances in Carrie's eyes as the camera spits out the photo.

"Sorry," Emmeline says. Carrie can't tell if Emmeline's being sincere. She holds the camera out to Carrie, the photo hanging out like a cigarette poised at the edge of a lip. Carrie goes to take it, then stops. She thinks about the Polaroid crammed into her wallet, her and Hayden and two strange kids.

"Keep it," she says. "Take some pictures."

"Of what?" Emmeline asks. "Hospital beds?" She sets down the camera, taking out the photo and shaking it in the air, because she's seen someone do that or because she heard it in a song.

"That doesn't make it develop any faster," Carrie says. "It's a myth."

Emmeline gives her a hard look and shakes the Polaroid more emphatically, checking regularly to see if the image has resolved.

"I have this thing to do today," Carrie says. "When I get back, we can go to the taco place on University Hill. My treat." Carrie smiles. Emmeline doesn't return it.

"When can we go wherever we're fucking going?" Emmeline asks.

"Soon," says Carrie. She worries it may not be soon enough. By now, the rest of the Bloom have found Martin and Thandi in the woods. Carrie's been going out at night, eavesdropping in bars and restaurants near the capitol for rumors of Faction agents sniffing around. She hasn't heard anything or seen anyone. Their best course of action is to get out quickly. The worst idea is taking an antsy teenager on a walkabout, invisible or not. She doesn't know who the other three in the Bloom are anymore. One might pick up Carrie's heat signature on the street, register her Kirlian aura or some shit. Invisibility isn't an absolute. There are other ways to be seen.

Emmeline holds up the photo, which is still milky and pale. Carrie's face is half obscured by her hand, like a celebrity fleeing paparazzi. Carrie smirks. "Sit tight a little longer," she tells Emmeline. "We're on the road as soon as we're gassed up."

Emmeline gives a full-body sigh. Carrie remembers making the same noise when she was that age. There's a five-year window when a person can produce that precise exhalation, like the high-pitched tones only young people can hear. You evolve out of it.

Waylon pulled strings to get them an apartment with separate rooms and a kitchen. He promised Carrie it was nice. When he said it, the grit of his teeth told her it wasn't, but it was the best that could be done. A shitty apartment in Boulder beat a vast estate in the middle of nowhere, or in some dead town with no plumbing or electricity.

The building is a dull brick among dull bricks along the southern border wall. *It might as well be a dorm,* Carrie thinks as she waits for the elevator. Three minutes of the up arrow blinking persuades her to take the stairs. At each landing, there are sleeping bags and belongings carefully arranged into personalized encampments. Tiny homes. She wonders about the delicate social contracts that allow these spaces to exist unattended, that protect them from being kicked to pieces by residents of the building tired of sharing space with squatters. She steps around them. She nods to the woman on the third-floor landing cocooned in her sleeping bag reading an old *Red Emma* comic, and the woman pulls her sleeping bag tighter around herself as if Carrie might steal it.

Her brother Brian answers the door in a ratty Pink Floyd T-shirt and boxers. His blank expression makes Carrie think she's forgotten to be visible.

"Fucking prodigal sister," he finally says.

"It's good to see you," Carrie says. She opens her arms to hug him, and Brian stiffly submits to it. He's too skinny and smells like he hasn't showered in days. He leads her into the living room. Dirty clothes are scattered around the floor. On the coffee table, an old laptop is playing porn, the sound muted, bodies mechanically pounding one another like fleshy oil derricks. The kitchen counter is covered in used dishes. Carrie sees one of the double inhalers used to snort Rez. When the user shoves both barrels up their nose, they look like they're wearing a fake mustache. Hong came up with the delivery system for the drug that way as a joke.

"Dad's in the back if you want to see him," Brian says. "I think he's almost done. Good days I've got enough painkillers to keep him out."

"Is today a good day?"

Brian leans in to check the time on his laptop. "He'll start moaning soon," he says. "It's not as bad as it was with Mom. Mom knew what was going on." He slams the laptop closed, not embarrassed but done with it for now. "One of your spies tell you he was dying?"

"I knew he was sick," Carrie says. "I'm here for something else."

"Spy shit," Brian says.

"Yeah," Carrie says. "Spy shit." He clears shirts off the couch to make room for her. She hauls the bag up and onto her lap. "I brought something for you," she says, pulling the Xbox out of the bag. "I stopped by the old house on the way out here. I was going to come right away, but I didn't. I felt bad about not coming before. Every time I thought of coming, all I could think about was how long it'd been. And the house. I hadn't been to the house since you left." She hands it to him, and he examines it while she extracts the controllers and various wires.

"Sweet," he says flatly. "I'll text all my friends and we can get a game of Fortnite going." He drops the console on the floor next to the couch. Carrie wants to lock Brian and Emmeline in a room together until they sarcasm each other to death.

"I thought it'd give you something to do."

"I have a job," Brian says. "I work with compost, in case you wondered. Raking and stirring mostly. Shoveling when my back's not bad. I'm off today."

"It is good to see you," she says meekly.

"You know what I think of when I see you?" he asks, turning to look at her for the first time. "I think of you standing in the doorway, telling me and Dad to get the fuck out of our house. I think about Dad asking *what about mom* and you stone-faced. So yeah, can't say it's awesome to see you. Go in and say goodbye to Dad and then go do whatever more important thing you have to do."

There's no point arguing with him. She has no right to show up here as if she's family. Whatever family she was a part of has been dismantled like the phone networks, denatured like gasoline. She leans across the couch and kisses Brian on his stubbly cheek. He bites his lower lip like he's about to say something, then opens the laptop and stares blankly at the couple fucking on the screen.

Carrie recognizes the smell of her father's room. It hides under the other smells at the hospice, smothered in antiseptics and the heavy perfume of aging nurses. This is how death smells in the wild, bad meat intersecting with metal. It's not human and at the same time intensely human, an element out of balance. *This is what it smells like when something has been kept alive too long,* Carrie thinks.

When Waylon relayed the message that her father was sick, Carrie imagined it would be something exotic, something befitting the strangeness of the world as it is. She wanted to be the cause of his illness so his sickness could be part of her story. It happened so neatly with Miquel. His breakdown was a result of their history, a scene in the movie of her life. But Carrie's father is dying of stomach cancer, the same as his father. He'd never been interesting in life. He's no more interesting in death. Lying in the bed, rail thin and face twisted by bad dreams, he's less a character in Carrie's life than a piece of scenery. The coincidence that brought her here was only a coincidence; any meaning she tries to attach to his death is hollow and post hoc. She takes the wedding photo out of her sack and props it on the bedside table. She looks for space on the table for the books and, finding none among the pill bottles and the picture frame, piles them under the edge of the bed. She sits in the folding chair by the bed, letting time stand in the place where feeling ought to be.

The raspy rhythm of her father's breath lulls her to sleep, and when she hears voices, she mistakes them for a dream of strangers negotiating in another room. Moving with an oneiric plod, she goes into the next room to investigate. Brian is talking in heated whispers with two men Carrie hasn't seen since the day they evacuated Deerfield. There's something right about them all being together now. Kenny was her favorite from that second Bloom, which sometimes had too much of a locker room vibe until Kenny reined everybody back in. Justin was the worst. He tried to convince Carrie she should sleep with him for the sake of group morale, and when she told him to fuck off, he tried the same lines on Thandi.

Carrie tries to push herself down into invisibility, but Kenny, who was always quick on the draw, extends his hand in her direction and her head fills with confetti. Her ability becomes a name she can't remember; her consciousness flails at it with no effect. Feeling neon, screamingly apparent, Carrie drops to a knee to go for the short blade in her ankle holster. Justin points his finger at her, a child's mimicry of a gun, and Carrie's body lights up with electrical current, cold and sustained. Every muscle convulses and lets go, dropping her to the ground like a puppet with its strings cut.

"Hey, kid," says Justin, who called her that even though she had the longest tenure in their Bloom. "Long time."

She tries to form a question, to ask Brian *why* or *what the fuck*. Her mouth gawps like a fish's as Kenny and Justin hoist her off the ground and drag her out, thanking Brian for his service and assuring him someone will be along to discuss his payment.

LOWER EAST SIDE/THROGS NECK

◇

Clay wears the pink Paul Smith button-down Dom got him three Christmases ago and a tight pair of midnight blue jeans and takes the B into Manhattan. They're meeting at a Mexican place Dom likes on Orchard. They used to frequent it when they were dating, before the war. Clay worked for a publisher, and Dom planned parties for the city's impossibly rich and dull. Neither had abilities; neither was special. Clay wondered what would have happened if the Pulse had changed one of them and not the other. None of the couples they knew split that way. There were couples who both resonated, couples who both didn't. Dom arranged a going-away party for the latter before the evacuation of New York, and Clay wouldn't go. He claimed someone had to watch Rai, but everyone knew he'd been in combat. There was no way to explain why he risked his life so some of their friends could be forced out of the city forever. Dom was relieved none of the soon-to-be evacuees showed up for the party. *It's better we all forget,* he said.

Everything about this lunch is planned to make Dom comfortable, but there's a risk that all these things will be poisoned: the shirt, the restaurant. Dom took Clay out to a Thai place in Williamsburg the night he confessed that he'd been fucking one of his chefs. The food burned Clay's tongue without tasting like anything. When they got home, Clay shoved the blazer he wore into the kitchen trash and threw up everything he'd eaten. This could be that all over again. Clay knows he's being irrational; he's put this off because the task will be painful. The aftermath will be better, but there's a chance it will fall apart. Never rule out the end of everything.

Dom got there before Clay, which already feels like a tactical disadvantage. He stands up when he sees Clay, straining not to run to him. Dom hugs him the way he used to when Clay came back from the front unharmed: a way that says *don't leave me again,* a hug that implies never letting go.

"How was your morning?" Clay asks as they sit down.

"Putting out fires," Dom says. "The wrap party for that war movie they're making is tonight, and now the director wants it to have a DMZ theme."

"Nothing says party like a combat zone," says Clay, sipping his water.

"He's this twentysomething wunderkind, but the closest he's been to war is an Oliver Stone retrospective at the Film Forum," Dom says. Clay realizes a beat too late that he was supposed to laugh. "The party's in a loft on Bedford," Dom adds. "Rai has choir till late; you could come for the early part. They won't break out the serious drugs until midnight."

Clay chuckles, which helps Dom relax. "No serious drugs?" Clay asks. "What's the point?"

"You and me, a night out," Dom says, missing the rhetorical question, taking every opportunity to control which parts of the conversation are serious and which are playful. "You used to like parties."

The way he says it, as if a few years ago was the distant past, as if all of their relationship is dead on the slab, makes Clay angrier than is warranted. The waiter comes over at that moment but sees something in Clay's face and finds other things to do.

"There's something I've been keeping from you," Clay says, taking the conversational reins.

"I got that," Dom says. He sits up straighter, ready to take confession, ready to be left, to be hit. "Is it someone I know?"

"It's not anyone," Clay says. "It's about Rai."

Dom relaxes, not because he doesn't worry about Rai, but because confused is better than sure. He can't imagine anything worse than Clay leaving him for someone else, so whatever this is must be preferable.

Clay tells him about the teacher's conference and the talk with Fahima at the Ruse. He lets Dom understand the time he's let pass, the duration of this secret. The waiter hovers nearby but has the decency not to interrupt. When Clay's story is over, the ice in their glasses is melted and fruit flies investigate the untouched salsa. The first thing Dom says will tell Clay everything. He'll know whether this has been a killing blow to them.

Dom takes a deep breath. "What are we going to do?" he asks.

"We'll take care of him like we promised we would," Clay says. "Like we always do." It doesn't matter that he has no idea how they'll do it. What matters is they'll be together in it. He slides his hand across the tabletop, and Dom grabs it, squeezing hard.

The DJ slides from the chopping beat of helicopter blades into the warping noises that introduce "Reflections" by the Supremes, and

Clay smiles, knowing the segue is lifted from some dimly remembered Vietnam drama his parents used to watch. His smug satisfaction at this *I see what you did there* moment is evidence he's already a bit drunk. The DJ punctuates the Motown track with digital bomb sounds that Clay can attest bear no resemblance to the real thing. A real bomb you don't hear with your ears; you experience it with your entire body, mostly in the liquid parts of your midsection. Flashbulbs go off at random intervals, and the entire loft is fugged with manufactured smoke and the burning plastic smell that accompanies it. Muscular waiters in ripped fatigues snatched up that afternoon by the garbage bag full at Kaufman's Army & Navy Surplus on 42nd and Dyer distribute trays of "meat bombs" dripping with red sauce and miniature cannolis made to look like empty bullet shells. The room is strewn with cargo nets and wooden crates with PROPERTY OF ARMY stenciled on them so recently that the paint glistens.

The bartender comes over to Clay. He's got streaks of blacking under his eyes and a red bandana pushing spiked hair back off his forehead, and he wears a desert camo jacket with no shirt underneath, the sleeves hacked off to expose gym-sculpted biceps.

"Get you another, soldier?" he asks, reaching for Clay's empty glass.

"I shouldn't," Clay says, shouting to be heard over a Jefferson Airplane song emerging from a murk of fighter jet whine. "I have to pick up my kid in an hour."

"Double, then," says the bartender, smiling so determinedly that Clay acquiesces. The bartender places a full tumbler of whiskey in front of him. "How old's yours?" he asks.

"Fourteen," Clay says.

The bartender projects an image of a toddler with perfect plaits directly into Clay's brain. She's gripping a hand-me-down stuffed rabbit and looking at the camera with a disdain for cameras that a runway model might aspire to. "She's three," he says. "I hate not being there when she goes to bed. But we haven't won the war on rent, so here I am."

"Can I ask you something?" Clay says, turning away from the rest of the room and leaning across the bar.

"Shoot," says the bartender as the digitized sound of handgun fire punctuates an M.I.A. song.

"What will you do if she doesn't have abilities?" Clay says. The bartender fixes him with that same bulletproof smile.

"She will," he says. "My girlfriend is crazy pyrokinetic. And I may not be much of a projector, but I—"

"It's not guaranteed, though," Clay says. "They don't know for sure. So I'm asking what if."

"I'd be freaked out," says the bartender. There are people waiting for drinks, but Clay has his attention.

"Practically," Clay says, "what would you do?"

The bartender straightens up, points a finger toward another customer, and leaves Clay waiting for his answer. The dull roar of the room fades into background noise as Clay fixates on his target, noting that the bartender doesn't look his way again until the bar is cleared. Then he leans in close, and for a second Clay imagines the bartender planting a delicate kiss on his cheek. "It happened to a girl I worked with," he says.

"No shit," says Clay. "What did she do?"

"There's a guy in the Bronx she went and talked to," says the bartender. "Kindred Network asshole, but he's got a soft spot for kids. He runs a rehousing program. She paid for it. I guess it worked."

Clay swallows an ice cube that feels like it's covered in battery acid. "Does she ever see the kid?"

The bartender shrugs. "She quit," he says. "Wasn't making enough. But I think it was because going to see him was expensive and she needed more money. So I guess she gets to see him."

"She have a name?" Clay asks. This puts the bartender's hackles up; he searches the bar for a customer he can take care of.

"I shouldn't say," he tells Clay. "I don't want to get her in trouble."

"Yeah, no, I get that," says Clay. He downs the remainder of his drink in two large gulps and places a twenty under the glass. On unsteady legs, he crosses the room, finding Dom dressed in a naval uniform so pristine that it glows purple under the blacklight. Dom is crystalline, and Clay knows it's because dark bags of worry have set in under his eyes.

"You leaving?" Dom asks.

"Soon," Clay says, aware there's a slight tire-leak sound in his *s*'s. Dom gives him a long look.

"Take a cab, okay?"

"I'm good," Clay says.

"This has been a lot for you to carry," says Dom. "I'm glad you're not alone with this anymore."

"Me, too," Clay says. He hugs Dominic, reveling at the solidity of Dom's crystalline form and at the same time pining for his husband's softness right now, something he could collapse into. "Who's the girl that quit recently?" he says into Dom's ear. "Has a kid Rai's age, maybe older?"

"Marietta?" says Dom.

"Okay, sure," Clay says.

"She asked for a raise," Dom says. "A big one. I said I couldn't, and she quit."

"You have her number?" Clay asks.

"What is this about?"

"Text it to me," Clay says.

"Don't do what you're doing," Dominic says. "Whatever it is, wait. Tomorrow, we'll sit and we'll come up with a plan."

"It's research," Clay says. "I promise. I won't do anything without you." Dom nods, takes his phone from his pocket, and reverts to dark, ordinary flesh. A few taps and Clay's phone buzzes, the information received. Clay takes Dom's hand and squeezes it as the DJ destroys a Clash song in a barrage of *rat-tat-tat* and *bang*.

Dom spends the morning gathering as much of their money as he can put his hands on. This isn't something they know how to budget for. Marietta wanted money to give up her contact, and the contact asked for three times that to set up a meeting the next day, without any indication how much more he might ask for. There's no ceiling to what they're willing to spend. If what they have isn't enough, they'll promise more. They'll find it, borrow it. They'll figure it out.

Clay walks Rai to school and then heads to work, partly to keep up appearances but also for a final bit of information gathering. For the first time since he's met him, Clay is happy to run into Thao on the train in. His enthusiastic "Hey man, good to see you" is enough to put Thao's guard up. Clay leans in conspiratorially. "Hey, you go over to the Bronx sometimes."

Thao looks around them. Everyone is packed into the train car, but no one pays any attention to anyone else. Knowing that doesn't alleviate the feeling they're all being watched.

"No, Clay," Thao says, too loud and formal. "I do not have any reason to be over there. And I certainly do not have the necessary clearance."

Then he leans in and whispers. "It's like the fucking Wild West over there, man," he says. "You can get *whatever*. Not in the sense of things as in material goods. But if you want to do something or you want something done to you? It is the free market." He pauses, considering. "I mean, I don't know what the options are for boys who like boys or whatever, but probably for you too."

"And getting over there is no problem?"

Thao shakes his head. "Not on a good day," he says.

"What's a good day?"

Thao shrugs. "It's not like 'Tuesday is a good day,'" he says. "A good day, whoever's working is slack." When people talk about Faction members, they make a distinction between *slack* and *taut*. There are Faction members on point all the time, constantly taut. They're directly connected to central authority, feeding information and receiving a steady stream of orders. They're elite. Attentive. *Taut*.

For every elite agent, there are ten guys who scrub toilets, high while doing it. It's not unusual to run into a Faction agent working an ass-end detail, staring into space when he's supposed to be manning the watchtower. They have a vacancy behind their eyes Clay associates with longtime addicts. Lights on, no one home. *Slack*. Trouble is, they can snap to without warning, pulled taut. There's no telling whether they're ever as slack as they seem. The ones who come off as slack might be the worst. You let your guard down thinking they've done the same.

"And you slip them a bill?" Clay asks.

"Try to be cool about it, but yeah," Thao says. "The thing is, when you're there, they will steal anything that isn't nailed down. I knew a guy who went over to see this Damp hooker." Clay feels a little sick that they've bonded enough for Thao to lapse back into using the slur. "He fell asleep after he fucked her and woke up in a tub of ice with a surgical wound where his kidney's supposed to be." Thao pulls up his shirt to indicate where a kidney belongs, and

Clay is half surprised not to see the story's scar there on Thao's own belly.

"That's an urban myth," Clay says. "That never happened."

"Didn't it?" Thao asks, winking with what he must imagine is an air of mystery. Clay thanks him, and there's a pause in which Thao might be waiting to receive money in exchange for the information. *Maybe this is what the rest of our lives will be like,* Clay thinks. *Paying out for phone calls and conversations. Carrying cash to slip to anyone who provides us any help.* The train pulls into the station, and Thao wriggles his way through the disembarking crowd, high-fiving Omars and assuring them *today is gonna be the day.*

They pull up in front of Berkeley Carroll in a car Dominic borrowed from the production team of the film, its hood pocked with precisely drilled bullet holes. Clay goes into the office to sign Rai out, feeding the receptionist some bullshit about a doctor's appointment. Mr. Castillo is in the office, running off copies, and Clay feels caught. But Castillo shies away from Clay as if they'd hooked up, and when Rai comes in from class, confused, Clay rushes him out of school and into the car.

"We going to the movies?" Rai asks. When he was little, Clay would kidnap him from school to hit up a matinee and binge at Shake Shack. It was a secret they kept from Dom, designed to secure Clay's spot as favorite dad. More than once, he's feigned enthusiasm for going to see a movie with Dom that he and Rai went to weeks before. Clay doesn't answer, and Rai looks confused when he sees Dominic sitting in the passenger seat of the unfamiliar car.

"Who's is this?" he asks as he gets into the backseat.

"It's from the movie," Dominic says.

"They gave you a car?"

Clay thinks about what Thao said about people in the Bronx stealing anything not nailed down and wonders if the film's producers will be getting this one back.

"Where are we going?" Rai asks.

"We're going to talk to somebody about our problem," Dom says.

"What problem?"

Dom looks at Clay, and Clay realizes that not only did Dom think he was the last one to know, Clay was working on the assumption Rai knew or suspected what he was. He's been using a different experience to understand what Rai's going through. When Clay came to the realization he was gay, when he admitted it to himself, he was discovering a fact he already knew, although he tried feebly to deny it. What Rai was or what he wasn't might be something else, a true revelation.

"Going to talk to a guy about a thing," Clay says. "Don't worry." Rai knows when Clay is shutting down.

"I'm not," he says. He takes out the Polaroid Clay saw him looking at a few nights ago, which he's kept in the front pocket of his school uniform. He looks at it for a second and, calmed, puts it back and leans back in the seat. He smiles, imagining this is an adventure, a grown-up version of their jaunts to the movies, with the added bonus of both his dads being present. At fourteen, anything beats being in school.

"Who's that?" Dom asks.

"Friend," Rai says, patting the pocket where the photo's come to rest.

At the checkpoint on Randall's Island, Clay eyes the Faction member on shift. If he was any more slack, he'd be asleep. Warily, Clay hands over his ID with a hundred-dollar bill wrapped around it.

"Coming over to see family," he says. "I feel bad for them, you know?" The kid doesn't respond, and Clay feels a nervous need to fill the dead air between them. "I try to come over once a month, but it's so depressing, right? Are you on the checkpoint often? I don't think I've seen you before."

"Yeah, it's fine," the Faction agent says, and waves him through.

"Did you bribe that guy?" Rai asks. Clay ignores him and takes the first turn he can, convinced that at any moment the Faction kid will snap taut and come after them. After a few blocks, he relaxes. He orients himself by putting Bronx Kill at his back and heads north to the address.

It's a three-story brick building on a block of abandoned shops, the only one on the street with lights on. Clay parks in the alley alongside the building, sure the car will be stolen by the time they come out. A pair of security goons work the door, more attentive than the kid at the checkpoint. One's got a shaved head that looks fitted onto his shoulders without the intervention of a neck. The other looks as if he's come right down from the mountain after killing something with his bare hands. Clay gives his name and watches to see if they hold their hands palm up waiting for another bribe. The men wave them in, Clay and Dom sandwiching Rai protectively between them.

The main room of the hall looks like a bar from an old gangster movie, oak with decades of tobacco smoke soaked into it, stained glass shades on the lamps hanging over the pool tables. What little natural light there is comes through glass block transom windows. The smell of fried food permeates. Men are gathered in booths; around the pool table, others are shooting as if it's a job they've lost their passion for. When Clay asked how he'd know his man, Marietta told him *hipster bigot,* and even if he hadn't recognized him, Clay could have picked Gavin Olsen out as the group leader. Rooms like this, dedicated male spaces, there's always a big man in the room, and Olsen's it. There's a knot of men with him, around which orbit others trying to pretend they're not waiting to see him. Clay wonders if there's security on the door when Olsen's not around. The bald security guy appears at Olsen's shoulder and says something that brings Clay, Dom, and Rai to Olsen's attention. He looks at Clay, then Dom, obviously confused, then opens his mouth with an *ahh* of understanding.

"I didn't realize this was an Adam and Steve situation," he says to Dom. "You don't sound queer on the phone. Anyone tell you that?"

"You talked to my husband," Dom says, gesturing to Clay.

"Do not care, man, do not care," says Olsen. "There was a time, I will tell you, that my opinion on this matter was more conservative, and now I am happy to let people do whatever gross fucking shit they want to one another and it's none of my business. This the kid?"

"This is Rai," Clay says.

Olsen stands up and walks over. For a moment, Clay thinks his entourage might follow him, but they just look on. Olsen sticks out his hand. "Nice to meet you, kid," he says. "I'm your new best friend. Rough luck for you." Rai shakes the man's hand warily. "Where's your stuff?" Olsen asks.

"What stuff?" Rai asks.

"He didn't bring anything," Clay says. "We thought this was more of an informational meeting."

"Oh, no, curriculum night's not till the middle of the semester," Olsen says. The men behind him chortle. He swivels on his barstool to face Clay. "You bring the kid and money and then you leave. It's an elegant system. Un-fuckupable, I thought. But then here we are."

"Dad, what is he talking about?" Rai asks Clay.

"So you're the dad and you're the mom?" Olsen says. "Sorry, I know I said I didn't care, but I'm curious by nature."

"We're not going to hand over our kid to a stranger," Dom says.

"That is by definition what you are going to do," Olsen says. "You are here to pay for that exact privilege. I assume from the fact you came to see me you are desperate. Who would leave paradise across the river and come here otherwise? If you're not desperate, that's fantastic, man. Good for you guys. Scamper on home. But I don't do informational meetings. I give not one shit about you. I will help your kid because he is a human being. You get no such consideration."

"We need him hidden until we figure out what to do," Clay says.

"That is not how this works," Olsen says. "We will house him. We will give him a home. There are people here who want children, because our children are no longer our own. The people we give him to will love this boy of yours. But they will keep him. Do you understand?"

"Dad, why are we here?" Rai says. He's asking both of them this time, pleading.

Clay does understand. There's a fear that dogs an adoptive parent that the child will be taken back. Rai's parents are long dead, and there was no family to be found. He belongs to Clay and Dom; no one has a claim on him. Clay has nightmares about a knock at the door, Maaya and Koyo waiting on the threshold with open arms. Blood trumps all, trumps love.

"I'm sorry," Clay says. He puts his arm around his son. "I think I've made a—"

Before he can finish, the mountain man from out front comes flying across the room, trailing his guts in the air like streamers. He smashes into the side of the bar near Rai's feet, already dead from the massive slash across his stomach. Clay shoves Rai behind him. Dominic becomes crystal and takes a wide stance. The door hangs off its hinges, and a Faction Bloom files into the Knights of Columbus hall. One has blades for hands, the left one covered in blood. All the men in the room turn to face them as one of them steps to the front. Clay recognizes her immediately. It's the girl who recruited him into the Black Rose Faction: Ji Yeon Kim, who once held the National Guard off for weeks with a barricade made out of old boats and Chevy fenders.

"We have a warrant for the arrest of the terrorist Gavin Olsen and any known associates," she says. "We are authorized to use lethal force against anyone resisting arrest."

Her hands are at her sides, bright blue spikes forming in her fists. With a motion so quick he barely sees it, she flicks the spikes at two men in the corner booth. Their heads snap back and forward again, and they slump off their seats.

"They were reaching for weapons," she says.

"I saw it," says the one with blade hands.

As the screaming starts, the rest of the Bloom mows their way through the lunch crowd. A pool cue spins in the air and drives itself like a spear into the holder's eye. A rush of heat radiates out from a lone drinker to Clay's right as the flesh of his face drips down his chin like hot candle wax and the air stings with the smell of burning hair.

"He sold us out," says the surviving security guard as the men around Olsen try to shuffle him toward the back exit through the chaos.

"I didn't," Clay says. Ji Yeon sees him and, although it takes a moment, manages to place him.

"You didn't sell them out, Mr. Weaver," she says. "But you should have. What happened to you? You used to be one of the good guys." As she says it, the severed head of one of the pool players rolls across the linoleum by her feet. "Being here makes you known associates," she adds, pointing to Rai and Dom.

She hoists another glowing spike in her hand, this one the size of a javelin, and Clay's world slows down. He remembers this, the cool moment of situational assessment that exists outside of time. He considers a bubble around himself and his family, but without knowing the nature of Ji Yeon's spikes, that might not save them. He reaches into Ji Yeon's neck and finds her carotid artery, thumping and pulsing, shoving blood up to the brain. He slows time, like putting his thumb on the edge of a record player, and before Ji Yeon throws, her eyes roll back and she collapses. It's not the worst thing he can do. There are things he could do that are so much worse.

When she drops, the rest of the Bloom stops as well. It gives Clay an opening to perform the same operation on them, dropping all four in as many seconds. They'll regain consciousness in a minute or two. He should do something more permanent, but he can't.

"Get out of here," he shouts to Dom, who grabs Rai and follows Olsen and his entourage in their rush out the back door. They spill into the alleyway and take off running. Olsen, out of shape, trails behind. The men who are supposed to protect him have decided it's not worth it.

"Wait," Clay shouts after him. "Our kid."

"Were you in there?" Olsen screams. He's out of breath, eyes wide with panic. "Nobody can help your kid. The cats are done worrying the mice. They're going to come kill us all. And your kid is one of us." He takes off down the street in a wobbly sprint.

"Dad," Rai says, shaking Clay's shoulder. "Dad, what's happening? What did you do?"

"She knew you," Dom says. "They can find us now. Oh, fuck. Fuck."

The midday sun is impossibly bright, and the screams of the maimed leak from inside the hall.

"We have to go," Clay says, herding them both toward the car.

"He said I'm one of them, but I'm not, right?" Rai says. Clay pushes him down into the front seat, buckling him in like he's a child, and closes the door.

ON WANDERING

◇

Emmeline has the feeling she's returning to herself. It's like a sleeping limb coming awake, pins and needles and uselessness. It feels like a sneeze that won't materialize, a name she can't recall. It worries her. She's afraid her ability will become too strong and the shackle she wears will short out under the strain of holding it back. She doesn't think that's what she's experiencing, but she can't be sure, and it frustrates her. She's been taking that frustration out on Carrie, which she knows isn't fair. But fair is a quaint idea, something for kids.

When Carrie doesn't come back that night, Emmeline is royally pissed. She asks Malcolm if he knows where Carrie's gone, but he's cagey. She doesn't like Malcolm. It's not the obvious fact that he hates her for what she is or that he spends the whole day sitting around waiting for people to die. He sweats a lot, and it makes him smell like her hands after she's touched old change.

Emmeline sleeps late the next morning and is awakened by the harsh sound of the buzzer at the front desk. She asked Malcolm why there was so much security, even made a weak joke about how people were dying to get in. Face expressionless, he told her that before the war somebody shot up a hospice in Denver. Ever since, all Colorado hospices have prison-level entry protocols. It's hard to think about tragedies that came before the war. How can she imagine a couple people shot to death in Denver now that all of Denver's been wiped off the map?

Assuming that the buzzer signals Carrie returning, Emmeline springs from her bed and throws her rucksack on, ready to ream Carrie for abandoning her and then, she hopes, leave. She rushes out to the front desk, where Malcolm looks nervously at a fuzzy black-and-white monitor that shows a girl not much older than Emmeline, smiling sweetly up at the security camera. Emmeline thinks of how her parents each told the story of the three little pigs differently. Her father gave the wolf a growl when he said *Little pig, little pig, let me in.* When her mother told it, the wolf implored. Her mother's version scared Emmeline more. The girl's face reminds her of her mother's wolf.

Malcolm turns to Emmeline. *Loading dock,* he mouths, pointing emphatically down the hallway. Emmeline goes far enough that she's out of sight but not out of earshot as Malcolm buzzes the girl in.

"I was hoping you could help me," the girl says. "A friend of mine is missing, and I'm trying to find her. She and I were roommates at boarding school." Her voice is a cheery singsong. Emmeline can barely keep herself from peering around the corner to confirm that the girl is Viola, her best friend from school. In their last days at Bishop, Viola was vacant, with slackness settled over her bright face. The chilly edge in Viola's voice the last time they talked is still there, and Emmeline knows if she could see Viola's face, there would be that same emptiness behind her eyes.

"We specialize in end-of-life—" His words are cut off by a quick hiss of breath, the sound of someone who's touched something hot by mistake.

"Are you sure you haven't seen her?" Viola coos. The faint smell of burning hair reaches Emmeline, and she creeps down the hall. At the end of it, one of the double doors opens onto the bright light of day. Alyssa's in the doorway.

"Come on," she whispers. "Quick."

"She's going to hurt him," she says.

"He knows what he's doing," Alyssa says. "He paged me as soon as she showed up."

"I thought he didn't like us," Emmeline says.

"He doesn't," Alyssa says. "But he knows there's good and bad, and he's decent enough he'll protect good ones from bad ones." She leads Emmeline down the alleyway behind the hospice. "Your name's not Esther, is it?"

"Nobody's name is Esther," Emmeline says.

"You're Emmeline Hirsch."

Emmeline doesn't answer. Alyssa nods and mutters what Emmeline hears as *fucking Fahima*. She goes to the edge of the alley and checks the street and then beckons Emmeline to come forward quickly.

They make their way through the city, and it occurs to Emmeline that although she's been chased for years, she's never had to run. No matter how close the Faction came to finding them, she and Kimani were always steps ahead, on the other side of the world before the agents were sure they had the right country. Every time they jumped, she was furious with Kimani, begging to know why they couldn't stay, wait it out, hope the Faction would sniff around and move on. Now she knows why, and it's too late to tell Kimani she's sorry, that Kimani was right. She's too late to thank Kimani for keeping her so safe when she was not yet able to manage safety on her own. She regrets every time she thought about not going back to the room when now all she wants is to see Kimani's door open in front of her one more time.

Paranoia is new to Emmeline—Kimani had carried the fear for both of them—and she isn't sure how to handle the feeling that everyone they pass is working with Viola and the Faction. Her steps keep threatening to break into a run, at which point Alyssa gives her hand a small squeeze and says "We're fine, walk." For as long as she can remember, the biggest threat to Emmeline has been what's inside her, the ability Fahima worried could rip the world open or do unspoken harm in the wrong hands. Now she's smuggling that ability away from whoever she's been hiding from this whole time and wishing someone had taken the time to tell her who the enemy was.

They end up at a warehouse that's been converted into apartments. Alyssa undoes a vertical series of locks, each one clacking open louder than the last, then lets them into the modest, warm space. The walls are exposed brick, hung with batiks, and there are bookshelves sagging under the weight of their contents. Where Kimani's room was spacious but airless, this room feels close but airy, a window open to the dry hot breeze of early afternoon.

"Have you eaten anything? Alyssa asks. "I can't imagine Malcolm's been feeding you."

Within minutes, Alyssa's apartment smells like canned tomatoes and garlic. Emmeline's dad would sauté garlic before her mom got home from work even if he didn't know what he was going to cook. The whole house filled with the smell. Her mom came in and said *Something smells good,* and her dad gave Emmeline a conspiratorial grin. The routine things about her parents, habits so ingrained that she learned to roll her eyes at them, are the things she misses most about them.

Alyssa keeps up the conversation as she cooks. It's small talk meant to keep Emmeline calm despite the people who are looking for her and Carrie's disappearance.

"Fahima talked about you all the time," Alyssa says. "You were one of her favorites." Water burbles in the pot. Alyssa gives the saucepan a toss, and the contents reward her with a fresh sizzle.

"How did you know her?" Emmeline asks.

Alyssa doesn't say anything for a few seconds. "We were dating," she finally says. "Practically married. I mean, we lived together for years."

"I didn't know she—" Emmeline trails off, unsure what she was about to say.

"Liked girls?" Alyssa offers.

"Yeah," Emmeline says, sure that hadn't been it.

"Fahima's good at compartmentalizing," says Alyssa. "She never talked about work. I think she only told me about you because . . ." It's Alyssa's turn to trail off.

Emmeline waits, then asks, "Because what?"

"Because you scared the shit out of her, frankly," Alyssa says. "Your ability."

"You don't have to be scared," Emmeline says, tapping her bracelet. "I haven't used it in forever."

"You promise not to rip open the space-time continuum in my apartment, I promise not to give you botulism," Alyssa says.

She drops the contents of a box of pasta into the boiling water. A tide of white bubbles rises above the rim and sizzles on the heating coil. Alyssa stares down into the pot, her back to Emmeline.

"You can't trust her," she says.

"Who?"

"Fahima tries," Alyssa says. "She looks at a situation and throws everything she has at it to fix it. But whatever the problem is, she sees one part of it. And because she's so smart and so focused, she thinks she can fire a laser at that one target and fix the whole thing."

"Am I the problem that needs fixing?" Emmeline asks.

"I think you're the laser."

LET ME STEAL
THIS MOMENT FROM YOU NOW

◇

Aspects of the room creep into Carrie's awareness: the blue of the fluorescent lights, the buzz close enough to the sound of inhibitors that for a second she thinks she's back at Topaz Lake. That year would be the perfect point in her life for her mind to break. Not like Miquel's, but shattered, the pieces reconfigured haphazardly and uselessly. But these lights buzz at a higher pitch. She can't feel it in her teeth or her stomach. She slides down, dips into a fuzzier state to be certain her ability is intact. She's slumped in a straight-backed chair with a ridge pressing into her abdomen. It's a familiar discomfort: a high school desk built to punish slouching. Carrie straightens up as if a teacher has caught her dozing. She thinks of Deerfield Middle, her school before Bishop. The memories are from another life. *I left my name here,* she thinks. *I wrote it in red so I could find it if I ever came back.* There's a motivational poster of a man crossing a tightrope between the World Trade Center towers. A fish tank, its water opaque. She wedges herself out of the desk. Her body is all ache and stiffness, and there's a burning behind her eyes.

The door opens, and Cedric Joyner, the man Mayor Pam claimed was here to heal all wounds, enters like a professor coming in after the bell. He moves as if he's come from somewhere important and has somewhere important to be. Carrie orients herself to her surroundings, but she reflexively goes slippy, becoming blurred edges around smoke.

"Don't bother," Cedric says. "I know exactly where you are. I took your knife, so don't bother with that either." He pulls it from his pocket, displays it to her, then puts it back. "Or this little relic." He holds up her iPod, the earbuds dangling. "I think the screen broke a bit when you fell. Such a shame. I imagine it'll be hard to replace." He lays it on the teacher's desk. Carrie lets herself rise up, fully visible. Cedric smiles. "That's better. Now we can be friends. Would you like to know why your brother sold you out?"

Carrie can see the smug look on Brian's face as Faction agents dragged her out of his shitty apartment, as if he'd one-upped her in a contest she didn't know they were having. "He wanted abilities," Cedric says. "I told him I could give them to him. I can't, incidentally. I've been trying with no luck. Once I found a boy with amazing abilities. I thought he was the key. I strapped him to a machine and pushed it so hard I killed a whole bunch of people, like that." He snaps his fingers, his face alight with glee. "That's how I ended up here."

"I read about you," Carrie says. "I knew I remembered that name. You murdered a bunch of people in the Bronx."

Cedric waves his hand as if shooing away a bug. "I was the first person since Emmeline Hirsch to induce Resonance in people who were otherwise . . . lacking. Not everyone who was part of the experiment lived, but that is what happens when you push boundaries. There are risks. Costs. But none of that made the news in Boulder. They've been happy to have me."

"That was years ago," Carrie says. "The mayor said you just got here."

"I may have done some editing in the dear mayor's head," he says. "Too much, I think. She's falling apart." As Cedric talks, he opens and closes drawers in the teacher's desk. He removes objects and holds them up like artifacts from a lost civilization, examining them from various angles. He gives off an air of indifference, letting Carrie know that none of this matters half a fuck to him.

He sits behind the desk, leans back in the chair. Carrie feels Cedric in her head. She remembers once when Waylon was drunk at a party and tried to persuade her to make out with him, his clumsy fingers pawing at her thoughts. This isn't like that. It's a mechanical spider climbing over the surface of her mind, poking with the sharp points of its legs.

Your thoughts are not an object to be observed and read. They are a process in which you participate. They're the fuel at the heart of a fire that burns constantly, a cool white flame.

"Your mind is a cool white flame," Cedric says, mocking her with his nasal intonation. "You're very good. Sarah Davenport taught you, right?" Carrie doesn't respond. "She taught me, too. And Fahima Deeb. I was one of Fahima's first students at Bishop. Her star pupil. I worked with her for a while after the war, trying to make everyone special. But Sarah was my favorite. So pretty. Everyone thinks she died in the fighting at the Bishop Academy, but Fahima hid her away. Fahima asked me to try to help her with her memories, but that's not the way my ability works. I learned a few things while I was rattling around in her head. Mostly about her brother. But there's not much there, and it isn't getting better. Imagine not being able to keep a memory. Moments flying by you like cupcakes on a conveyor belt. You grab at them but you're a second behind. Starving forever." He shakes his head.

"I thought Fahima might have sent you. I was flattered Fahima would send someone to kill me. And someone so impressive. You've done some unpleasant things. Although they weren't always your choice, were they? There's something in your head like a broken transmitter. A radio on the fritz. But then there are the things you did all on your own, Carrie Norris." Carrie's startled by the sound of her name in Cedric's mouth. "Your mind might be a cool white flame, but I can read your name like an appetizer off a dinner menu."

For a second Carrie flashes on Emmeline. She throws the image into the flame.

"*That's* who I'm interested in," Cedric says. "You are a small-time smuggler, but that girl you're thinking of is relevant to my interests. I would greatly like to speak with her. If you tell me where she is, I have no reason not to let you go. Your brother, too. He's not of any particular use other than as one more guinea pig."

"You can keep him," Carrie says.

Cedric shakes his head sadly. "Carrie Norris, do you know where you are? You're in the New Vista High School. Former, that is." He looks around. "I believe this was a social studies classroom. But in another sense, Carrie Norris, you're in Room 101. You get that reference. You're very well read. I can see that. But watch this." Cedric touches Carrie's forehead with his thumb like a priest administering the ashes.

"Do you know where you are, Carrie Norris?" he says. "You're in Room 101. Do you get that reference? Do you remember Room 101?"

She doesn't. She can see the book, its cover white except for the title and the author's name. An eye; she remembers an eye. She can't read the text; it's smeared and out of focus. Room 101 is something terrible; as a kid it terrified her. But it's gone.

"It's *1984*," Cedric says. "You read it three times in eighth grade. You underlined passages. You woke up from nightmares of rats gnawing at your face. I ate it out of your brain. I ate all of your Orwell, just for kicks. That's what I do. I eat people's memories. Like those rats chewing on your cheeks. Like cupcakes on a conveyor belt." He mimics shoveling food into his mouth with both hands and grins at Carrie, cheeks puffed out like a chipmunk's. Carrie can't move. For a second she thinks she's forgotten how. The terror of this feeds into the fear that holds her in place; when her mind lets the thought go, she's pinned. "That's how I came to be Fahima's star pupil. I went on a little tour. I met with the greatest scientists in the field, and I ate everything they knew. And still she kicked me out. Aired my dirty laundry in public. What she didn't tell them is that I was close, closer than she ever got. If I had Emmeline Hirsch, I could do wondrous things. Things Fahima Deeb can't. I'd be welcomed back as a hero."

Cedric clasps his hands together. "I would love to be able to spend the whole day with you, Carrie Norris," he says. "But I need Emmeline Hirsch. I can't see her directly. She's slippy. Is that your word? Emmeline is naturally slippy. But you know where she is. I'm going to give you some time. I want you to think about what else I could take. The day you and your friends spent at Coney Island in the cold. Your mother. Your name."

He throws Carrie a wink.

"I just want the girl," he says. "I'm not going to hurt her. When it's done, I'll take her out of your head. Betrayal leaves a phantom pain. I hate thinking of anyone suffering that way. The girl will be like George Orwell and Winston Smith and the rats." He snaps his fingers again. "Gone."

SCHOOL'S OUT FOREVER

◇

Carrie drifts in and out of consciousness, bleeding from fresh wounds in her memory. When she feels stable, she assesses the room. Ideally, there would be something sharp: a letter opener or an ancient pair of scissors. But high schools are like mental institutions and prisons. There's nothing that can be repurposed as a weapon for fear a student might turn it against a teacher. Carrie considers the effectiveness of sharpened pencils when she sees the defibrillator pack by the door.

She stands up, her legs unsteady. It seems unlikely the defibrillator will carry a charge, but she clicks the pillbox case open and sees a light blinking green. At the same time, she hears voices in the hall. Not Cedric but Kenny and Justin, the ones who came for her in Brian's apartment. Carrie drops into slippiness, bringing the paddles of the defibrillator with her. She stands behind the door.

"Cedric's going to be pissed if you even touch her," says Kenny.

"She killed Marty and Thandi," Justin says. "You don't want to see her pay for that?"

"He's going to hollow out her brain," Kenny says. "That's bad enough."

"I want to give her something to remember," Justin says.

"I'm telling you she's not going to remember shit," Kenny says. "What are you going to do, rape her?"

"She used to want it so bad," says Justin.

"Not from you," Kenny says.

"I'm going to scuff her up."

"Fuck that," says Kenny. "I'm going to grab dinner."

"I'll catch up," Justin says.

Carrie listens to footsteps heading down the hall. She wants to cry out to him for help, hoping whatever part of his humanity is still there will respond. She wants to scream at him for looking the other way. The doorknob turns, and the door swings toward her. Carrie moves toward its edge. Justin closes the door behind him. She worries the defibrillator won't have any effect because of Justin's ability with electricity, but there's nothing else at hand. She waits for him to take another step into the room, then puts the paddles on either side of his head and fires a charge. He lets out a gargling noise and shudders to the ground. Carrie's on him immediately, straddling his chest. The paddles hum and whine as a second charge builds. He looks at her, dazed, and shakes his head to clear it. His eyes come into focus, welled up with tears.

"Do it," he says. She feels his arms struggling weakly against her legs. "Do it now." His face quivers with sobs. "There's someone else in my head with me. There's less of me every day. We used to be good. Carrie. Please. I don't know how long I can—" His pained expression twists into a smile, and his face firms up in cruel resolve. "That wasn't very nice." His voice changes, calms and drops half an octave in the middle of a sentence. Something milky and black swims over the surface of his eyes. It frightens Carrie backward so she's sitting on his legs rather than his chest. Justin or whatever's controlling him sits up. "Can't you hear me anymore, Carrie? I've been calling y—"

Carrie presses the paddles against Justin's forehead and releases another charge. The scared boy surfaces again. "Please!" he says. Carrie feels a humming vibration coming from him, an echo of the paddles' building charge. His hands spark and crackle. She jumps off his legs as he brings his hands up to his face. The room fills with the smell of ozone, a storm about to break. "I don't want to be this." He presses his face into his palms, muffling his scream. Sharp ozone is blanketed by the low smell of cooked meat and singed hair as his body slumps backward, hands welded to his face.

Carrie doesn't give herself time to register the horror of it. She files it away with other horrors. She'll revisit it in dreams, in moments when she feels safe. She's up and out the door, leaving Justin's body smoking on the classroom floor.

She runs down the hall. The lights are off. There's a thrill in being in a school after dark, even as an adult. She imagines pranks, flasks of cheap booze consumed in the bathroom while classmates slow dance in the gym. It's the stuff of teen movies, and Carrie worries her mind is filling in gaps where actual memories had been with scripted fictions. *Sneaking into Bishop,* she thinks. *Miquel and me. Bryce and Waylon behind us, holding hands. Did we do that?*

Carrie hears sustained cries of pain coming from down the hall. The ground floor of every high school centers on the gym, like spokes feeding into a hub. Carrie can hear it in the quality of the screams, an echo and a space she remembers from Deerfield High. She associates it with the squeak of sneaker soles on hardwood, the shrill enthusiasm of pep rallies bouncing off cinderblock walls. She continues down the hall, toward the center. The gym doors are closed, but light and sound leak through around the wooden doors. Knowing it will draw attention to her but unable to stop herself, she pushes the door open.

The gym is set up like a triage unit. Rows and rows of hospital beds, teenagers and old people strapped to them. Some sleep, some writhe, some scream. There must be a hundred beds.

The door eases shut, and Carrie watches attendants make their way through the rows. She focuses on the one nearest. She's middle-aged with the weary air of a mother. She wears saddlebags, one resting on either thigh. She stops at each bed and pulls something out of the left bag. A small metal cylinder, no bigger than Carrie's pinkie finger. Carrie recognizes it immediately. These little canisters were how she made a living for years. The nurse discharges the canister of Rez into a tube that runs up each patient's left nostril, then puts the spent canister in the other saddlebag, where it clinks against the others. As the dose hits, each patient slams against their restraints, their body pushing heavenward only to get pulled back down. The attendant moves on to the next patient.

In the far corner of the gym there are beds with sheets thrown over them, the uneven terrain of bodies beneath. Creeping through the rows, Carrie moves toward them. As she does, she brushes the starched sheets of one of the patients, who startles and grabs her by the wrist. His skin is translucent; she can see the fascia underneath, the blood vessels surging like leeches fattening themselves. She'd have no way to recognize him if it weren't for his Deerfield High T-shirt, stained with vomit around the collar, hovering over the gory insides of his body like an angel resting on wisps of cloud. Brian stares into her eyes, and Carrie is at once sure he can't see her and positive he can.

"Doctor," he croaks. "I don't think it's working."

Carrie shakes her wrist free and stares at her brother. He's in no state to run. She'll have to carry him out. She hurries to the makeshift morgue. There's a metal tray of autopsy tools, scalpels of various sizes. She grabs three and holds them folded along her forearm. She goes back toward where Brian is to cut him loose.

The door swings open, and Cedric enters with Kenny.

"That's enough now, Carrie Norris," he shouts to the entire room. He can't pinpoint her. It's her only advantage, but it's not enough to save her and Brian.

The doctor panics and runs from the room. Carrie leaps over one of the bodies and zigzags toward Cedric and Kenny. She doesn't need the white flame meditation now; her mind is a flitting piece of malice moving across the room. She focuses on Cedric, watching his glance dart around the space, occasionally picking up on the spot where she was.

Everywhere you think I am, I'm not.

Scurrying under a gurney in a low crouch, she comes up between Cedric and Kenny. She raises two of the scalpels and stabs both into Cedric's eye. His head jerks back, pulling the weapons from her hand as he falls to his knees, screaming. Carrie grabs Kenny by the neck and shoves him up against the lockers, the last scalpel drawing blood from his stubbly neck.

"Why are you doing this?" she says. "What the fuck does the Faction want experimenting on these people?"

"It's Davenport," he says, tapping the side of his head. "He wants everyone like us." He's sobbing, watching Cedric on the ground trying to free the metal from his orbit.

Carrie feels a thrashing inside her brain. Cedric, wounded, lashing out, trying to grasp at her memories and shred them. She lets Kenny go and delivers a swift kick underneath Cedric's jaw. She kneels down and finds her knife in his pocket, realizing that her stolen iPod sits on the desk in the classroom upstairs. She tucks the knife back into its holster.

She winds through the beds, looking for Brian or whatever's

left of him. When she finds him, she yanks the needles out of his arm and hoists him onto her shoulders, grateful he's such a bag of bones. She carries him out of the gym and down the hall, hoping it's in the direction of an exit. Behind her, the pained moans of the patients in the gym, the choked gasps of Cedric trying to scrabble back to his feet and regain his breath. For an instant, she's back in the camp at Topaz, the brief return of her ability and the promise of escape for some of them. She should get everyone out, but there's no way and no time. Hunched under Brian's weight, she walks out the school's front doors.

SAMPLES

◇

Fahima isn't used to butting her head against a problem, but it's happening more and more lately. Project Tuning Fork is the obvious example, but then there's this one: she needs a way to objectively study Hivematter. This is roughly like saying she needs to autopsy a dream or throw a wish into a mass spectrometer. What's wanted is a version of Kimani's room she can fold around herself like a deep sea diving suit. Once, she would have been able to imagine the workings of such a thing and sketch it out on a napkin, but now even the concept makes her head hurt. The Hive is transspatial, which is how Kimani's room travels and the answer to how she can be in two places at once when she's not anywhere at all. She thinks the key might be thinking of what Kimani's room looks like from the outside, but where would you stand to look at it? It abuts the real world only at the door. What's on the other side of Kimani's walls?

If she could dream up a suit, she could fold into the Hive and pick one of the black flowers as easily as stealing a peony in Central

Park, but she's stuck dropping her mind into the Hive, interfacing with the flowers there only through her Hivebody. No data, no instruments. Lying on the couch in the headmaster's quarters, Fahima lets her mind go in, her Hivebody manifesting at the same place it always does: the spot where they rescued Emmeline Hirsch from a cage of onyx, the first time Fahima saw the black substance in the Hive or anywhere else. It's grown over with snakes of black vine, but Fahima can see the spot at the center where the cage Emmeline was held in had burst like a pustule, freeing the captive girl inside.

Knowing what's coming and bracing herself for it as best she can, Fahima grabs one of the black flowers with the bare hand of her Hivebody. The first time she ever touched the black substance in the Hive, it flooded her head with memories of her mistakes, shame at things she'd done. *Bring it on, fucker,* she thinks. *Shame is basically where I live.* But the feeling that invades her mind when she grips the bloom isn't about anything that's already happened. It orients her thinking toward the future and finds nothing there. Not a dystopia, not an earth in ruins, but nothing. Eschaton. She lets go of the flower, but the hopelessness lingers, a nihilistic certainty that all of this is pointless. She looks at her hand, expecting to see burns, some physical remnant of the harm the flower's done to her mind, her heart, but the skin is intact, unblemished.

Fahima remembers the object Kevin Bishop created in Revere before he died, an inverse of the black glass. Touching it made her feel powerful; it kicked her ability into an unsustainable overdrive, one she wouldn't feel again until the first moments after the Pulse. But along with that power, there'd been a feeling of hope, of the limitless potential the future held. It was what she felt was at the core of Bishop's message: that Resonants were an embodiment of some future promise. Not a destiny, because destiny was limited to a single preordained path. It was a multiplicity of futures, branching and ever-expanding possibilities.

Now she struggles to recall that feeling. It seems cheap and naïve, and she can't help thinking it might be permanently eclipsed by this one. With a sense that she's lost something, Fahima brings herself up out of the Hive, back into a lab she thinks of as Remote Site Minus One. It's not on any of the Bishop Foundation's paperwork, and except for the Omars, only four people outside the site know about it. Some days four seems like too many.

The sample swims in a jar on her desk, twisting itself into shapes as if trying to relay a message or spell out its name. She hasn't said it out loud, but in her head she's been calling it Yorick.

She sliced pieces off it and ran them through every test from gas chromatography to Kirlian photography. The latter was terrifying: the entire plate came out exposed, as if the tiny slice of Yorick implied a ubiquitous presence. More traditional tests yielded two incompatible results: Yorick was organic matter that shared Patrick's DNA, but Yorick was also inorganic matter with the same structure and chemical composition as black glass. It tells her nothing. It's brought her no closer to understanding what's wrong with Patrick than she was the day of the riot, the first time she saw something foreign looking out at her from behind his eyes.

She's theorized that he's infected with something, that constant contact with the black glass has had a permanent effect on his mind. She's imagined that his own personality, his psyche or whatever you want to call it, has become diminished by shearing off tiny pieces like Yorick here and inserting them in the brains of Faction members like poor dead Heidi. She asked Omar if it felt this way when he had too many duplicates out in the world, as if his essential self was a limited amount of water poured out in drams into dozens of smaller containers, leaving the main one nearly empty. Omar said it didn't work like that but refused to explain further. The two theories could work in tandem: Patrick lessened by division and then infected. But neither told her anything useful.

Fahima sits, staring at Yorick, which floats sleepily in formalin. Next to the jar, a martini with a twist swimming in it, yellow echo of Yorick's black. Fahima keeps thinking what a poor game of chess she's played. She's near the point where the only option is to flip the board, send the pieces flying.

She worries that Patrick can sense it, that it calls out to him, maybe even wanting to rejoin him. Yorick hasn't given up much in the way of information, so it would be a shame if he blew their cover. Thinking about it reminds her how likely it is Patrick already knows about this place and tolerates it. Feeling as if she's being watched, she puts Yorick back on the shelf, leaning a copy of *The Feynman Lectures* against it. She picks up her martini, starts up the Gate she's secretly kept here, and in the deafening roar that follows steps through into the headmaster's quarters at Bishop.

Sarah wanders in from the bedroom without any real purpose. The Omars here are good with her, although some are better than others. As he has with the ones at the lab, Omar has been letting more of his duplicates persist autonomously. They're growing into actual people, whereas Sarah is static.

"Working?" she says.

"Not really," Fahima says. "You want anything?" She points at her martini. "I could make you one of these."

"I don't think I like those, do I?"

"No," Fahima says. "You said they tasted like pine needles soaked in paint thinner."

"Then no, thank you," Sarah says. She stands in the doorway, awkward, waiting for something.

"What's on your mind?" Fahima asks. As soon as she does, she regrets the wording.

"I asked . . . the man . . . a question," she says. Some days she remembers Omar's name, but not today. "He told me I had to ask you." Fahima nods. She already knows the question. They go through this once a month. Sarah is an assemblage of loops, certain conversations repeated at intervals.

"What happened at Bishop that day?" Sarah says.

"You don't want to talk about that," Fahima says.

"It's the only way I can remember."

"Maybe it's better not to remember."

"Sometimes I wake up and I don't know how we got here," Sarah says. Her hand trails back to where Cortex used to sit at her heel. Her fingers trace the outline of where the dog used to be, a memory written into the nerves of her arm. "What's in the jar?" Sarah says.

"Patrick," says Fahima. "Or maybe not; I don't know."

"Do you think he's gone?" Sarah says. "You still talk to him, don't you? Or work with him?" Since Cortex was killed, Sarah has trouble keeping track of things. Even the things she remembers, she's unsure of. She's at most a hundred memories held together by a handful of personality traits. It's like watching someone give a poor performance of her friend. She's lost Patrick because he's becoming something more, and she's lost Sarah because she's becoming something less.

"*He* says it's still him," Fahima says. "He makes a point of telling me every time we talk. *It's still me in here, Fahima. Your old buddy Patrick*. He must think it's what keeps me from killing him."

"Is it?" Sarah says.

Sarah and Fahima have gone over every memory Sarah has of Patrick, all the ones she's kept: the two of them swimming off the coast of Maine or backpacking through the Swiss Alps on their parents' dime. They're beautiful and dear to Sarah because the truth of what Patrick is now doesn't stick with her. Fahima's mem-

ories of Patrick are tainted with the present. She wonders which
would be worse: knowing their friend is dead or knowing their
friend had done the awful things Patrick's done. But it's not as if
Fahima's hands are clean. Once again, she's bought time. More of
it, but at a higher price. The bill is coming due, and she needs a way
to cheat the Devil. She hoped Yorick might be the key, but she has
nothing.

"What keeps me from killing him is I don't know how," Fahima says.

ON ESCAPE

◇

Emmeline rejects several activities Alyssa proposes out of loyalty to mothers she's had before. She did the same thing to Kimani at first, refusing to be read to not because she was too old for it but because it was a thing she used to do with her mom. It wasn't until Paris that Emmeline had submitted, allowing Kimani to read her *Les Misérables* under the stipulation that they take turns so there would be an alteration from the way it had been with her mother. With the separation still fresh, everything Alyssa suggests reminds Emmeline of Kimani. All board games indicate chess, which is *their* thing. Alyssa's collection of DVDs has no overlap with the library they had in their room—Alyssa favors rom-coms and early 2000s medical dramas, whereas Kimani preferred noir and turned her nose up at television—but watching a movie with Alyssa feels like a betrayal. In the end they listen to some sad singer with a deep baritone and Emmeline pages through a 1950s nurse novel, one of dozens of paperbacks on Alyssa's shelf.

"I used to collect them when I was a kid," Alyssa says. The apartment is surprisingly full of knickknacks, and the kitchen is stocked with culinary gadgets and other ephemera. It clashes with Emmeline's understanding of how the evacuations had worked. She thought everyone left with only what they could carry.

"I was special," Alyssa says. "Fahima gave me everything I could want. She kept me like a princess in a tower. Some of it's mine from before." She picks up a brass statuette of a man with an elephant for a head and runs her fingers over it before putting it back on the shelf. "Some of it must have been looted from houses back east." She looks at the kitchen as if it's haunted.

"She sent you here?" Emmeline asks.

"Not at first," Alyssa says. "I was in Chicago, then someplace else, all by myself. I got tired of being a bird in a cage, so I came here. She helped. Found me the apartment. Got all my things here, and all the things she found for me. I guess this is where she put things she thought she might need later."

The small empty space between songs is broken by a rattle of the front door lock. Alyssa goes to the kitchen, looking for the most menacing knife she can find as the dead bolt shoots back. The door swings open, revealing no one behind it. It slams shut again, and Carrie appears in the middle of the living room, face and clothes streaked with blood, carrying a boy on her shoulders. She's clutching two thin pieces of metal in her hand.

"Help him," she says, collapsing to her knees under the weight. The boy rolls off her, a jumble of limbs. He looks sickly, impossibly pale, as if his skin is made of rice paper.

"Jesus," says Alyssa.

"Blood's not mine," Carrie adds. "Drugs. Help him."

Alyssa straightens the boy out, laying him on his back and checking his breathing, his pupils.

"Rez," Carrie says, pointing to the boy. "A ton of it. He's over-dosing people. Trying to get them to resonate."

"Who is?" Alyssa asks

"The man with the mayor," Carrie says. Her mouth shapes a sound, possibly an *s*. "He was there, at city hall, with her when I met her."

"There wasn't anyone with the mayor," Alyssa says.

"He was right—" Carrie stops. "He eats memories," she says. "You met him, but you don't remember."

"Okay, that's enough," Alyssa says. She pulls a flip phone from her pocket and dials. She stands, impatient, with one hand on her hip, waiting for someone to pick up on the other end. When they do, she launches in.

"How is it you're still in the business of fucking up my life?" she says. "I'm supposed to be back among normal people, Fahima. But I'm standing here in my apartment with a girl you told me was dead and another girl who says somebody ate her memories, and none of it feels remotely normal." There's a pause before Alyssa repeats *ate her memories,* then another pause. Alyssa puts her hand over the phone.

"The man with the mayor," she says to Carrie. "What was his name?"

"Cedric Joyner," Carrie says. "He's running a lab. He's doing experiments on people."

"I know who he is," Alyssa says. She turns away, as if turning her back will silence her conversation, but she's still audible. "It's him," she says. "She says I met him and I forgot. He could have been here the whole time." She turns back, hand over the phone again.

"Did he know about Emmeline?" she asks.

Carrie nods.

Alyssa leaves the room to finish the conversation. While they wait for her to come back, Emmeline checks on Carrie, doing the things she imagines she's supposed to do for someone in shock. She asks her the date, which Carrie gets wrong by three days, and has Carrie follow her finger with her eyes. She wets a washcloth and cleans away blood to be sure there are no wounds underneath.

"Who is he?" Emmeline asks once she's convinced Carrie's okay. "Another job?"

"He used to be my brother."

Alyssa makes another call from the landline in the kitchen, and within ten minutes paramedics show up from the hospital to take Carrie's brother. He's in and out of consciousness, muttering about comic books and a room made of black bone. Carrie stops one of the paramedics, grabbing him by the arm.

"Can you do one more thing?" she asks. "Can you send someone to get my dad? He might already be . . ." Carrie trails off. "He's all alone, and I don't think he has long left. I want to know someone is taking care of him."

"Of course," he says. Carrie writes down the address for him, but Emmeline can see her struggling to recall it. Alyssa goes back into her bedroom with the cellphone and comes out with a suitcase that's been sitting, packed, for when this moment came.

"Is the car ready?" Carrie asks. "Even if there's not enough gas, we can start back."

"You can't go back east," Alyssa says. "We don't know how much he pulled from your head, but we have to assume he thinks you're taking her to New York."

"I know sixteen routes to get us back across—"

"He could know all of them," Alyssa says. "Anything you thought you were going to do is compromised. Fahima has a plan.

She always does. Apparently I'm fucking part of it." She hoists her suitcase. "Grab your gear. We're meeting one of Fahima's people downtown in an hour."

"Wait," Carrie says, shaking her head like she's trying to remember something else she's lost. "Fahima Deeb?"

Alyssa stares at her blankly. "Who did you think you were working for?"

"Part of the job is you don't ask," Carrie says.

Alyssa's expression softens, and Emmeline can see the moment when she wants to be kind. Once, this woman probably had it in her to be kinder than she is now. Her face sets into a cold resolve. "That's a stupid job, kid," she says. "Get your stuff. Let's go."

Emmeline grabs her rucksack and looks at Carrie, who has nothing.

"All your stuff," Emmeline says.

"It was just some clothes," Carrie says.

"You had books and a picture," Emmeline says. "Your music thing." She mimics the way Carrie holds the gadget and traces circles on it with her finger.

"That I'm not happy about," says Carrie. "But I'm not going back to that place. Not ever." She doesn't look scared or shaken. She looks as if she's seen lots of horrible places and has learned to put them someplace in her head once they're behind her.

Under the cloak of Carrie's ability, they ride bikes downtown, passing the Boulderado Hotel. Emmeline slows her pedaling as they go by. She wants to go in and check to be sure Kimani isn't there, but she knows Carrie's right. The hotel was never her home, only Kimani's room, and that isn't there anymore. Emmeline's vision flutters, and she thinks it's tears until she realizes she's become visible again, with Carrie and Alyssa well ahead of her.

"Keep up," Carrie calls, and Emmeline pedals hard to get back under the umbra of Carrie's ability.

A tour bus waits for them in the loading zone of the Fox Theatre, its windows opaque. It idles like it's trying to build suspense. Roadies load gear into the compartments underneath, some of which are filled with large plastic tanks of gas. The front door folds open like a curtain drawn back, and Hayden Cohen descends the stairs in postshow attire of ripped jeans and a hoodie, holding their arms open.

"I am so fucking happy to see you," Carrie says, rushing over and sweeping Hayden into a hug. She sobs, the sound muffled by Hayden's shoulder.

"Easy, hon," Hayden says so quietly that Emmeline barely hears them. They wrap their hand around the back of Carrie's head, knitting their fingers into her hair. It's the first time Emmeline considers what Carrie's gone through since she got here, how much has gone on outside her own attention.

"Rafa," Hayden says. "Throw their things in with ours."

"I'm a guitarist, not a roadie," says an olive-skinned boy with a greasy hank of hair concealing a patch over his right eye.

"Fuck you, man," says one of the women telekinetically lifting an amp onto the bus. Rafa seems to think this is a valid point. He flashes Emmeline a smile as he eases her bag off her shoulder.

"Rafa, no," Hayden shouts the way they might at a dog considering getting into something it shouldn't. He shrugs, smiles sheepishly, and takes the bag to the luggage bays under the bus. "That's Rafa; he's mostly harmless," they tell Emmeline. "Don't take anything he says seriously."

Emmeline nods. Hayden rubs their hands together. "Apparently one of you is supposed to tell me where we're going," they say.

"The fuck out of here," says Carrie. "Faster the better."

"I got that part," Hayden says. "High-speed getaway, check. But I was told you know where we're going. Compartmentalization of intelligence. It's like Fahima's pickup line."

"I know," says Alyssa.

"Who are you again?" Hayden asks.

"Alyssa's our friend," Emmeline says.

"Cool. I love putting my complete trust in strangers," says Hayden. "So where are we headed?"

"Phoenix," Alyssa says.

"That's fucked up," Rafa says. The crew congeals around Alyssa, arms folded.

"A lot of us lost people in Phoenix," Hayden says.

"There's nothing there," says the roadie.

"Your people—" Rafa starts, but Carrie cuts him off.

"Phoenix is gone," she tells Alyssa. "I've seen it. The Gate at the school there collapsed. The whole city—"

Alyssa shakes her head and waves them off. "Fahima hid it," she says. She looks at Emmeline. "She's very good at hiding things."

"A whole city?" Carrie asks.

"Fucking look around," Alyssa says. "She sets me up down the block from Emmeline—who is supposed to be fucking dead, by the way—for years, just in case. She sends you out here"—she points to Carrie—"without telling you fuck all and sends in a whole goddamn rock tour as a backup plan, just in case. You think she couldn't hide a city?"

The crew look at one another, and Emmeline wonders about the extent to which they understand that they've been working for anyone other than Hayden. Compartmentalization of information, after all. As seconds of silence tick by, they turn from each other to Hayden, waiting to be told what to do. Hayden shrugs.

"Westward ho," Hayden says. "Rafa, you've got first shift. Let's get a couple hours away from the city at least."

Emmeline climbs up onto the bus, which smells deeply lived in. Rafa starts the engine and puts *Aladdin Sane* on the stereo. Emmeline curls up on a bench. Hayden distributes beer from a mini-fridge, motioning to offer one to Emmeline before Carrie wards it off. Alyssa declines, opting to sit by herself. Hayden clinks their bottle to Carrie's as the lights of the city recede and the bus moves into the darkness of the Wastes. Even with the path clear, the trip has a doomed feeling. But if they're fucked, at least they're among friends.

THE LOVE SONG
OF KEVIN BISHOP

BE SURE TO WEAR
FLOWERS IN YOUR HAIR

1968

when thou bringest food
I howl my joy, and my red eyes seek to
    behold thy face—
In vain! these clouds roll to and fro, and
    hide thee from my sight.

—WILLIAM BLAKE,
America a Prophecy

Kevin was surprised when he rechecked the address Raymond had given him and found it was in a burned-out block on Haight, between Buena Vista and Golden Gate parks. He could see the seedlings of the San Francisco counterculture he'd read about breaking through the soil. Cheap real estate had drawn artists and bohemians until the concentration hit the point where businesses that catered to them became viable. Kevin asked for directions in a shop that sold marijuana, LSD, and substances he hadn't even heard of alongside spinner racks of comic books that ranged from superheroes to sex dreams. The girl behind the counter, pupils like saucers, looked at the address and practically shrieked, "I live there!"

"This is the home of Professor Raymond Glover," Kevin explained in a voice that bordered on condescension. "He teaches physics at—"

"It's the professor's house, but we all live there," said the girl. "We're so glad he's back. Are you going to live there, too?"

Kevin bought a pack of gum and, worried it might be laced, threw it in the trash. Haight Street was full of the lost: some burned and broken, some merely searching. Kevin reached out, looking for other Resonants. There were communities forming in knots and whorls: a block in Chicago, a seaside cul-de-sac in Maine. This wasn't one of them. The people on the street were only people, nothing special about them. He felt the pull from the house at the end of the street, the top of the hill. It called to him the way other Resonants always called out to him: a voice in another room. This time it was louder. Resonants had an amplifying effect when they grouped together, and it was that multiplied call he heard from the house at the top of the hill.

A stunning young Asian boy opened the door wearing a silk tunic and torn faded jeans. He smiled beatifically at Kevin, then pulled him into an abrupt, awkward hug. "You're the professor's friend," he said into Kevin's ear. "He told us you were coming."

"Bowen, let him go," said Raymond, coming down the hall with his brisk long strides. "Mr. Bishop is joining us from the East Coast, where there are stringent rules about physical affection."

Bowen released Kevin. Raymond extended his hand formally, which broke a tiny piece of Kevin's heart, but the moment he took it, Raymond promptly swept him up in an embrace. "It is so good to see you," Raymond said. "Talking in our heads is not the same as having you in my arms. Nothing is."

"I've missed you, too," Kevin said. Something trembled and fluttered in his throat like a trapped bird. Since the last time they had seen each other, he had shared psychic intimacy with hundreds of people but only a scattering of awkward physical encounters. His biggest fear was that Raymond no longer felt that way for him, that his mask of heteronormalcy had become his face. To have Raymond say exactly what Kevin thought meant the world to him, so much so that he never questioned the preciseness of it, the mirrorlike quality of his own words coming from Raymond's perfect mouth.

"Did you solve the problem you mentioned?" Raymond asked as he led Kevin down the hall. In one room, a group of young people lounged on tatty couches, smoking cigarettes that gave off the sweet smell of campfires. A boy with no shirt and carved muscles levitated a silver tray across the room to a girl who licked her finger, pressed it to the tray, and came away with a square of paper tinier than a postage stamp, which she laid gently on her outstretched tongue. Their thoughts flowed together into a pool of glowing liquid, swirling with color so that Kevin could not tell where one of them began and the others ended. He paused in the doorway of the living room and watched as one of the boys knelt in front of the shirtless boy, unzipped the boy's pants, and delicately placed his cock in his mouth. Raymond and Bowen were a few steps ahead by the time Kevin wrenched his attention away.

Kevin looked at the couple engaged in oral sex and at Bowen. "I dealt with it," he said. One of Raymond's more annoying habits was leaving it to Kevin to handle problematic Resonants as they emerged and taking the high hand when it came to how Kevin handled them.

"I have some data I want you to look at," Raymond said. "Are you staying a few days? You could come to the labs with me on Monday."

"I could stay a little while," he said. "The real estate deal in New York that Davenport set up is supposed to close next week. There's paperwork."

"It's hard to imagine you working with Davenport," Raymond said. "He's a bit unscrupulous, isn't he?"

"He's a swindler," Kevin said. "He's secured me an entire block of Manhattan for the kind of money you could find in the cushions of a couch. But it's for the greater good."

"The school, yes," Raymond said, waggling his eyebrows. "But what about the little place he sold you up in Maine? Cui bono, my dear?"

Kevin blushed. He wasn't planning on telling Raymond about the bungalow on Oceanside Drive yet, and he'd never intended to tell him how he'd gotten it. Davenport had psychically bullied every owner on the street to sell at pennies on the dollar, as he had with the block in New York, and sold it back to Kevin at cost, hoping for a favor down the line.

"It was meant to be a surprise," he told Raymond. Raymond smiled, the smile that had always marked the end of Kevin's resistance. "Are you disappointed in me?" he asked. "Consorting with such low company?"

"I'm proud of you," Raymond said. "You've developed a pragmatic streak. And I can't wait to see the place." He kissed Kevin on the cheek like a priest absolving a sinner.

"Where's Mona?" Kevin asked. "I thought she'd be the first out to greet me."

"She's around somewhere," Raymond said, waving a hand dismissively. They passed the kitchen, where a young couple were sculpting a great swan out of water, their abilities working in concert.

"What are you up to here?" Kevin asked.

"A school of my own, I suppose," Raymond said. "A house for independent study. We do a lot of meditation work. Self-actualization. Nothing compared to your plans, of course."

"They're all so young," Kevin said. "And so pretty."

"None as pretty as you," Raymond said, but it had the flat tone of a bored, placating husband. "Come on; there's a girl upstairs I want you to meet. And Kevin, I'd like you to help her rather than *deal with* her."

The door looks out of place. The house was built on the cheap, and the doors were flat pieces of pine with brushed metal knobs, the same kind Kevin had had in his family's cramped Brooklyn apartment growing up. Except this one. It was made of rich dark wood, the handle burnished brass. When Raymond rapped a knuckle on it, it sounded like a bass drum being struck.

"Miss Moore?" Raymond said. His voice was gentle, solicitous. "I have someone here I'd like you to meet."

"I'll meet him at dinner," said someone inside.

"You haven't been down for dinner all week," Raymond said, a hint of chiding creeping in. "My friend is only on a brief visit. It would mean a lot to me if you'd speak to him."

There was a long pause before the doorknob turned. A young woman poked her face out of a thin sliver. She was black, not older than twenty, with high cheekbones, skeptical eyebrows, and her hair in the natural style popular on campuses, like a cloud of dark steam emanating from her head.

"This your friend?" she said.

"This is Mr. Kevin Bishop," said Raymond. He never missed an opportunity to highlight the fact Kevin never finished his degree. "You've heard me talk about him. He helps people like us when we have problems."

"I don't have problems," she said.

"Then step out and say hello," Raymond said. The girl glared at him as if Raymond had dealt her a cruel blow that Kevin didn't understand. She stepped back, and the door swung open. The room was dark inside, framing the girl.

"Come on in," she said, dejected.

Raymond nodded. "You two talk for a bit," he said. He handed Kevin a pair of candles and a book of matches, which Kevin looked down at, puzzled. "I'm going to check on dinner, and I'll be back up in a little while." He headed down the stairs, leaving the two of them standing on opposite sides of the threshold. The sound of two people aggressively fucking could be heard from the next room.

"Joey and Merilee," said the girl. "Or Joey and Tall Stephen. Or Joey and Veronica. Joey's basically a hard-on with legs."

"Sounds like a suboptimal housemate," said Kevin.

The girl shrugged. "Can't hear him in here," she said.

"We can talk like this if you want," Kevin said. "I don't have to come in. Also, I'm . . . not a hard-on with legs."

The girl laughed. "It's cool," she said. "Light that and come in."

Kevin pocketed one of the candles, then fumbled to light the other. When he managed to apply a lit match to the wick, he held the meager flame up for the girl's approval. "I'm Kimani," she said, giving him a hand wave in.

"Kevin," he said. He stepped over the threshold tentatively, as if he were crossing an invisible boundary rather than entering a closet.

"It's tiny," Kimani said. "It used to not be, but it's gotten smaller."

"Your room is shrinking?" Kevin asked. He explored the corners of the room with the candle. In the paltry light, it was difficult to make out colors, but the walls were black: they barely reflected the flame, casting back a portion of it and consuming the rest.

"It used to be a regular room," she said. "I used to be able to leave."

"You can't leave?"

"No."

"Have you tried?"

"No."

"You just know you can't?"

"It's like that," Kimani said. He caught hints of her expression in the candlelight. He took the other candle out of his pocket, lit it from the first, and handed it to her. She held it near her chin, lighting her face.

"Better," Kevin said. Kimani smiled. "How long have you been staying here?"

"Couple months," she said. "I took an intro to physics class with the professor. I'm studying to be a filmmaker."

"They have a whole program for that?" Kevin asked.

She tipped the candle side to side to indicate a shrug. "Probably have to major in English or something."

"When I was in school, there were fewer choices," said Kevin.

"And zero black people," Kimani said.

"A handful," Kevin said. "No black women that I can remember."

"I'm on a leave of absence," Kimani said.

"I took one of those," Kevin said. "Never went back."

"That's not really what I wanted to hear."

"I know it's not polite to ask," he said, "but what is your—"

"I don't have one," she said. "Professor swears I'm like you all, but I can't do anything special."

Kevin ran his hand along the wall. It was cold and bumpy. "Can I ask you a weird question?" he said. "This room. Did you pick it out yourself? When you moved in?"

"It wasn't this small when I picked it," she said defensively.

"I don't think it was here before you picked it," Kevin said. "I think this room is your ability."

"My ability is being trapped in a janitor's closet?"

Kevin let out a little laugh. "I know this keeps being weird, but can I come into your thoughts?"

Kimani considered for a moment, then shrugged. Kevin went into her mind and immediately saw the piece of her where her ability lived. He was looking at something he thought was impossible. Kimani's ability was connected directly to the Source, but it operated on some space that was between the source of where their abilities came from and the actual world. He pulled back out of her mind and looked around the room. He tried to orient himself, north-south, even up-down, and found that whatever cues he normally relied on were missing.

"We're in it right now," he said.

"In what?"

"Nothing I am about to tell you is going to make any sense," Kevin said. "When you opened that door, you pushed a bubble of the real world into a space that . . . isn't in the real world. There is some way that we can recognize each other as having abilities, and I think it's across an interstitial space. I think we're in that space right now."

"Cool," she said. "Can I leave?"

"I don't know," Kevin said. "But I think what's happened is that space is pushing in on this one. I think that space is bigger than space the way we think of it, and it's crushing your bubble. It's a matter of pressure."

"You were right about this making no fucking sense," Kimani said.

"Push back," Kevin said. "Instead of focusing on getting out, push the walls away from you. You should feel a tingle. It will feel like it's at the spot where the back of your skull meets your neck, but it's deeper than that. It's in what's called your parahippocampal gyrus. Can you do that?"

"Yeah, parahippo whatever," Kimani said.

Kevin waves this away. "Push out," he said. "Give yourself space."

Kimani stepped to the nearest wall and laid her palm against it. "Not like that," Kevin said. "In your head. Imagine this bigger."

In the sputtering candlelight, Kevin could see her eyes were closed, her forehead furrowed as she concentrated. He felt a shiver through everything as her ability moved out from her, shoving the walls backward until the room was too big to fit in the physical space it occupied.

Kimani opened her eyes and looked around. "Holy shit."

Kevin licked the tips of his thumb and forefinger and reached out to pinch the flame of Kimani's candle between them. He blew out his own flame, leaving them in the dark.

"What'd you do that for?" she asked.

"Imagine us a light," Kevin said.

"After that should I invent you a sandwich?"

"Imagine a light in between us," he said. "Or pull a floor lamp up from the ground. It doesn't matter. Everything within this space is yours to shape."

Kevin felt something move underneath his foot, and the dimmest light appeared at the height of their shins. It was the tip of a white tendril growing up from the black ground. As the tendril grew, so did the tip, and so did its light, until it was an ivory stalk with a glowing yellow globe perched on top of it.

"It's sort of phallic," Kimani said.

Kevin laughed. "So fix it," he said. Kimani closed her eyes. He could watch her now, see how little effort the shaping took her. Three branches extended out from the main stalk, each one dangling a light like a ripe fruit.

"That's better," she said. She circled around the tree, examining her work. "So this is my ability? I can shape the room I'm trapped in?"

Kevin rested his hand on the wall again, and the black calcified coating melted under his hand, running down like snot and revealing ivory walls underneath. "I don't think that's even the beginning."

At dinner, Kevin met Joey, the hard-on with legs, and Cassidy, the girl from the head shop whose Resonance had been so muffled by the acid she took at the start of her shift that Kevin hadn't noticed it when they met. He sat between Raymond and Bowen, who was kind enough to keep reminding him of the names of the twenty Resonants seated around the table, passing bread and vegetarian dishes back and forth like an elaborate card game. Raymond, who didn't seem to eat, pontificated on shifts nascent in the social strata: the death of capitalism and the end of mere humanity, the birth of the world to come.

"In Mesoamerican literature, the universe repeatedly dies to be reborn," he said. "Each time, there are new gods at the ready to take over from the dying ones. The 'gods' aren't beings or entities the way we think of a Judeo-Christian god as an omnipotent Santa Claus in the sky." This got giggles from the room. "They're idea sets. Ideologies that run their course, exhaust themselves, and die. We see these dying gods staggering in their last steps all around us. The God Money. The God Nation. The God Sex. As they die one by one, what new gods rise to take their place?"

The shirtless young man who'd been on the receiving end of the public blow job raised his hand tentatively.

"Us?" he offered.

"No, Arthur, and you don't have to raise your hand," Raymond said. It felt like a Sunday school class, not a discussion but the impression of knowledge on minds too young to comprehend it. These were children, absorbing rather than digesting the things Raymond told them. "Not us but the ideas we provide. New models for living in the world."

"So what are they?" Kevin asked, seated at Raymond's right hand. Raymond looked at him, flustered, startled to find another shepherd among his sheep. He considered the question, then gestured to the room.

"Look around, Kevin," he said. "You want to build a school. You want to replicate the old. Teachers and students. Knowledge poured from a pitcher to a cup like wine that's gone sour. How does newness enter? Where is the space for novelty and innovation? Here we learn from each other. We allow our ideas and experiences to combine, hybridize, in the pursuit of metamorphosis and breakthrough."

Kevin considered mentioning the evangelical dynamic Raymond had established with these kids or saying that every "hybridization" he'd seen was in pursuit of nothing more glorious than an orgasm. Instead he said, "It's a noble experiment, Raymond," and sipped the bathtub gin Raymond's disciples had made for his visit, which tasted so much like lacquer that he worried it would harden in his guts.

"We're so glad the professor is back," Bowen whispered to Kevin as people cleared the table.

"Where did the professor go?" Kevin asked loudly enough for Raymond to hear him. Before he could get an answer, Mona came in, looking harried. She carried a bag of groceries in one arm and in the other had a bundle that was unmistakably a baby. The rest paid no notice, but Kevin jumped up to greet her, rushing around the long table.

"Oh," she said. "I didn't know you'd be here." Kevin kissed her on the cheek, and she received the kiss numbly. "I was out getting groceries."

"Mona," said Kevin. "Who is this you've got with you? Raymond, how did you not tell me?"

Mona pulled the baby closer and lowered the grocery bags to the floor. "This is Laura," she said. "She's . . . a couple months old?" She seemed confused and embarrassed.

"May I see her?" Kevin asked. Mona looked to Raymond, who nodded with an expression of minor annoyance. Mona handed the baby over to Kevin, and he shifted her into a comfortable hold-ing position without waking her. "She's so beautiful," he said to Mona. "How could you not tell me?"

"You move around so much," Mona said. "We never know where to call." Kevin heard the words in his head a half beat before she spoke them, broadcast from Raymond to Mona, a script to be read aloud.

"There's more in the kitchen," Raymond told her. "Why don't you make yourself a plate while Kevin and Laura get acquainted?" Mona nodded and disappeared with the groceries.

Raymond resumed his sermon, and Kevin allowed his suspi-cions to fade in the face of little Laura, an entirely new thing in the world. He speculated whether she would be like her father or her mother, a common question that carried great stakes. This too faded, concern over what she might be subsumed in the miracle of what she was already. Laura demanded presence; she grounded Kevin in the moment and gave him an immediacy he hadn't felt since the night of the Trinity test. It was the feeling of the future pressing itself into the present so heavily that the two merged, the present became charged with potential. Everything was possible for Laura. Everything began with her.

All around Kevin and Laura, Raymond and his disciples rat-tled on, oblivious to the fact their replacement slept soundly in their midst.

Mona went to bed early, giving Kevin barely enough time to catch up. "I get tired lately," she said, looking mournfully at Laura before ascending the stairs. The rest stayed up drinking and philosophiz-ing, their numbers dwindling as people left in pairs, threes, and fours. Somewhere around midnight, the effort expended working with Kimani caught up with Kevin, and he excused himself, hoping Raymond would follow. Raymond responded with a curt good night and a kiss on the cheek and told Kevin he could take the third room on the second floor.

The room was furnished with a banker's lamp and a mattress on the floor that probably had been host to a dozen couplings or whatever one called the permutations beyond couplings. Thankfully, there were clean sheets folded at the foot. Kevin made up the bed and climbed in, clicking off the lamp. He replayed the last conversation he'd had with Raymond in his head. Had Raymond invited him? Was this intended to be more of a house call than a visit? Not telling Kevin about the baby was such a huge mystery that it shocked Kevin every time his mind came back to it, wounding him anew. His body was spent, but his mind reeled with anxiety, the psychic clamor of young people in enthusiastic lust creeping into the edges of his mind. Kevin lay awake for hours before he heard the creak of the doorknob turning, saw the hall light falling across the bare floor of the room.

"Are you up?" Raymond asked quietly.

Kevin sat with his back against the wall, and clicked on the lamp. "What are you sneaking around for? Can't you sleep with who you want?"

Raymond smirked and climbed in under the covers next to Kevin. "Are you jealous?"

"Of which one?"

"Of me for having my pick."

"What makes you think I haven't been out in the world having my pick?"

"I know you," said Raymond.

Kevin rested his head on Raymond's shoulder. "What are you doing here?" he said. "These children. An actual child!"

"I was worried you'd be upset," Raymond said.

"I am upset."

"It was an experiment that failed," Raymond said. "Last year Mona was ready to leave. I should have let her. But I wanted to keep her happy. It's not as if there wasn't an easier way. But I'd been trying to keep her leash slack."

"Her leash?"

"I thought a baby would be good for her," Raymond continued. "She was nearly too old to have one. She'd have someone to care for. I've never been that for her. Never needed her, really. I needed a person to fill a role, but it didn't have to be her. I think she forgot we were playing roles."

"She can't be happy here," Kevin said. "All this. It isn't like her. It isn't like *you*."

"It *isn't* like her," Raymond said. "I'm not certain it works for me either. It feels like a half measure."

"I'd hate to see the full measure," Kevin said. "Where did you go? They keep talking about you being away."

Raymond took Kevin's hand in his and ran his thumb along his forefinger. "Japan," he said.

Kevin sat upright. "Did you find it?"

Raymond nodded. "I found it years ago," he said. "I was back for a visit."

"You'd already found it?"

"Mona and I went to Tokyo in 1961," Raymond said. "There were rumors of a performance troupe that had been through the city doing impossible things. I caught up with them in Niigata. They'd heard me coming for days. They said they heard my song. They came from a village south of Hiroshima. A tiny fishing village on the coast called Onomichi." Kevin formed the name with his lips; it felt like a magic word in a storybook. "Everyone in the village was like us, Kevin. They don't call it Resonance. They speak of it in terms of song. Your ability. Your song."

"That's incredible," said Kevin. They had talked about the possibility that the bombs had induced Resonance. If it was true, there would be pockets near the bombing sites in Japan, not to mention Atomgrad, Monte Bello, Reggane, Lop Nur.

"We were even close about the distance," Raymond said. "Sixteen miles from ground zero. There were only a hundred people there, but *all of them,* Kevin. It's where the idea for this house began. I felt stronger there, away from *humans.*" There's a contempt in the way he pronounces the word, one Kevin hasn't heard from him before. "Surrounded by our people, my ability, my sense of identity, felt stronger."

"Was Mona with you?"

"I left her in Osaka," Raymond said. "I told her I'd be back in a day or two, but I was gone for a month. I couldn't bring myself to leave. I feel as if my heart is still there."

"We should go," Kevin said, taking Raymond's face in his hands. "You and I. And Laura. Laura must be like us. I can feel it from her, can't you?"

"No," Raymond said. He put his head onto Kevin's shoulder, and something between them was momentarily reversed. He couldn't tell what Raymond was saying no to: the possibility of them going to Onomichi together or the possibility that Laura was like the two of them.

"I went back a few weeks ago," Raymond said. "It was right after Laura was born. I can't explain what I thought it would be like becoming a father, but whatever I believed it would be, it wasn't. I didn't *feel* anything. Or if I did, it didn't compare to the feeling I had in Onomichi. I left instructions with the children here to take care of Mona and Laura. They think of them like pets. Basic feeding, cleaning, and occasional expressions of affection. I left enough money to keep everyone alive. I took leave from the college. I had no intention of coming back."

Why didn't you call for me? Kevin thought. *I would have left it all too. The school, the idiot role of itinerant savior. I would have thrown it all over in a second.*

"It was gone," said Raymond, as if in answer to Kevin's thought. "Burned. Abandoned. I hope it was abandoned. I didn't find bodies, but Kevin, everything was ash. Even if all of them had been in their houses, there would have been nothing left. I reached out in the Hive to find them, any of them. Nothing."

"The performing troupe," Kevin said. "They might know—"

"The troupe got lazy," Raymond said. "They came back, too close. They played two weeks in Takahashi. Long enough. It's on a different island, but it's only a ferry ride away. The fishermen there had seen things. They suspected things about the village. When the troupe appeared, they put two and two together." His body was rigid, and tears escaped like water from the fingers of a clenched fist. "That's how it will happen, Kevin. Someone will put two and two together, and then they'll burn us all."

Kevin held Raymond until his body relaxed. He kissed the top of Raymond's head, his thick blond hair. It had occurred to both of them in the last few years that they were aging slowly. He wondered if Raymond having Mona in his life made that more noticeable, a youthful Dorian forced to hang his weathering portrait in the living room for all to see. He lifted Raymond's face and kissed him, and grief transformed into a need that wasn't passion or lust. Kevin had suffered a loss, too: the promise of a heaven he hadn't seen burned to ash before he could witness it. The connection of their bodies was a substitute for that one, the volatile form of a more stable element. It was what they had and what they had to settle for.

When it was over and Raymond collapsed against his back, letting Kevin bear his full weight, Kevin looked back and saw that the door was open. Mona watched them from the hall, her expression blank. Upstairs, a baby was crying.

THREE

BLANK GENERATION

If home is the question,
the honest answers must all be elegant
forgeries.

—KAVEH AKBAR,
"The New World"

ON HOME

Emmeline has few places she thinks of as home. The house on Jarvis Avenue where she grew up. Kimani's room, wherever and whenever it is in the world. She never considers the Bishop Academy home. She was so nascent, barely a person, and the place became part of her. People say *I found myself there* as if there's a preexisting self to be discovered, left for them by someone else. Emmeline didn't find herself at Bishop. She built herself out of Bishop. She used it the way a house uses a forest; the two were contiguous, the latter an earlier stage in the life of the former.

For these few days, Hayden Cohen's tour bus is home. It's what Bishop would have been for her if she had stayed, what Bishop was for Carrie and Hayden. She's a whole person, fully formed but open to change, and she's in a place where she's accepted and loved. How else could she define home?

They make their slow way west as if no one told them they're running. When Emmeline says as much to Rafa, he laughs.

"Touring musicians are always running," he says. They sit together on the long bench near the front of the bus. Emmeline twists to look out the window behind her. Rafa plays with a ball of multicolored light between his hands, turning it this way and that so different facets shine.

"Running from what?" Emmeline asks. The way she sits means that when she turns toward him, they're nearly touching, and when he looks at her, their faces seem poised to kiss.

"We are running from ourselves," he says. His voice has a faux depth to it, and he gives Emmeline a look like he's said something incredibly deep, which cracks her up. It isn't the first time she's laughed at a boy flirting with her. There were boys in the Boulderado Hotel who tried to chat her up in the lobby, an unavoidable inconvenience. They threw out their lines, and when Emmeline laughed at them and not with them, they crumpled, defeated.

Rafa smiles and doubles down. "I haven't caught me yet," he says. He stands up and does a shoot from the hip gesture with his fingers, complete with *pew-pew* noises and a three-second rendition of the running man. He looks around as if to go, then remembers they're on a bus with no place to retreat to and sits back down. "So what kind of music are you into?"

Flirting is the lingua franca of the bus. It takes time to get used to. At first Emmeline assumes everyone is sleeping with everyone else. But the flirting is about play and making each other feel good. It's never lecherous, rarely even sexual. An outsider watching Rafa might think he was trying and constantly failing to fuck everyone on the bus. Kristal, the bass player, assures Emmeline it isn't so.

"Bad dynamics, fucking on the bus," she says, gnawing on a hank of homemade jerky a fan in Boulder gave them. "Rafa knows that; he's a good boy. We do a show, he'll chase down three, four girls a night, but he always seems sad about it. Doesn't keep score. I think he's in love with Hayden, but who isn't?"

Kristal is ace but has what she calls a "cuddling arrangement" with Newton the sound tech that she swears does not violate the "no fucking on the bus" policy. Jerrod the drummer has a boyfriend back home with whom he has a "loyalty arrangement" he claims is too complicated to get into.

"Cheating's like obscenity," he says while Daniel, the waifish costume manager, lounges in his lap. "I know it when I see it."

"And both of them look like a throbbing cock," says Hayden, throwing the whole bus into hoots and hysterics. Emmeline suspects that Hayden shifts their features, riffling through faces like a children's flip-book, their aggregate allure never in a single place. She's seen the big photos of Hayden postered in Boulder and knows it isn't true, but it feels right. When she closes her eyes and pictures Hayden's face, something is missing, the keystone against which disparate elements lean and hold. Hayden is stunning even before they speak, but their voice bypasses senses and travels nerve pathways that snake through pleasure centers like a river that winds through parched towns. Once they speak, no matter what they say, it's impossible not to fall in love with them. On their first full day out, Hayden harangues Lana, one of the roadies, with a string of expletives over a pedal rig left behind in Boulder. When Hayden walks away, Lana, in tears under the verbal assault, watches them go the way a puppy watches its owner leave for work.

Carrie expands her mandate so she's no longer Emmeline's keeper but everyone's. She takes stock of supplies and interviews each member of the band and crew on their abilities, assessing defensive potential, which for most of them is zero. Emmeline watches Carrie make her way through the passengers on the bus like a vulture circling overhead. Inevitably one night, Carrie comes to Emmeline in her bunk.

"There's something we need to talk about," she says.

"I'm sleeping," Emmeline says. She's not tired, but she likes hiding in the bunk and listening to the way the rest of them play off one another, improvising filthy songs and laughing at unfunny in-jokes.

"It sucks, but I have to ask," Carrie says.

"I can't do anything," Emmeline says, rolling over to face away from her. "My ability is broken."

"If they come for us again, I need to know what we have in our favor," Carrie says. "I need to know who can fight."

"Not me," Emmeline says. She wraps her hand around the shackle on her wrist, assuring herself it's still there. She has dreams in which it's gone, and she wakes gasping and grabs for it, sure the world is about to collapse into her.

"Hey, Carebear," Hayden calls from the front of the bus. "What's that Mountain Goats song about I hope we die?"

Carrie sighs, understanding that she's gotten all she's likely to. " 'No Children,' " she says over her shoulder.

"See, I knew she'd know it," Hayden says. "C'mere, sing the first line. I think it starts in C." Carrie lets the curtain drop. Alone in the tiny dark space, Emmeline listens to them singing, disjointed and off-key, bitter lyrics set to a joyful tune.

On the lunar landscape of Utah, Hayden insists on a detour into Monument Valley. Carrie argues against it, but she's outvoted, the first instance in which the bus has to resort to democracy rather than consensus.

"Play that Arthur Russell song about the moon," Hayden tells Carrie as the bus sails through an abandoned parks department checkpoint. They hold out the audio cord plugged into the bus's stereo system.

"I lost my iPod," Carrie says, patting her pockets. "It's at . . . it's back in Boulder."

"Oh, that *sucks*," Hayden says, dropping the cord. "You had that forever."

"Yeah," says Carrie. "Sucks."

Emmeline recognized Monument Valley as the backdrop for a bunch of the Westerns Kimani made her sit through. "It's like New York," Hayden says. "It's part of this mythic America, but also it's a real place. Everybody's been here before."

Hayden declares a mandatory picnic, proving the bus is not a pure democracy but a benevolent dictatorship. With Alyssa at the wheel, trying to find an appropriate spot, the rest gather looted snacks into something resembling a meal. When they stop and get out, Carrie reconnoiters the perimeter, checking for points of potential attack, divining escape routes. Lana and the roadies go into setup mode, laying out blankets on the clay-rich dirt. Everything burns bright red and orange. Kristal pantomimes giant slow-motion steps, and Newton talks into his curled hand, broadcasting bad pickup lines from mission control. Alyssa squints at the sky, where clouds float like dumplings in soup and the sun bears down full bore.

"We should find some shade," she says, shaking her head at the spot where the roadies have laid out the food. "Or some SPF one million."

"Nobody's going to live long enough to die of cancer," Hayden says, lighting a cigarette.

Emmeline makes them clump together for a selfie with the Polaroid in front of the bus, with a striated outcropping the shape of a perilous stack of quarters rising behind it. Rafa holds the camera because his arms are the longest. He balances it on an outspread palm. Emmeline worries it will fall and shatter in a spray of broken plastic, but he gets his thumb on the shutter button and snaps the picture as they all shout "moon!"

They huddle around the picture as it develops, their faces rising out of the surface. It looks as if all of them are singing, their lips pursed like a choir's.

"It doesn't really get the colors," Rafa says before the picture has fully resolved. Emmeline sees something unbearably beautiful in the photo, an iteration of the way she feels. Unwilling to let anyone else criticize the picture, she takes it from them, hiding it with the picture she took of Carrie in the hospice by accident.

After the picnic, everyone's exhausted and no one is willing to take a driving shift. Lana points out that it's Daniel's turn, and he says he's happy to do it if no one minds dying in a fiery wreck. They decide to stay the night in Monument. Some of them build lean-tos out of sheets, and others bunk on the bus.

Her skin sunbaked until it feels like the crust on bread, Emmeline is lured out of her bunk by the sound of Hayden playing guitar, something in a minor key, softly strummed to avoid waking anyone. They're singing quietly enough that the sound is a cloud around them. Emmeline approaches, trying to hear the words, but as soon as she's close enough to discern them, Hayden stops. They look at Emmeline and smile.

"Hey, Em-Bomb," Hayden says. "Did I wake you?"

Emmeline shakes her head. Maybe they had. The guitar wove into her dream; there was no telling if she came up from sleep to find it or if it burrowed into her and pulled her to waking.

"Carrie'll kick my ass if she thinks I'm keeping you up," Hayden says. "She thinks if you get enough rest, you'll be a weapon."

"I'm not a gun," Emmeline says.

"It's not such a bad thing to be," said Hayden. "Carrie and me, we were guns for a while."

"You fought?" Emmeline assumed Carrie was in the war. It's the only way she can understand the way Carrie is. She imagined Hayden outside of things like politics and time.

Hayden shrugs and strums the guitar. As they speak, their words lilt along melody lines, turning their story into a song.

"We fought to get out," Hayden says. "We were in the camp at

Topaz Lake together. Me and Carrie. Her boyfriend, Miquel. When the Pulse happened, some of us got out."

A small ember of pride glows inside Emmeline. *The Pulse didn't happen,* she thinks. *I did that. I helped get them out.* "Did you kill anyone?" she asks.

Hayden focuses on their left hand, leaning close to it, shaping it into an intricate claw. "People got killed," Hayden says. "Not nice people. But I don't know. Maybe no one deserves it. We didn't know where we were. We didn't know where to go. Everything was in flux. Going home wasn't safe. We didn't know if they were coming after us. The camp we were in was run by a private company. A conservative television network called Kindred. We didn't know how much they were linked up with local law enforcement or the feds. Somewhere along the way the camps were made official, which was a holy shit moment for us. We knew exactly who was after us, and it was everyone. The law didn't create the camps; it put the stamp of approval on them. The same assholes who kidnapped us in their plainclothes could do it in their uniforms. We were scared. We holed up in a motel, watching the war start at Bishop. We were watching our country attack the place we grew up."

The chords they're playing lift into a major key for a moment, then slink back.

"Ji Yeon Kim found us," Hayden says. "She was gathering troops, I guess. It wasn't technically the Faction. They never . . ." Hayden lays their hand on the side of their face. Their ring finger curls into their ear, and they wince uncomfortably. "She was finding people who'd be useful in combat," they continue. "I'd heard of Ji Yeon because of Revere. She was putting together liberation squads. That's what she called them. Groups to free the camps. It worked for me and Carrie. We wanted Topaz at the top of the list, but there were bigger camps down the California coast. Up in Bumblefuck, Montana, serious militia country. Ji Yeon promised we'd get there.

"We took out camps in Crater Lake and Emerald Bay. The men at Krupp Hollow laid down their guns and walked away, which was funny. I mean, not laugh out loud funny but funny they knew which way things were going. After Krupp Hollow was Chimney Park. I went into the mess hall wearing the commanding officer's face; Carrie had snuck up on him in his quarters that morning. A syringe full of methylprylon in the neck. Signature Carrie move." They smile and chuckle, recalling a fond memory. "I went in and 'inspected the kitchen,' which meant dropping thallium in the oatmeal. Poisoned breakfast for forty guards. By lunch they were doubled over with the shits. We walked back out and waited, then strolled right through the front gates."

"What about Topaz?" Emmeline asks.

"Carrie led twenty of us in," Hayden says. Something crosses their face, the inverse of the look they got remembering Carrie injecting drugs into people's necks. Antinostalgia. "They were *liquidating the stock*. That's what they called it. They lined people up in the yard and shot them. It was slow work because they had to drag off the bodies to a quicklime pit at the south fence. They didn't want anybody to know. We saw the pit before we got to where they were executing people. Carrie assumed Miquel was already dead."

They turn to Emmeline as if they had forgotten she was there. "They've been together since Bishop. They got married while we were in the camp. I almost forgot that." They smile, but it's a tiny, sad smile. "She lost it," Hayden continues. "She tore through guards with a knife, except you couldn't see her or the knife. The guards didn't know what was happening. They'd look down at themselves and"—Hayden stacks their hands on their belly, then looks down and opens them, palms upward, like they're catching a ball—"*oh, shit, my guts are on the outside.* One of them figured out someone was doing it, so he started firing at his friends. All of them, shooting at one another, and Carrie in the middle working her way through them with her knife. When it was over, we looked for survivors. There weren't many. Carrie went looking for Warden Pitt, who ran the place. Slimy fat nothing. He had to be there because he'd given the kill orders. He had to be around to make sure they were carried out. Carrie went into the trailer where he had his office. She came out drenched in blood."

"Was Miquel dead?" Emmeline asks.

Hayden shakes their head. "He locked himself and some of his kids in a fallout shelter under the community center. He was a teacher at the camp. They were in bad shape, but they were alive." Hayden looks around to see if there's a beer nearby, but there isn't. "Hey look, Em-Bomb, I'm going to turn in, all right? You should get some rest."

They lift Emmeline's curls and kiss her forehead, then head toward the bunks. Emmeline looks away before she sees which one Hayden climbs into, whether they're alone or joining someone. She picks up Hayden's guitar and plucks strings, disappointed they don't work under her fingers the way they did under Hayden's. She rests her forehead against the window. The spot Hayden kissed presses on the glass, transferring the kiss to the starred skyscape outside.

WICKER PARK

◇

It's easy to abandon everything once they make the choice to do it. On the drive from New York to Chicago, Clay has trouble thinking of things he'll miss. Their apartment, which, though small, was home. Coffee at Grumpy on the way to the Ruse. Mission Cantina for lunch and the twice-a-year splurge for dinner at Café Colette. The silver tabby that wanders the aisles at Molasses Books, which was reopened by one of the clerks after the owner left for the Wastes. The selection of otherwise impossible to find movies at the Video Vortex, owned by a couple, the wife a former festival curator with perfect visual recall and the husband with the ability to digitally encode other people's memories. Nothing couldn't be replicated. He didn't know much about Chicago, but they must have coffee and cats.

It's tougher for Dom; friendships are his profession. His network of contacts in New York and within the Bishop Foundation is a key part of his skill set. The move renders him professionally useless, starting him back at the bottom with a handful of leads.

Clay liked his coworkers well enough, but Dominic had a true affection for the people he worked with. They hung out outside of work; they came to one another's apartments for dinners and game nights. They bought presents for Rai on Christmas and sent cards to Clay on his birthday. They were friends without labeling themselves as such, and it pained Dom to leave them behind.

Rai has it worst of all. His friends at Berkeley Carroll were his whole world, and he's sullen the whole trip. There's a second loss he's mourning, too: a promise regarding his future, an idea of who he was going to be. After what happened in the Bronx, he asked Clay about it.

"So I'll never?"

"What we don't know adds up to more than what we know," Clay said. "But my boss is the expert to end all experts. And she thinks the people who weren't affected by the Pulse, no matter how old they were, aren't going to change."

"Did you ask her about me?" Rai said. "Did you ask if she could help?"

Clay promised he would. He'd gone through the elaborate steps of setting up the meeting in the Bronx rather than asking Fahima because he was spooked by the idea she'd report him. The loss of whatever potential ability Rai imagined for himself paled next to the pain of being severed from his friends. He held Clay responsible for both.

They pull up in front of a nightclub in Wicker Park that looks, by Clay's New York standards, divey and tacky. It's owned by his cousin's boyfriend. Clay wasn't close with his cousin growing up; his aunt and uncle claimed he ran away in his early teens when he'd been sent to the Bishop Academy years before the war, before most people knew about Resonants. Clay sheepishly tracked him down after the Pulse, and his cousin had been a sounding board for him since. When Clay told him about the situation with Rai, he chastised Clay for not coming to him first. "You messed around with those Nazis before you called me up?" But his anger was feigned; he told Clay to get them all to Chicago immediately and they'd work things out from there.

"Is this where we live now?" Rai asks. Two women who might be sex workers share a cigarette in the doorway.

"We have family here to help us out," Clay says. Dom makes a point of checking that the car doors are locked. One of the women gives them a neighborly wave as they enter the stairwell to the apartment above the club.

Bryce greets them from the top of the stairs, his natty outfit and pale birch bark skin making Clay instantly aware that the three of them look like they've been driving for days. "Get on up here; I want to see this kid of yours." He makes a big show of hugging Clay and Dom. "How was the drive?"

"Family road trip," Clay says. "Real wholesome stuff."

Bryce opens his arms to embrace Rai, but Rai holds out a hand stiffly. A new, fresh bitterness wells up in him. Bryce wears his Resonance on the outside, a reminder of what Rai might have been but now won't become. Bryce shakes Rai's hand respectfully and guides them into the apartment.

Bryce's boyfriend, Waylon, is so kind that it's nearly overwhelming. He's cooked them a big dinner, a huge roast with broccoli and biscuits. He's found a house for them but insists they can't go until they're stuffed. He pours generous glasses of wine for Clay and Dom and a thimbleful for Rai without asking. Rai looks at his dads, daring them to say he can't have it. Dom turns away toward the window that looks down on the street. All of the sudden, he makes a break for the door.

"They're stealing the car," he says.

Bryce holds him back with one massive arm.

"Those are my people," Waylon says. "They're moving the luggage over for you. Everything's taken care of."

Dominic chafes at having everything tended to this way. He's used to being the one who makes things appear and disappear with barely perceptible gestures. Before dessert, Waylon wins him over. "Bryce says you were in event planning."

"Bishop Foundation stuff, mostly," Dom says. "Office parties, that kind of thing."

"Bullshit," says Waylon. "Excuse my language. You did the Hassie Whitehead premiere and the gallery opening for Isidra Gonzalez. I do my research." Dom blushes. "My booking agent is leaving me at the end of the month. He wants to DJ full time, which is apparently a life choice people still make. It's not as glamorous as what you've been doing, but it's work if you want it."

"I would be thrilled," Dom says.

"So that's done," Bryce says. "Which brings us to you, Rai."

"I don't need a job," Rai says through a mouthful of broccoli.

"You need a school," Clay says.

"I teach at the Unity School in Hyde Park," Bryce says. "It's a pilot project, fully integrated."

"I'd have to go to school with people with abilities?"

"You *went* to school with people with abilities," Dom says.

"When I thought I was going to get some," Rai says.

"It's a normal curriculum," Bryce explains. "History, math, science."

"Sounds boring," Rai says.

"It's school, man," Bryce says, which gets him a halfhearted smile from Rai. "It'll get you papers to be anywhere in the city. If you hate it, you can play hooky and wander the streets."

"No, you can't," says Dom.

"What papers?" Clay asks.

"You have to understand, Chicago isn't the nonstop love-in people want to make it seem like," Bryce says. "The Accords mean the city is integrated, but the Faction can hassle you if you're a non-Resonant without papers."

"Sounds fucking great," Rai mutters.

"Rai!" says Dom, but Clay pats his arm to let it go.

"There's been a lot more Faction in town than we're used to," Waylon says. "Willis Tower's like an anthill, people going in and out all hours."

"He's being paranoid," says Bryce.

"I'm being straight with them," Waylon says. Rai gives a huff of a laugh under his breath, and Clay remembers the period in middle school when Rai decided he hated having gay dads. It clearly came from someone else, and it went away quickly, but this was the echo of when Rai was cruelly homophobic because their queerness made him different. "It's not just more Faction," Waylon continues. "People are split on keeping the city integrated. The divide between people who are for it and against it is getting more pronounced."

"We're getting protesters at the school from both sides," Bryce says. "That never used to happen."

"If this isn't going to work out, maybe we should keep moving," Clay says. "I don't want to be part of an exodus out of Chicago. We might as well get a head start."

"There's no better place for you to be than here," Bryce says. "You go west, they're not going to want you or Dom around. You go back east, they're not going to want Rai. You want to be a family? You stay here. Don't worry about Chicago. Chicago can keep its shit together."

I'M ON FIRE

◇

Carrie wakes in the middle of the night to a faint sound of music, thin and tinny. Emmeline is at the window watching the desert go by, one headphone in her ear and the other dangling at her waist. She's holding an iPod, the unmistakable blue-green glow of the screen lighting the underside of her chin.

"Where did you find that?" Carrie asks.

Emmeline turns around, surprised. She pulls out the earbud.

"It was in the bench," she says, holding it out to Carrie. "Down between the cushions. You can have it back. I was listening to the song Hayden was talking about, about the moon." Carrie takes it and scrolls the click wheel through the list of albums, although she knows from the pattern of scuffs on the metal back this is the iPod the bad man took from her in Boulder. A tenuous connection forms in her mind. Carrie pulls the Polaroid out of her wallet and shows it to Emmeline.

"Who are these people?" she asks.

Emmeline examines the picture. "You and Hayden and some random kids," she says. "You look like shit."

"I have a scar," Carrie says, pointing to the forked line that runs down her face in the photo. Emmeline looks at it, then at Carrie's face, as if the scar might have been there the whole time.

"In the picture you do," Emmeline says. The girl is a brick wall, which reminds Carrie how defenseless Emmeline is in other ways.

"Are you up?" Carrie asks. Emmeline nods. "There's something we need to work on."

"My ability is broken," Emmeline says. "It's not coming back. It's not getting fixed."

"This isn't that," Carrie says. Her hand rests on the lump the iPod makes in her pocket. She wants to add *I don't believe you,* but she needs to have Emmeline on her side. "There's something I need to teach you. In case something happens."

Emmeline eyes Carrie skeptically. "The people who came after us in Boulder didn't have psychics with them," Carrie says, "but they're going to figure out that was a mistake. When they restaff the Bloom, they'll add at least one reader. You need to learn to mask yourself psychically. There's this technique they taught us in school—"

"My mind is a cool white flame," Emmeline says, rolling her eyes.

"You said you never learned it."

"I said I never had class with Sarah," she says. "Kimani taught me. I'm not as helpless as you think."

"I don't think you're helpless," Carrie says. It's not optimal; learning psychic defense without a psychic to defend against is like learning to kiss by watching rom-coms. But it's not as if having Carrie training her would be any better.

"What did you mean, restaff the Bloom?" Emmeline asks.

"A Bloom is always five," Carrie says. "When an agent is decommissioned, they restaff."

"How many did you *decommission* in Boulder?" she asks. She's cautious with the word, as if it might break open and reveal what it holds inside.

Carrie flinches. It's an easy question to lie about, but she's gotten away with enough omissions with Emmeline. "Three," she says.

"My friend is one of them," Emmeline says.

"One of them is a friend of mine, too," Carrie says, then catches herself. "You have to not think about them that way. They aren't who they are anymore."

"She's still my friend," Emmeline says.

"When you join up, they put something in your head," Carrie says. Her hand goes to the side of her face, covering her ear. "It's this voice that tells you what to do. Sometimes. Even when it's not telling you what to do, it makes you feel bad. It makes you angry all the time."

"You have one," Emmeline says. She reaches out and rests her fingertips on Carrie's face above the eye, where the scar is in the picture. It's gentle but makes Carrie flinch.

"Yeah."

"When?" Emmeline asks.

"After Topaz," Carrie says. "Miquel and I and Hayden, we went back to Chicago. There wasn't as much fighting there; we were trying to keep the peace. But I didn't *want* peace. I was still angry. It might have been easier if they'd killed Miquel. When I thought they killed him, then got him back, that was worse. He was in bad shape, more than I could handle. But it was more like I made a decision to be this person who needed revenge. I became her. And then I didn't need to be her anymore, but I still was. I didn't stay in Chicago more than a week. I went and joined up with the Faction for real. They put this thing in my head. They said it was for communication. But it made me feel different, like I wasn't myself."

"It's still there?"

"Not the first one," Carrie says. "We went into the school in Houston. The army or whatever was holding it. They had kids hostage. The whole school was rigged up with a blast inhibitor. One big flash and my ability was gone. I got out before they blew up the building with everyone in it. All the kids. The rest of my Bloom.

"But the little voice was gone, too. For the first time in months I wasn't getting orders. No one in my head but me. I wasn't in a place where I could make decisions for myself. They found me wandering around. They put in a new one, and I was joined up with a new Bloom. Thandi and Martin. Martin I knew from school. Thandi joined the Faction after Houston. She was kind at first. Kinder than I was. I liked her. When I saw her in the woods, all that kindness was gone."

"It was like that with Viola," Emmeline says. "My friend. Like something was missing."

"She must have replaced me after I left," Carrie says.

"How did you get out?"

"The war was over," Carrie says. "We wiped out Denver; they bombed Boston. We could have kept going like that until everyone was dead, but they gave up. Separation was the main condition of the Armistice. We got the east, up to Chicago. Whatever was left of the West Coast had been out of anyone's hands for months. They got everything in between. Millions of people had to get out because the country wasn't theirs anymore. We were evacuating towns and cities. It was ugly. People were so beaten down, so helpless. The little thing in my head buzzed constantly, egging me on. When I pushed against it, it pushed back. It was easier to listen. We cleared out my hometown. My dad and my brother, I chased them out of their house.

"Once everyone who could move was gone, we started going through the hospitals. They'd gotten everyone out they could, but there were people they left behind. The generators were running; they had set things up so people would last as long as possible. I wish they'd—it would have been simpler for the doctors to go through with morphine or whatever and—I knew when we got there. I knew this was the hospital where my mother was. That thing in my head kept showing me memories of her, all the worst things she ever said to me. It pulled up moments when I wanted her there and she wasn't. It wanted me to understand my mother as an absence in my life so I could go into that hospital and do what it wanted me to do.

"I pushed back as hard as I could. I've heard that some of the replacements, right after Houston, never worked right. The first ones, Patrick put in himself. These, they had racks of test tubes. They poured them in." She touches her ear again. "Maybe I was lucky. I did what Sarah taught me and imagined my mind as a cool white flame. I pushed down and became as invisible as I possibly could. I wasn't sure I existed anymore. That would have been better, to stop rather than to go in. It felt like slipping my head out of a noose. It felt like when you pull the headphones off and the whole world of sound comes rushing back in."

"Do you still hear it?" Emmeline asks.

"It's mostly static when I do," Carrie says. She cups her hands in front of her mouth and does an impression of a shitty radio signal. "Do you read me—*zork*—this is—*brrzzzk*—Ice Station Zebra, command control, do you read?" Emmeline smiles. "More often it's a feeling. An anger I'm not sure is mine. That's harder."

"Maybe Fahima can fix it," Emmeline says.

"Maybe," says Carrie. She wonders if she wants it fixed. It's been years, and she hasn't done anything but manage it. She thinks of Miquel as the one who's broken, ignoring the cracks in herself.

Carrie taps the iPod in her pocket. "Thanks," she says. "For finding this." She goes to the front of the bus and takes the seat next to Rafa. "Where are we?" she asks.

"You familiar with nowhere?" he says. "We're somewhere near the middle."

"We need to make a stop."

Rafa shakes his head. "Already talked with Hayden about it. The Grand Canyon is overrated, and I am ready to be done with this magical mystery tour."

"It's right off the highway near Flagstaff," Carrie says. "There're people I want you all to meet."

TAKEOVER

Fahima prefers to work underground. She thinks of it as hiding what she does from the eyes of God. When she putters in a basement of the Ruse reachable only via a staircase left off any blueprint of the facility, which she accesses through a false back wall in an unused supply closet, divine eyes aren't the ones she's hiding from. She wonders if the reason none of the Tuning Fork devices upstairs work is that they were conceived and built in the cold light of the sun. Their progenitor was made in the basement at Bishop, and it worked like a charm.

Fahima cleans up at the utility sink and climbs the stairs. She waits a moment in the closet, hoping she can exit unseen. She presses a button built into the necklace she's wearing, and the world goes into soft focus. It's a new device, and she isn't happy with it yet. It approximates the ability of one of her old students, but it doesn't make Fahima invisible, only slightly less noticeable. Before she opens the door, she knows something isn't right. It's loud in the hallway, the normal bustle of voices amplified, electric.

With the device on, she'll be seen but not noticed, so Fahima opens the door.

Her math teacher at Bishop, a Stanford professor who dropped out of his "normal" life when a student discovered his ability, told them there were different sizes of infinities. The infinite set of whole numbers contained within itself an infinite set of even numbers, half as large but infinite. Between any two whole numbers lay an infinitely regressing set of fractions, a Zeno's paradox of tinier and tinier steps between 1 and 2. The teacher delivered this concept with revelatory weight. He built pauses into the lecture so he could hear the soft poofs as teenage minds were blown. It was a sermon to convert them to the gospel of math, turn students into acolytes. This was God winking at them from between digits.

Because she had been raised Muslim, the idea of the infinite wasn't news to Fahima. But she was intrigued, obsessed with infinities that varied in size. Were they nested like Russian dolls? Was there one infinity studded with others like fruit in a Jell-O mold? It was intuitive: the set of even numbers would have to be half the size of the set of whole numbers. At the same time, it was completely ridiculous. Infinity should be an end point. There ought to be nothing beyond.

As she steps into the hallway, this teenage revelation returns to her as applied to chaos. Chaos ought to be an ultimate state, the complete lack of order. But the Ruse is a broad chaos dotted with smaller ones. Tendrils of it pull passengers from the train car, eager to infect them. It wants to speak its gospel, share its news. Each little chaos is a mechanism in a sprawling, encompassing chaos, which is an entity entirely its own. It takes the form of a frenetic stasis. People move around doing nothing. A public address system Fahima wasn't aware that the Ruse had chimes. A deep baritone voice speaks.

"Employees of the Roosevelt Island Research Facility," it says.

"Please proceed in an orderly fashion to the New Deal for a presentation. Refreshments will be provided." Another chime signals the end of the message.

The employees of the Ruse herd themselves back toward the entrances and into the New Deal. By this point, most have stopped chatting among themselves. Speculation is no fun with a total absence of facts. To continue, they need a couple of clues: something strange an Omar said, a blind item news story. Fahima joins the silent march to the bar. She falls in with a group of Omars, and when the opportunity presents itself, she tugs on one of their sleeves. Omar Six turns and looks at her, puzzled for a second.

"Why are you here?" he says. "And why are you all fuzzy?"

"What's going on?" Fahima asks.

"We have no idea," he says. "But it can't be anything good."

"They're gathering us up to liquidate us," says Roxane, one of the Tuning Fork operators, once they're crammed into the New Deal. "Project's over, and we're security risks. Bet on it." Fahima wants to tell Roxane this isn't true, but she's not sure herself. Everyone is cheek to jowl. Each individual's nervousness conducts itself into those they're pressed up against until the room is one antsy, twitching mass. Waitresses weave and squeeze their way through the anxious crowd, holding trays of champagne flutes aloft. Roxane takes one when they come around.

"It's ten-thirty in the morning," Marlon says.

"This is the cigarette they give you before the firing squad," Roxane says. She drains her glass and signals for another, but the waitress is a hand supporting a tray, bobbing above a sea of human heads. With the addition of alcohol, the anxiety softens and turns benign. There's a buzz in the room as if a piece of art is about to be unveiled. Whoever's making the decisions is waiting until everyone is some combination of worked up and intoxicated. The Ruse's employees get loose and chatty about whether they're all about to be killed or fired. *Get on with it already*, Fahima thinks, tired of being an audience member for a show she's supposed to be directing.

The front double doors of the New Deal open, and Ji Yeon's Bloom enters, restaffed back up to a full five. They're grouped around two figures Fahima can't make out from where she's standing. The crowd parts to make room for them, compressing to a higher density to avoid making any physical contact with members of the Faction. When the Faction went through its first big expansion two years after the Armistice, there were rumors that they could recruit you by touch. Those rumors evolved into a superstition that if a Faction member touched you, they had surveillance on you forever, like a witch leaving her mark. None of it's true, and no one *really* believes it. They shy away all the same.

The Bloom parts like a curtain to reveal who they've escorted here. Standing next to Patrick Davenport, who looks as if he has a bad flu, Cedric Joyner smiles out on the crowd. The shudders and gasps of the Ruse employees are muted by the fact that he's been escorted here by the Faction and the fear of being seen by a full Faction Bloom as noncompliant, but the return of the disgraced Cedric Joyner, the Ruse's own private Mengele, to Roosevelt Island is received like the sudden appearance of a ghost. Coupled with a rare public appearance by Patrick Davenport, it's enough to distract the employees from any concerns about their own well-being.

Cedric wears a suit tailored so tight he looks bound up in it, fifty-some snakes compressed into an Armani. He'd always had a primness to him, the look of an ascetic and self-flagellant. Cedric and Fahima were both true believers when it came to Resonance, but Cedric was less interested in the superiority of Resonance than in the inferiority of Damps. Creating a new Resonant was a way of wiping out a Damp—universal Resonance as a socially acceptable form of genocide. The patch Cedric sports over his right eye is new but fitting. *You finally look the part, you vicious fuck,* Fahima thinks.

Patrick steps forward to address the crowd. "Ladies and gentlemen," he says. "I know it must come as a shock to see myself and members of the Black Rose Faction here. The Black Rose Faction has always respected the sanctity and independence of this facility, and I personally consider the work done here of the highest importance. Truly, the vision of who we are going to be as a nation is being birthed here." He holds out his hands and applauds them all with a dainty golf clap. "In particular, the progress of Project Tuning Fork has been of interest. I believe success in this project is all that separates us from a lasting peace with the rest of the world. Which is why it's pained me to see the project struggle. I've decided it's time to involve myself directly. I've been lucky enough to secure the talents of someone who is intimately familiar with what you've been doing here. Cedric Joyner will be the new interim director of Project Tuning Fork. Mr. Joyner, would you care to say a couple words?"

"My friends," Cedric says. "I cannot express how good it is to see you all again. I wish it were under better conditions. Given the volatile juncture at which we currently stand, the Black Rose Faction recalled me from my studies to come back and contribute my knowledge to the project and help us reach the goals that are so near to our grasp."

Fahima waits for someone to speak up. Cedric's sins weren't just horrible, they were public knowledge. When Cedric disappeared, there was no rumor too atrocious to be true. The most horrific theories were favored because they fit with what people already thought of him, and the truth about what he'd been doing in his satellite lab in the Bronx was on par with people's worst imaginings.

One night, Fahima got Omar Eleven drunk and asked him

about it. Eleven had been on the crew that was sent in to clean up after Cedric. "Sci-fi horror show shit," Omar Eleven said. "Resonant limbs Frankensteined onto Damp bodies, flaming red with infection at the graft site. People still alive with their skullcaps popped open, waiting for him to try different brains on them like hats. A couple of us asked to be reabsorbed after. I still see shit sometimes."

Cedric's voice drips with the glee of someone who's gotten away with something, or who's gotten caught and still profited from his crime. Fahima can't help but imagine he's speaking directly to her, rubbing his victory in her face. "In the next few days, Mr. Davenport and I will be talking with all major stakeholders to plot our course moving forward. Mr. Davenport and the Black Rose Faction are making efforts to secure us certain resources that were previously thought out of our reach, and they will be working closely with us until the project is complete. Which, given a broad assessment of the data, I believe will be on a much shorter schedule than any of us dared hope. I'm so impressed with the progress you've made while I was away."

A murmur passes through the crowd, quickly chilled by a minor motion from one of the Faction agents that could have been a lunge. Cedric has accidentally strayed close to one of the open questions about him. Where did he go? He should have been in prison. Fahima enjoys imagining that he lost that eye to a jailhouse shiv. But he's come back an all-conquering hero, complete with an honor guard. So from where?

"I'll be calling several of you in for meetings this afternoon," Cedric continues, "but I don't mind if things are a bit candid. Please, enjoy yourselves. Think of this as a celebration of how far we've come and a moment to contemplate the brave new world that lies ahead. Thank you all for your time."

Tepid applause follows as Cedric begins glad-handing through the crowd like a candidate for local office. Even those out of his earshot don't seem inclined to talk. With the Faction here, the notion that anything on the Ruse is out of earshot now seems naïve. People talk niceties, aware they are being watched. The funny thing is that they talk like this all the time. The expectation of listening devices and eavesdropping psychics is a way of life. It's only when people notice the red light blinking on the security camera or catch a stray thought that isn't their own, mental chaff from a clumsy psychic scan, that they become aware they're self-censoring.

"Now we're going to get somewhere," says Thao Bui, one of the last operators Fahima hired. He's a blunderbuss, no focus. "Now we're going to see some serious weird science shit. Did you hear him all Brave New World? That is what I'm talking about."

"Yeah," Roxane says. "Hooray for us." Fahima reaches out, about to put her hand on Roxane's shoulder, but she doesn't have anything comforting to add. She thinks about the device hidden in the basement, about the data she's been fudging, making some of the operators, like Thao, look less effective until she can get their fatality rates down. She wonders where Emmeline Hirsch is at that minute and how much time any of them have left before a whole lot of people die.

ON COMMERCE

◇

It's morning, and Hayden has promised this is the day they hit Phoenix. Rafa's been driving all night but insists he's fine, and when the van veers toward an off-ramp near Flagstaff, Emmeline immediately checks to see if he's nodded off.

"What are we doing?" Hayden calls from the middle bench.

"Carrie wants to go shopping," Rafa says.

"It's a little stop," says Carrie. "We'll stay the day and get back on the road tomorrow."

Hayden looks at her, their face pleading. "Can't we just get there?" Hayden asks. "Can't we be done?"

"One stop," Carrie says. Exasperated, Hayden heads back to the bunks. Off the expressway, Rafa routes the bus toward a massive sprawl of a building. It's been so long since Emmeline's seen a mall, she has trouble recognizing it for what it is. The word comes back to her and feels strange in her mind, like a word in a dead language, something a tour guide says as he leads you through ancient ruins.

"That's it," Carrie says.

"Where should I park?" Rafa asks. The parking lot is half full, studded with cars rusting out on flat tires.

"There," Carrie says, pointing to a white arch over one of the entrances that doesn't go directly to a store. She grins broadly, which Emmeline's sure she's never seen. Emmeline wonders what would happen if the thing in Carrie's head took over. Maybe it would put exactly that grin on her face.

They get out of the bus, and Emmeline's unsure whether to take her things with her. Carrie's the first one out, but since she doesn't have anything, Emmeline can't use her for guidance. They fall into a triangle formation like geese, with Carrie in the lead. She approaches the doors, and Emmeline gasps as they slide open on their own. It's everyday magic, but she forgot about it, along with malls and school and all the other things she used to take for granted.

The hallway of the mall feels vast and bright, vaulted ceilings of reinforced glass honeycombed with supports like a cathedral made of crystal. It isn't only the sunlight through the ceiling: the fluorescents are working, too, and as she feels the cool air on her face, Emmeline recognizes the thrum of commercial air-conditioning.

"Guys, it's me," Carrie yells. "I brought friends. Come out and say hi." Her words echo in the empty space, nearly drowned by the whoosh of cooled air. Four boys, each younger than Emmeline, emerge from around the corner, in the main concourse of the mall. They're dressed in overly large business suits cinched with belts and clumsily tailored.

"Killer Carrie!" one of them shouts. "What are you doing out this way? Come on out, y'all, it's Carrie." He hugs Carrie in the enthusiastic three slaps on the back way boys hug one another. Emmeline detects movement from every direction. From each shop, packs of teenagers are watching them, peering out from behind empty display racks for vitamin supplements and hair care products. They all look as if they've been outfitted from their parents' closets. Prom dresses and pantsuits, pleated khakis and tuxes.

Carrie takes Emmeline's hand and pulls her forward. "This is Tuan," she says, introducing the boy she'd hugged. "He's sort of in charge."

"Nobody's in charge of anything," Tuan says. "I'm the one Carrie doesn't scare shitless, so they send me out whenever she breezes into town."

A group of kids hovers around Hayden, hanging back and starstruck. One of them glows, a purple aura radiating from her skin.

"You're—" Emmeline starts. Tuan nods. He draws a circle in front of him, his finger tracing a bright line in the air. When the circle is complete, the space inside it shimmers like a pool of mercury. He reaches his hand through, and it disappears. At the same moment, a finger taps Emmeline on the shoulder. She turns to see his disembodied hand emerging from an identical circle, waving at her. He pulls his arm back, and both circles disappear. Some of the girls near Hayden giggle.

"Everybody here is," he says. "We're a sort of . . . home for wayward Resonants."

"They all resonated out here in the Wastes after the war," Carrie explains. "Tuan and these guys find them and bring them here."

"Not all of them," Tuan says. "We only have so much room. And some we don't get to in time."

"Carrie helps," chirps a girl in an oversized University of Arizona football jersey. "She brought me here."

Carrie blushes and looks at her shoes. The girl sees her opportunity and rushes over to hug her. These moments of sweetness and vulnerability from Carrie keep catching Emmeline off guard.

"Let's get you all some food," Tuan says. He eyeballs Carrie's outfit. "And some clothes. You look like ass."

Clothing, it turns out, is one resource they haven't run short on. The retail stores were stocked up for the holidays when the mall shut down, and there's enough Brooks Brothers and Laura Ashley to keep everyone comfortably, if unfashionably, clothed. There's a barter market on upcycled outfits made by the handful of residents with an eye for design. Fashion subcultures have developed: pseudo-punk tearing and staples as stitching, glam pirate aesthetics, maximum skin exposure.

"We picked here because it was easier than trying to get a hundred houses up and running again," Tuan explains. "Heating and cooling, air filtration, plumbing. The mall's practically its own grid. It's like a spaceship in the suburbs."

"There's a sick bay up in the Metro Mattress on the second floor," Carrie tells Alyssa. "They've patched me up a bunch of times. Maybe you can give them some tips."

"I bet it's a horror show," Alyssa says, but there's a note of excitement in her voice. She's been disconnected the whole way out, and Emmeline figures she's used to being more useful. She asks one of the suit-wearing boys to take her right there while the rest of them head to the food court.

"Don't get your hopes up for Arby's or whatever," Tuan says. "We burned through most of the food supplies in the first couple weeks, anything that wasn't spoiled. The saddest thing was, when we still had it, no one knew how to cook anything. You'd be amazed how many ways you can fuck up a frozen Burger King patty."

"So what do you eat?" Emmeline asks.

"We raise vegetables in the atrium," he says. "A couple kids can transmute raw material into organics for proteins. It's not good, but if you cook it right, it's edible."

At the counter of a Johnny Rockets, a teenage boy in an apron and hairnet serves them each a tray of broccoli studded with cubes of something spongy that reminds Emmeline of the tofu her mother used to force on them when she got on a health kick. It's drowned in a brown sauce that's thick and salty and is the greatest thing Emmeline can remember eating. She wolfs it down, eliciting a respectful nod from Tuan, and sheepishly goes back for seconds. "It's really great," she tells the kid behind the counter, who goes tomato red as he refills her tray. As she goes back to her seat, she notices kids leaning over the railings of the mezzanine, watching them. *They're watching Hayden,* Emmeline corrects herself, and to prove her point, a trio of girls approach Hayden with a poster and a Sharpie.

"I'm in the band, too," Rafa says through a mouthful of broccoli, but the girls don't seem to hear him or care.

"My parents kicked me out as soon as they figured out what I was," Tuan says, answering a question no one has asked. "Some of these kids lost their folks in the war. Rest of our folks didn't want us. So fuck all that. Blood's got nothing to do with family anyway. Not anymore."

There has to be some word past *friendship,* short of *family,* Emmeline thinks, that accounts for the bonds these kids have. She thinks about Kimani, her almost-mother, and how often her mind strains at the borders of language, wishing she had the proper term for the enormous love she felt, a word that wouldn't wipe away the memory of her real mother but put the two in a mutual orbit, memory and presence in a constant spiral around her heart.

Alyssa has found her happy place, organizing and labeling supplies in the mall's makeshift medical wing. Hayden allows a group of kids to talk them into playing a set in the center concourse. "I feel like a pop star from the nineties," they say to Carrie as they rally the troops to load in gear from the bus. Emmeline doesn't necessarily want to join Carrie looking for clothes; the idea of spending a couple hours apart is certainly tempting. She also has to admit her clothes are not in the best shape, so they set off exploring.

The first clothing store they pass specializes in bridesmaid and prom dresses, but they go in anyway. Emmeline holds up a bright yellow dress with puffy arms for Carrie, who winces. Emmeline tosses it aside and keeps searching the rack. She finds something navy blue that she can imagine her mother might have worn. "This might work for you," she says. "It's almost black."

"I don't always wear black," Carrie says. "You've only seen me in this one outfit."

"One *black* outfit," Emmeline says.

"I want T-shirts and jeans," Carrie says. "This mall has got to have an Old Navy or something."

"I'll give you five bucks to try this dress on," Emmeline says.

"What am I going to do with five bucks?"

"I thought that's how you work," Emmeline says. "You do jobs for money. Like a mercenary."

"I don't do jobs for money," Carrie says. "I get paid most of the time, but that's not why." Carrie holds out a dark red dress that flares out at the waist. Emmeline takes it, running the cloth through her hands.

"That color's good," Carrie says. "For you."

"Short sleeves," says Emmeline. She hands it back.

"It's a hundred fucking degrees out," Carrie says.

"I don't wear short sleeves." Rather than try to explain, she rolls up the sleeve of her sweater and shows the scars above her bracelet. Carrie takes her forearm in her hands and inspects it the way a jeweler inspects a diamond, looking for a flaw.

"Water burn?" she says. Emmeline nods. Carrie lifts her shirt to expose her midsection. There are two puckered scars, like eyes squeezed tightly shut. "Stab wounds," she says. "Bayonet from when we liberated the camp at Alta Mons in Virginia. The guards were Civil War reenactors. They were shooting at us with fucking muskets." She reaches her left hand around the side of her head and pulls her hair up and back. When it's held taut, Emmeline can see a line snaking from her temple along the back of her skull. "Kenny, the other guy in my Bloom, accidentally hit me with a bolt when we were evacuating . . . Detroit, maybe. Could have been Buffalo. Some place that sucked to begin with. Thandi had to drag me out of there. I was unconscious for hours."

"Thandi who you decommissioned," Emmeline says. "And Kenny who is probably still after us." Carrie nods. "Is there a lesson in all this?" Emmeline asks, rolling her sleeve back down.

"They're just scars," Carrie says. She lets her hair fall back and folds the navy dress over her arm. "We all get hurt, and we all get up."

Emmeline continues along the dress racks, but all the dresses are for summer weather. She wonders who it is she's hiding the scar from and if there isn't something beautiful about it that she's misunderstood her whole life.

"Why'd you bring us here?" she asks Carrie.

"The dress store?" Carrie says. "I thought it'd be funny. Seriously, I want to find a Gap or something."

"Here, to this mall," Emmeline says. "We could be there already."

Carrie picks another dress off the rack, a floral print Emmeline can't picture her ever wearing. "I wanted to give you the option," she says. "You're older than the other kids, but you could stay if you want. You could stop here and stay."

"What about your job?" Emmeline says. "What about whatever I'm supposed to do?"

"You could forget all of that," Carrie says. "Spend some time today, think about it. In the morning, if you want to keep going, we keep going. If you want to stay, we leave you here and I tell Fahima I couldn't finish the job."

Emmeline considers what she'd be giving up if she stayed here, but she has so little conception of what anyone wants from her. She thinks about her role in the Pulse, how important that had been and how much it changed things. If she could do something on that scale again, she owed it to the world to do it. Except she can't say the Pulse had been a good thing. It set all this in motion. People died because of it. She wonders if she can judge a thing like that, if she can take in the full scope.

"Come on," says Carrie. "I think I saw a Hot Topic downstairs. They do great outfits for the young and brooding."

Not sure whether Carrie's talking about Emmeline or herself, Emmeline follows.

I THINK WE'RE ALONE NOW

◇

The band plays nine songs: four of their bigger hits from the first couple albums, three new songs, and two teenybopper pop covers Hayden taught the band that afternoon. The set runs forty minutes, but it's twice that long before Hayden can extricate them from the crowd.

"You need to find me a place where I can hide," they tell Carrie. Rafa and Kristal decide to hang out with the fans while Jerrod, stricken with the munchies, scopes out the food court for snacks. Hayden pokes Rafa in the chest with a finger before they leave. "Jail. Bait." Carrie wonders if Rafa is a huge slut or if these are roles they play on the road, easy ways of being with one another.

She leads Hayden to the third floor, where there's a security office with a door that locks. Inside, there's a wall of nine monitors and posters listing the maximum penalties for shoplifting. Carrie sits in the high-backed armchair in front of the monitors and presses buttons on the keyboard until they all come to life, casting a gray pallor over the small room. Hayden glistens with sweat, their hair askew after the pogo dance they did during the encore's rendition of "Call Me Maybe."

"You know I'm really proud of you, right?" Carrie says.

Hayden looks at her and rolls their eyes dramatically. "Thanks, Mom."

"Out of all of us, you became exactly who you were supposed to be," Carrie says. "None of it affected you."

"It all affected me," says Hayden.

"It didn't stop you," Carrie says. "That's all I meant."

"Did you know there's a thing your face does when you're not telling me something?" Hayden asks, touching the corner of Carrie's mouth. "A pout of your lips right here. You do it when you talk about Miquel. You do it when you talk about the war."

"And now."

"No," Hayden says, "but I thought I'd mention it right this minute. So what are you leaving out?"

"I'm worried we're into something too big," Carrie says.

"We might be," Hayden says. "I don't know, because you haven't told me anything about what we're doing. Or why I haven't talked to you in forever. Where have you been, Carrie?" Hayden strains their neck forward, nodding and breathing through clenched teeth. "It's been three fucking years." It's a quiet shout, a reprimand and an accusation. Carrie's first impulse is to push against it, to shout back.

"It's hard to see you," she says. "It reminds me."

"Bryce was there, too," Hayden says. "He gets to see you all the time." They're pleading, as if Carrie can give them back those years. Bryce *was* there. Hiding in the woods for days while guards from Topaz Lake tracked them down with dogs. Watching the fighting break out at Bishop from a hotel, trying to decide if it was safe to go back to Chicago, even to contact Waylon and let him know they were okay. But Bryce had wisely noped out when they joined up to free the camps and encouraged Carrie to do the same. Carrie insisted it was about Miquel when it wasn't. Bryce took a ride back to Chicago. He and Waylon had started building the support structures people would need after the war was over. He went and did the hard work while Carrie and Hayden did the easy, ugly work of revenge, and when that was done, Hayden found their way out, too. Only Carrie went back.

"I don't like thinking about it either," Hayden says. "But you could have called. We could have been working through it together." She hasn't talked to Hayden, but she's talked to Bryce *about* Hayden. She knows Hayden's done more to work through those months than she has; her solution was to avoid the subject.

"I know," she says. Hayden weighs this to see if it'll pass as an apology and decides it's the best they're likely to get.

Hayden tents their fingers, and because Carrie knows Hayden, she knows some version of what they're about to say. "Listen. Let's fuck off out of all this. Fuck Phoenix. Let's load everybody back into the bus and go. You can tend the sick and lame. I can preach to the masses. Or we can get drunk and fuck groupies. Take a couple weeks. The whole shitty world will be here when we get back."

Carrie wants to think this way, but she knows that even Hayden doesn't believe what they're saying. They want to keep Carrie safe. They don't want her to come back to the fight because this time there might not be a moment of clarity. This might be the time Carrie doesn't come back.

"I don't know what I'm doing," Carrie says. Hayden stands up and comes to her. They wrap their arms around her, and it feels as if Hayden changes the shape of their body so that more of it can be in contact with Carrie's. As if Hayden could fuse Carrie's broken parts back together like scraps of soap into something useful again.

"Come with me. We'll figure it out." Hayden's embrace loosens, and it's a way to give Carrie the space to decide. She knows

Hayden would run out of here if she said yes. The look in Hayden's eyes says they'd do anything for her right now, and she kisses Hayden because it's the only thing that makes sense to her. When she stops, Hayden closes their eyes and looks hurt.

"Are you sure? You are my best friend, and I have to be so careful with you. Are you sure?"

Carrie wants to say yes, but she isn't sure of anything. She kisses Hayden again, not to move things forward but to hold them where they are. Their lips come apart, and Hayden says her name in a way that could mean anything, that strains under the possibility it holds. Carrie opens her eyes again, and before she can speak, she sees a flicker of motion on one of the monitors. She puts her hands on Hayden's shoulders, moving them aside so she can confirm what she's seen.

"Oh, shit," she says. "Where's Emmeline?"

ON CLARITY

◇

The feeling of air on the bare skin of her arms is something people take for granted. It's a thing about being normal: you never think of it as being made up of parts, things that can be separated out. For some people, there's only the experience of being without the need to analyze constantly, without the pressure to also look in at yourself and your experience from outside or above. For Emmeline, this little thing is thrilling and new, the sense of her arms exposed not only to the air but to eyes, to a million people. It's terrifying, but she can also feel strength in carrying it. Some weights make you stronger. Certain burdens hold you up.

Tuan finds Emmeline in a Foot Locker, trying on sneakers. She's evaluating them on the basis of what they'd be like for running, which is entirely new to her. He sits down on the bench next to her. There's a mirror attached to the legs, angled up so she can see the shoes she's trying on. Tuan bends down, looking into it, picking broccoli from between his teeth. "You want to go see a movie?" he asks. "We have, like, twenty movies we show on repeat. Whatever was playing here when it happened."

"Anything good?" Emmeline asks.

Tuan shrugs. "Once you've seen something a hundred times, it's past good or bad. It's like the Beatles. You hear them all the time, and you know them, but nobody like loves them."

"My dad loved the Beatles," Emmeline says. Sometimes she says things about him when she can't remember if they're true. As if she's trying them out. As if the sound of them out loud would tell her something about their truth value.

"Oh," Tuan says.

"I'm sorry," Emmeline says. "You probably don't like talking about parents."

He shrugs again. "Don't mind. It doesn't make me sad or anything. My parents were assholes, that's all. They weren't going to kill me in my sleep or anything. But they didn't want me. They didn't know what to do with me. I doubt they're any more broken up about me running away than I am. Sometimes it's easier for everybody."

"If it helps, both my parents are dead," Emmeline says.

Tuan gives her a strange look and busts out laughing. "How would that help?" he asks.

Emmeline thinks about how much she wants to fit in here, maybe more than she wanted to on the bus. She's adopted the mannerisms and speech patterns of someone younger than herself, joshing and shoving in the preflirtatious way kids do. And now offering up her dead parents like a membership card. It isn't funny enough to laugh about, but it makes her smile.

"Come on," Tuan says, standing up. "Let's go see what's playing."

They arrive as the lights are going down. The theater's full enough that they have trouble finding seats together, climbing over legs to get to the middle. The coming attractions title card appears on the screen.

"Oh, come on, Nyla," one of the kids yells back at the projectionist's booth.

"Nyla thinks the coming attractions are hilarious," Tuan explains. "All these movies they spent millions of dollars on, and they never got finished or no one ever got to see them or whatever. She always plays the preview reels."

He offers her popcorn, of which he assures her there's a nearly infinite supply. On screen, an action star whose name Emmeline can't remember leaps off a bridge and lands on the roof of a car. She remembers one movie they made about Resonants after they'd become public knowledge but before the war. She watched it in the Bishop common room with Viola and everyone else from their floor. It was a tense family drama about parents whose kid turned out to be a Resonant. The kid was the plot device, a reason for the drama rather than someone who experienced it. They'd watched it, cracking up at the corniness of the lines, the melodramatic angst of the parents.

White letters on a black screen announce that the film is coming next summer, a summer been and gone. In the patch of quiet between the trailers, Tuan leans over toward her. Emmeline's afraid he's going to try to kiss her.

"Do you want to stay?" he asks. "I mean, you could stay here with us."

"Did Carrie tell you to invite me?"

He shakes his head. "But I can tell it's why she brought you."

Something explodes on the screen. Looking at Tuan, Emmeline missed what the thing used to be; she sees it only as a fiery blast.

Finally, the last of the previews ends, and the title card comes up for the actual movie. The audience cheers. Some of them sing along to the opening theme song, a big sweeping orchestral piece. As soon as a character speaks, it's clear to Emmeline that all of them have seen this movie a million times and committed it to memory. Sometimes Kimani's lips would move in sync with the dialogue of movies she especially liked. These kids aren't so quiet about it. They speak every line. They heckle and argue with the characters, warn them when they're making bad decisions. The characters continue on, oblivious. As the plot continues, the audience quiets down not because they're tired but because they're drawn in. The magic of it wins them over.

The house lights come up suddenly, searing Emmeline's eyes. The audience erupts in a chorus of *what the fuck*s as the back door to the theater swings open, revealing Viola, who is wearing the same mean smirk Emmeline saw in the hospice in Boulder, and a man Emmeline deduces must be Kenny. Emmeline's eyes dart around the theater, wondering where the other three are going to come from, the ones who restaffed the Bloom after Carrie killed the others, but there are only these two.

Emmeline's head fills with static, a loud buzzing and scraping that makes it hard to hold a thought. It's Kenny throwing noise into her skull.

"Hi, Emmeline," says Viola. "I've been looking for you for so long."

"Everybody else out," Kenny says. "We want the girl, and we give zero fucks about the rest of you." Everyone is too scared to move, and Kenny rolls his eyes in annoyance.

"Emmeline, come on," Viola says. There's something fundamentally changed about her. A light has gone out. Her smile is a sneer, a cruel thing for a girl who was never cruel. Emmeline can sense what it is, and she knows it's her fault. The thing she did, the

Pulse, soured something in all of them. It made them mean when they should have been kind. "It's me. You know you can trust me." Her hands glow in the dim like the coils on a stove. "Come here and give us a big hug."

"You're not really like this," Emmeline says.

Viola takes a step toward her. The other door to the theater opens, and Carrie and Hayden are there. Carrie's knife is already drawn, but as soon as she takes her first sprinting steps toward Kenny, she clutches her head and stumbles like a drunk.

Zeroing in on one task, reaching through the noise, Emmeline grips the shackle on her wrist. Her fingers find the clasp, and for a second she doesn't think it'll come undone. It hasn't come off in years; maybe it's rusted shut, permanently attached to her arm. She hears a small pop as the clasp gives. She lets the shackle drop to the ground. For the first time since the day she caused the Pulse, Emmeline slips into the Hive, pulling Viola and her partner and everyone in the theater in with her.

Her Hivebody crashes into a briar patch of black vines. They burn cold where they touch her but melt into air. Viola's Hivebody looks the way Emmeline remembered her, petite and pale. The other man looks like a cloud of ticker tape raining down in an old-time parade, but his face registers the shock of being dragged into the Hive against his will.

"You've got your ability back," Viola says. "That's great, Emmie; that's really exciting."

"You're not really like this," Emmeline repeats. She sees it in them, a coil of darkness inside. It whispers to them, tells them they're terrible and deserve nothing better than acting this way. It tells them nothing better than this is possible.

"Emmeline, let's go somewhere and talk," Viola says, coming closer. "You never liked it in here, did you? We're going to take you to New York. We'll get coffee. Or cupcakes, like we used to."

"He put something in you," Emmeline says. "I can see it, Viola. I can take it out."

"I don't want it out," she says. "It's who I am."

"It's not," says Emmeline. "Let me show you. Let me remind you."

Emmeline can feel the part of Viola that isn't her. She can feel it in both of them. She can reach out and touch it, so she does. It floods her head.

Orphan, it says. *Stupid little orphan girl, hunting for your parents in the graveyard, sleeping on their shrouds. It's not just your parents, you know. Your friend Kimani is dead. Your little schoolmate's a killer. And you, you're not special. You're a stupid little orphan girl.*

It speaks to her in her own voice, or tries to. But Emmeline has been hearing her own voice speaking to her for her whole life. She isn't tricked by a tin-can devil. She grabs the thing in them that isn't them and pushes against it. It holds fast. It's strong, stronger than she remembers it. She's been hiding, and it's been expanding, building itself up. She hears a voice that is hers, her true voice, telling her she can do this. She feels the thing in them give, feels it let go so suddenly that the force she's directing at it keeps moving outward, radiating.

All around her in the Hive, the black flowers blow away like dandelion seeds, exposing the milky ground beneath. Hayden and Tuan look like they've come up from underwater, and Carrie falls to her knees, clutching her head. Emmeline feels something push back, as if she's hit a wall, and moves toward the object, toward the blockage. It's a spire, a tower she saw once before in a dream, a terrible vision she had once in Central Park with her parents before everything unraveled. It runs through the Hive like a skewer, pointing outward on either side into the real world, into the Source.

The black flowers and their tentacles scrabble, spreading from the base of the spire, trying to reclaim purchase on the ground. She tries to hold the spire in her mind. She wraps her thoughts around it, and it creeps into them, the voice louder now and closer to the sound of her own.

You scared your mother shitless; she thought of you as a creature, it says. *Your father's body lay unfound in the attic until it bloated and burst like a gangrenous balloon. He'd been there dead for days because you couldn't be bothered to find him. His last thought was that all of this was your fault.*

It might all be true. It might be lies. Emmeline doesn't care. She pulls back from the spire. She scoops up the little bits, the tiny malignant blooms inside Viola and Kenny and Carrie. She squeezes them with her grief and her love and her fear and her hope. She feels the cold burn of the black glass against her heart, and then they break. They shatter into a million pieces, and Emmeline remains whole.

ROGERS PARK

◇

The house Waylon found for them is up in Rogers Park, a neighborhood that was once considered practically a suburb and is now home to mostly harmless youth gangs that play elaborate ongoing war games in the abandoned houses. "But not this one," he assured them. "Nobody touches this house."

"Why not?" Rai asked.

Waylon and Bryce looked at each other for a moment. "The kids say it's haunted," Bryce said.

The worst Clay can tell about the house on Jarvis Avenue is that it's suffering from neglect. The lawn is waist-high, and hunks of the stucco siding have crumbled off, exposing the faded logos on the sealed Sheetrock beneath. Something domestic in Dom stirs to life as they enter the house. He's never talked about home ownership before; it's not something they could think about without leaving New York. Now, with a whole house that's theirs, he has a flurry of ideas about design and repair, little fixes they can do.

It's a way for Dom to make this place feel permanent, but Clay can't get excited the way he is.

Unfortunately, Dom is all enthusiasm and no time, whereas Clay has nothing but time and zero enthusiasm. While Rai's at his new school and Dom's learning the ropes at Waylon's bar, Clay mopes around the house, sometimes not showering until the last moment in the afternoon he can do so and be dried off when Dom gets home. Waylon sends Dominic home each night with enough food for the three of them, so there's nothing Clay has to do during the day. His hours go pear-shaped, and he wants more than anything to call the Ruse, to see how things are going, to find out who's occupying Theta Bay.

He wants to know who's been sitting in his Chair.

At night, they listen to bands of youth rove the neighborhood, shouting taunts and catcalls, banging on every door in the neighborhood but theirs. Clay hasn't seen any of them out during the day. He hasn't seen them at all, but the sound of their games eases him to sleep.

He explores the house on Jarvis Avenue, putting together the history of the family that once lived there from what they left behind. There isn't much. They were a mixed-race couple with a daughter whose room Rai now occupies, but something about the house gives Clay the sense that the wife and daughter had left. There was a bachelor disarray to the house, one he recognized from the way he let the apartment degrade when Dom and Rai weren't around for a couple days.

On the second day he finds the drop-down door to the attic in the upstairs hallway. Thinking about wardrobes that lead to fairy kingdoms and beanstalks that stretch into the clouds, he climbs the stairs. The attic has been repurposed into an office with certain notes of a man cave: the record player and the dumpster-dive vibe of the furnishings. Feeling like he's committing theft, Clay peruses the record collection and puts on A Tribe Called Quest, the lone hip-hop album he can find. Instantly relaxed by the sound, he feels licensed to intrude further.

He boots up the ancient computer on the desk, tapping the keys impatiently as it struggles to come to life. The desktop is a clutter of document files. Clay picks one at random titled "NULL." "On December 4th, a young Resonant named Owen Curry opened a hole in the world and fed nineteen people into it," he reads. What follows begins like a piece of investigative journalism, but as it goes on, the writer becomes more and more integrated into the story until the story is no longer about a monstrous Resonant named Owen Curry but a sad, lonely man named Avi Hirsch who pursued Curry at the cost of his marriage and his friendships. The first time he sees the name, it feels impossible, but it's quickly apparent that he's in the house where Emmeline Hirsch grew up. He feels as if he's violating sacred ground and tells himself he should shut off the computer, leave the attic, and move all of them to a less important place. Instead, he keeps reading.

The A side of the album runs out, the needle scratching on the label. Before he can make it to the end of the story, Clay catches a reflection in the corner of the computer screen, a young woman with a headful of corkscrew curls. He whirls around in the desk chair, but the room is empty. Laughing at himself for being so easily spooked by Bryce's mention that the house is haunted, Clay turns off the computer and the record player and goes back downstairs.

That night Dominic comes home with a large tray of tiny hamburgers. "They found a body in Pilsen," he says as he sets it on the counter. "Eito Higashi."

"Should I know who that is?" Clay asks.

"No, you wouldn't," Dominic says. He picks up one of the burgers and takes a dainty bite. "He was one of the guests at that thing the night of the bombing. Went missing after. Waylon's guys say he washed up on the north shore of the South Branch this morning. He'd been . . ." Dominic looks at the burger in his hand as if reconsidering. He sets it on the counter, next to the tray, half eaten. "Bad stuff happened to him between then and now."

"Bad stuff's happened to us between then and now," Clay says.

"Not all of it is bad," Dominic says. "It's new is all. And none of it is your fault."

"Tell the kid that," Clay says.

"You tell him," Dominic says. "You've barely spoken to him since we moved out here."

"He's barely spoken to me," Clay insists.

Dominic smiles at him. "But you're the grown-up." He puts a half dozen tiny burgers on a plate and holds it out to Clay. "Go be the grown-up."

Shoulders slumped in a posture Rai's adopted too many times to count, Clay takes the burgers upstairs. From outside Rai's door, he hears Rai talking to someone inside. He hesitates before knocking, but the talking stops. Clay knocks on the door. "Yeah," says Rai. Taking it as an invitation, Clay goes in.

"You on the phone in here?" Clay asks.

"What phone?" Rai says, crossing his arms. "You all talk through the Hive, so who needs phones?"

"I thought I heard talking," Clay says.

"I have to give some bullshit presentation tomorrow," Rai says. "I was practicing." Clay smiles, thinking about how even when Rai tries to rebel, he still does his homework. He holds out the plate.

"Your favorite dad brought these home," he says.

"Don't say that," says Rai.

"Calling it like I see it lately."

"It's not like that," Rai says.

"So what's it like?"

"Why'd you fight in the war?" Rai says.

"A lot of us—"

"Why'd you?"

Clay considers this. There are the reasons he tells himself, bullshit about injustice and oppression. But none of them feel sufficient. None of them ever did.

"I grew up watching movies about people standing up for themselves," he says. "All the movies. All the books. There's a moment someone has to decide who they are, even if it's a risk. People say things like *If I was alive in Nazi Germany, I would have joined the resistance.* You can say that, and it doesn't cost you anything. Before the war, things were getting bad. Nazi Germany bad. And it was like, *Here's what I said I'd do in this situation. And here's the situation.* And I didn't do anything. I went to a couple protests. I called my senators, and I donated money when I could. Then I stopped even doing that. I went online and complained and said how bad it all was, but that was all I did. I felt powerless. All the time.

"Then the Pulse happened, and I wasn't powerless," he continues. "And the situation was the situation, and I always said I'd fight. Maybe it was because I hadn't before. But I decided, *Yeah, now I fight.*"

He looks at Rai, knowing his answers are insufficient. But Rai nods as if this jibes with what he thought he knew. He nods as if it's okay.

"That stuff you did in the Bronx," Rai says. "It was scary."

"That was different," Clay says. He sits down on the edge of the bed next to Rai, putting one arm around him in the way they've become comfortable with since Rai hit adolescence, then, impulsively, throws the other around him, pulling the boy in. "That time I was protecting you. That time I didn't think about it at all."

I'M BEGINNING TO SEE THE LIGHT

◇

Buzzing with euphoria, the kids refuse to go to bed. They get the roadies to help them wire a phone into the amps and stage an impromptu dance party in the main concourse, thrashing and flopping around with abandon in their mangled formal wear. Carrie is alone on the balcony, leaning over the railing and watching them. She hears footsteps coming toward her, and all her instincts kick in; her hand goes to the handle of her knife. She's angry the instincts are still there, wishing they'd shorted out along with the thing in her head. The ghost of a voice, the pulsating bit of hate that lived in her is gone, but it left behind violent neural paths that networked her body. It left guilt and recrimination and the blurred line between what that thing might have forced her to do and what she did willingly.

"It's me," Emmeline says. "You okay?"

Carrie nods halfheartedly.

"The thing in your head is gone," Emmeline says. "I squashed it. I think maybe that's how they found us."

Carrie huffs a single laugh. "I was supposed to be keeping you safe, and I got you caught."

"I didn't get caught," Emmeline says. "I got my friend back." She points at Viola down on the dance floor, her arms folded around her body as she sways gently to the music. She sees Emmeline and gives a wave, which Emmeline returns. "I helped you." She's asking, looking for affirmation she's done the right thing.

"You did," Carrie says.

"And now you're going to go."

"I talked to Kenny," she says. "The Faction is going to evacuate non-Resonants in Chicago. He says it won't be as gentle as the last time, and the last time wasn't gentle at all. My friends there are in trouble."

"Your friends here are in trouble."

"You can handle it. I think you can handle anything."

"I don't think I can," Emmeline says.

"I know you can. Come here." Carrie gathers the girl up in a hug, wondering at the slightness of her. "But you don't have to," she says. "Whatever they want you to do, you don't have to do it. You know that, right?"

"I want to help," Emmeline says. "Even if that means fighting."

"If it means fighting, fight," Carrie says. "Just, don't turn into someone you wouldn't fight for. Don't let yourself become someone you don't even like."

"You're not a bad person," Emmeline says. "Here." She holds out the bracelet she wore on her wrist, wide and silver with beautiful stones and script. "Your payment. I'm sure Fahima was going to give you this, or one like it."

"It shut you off."

"For a long time, yeah," Emmeline says. She lifts one of the red stones to reveal a switch. "This is how you turn it on. It gets power from moving it around. But you have to check it before you go to bed." Under another stone, there's an LCD readout. "This tells you how long the battery has left." She clicks the stone back into place and runs her finger over the Arabic letters inscribed there. "The word on it means *time*."

"I can't take this," Carrie says.

"I don't need it anymore," Emmeline says.

"I didn't finish the job. I was supposed to get you where you needed to be."

"I think you did," Emmeline says. She presses the bracelet into Carrie's hands, then runs off down the hall, past Alyssa, who's been standing in the doorway.

"It's not a blessing," she tells Carrie. "Best case, it's a stopgap. Fahima used to say every time she looked at that thing, it reminded her there was one more problem she couldn't solve."

"Maybe my problem's not as big," Carrie says. "Maybe for him this is enough."

"There's a mattress store downstairs," Alyssa says. "There's probably twenty teenagers fucking like rabbits in there, but I bet you could find noise-canceling headphones and an empty bed."

"I need to get going," Carrie says. She feels light and heavy at once. Alyssa looks at her like a mother.

"You need rest," Alyssa says. "We all do."

Carrie shakes her head. "I gotta go."

"Every time I get mixed up in Fahima's life, I feel like I'm watching a movie with the subtitles off," Alyssa says.

"Don't let her—" Carrie starts, but she's not sure what she's worried about. She wants to know that Alyssa will protect Emmeline from Fahima and Hayden will protect all of them from everything else, but she doesn't know how to ask.

"I won't," Alyssa says.

"Could you tell Hayden thank you?" Carrie says. "I didn't mean to leave them with this mess."

"Not your mess," Alyssa says. "You haven't told Hayden?"

"I can't. I'm going back to Chicago, and there are people there I need to finish things with." She runs her fingers over the inscriptions on the bracelet. "Whatever this is," Carrie says, waving her hand toward the center of the mall, which throbs with bass and the shouts of young people, "I don't think I'm a part of it anymore."

"I'm not a part of it, and I'm still going," says Alyssa.

Carrie thinks about the baseliners who've been in her life since she left home for the Bishop Academy. There weren't many: her parents and Brian, the guards at Topaz and the people she fought in the war, the people in Jonathan's neighborhood who eyed her sideways when she left his apartment and the people in New York before the war who did the same, the ones she brought food and medicine to in the Wastes who mumbled thank you or gave her looks that said *is this all?* Who among all of them had been kind or caring? Who bothered to look past what she was to who she was, and who would have fought alongside her?

"Thank you," she says to Alyssa, and the words feel insufficient, as if she should explain what for. She doesn't have time to list the little kindnesses or the absence of kindness that makes each of them stand out. She hugs Alyssa and walks to the escalator.

She finds Tuan sitting on the counter of an ear-piercing kiosk, nodding his head in time to the music, assessing the dance floor like it's a pool he thinks might be too cold to jump into. Carrie grips his knee to get his attention.

"Hey, Killer Carrie," he says. "Your girl there make any decisions? She's got some fans here after whatever she pulled in the theater."

"I'm not sure," Carrie says, but she is sure. Emmeline's like her a little bit. Emmeline will do what she has to. "I need to get back to Chicago fast."

Tuan's eyes go wide, and he looks at Carrie like he's trying to guess her weight. "You know I can't do that anymore," he says. "Too much distance and too much—"

"Don't," says Carrie. "I know it sucks for you, and I know it's going to make you feel like shit for days. But I need to be there now or people are going to get hurt."

He sighs deeply and hops down off the counter. He draws a circle in the air, then grips its edges, stretching them up and down, left and right, with obvious physical strain until the portal is tall enough and wide enough for Carrie to fit through. Its surface looks like rain pouring down a mirror. Tuan wipes away a trickle of pink liquid dribbling from his nose.

"Thank you," Carrie says. She's about to step through when she feels hands wrap around her waist, a body press against her back.

"Nice fucking try," Hayden says in her ear, then nips Carrie's earlobe with their teeth and plunges them both through.

GRADUATION

◇

Fahima's glad her last entry to the Bishop Academy has the feeling of finality. Knowing she'll never be back helps her attend to all the details. As she pushes through the revolving door, she notes the place where it scrapes the tile, slowing in its spin. She closes her eyes and lets the acoustics of the lobby fill her mind with a sense of its space, the height of the ceilings, and the distance of every wall. She takes a deep breath and tastes lemon-scented cleaning products, the sour milk and soil smell of adolescent body odor, and the high burn of ozone as a student arcs across the room as a blur of electricity. When she started working here, no one was allowed to use their abilities in the lobby. Now they're all free to be their whole selves everywhere. Fahima tries to remind herself that this is a victory. She tries to feel as if she's won.

She stops when Shen says his standard "Hello, Dr. Deeb." She stands between him and the elevators, playing his words back in her head, listening for a sign he's lost to her. She'd told herself if they took Shen, it was over. But she'd told herself that about Omar and Ruth. She'd said *As long as Emmeline is safe* and *As long as nothing happens to Alyssa.* All of these were predicated on the idea that she'd be the one to make choices, that she got to draw those lines.

"Have you heard anything about the Mexican place on Orchard?" she asks Shen.

"Mission Cantina? I hear it's not bad," he says. "Not as good as Toalache."

"I thought Toalache's overrated."

"It would be impossible to overrate Toalache."

"I'm thinking I might go there tonight," she says. "You want me to bring anything back?"

"The short rib and bone marrow tacos are fantastic," he says.

"Tacos it is." She smiles at him because she can't let him see her cry over tacos she'll never get to deliver. The elevator doors shut in front of her.

Upstairs is too quiet. She moved Sarah out last night, and not being greeted by a full report from a guardian Omar when she arrives makes the place feel abandoned. Fahima clears papers off her desk, grabbing heaps and stuffing them into a messenger bag. She stops at the Polaroid she found taped to the window, the image of the street below. She knew what it meant as soon as she saw it. It was a message to start, the date and time written on the bottom indicating the last moment before it would all be too late. The message could have been wrong. There would be some comfort knowing she'd started too late. There would be someone else to blame. Fahima puts the Polaroid in the bag with the rest of the papers: the schematics for useless devices, the notes toward ineffectual plans.

She's so busy packing, she fails to notice Ji Yeon standing in the doorway, flanked by all four members of her Bloom.

"Do you have a minute?" Ji Yeon asks.

"Not really," Fahima says, continuing to pack. "I'm supposed to meet with Cedric in an hour to give a full accounting of where we stand with Project Tuning Fork, which is suddenly everyone's highest possible priority."

"It's always been the highest priority," Ji Yeon says. "It's the end of everything we've worked toward." Something in the cadence of her voice puts Fahima on edge. "That's why we were surprised to find out you'd been altering the data."

"I don't know what you're talking about," Fahima says.

"Cedric's had technopaths running through all the files," Ji Yeon says. "They say it was sloppy work, as if you wanted to get caught."

They were half right. Fahima had never been too careful when she rewrote files at the Ruse not because she wanted to get caught but because she thought the Omars were the only ones who'd ever see them.

Fahima sorts the papers, trying to make it look like she's looking for something in particular.

"We understand," Ji Yeon says. "You were being cautious. Too cautious, maybe. None of that matters now. We're here to talk about something else."

Fahima drops the papers and turns on Ji Yeon. "What happened to you?" she asks. "You were a good kid. You were a prick, but you were a good kid."

"You always saw me as a kid," says Ji Yeon, smiling her tight smile.

"It's not so bad, being a kid," Fahima says. "It means you're not all full of adult bullshit."

"Like you?"

"Exactly like me," Fahima says. "I thought you were going to change the world."

"Like you?"

"Better than me. Better than this."

"I like to think I am changing the world," says Ji Yeon.

"Are you even still in there, Ji Yeon?" Fahima asks even though she knows the answer.

Ji Yeon looks confused for a moment, even scared. She opens her mouth to speak and then snaps it shut. Her face goes deadly calm, all fear, all feeling gone.

"There's a flicker," Ji Yeon says. Her voice is different. Deeper. Fahima stops and looks at her, searching for the last bit of the girl she met behind a barricade in Revere, Massachusetts, ready to give her life for a noble and futile cause. She can't find it. "We're mostly me now."

"Which one?" Fahima says.

"All of us," the five members of the Bloom say in unison.

"What do they do?" Fahima asks. "The little pieces you put in their heads?" She circles Ji Yeon like she's examining a statue in a museum.

Ji Yeon's mouth pulls up into a wider smile. "Focus on the little pieces and you miss the big picture."

"That's droll," Fahima says. "Patrick isn't droll."

"I'm barely Patrick anymore," says one of the ones behind Fahima. The beanpole of a boy with acne scars. "You've figured that out at least."

Fahima keeps her attention on Ji Yeon because it's easiest. "You're Raymond Glover," she says.

"You know my name," says the soccer mom on Ji Yeon's left, "but I'm guessing you don't know a thing about me. Kevin never told you. He was keeping secrets."

"You were one of the first," Fahima says.

"I was *the* first," says Ji Yeon. "Kevin and I. Created at the same time."

"Where've you been, Ray?" Fahima says.

"Doesn't matter," says the beanpole.

"Tell me where the girl is," says the soccer mom. She slams Fahima's suitcase shut.

"I don't know," Fahima says.

Ji Yeon places her hand on Fahima's cheek. "Tell me or I will crawl into your skull and find out."

"You promised me you'd never," Fahima says.

"*Patrick* promised you," Ji Yeon says.

"You're scared of her," Fahima says. She watches for a flinch, but Ji Yeon is only a mask. Even more than Patrick's face. Raymond is elsewhere.

"She's the solution to our problem," says the beanpole. "Think of the lives we could save with her help."

"You could save them by waiting," Fahima says.

"I am so tired of waiting," says the beanpole.

"I've been waiting such a long time," says the pudgy one.

"Ask me again about the little pieces," says Ji Yeon.

"What do they do, Ray?"

"They're a stopgap," Ji Yeon says. "They're tin cans and a string."

"This?" the beanpole asks.

"What I'm doing right now?" the pudgy one asks.

"It's painful to do it this way," Ji Yeon says.

"Don't show off for my benefit, Ray."

Ji Yeon smiles that awful fake smile again. Fahima circles her. "I like you, Fahima," she says. "You're so practical but idealistic at the same time. It's made you very easy to work with."

"Ray?" Fahima asks.

"Hmm?" She can't tell which of them it comes through, a querying sound that hangs in the air for a second.

"You should've called me upstairs for this little meeting," Fahima says. "You could have had home field advantage."

She presses a button, and the overhead lights begin to hum.

They turn a sickly green, and each member of the Bloom trembles and goes slack, dropping to the floor like the bones have gone out of them. It's a temporary fix, but it gives Fahima enough time to climb up on a chair, remove the corner panel of the door, and turn on the Gate. She grabs her bag and steps through. Two Omars are waiting on the other side.

"Brick the Gate," Fahima says. She's texting Ruth two sets of coordinates: an extraction point and her current location.

The Omars hesitate. "Shouldn't we wait for them?"

"They'll have to come by air," she says.

"Do you think Ruth can get them out by air?"

"She'll fucking have to!" Fahima shouts. "She can do it," she adds quietly.

One of the Omars enters a code into the Gate panel, and electronics burn out like dying stars. The image of the headmaster's quarters in the doorway strewn with the unconscious bodies of Ji Yeon and her Bloom ripples, wavers, and fades. At both ends, the Gates become inert, useless arches of metal, their connection severed.

THE LOVE SONG
OF KEVIN BISHOP

FAIRY TALE OF NEW YORK
1989

Rise and look out; his chains are loose, his
dungeon doors are open.
                                    —WILLIAM BLAKE,
                                    America a Prophecy

Kevin wondered how it could have happened without his noticing. He was nominally aware of every Resonant in New York City at any time, and Raymond Glover's presence had been a high thin note at the edge of his consciousness for fifty years, so constant he often forgot it was there. When he got a call at the school from an office ten blocks away inviting him to a meeting with Raymond Glover, CEO of Harmonic Solutions, he had to ask himself if Raymond had been hiding from him.

Bitter about the way he'd been summoned, Kevin left the school at the time of his appointment and walked from 57th and Lexington to the financial district, where Harmonic Solutions was housed in a newly built tower that gleamed with all the idealism of New York that year. Kevin had heard the promises about a rising stock market lifting all boats, but he wondered about the cost. It was as bougie to wax nostalgic over the days he might score shake weed or an anonymous blow job in Times Square as it was to slaver at the prospect of spiking rents and franchise restaurants on every block. Kevin had been an occasional tourist in that darker dream of the city; he looked like a man striding into his midforties and a veteran of a debaucherous downtown heyday, but he had turned eighty last month. The slow aging was an unexpected side effect of his ability, one not all Resonants shared. Kevin had been called to the bedside of some of his oldest friends, the first Resonants he met in his wandering years after the war. When their minds began to go and they worried about the harm their abilities might cause, they summoned him to ferry them over the Styx. Some of them made it no secret they resented his youth, and others saw it as a reason for hope. They were leaving, but Kevin Bishop would carry on.

Security on the ground floor called upstairs to confirm his arrival and issued him a visitor's badge. The receptionist for Harmonic Solutions on the twenty-first floor was the type of skinny blond boy Raymond seemed to have at least one of around at all times. *Is this why you stayed hidden?* Kevin wondered. *Didn't want me to meet your latest boy toy?* Kevin might have the body of a man younger than he felt, but the spark of the young had long gone out in him. If that was what Raymond wanted, he'd be looking elsewhere.

"Here at Harmonic Solutions we offer a dynamic program of healing and self-actualization designed personally by our founder, Mr. Glover," said the receptionist. His voice was a thin reed trembling in the light breeze such a small body could muster. Kevin dipped down to Hivescan him and found nothing. The boy had no Resonance. A quick survey of the building showed there were no Resonants here other than him and a dead spot that must have been Raymond. While Kevin tried to figure it out, the boy's voice dropped a half octave and his expression of enthusiastic conversion to a New Age cult became more playful.

"Don't be nervous, Kevin," the boy said in this voice. "I wanted you to see my new project. It's an urban farming experiment. I'm going to let go of Adrian now, and he'll bring you back. And no, Kevin, I'm not fucking him. Jealousy's a bad color on you."

"Raymond?" said Kevin.

The boy blinked at him like a dreamer awakening. "Well, he's Mr. Glover to me," he said, his voice again a high treble. "But he told me you were old friends, so I suppose he's Raymond to you." The boy looked around as if he'd said a cuss word, then grinned at Kevin conspiratorially.

"Yes," Kevin said. "Very old friends."

Adrian came around the desk to lead him down the hall. There were pictures on the walls of Raymond with people Kevin recognized: prominent businesspeople, the occasional television actor. He'd seen this type of picture before. He recognized the dynamic in which the person attempted to play it as if they were equal to the celebrity they were stealing the shot with. In these pictures it was clear Raymond held the power. In one, the deputy mayor had his arm slung around Raymond's shoulders and with the other hand he pointed at Raymond as if to signal, *check it out,* the *Raymond Glover, here with* me.

At the end of the hallway was a room with glass walls, letting all the light from the outer windows flood the space. Inside, Raymond sat on a chair with two dozen men and women in business attire rapt at his feet. When he visited Raymond's hippie commune in the Haight, Kevin had the sense he was watching a professor dole out wisdom to his students under the guise of egalitarian exchange. That had been stripped away. Raymond looked like a kindergarten teacher reading a picture book to toddlers, and the listeners looked the role of toddlers, their faces upturned and rapturous.

"I don't know if he wants you going in," Adrian said. "The content of the curriculum is copyrighted and, to be honest, expensive."

"It's fine," Kevin said. "I can wait." Inside, Raymond looked up and spotted Kevin. His face lit up in a grin. In eerie unison, twenty of his listeners turned their heads, smiled, and waved, then stood up and filed out of the room.

Everything about Harmonic Solutions, every aspect of the most recent life Raymond had built for himself in a span of months, called Kevin's attention to how average his own life had become. He looked out the window onto Fifth and thought about the clutter of his workspace, how filled it had become with student incident reports and teacher evaluations. He saw Raymond's photos from the desert at Joshua Tree and the neon-streaked streets of Tokyo and thought how the only trips he'd taken in twenty years had been when he was whisked somewhere by Kimani Moore to attend to a problematic Resonant—to bring them to the school or take them off the board.

"It's the life you wanted," Raymond said.

"Stay out of my head," Kevin muttered.

"I'm only saying, you chose it," Raymond continued. "I think it's beautiful for that, your shabby little school. I admire the self-abnegation it takes to go there every day and wipe the noses of the next generation of . . . well, that I've never been clear on, really. What is it you're raising these children to be?"

"Did Davenport sell you this building?" Kevin asked.

"Davenport's a pickpocket," Raymond said. "I rent at a market rate. This floor and three above it. I'd like to open a second location, but unfortunately there's only one of me."

"What is it you're doing?" Kevin asked. "Scamming them out of their—"

"I'm not taking anything from them they don't pay for up front," Raymond said. "And they are getting something back in exchange."

"Your voice in their heads?"

"It's no secret people don't want to be in control all the time," Raymond said. "It generates guilt and doubt. I promise them that every once in a while they can go through a day of their life without making choices, without exerting control. They can sit back and watch."

"And you get the control they give up?"

Raymond laughed. "Why would I want control of their drab little lives?" he said. "I'm supposed to get excited about fucking their flabby husbands or their sad mistresses? Playing catch with their idiot kids or chewing out their employees? None of it is about them, Kevin."

"What, then?"

"Practice," Raymond said. "A chance to expand my abilities. Right now I'm five other people while I'm talking to you. I'm watching out of seven pairs of eyes on top of that. And look at me." He holds out his hands. "Not missing a beat." As he said it, a thin trickle of pink fluid ran from his nostril, and he quickly wiped it away.

"You're not well, Raymond," Kevin said.

"I'm extremely well," Raymond said. "But how are you? Do you even *like* what you are, Kevin? Do you hate it so much that you'd keep us all in the closet?"

"Why am I here, Raymond?" Kevin asked. "You had to know I wouldn't be happy with what you're doing."

"Oh, I expect you're going to be very unhappy," Raymond said. "You care about them so much. You think you're protecting our people, but the whole time it's *them* you're keeping safe from *us*. They're not important, Kevin. They're walking dead. Here. Watch."

Kevin felt the world ripple as Raymond's ability moved through it. There was no message Kevin could discern, only malice. It passed in an instant and left him puzzled. Then Raymond pointed him to the window. Kevin looked out onto Upper Manhattan as a body plummeted past him. He caught a glimpse of the man's face as he went, calm, with a smile that mimicked Raymond's. Kevin was about to turn to ask what was happening when another body fell. He recognized the face of Adrian, the receptionist, as it toppled past him, grinning, followed by others.

"The trick is to pull out of their heads before they hit the pavement," Raymond said. "The ride down is a thrill."

Kevin stepped toward Raymond, moving against his mind to stop him, but he felt a strong push back and then an overwhelming sense of calm. The visceral horror of what he'd seen was gone. He couldn't remember what he'd been about to say.

"Why am I here, Raymond?" he asked, although he had a feeling he already knew.

"I missed you," Raymond said. "Both of us are so busy, we've hardly made any time for each other. Maybe we could go up to the coast some time. You still have the house?"

"I've always thought of it as ours," Kevin said. "I'd never sell it without consulting you."

"We should go."

"The academy's out of session the last week of June," Kevin said. "I'll be up there unless something dreadful arises."

"The last week of June, then," Raymond said. He took the back of Kevin's neck in his hand and kissed him, a hard press that Kevin felt not only on his lips but as a pressure on his mind, feeling him out. For a second he considered handing himself over to Raymond. Then the kiss ended, his body and mind his own again. He took the elevator down and stepped out the front door, ignorant of the dozen bodies on the sidewalk, of the police cars and ambulances. The sun had come out, and it was shaping up to be a beautiful afternoon.

FOUR

THE REASONS WE FIGHT

All of us turning from being alone (at best
Boring) because what we want most is to be
Interested.
> —Delmore Schwartz,
> "All of Us Always Turning Away for Solace"

I NEVER ASKED FOR THE TRUTH, BUT YOU OWE THAT TO ME

◈

Carrie forgets there's a pause when she moves through one of Tuan's portals, like a singer taking a deep breath before hitting a final note. In that moment, she's neither where she left nor where she's going. She wonders if she ceases to exist and pops back into being at her destination.

The collision with Hayden and the disorienting pause land them on the floor of Carrie's apartment in a tangle of limbs—Carrie facedown and Hayden lying on her back. It's not an adorable rom-com jumble that segues into kisses but a bruising fall that narrowly avoids the coffee table's sharp corners.

"I did not like that," Hayden says, rubbing an elbow that struck the hardwood floor.

"Faster than the bus," Carrie says.

"This is your place," Hayden says. "I haven't been in your apartment in . . ." They trail off. The last time Hayden was here was the last time Carrie and Miquel had guests in the apartment. They were just graduated from Bishop, experimenting with new selves in the bright lab of possibility, and something went wrong. Carrie never regretted what they did, but the morning after she felt exposed in a way she never had before. After years struggling to be seen, when she woke up in the bed with Miquel and Hayden and Jonathan, every bit of her, each flaw and secret, glowed like a halogen bulb, and whichever of them woke up first would see all of it. Whatever Hayden saw that morning made them leave, confirming every fear Carrie harbored about herself. She didn't know at the time that Miquel's ability had started to overwhelm him, but the two things together led to the apartment becoming a cloister, the closed space where they retreated from everyone, even the people they loved. After Miquel moved out, Carrie kept the apartment shuttered to the outside world.

"Hey, Miquel, I brought your wife home," Hayden shouts to the empty apartment. When they get no response, they look at Carrie, confused. "Is he here?"

"He doesn't live here," she says. "He hasn't for a while." The breadth of how much—and how often—she's hidden from Hayden settles on Carrie in those words, *a while*. It's six years of unanswered texts and canceled plans, unused comp tickets and half-assed excuses.

"What are you talking about?" Hayden asks. "You split up?"

"He was falling apart," Carrie says.

"The couple times I saw him after Topaz he was shaken up," Hayden says.

"He came back broken, Hayden," Carrie says. "It started getting bad around when you were leaving. Waylon built him a room under the bar with an inhibitor. It helps."

"Sticking him in a basement helps?"

"He couldn't tell what was him anymore," Carrie says. "He had no defenses."

"Honey, why did no one tell me?"

"I asked them not to," Carrie says. "Everything was good with you. Out of all of us, you became this perfect beautiful thing. I was worried if we told you, you'd come back and help."

"Of course I would have."

"But you couldn't," Carrie says. "You would have given up every amazing thing you were doing, and it wouldn't make any difference." Carrie shows Hayden the shackle. "This will," she says. "That's what all this has been about. It turned bigger than I meant it to, but the whole trip was supposed to be a quick courier job to get this."

"That's Emmeline's," Hayden says.

"She gave it to me," Carrie says. "Fahima was going to give me one when I got Emmeline to Phoenix, but Emmeline cut out the middle man."

"You're going to shut him off?"

Carrie notices how Hayden watches the shackle, how they avoid touching it. She remembers how bad it was for Hayden under the inhibitors at Topaz, how, more than any of them, Hayden has an ability that ties to who they are. Carrie will never be able to explain to Hayden why she needs to shut Miquel off. She'll never be justified in Hayden's eyes, but she has to try.

"It's killing him. It's killing us. Everything's gotten so bad. I keep fucking up."

"You and I last night?" Hayden asks. "Was that fucking up?"

She wants to tell Hayden that kissing them was the first decision she's felt sure of in as long as she can remember. That's the problem with fucking up: it plants doubt that spreads into everything. Where's the line she can draw between sleeping with Jonathan, which was as much about punishing herself as it was about sex, and kissing Hayden, which felt like she was finally making a choice? Carrie distrusted everything she did to the point where feeling sure of something was the surest sign that something was wrong. With Hayden next to her on the floor and Miquel a life-time away, part of her insists that if she wants something, it must be poisoned.

Carrie picks up the shackle. "This could be a new start for us," she says, wondering who it is she's speaking to and who she means by *us*.

"This could be, too," Hayden says. Carrie doesn't believe them any more than she believes herself. No one gets to start over. You bring every terrible part of your past into the next day with you. "I should go," Hayden says when Carrie doesn't answer.

"I don't want you to go," Carrie says. Her voice is small and fad-ing.

"You don't want me to stay either," Hayden says, letting go of Carrie's hand. "I can't do both. Go find him. See if you can fix it or if you even want to. Let me know how it . . ." Hayden trails off, and Carrie knows this is the thing that's always scared her, too: that she and Hayden might reach a point from which they can't move for-ward. "Don't shut me out anymore," Hayden says. "Whatever hap-pens, I want to know."

Hayden stands up and looks around as if to gather their things before realizing that they don't have any things to gather. They dived through the portal with Carrie and landed in the middle of her old and broken life with nothing to show for it but some bruises, exactly what Carrie knew would happen.

"Where will you be?" Carrie asks.

"I'll be around. I'll find you," Hayden says. "I always find you." Hayden kisses Carrie on the cheek and Carrie holds them around the waist, wishing she had it in her to pull Hayden closer and make them stay.

The shyness and elation Carrie feels as she descends the stairs remind her of the days before she and Miquel were dating. She's clutching to a secret she wants to broadcast, playing hide-and-seek and aching to get caught. She knocks on the door, the shackle held behind her back. In the time it takes him to answer, her mood curdles into dread. *He's gone,* she thinks. *The Faction came and took him or he's in there, dead by his own hand, because I was gone, because I took too long and came back too late.*

Then he's at the door, drying his hands on a dish towel. He reaches out and pulls Carrie into the room by her shoulders, enfolding her in his arms as soon as they're both under the humming green lights. She hugs him back, the shackle in her right hand, her arms crossed at the wrists behind his neck. "Oh, thank God," he says. His embrace is as enthusiastic as it can be while being delicate about not touching skin to skin. "I thought Waylon was lying about not knowing where you were, but he's such a terrible liar, I knew that couldn't be it." He's holding her so close and tight that she can't stop herself breathing in rhythm with him, full, deep, and fast. His lips come near enough to almost graze her ear, and she hates herself for thinking about Hayden nipping her earlobe as they dived through the portal together like pirates leaping from the crow's nest.

"I figured you ran off," Miquel whispers.

"I'd never do that," Carrie says.

Miquel pulls back from their embrace and grins at her sadly. "Carrie, you ran off on our wedding night."

He's never phrased it that way before, never reprimanded her for the decision she made that night, even if he has every right to. Calling her out on it would put her in the position of needing to apologize, which he knows she won't do. If she did, she wouldn't mean it.

"Come on in," he says, guiding her with a hand on her hip. "There's food. Have you eaten?"

Carrie sidesteps into the room, rotating to keep the shackle behind her back. "I'm sorry I didn't tell you where I was going," she says. "A job came up, and I had to leave right away."

"You freaked everybody out," he says. "Waylon was giving himself nosebleeds trying to scan the Wastes for you. He went into the Hive looking. Sometimes you forget how much we all care about you."

It's an echo of what Hayden said to her when they came back to Chicago after liberating Topaz. Hayden must have seen Carrie's eyes on the door. *Don't forget how much we care about you,* they said. Carrie never forgot. The caring was the reason she had to go. There was so much of it, and it wasn't enough. The problem couldn't be her friends who loved her fiercely, so the problem had to be Carrie.

"You want to show me what's behind your back?" Miquel asks.

Carrie takes a deep breath. She holds the shackle out to him in cupped hands as if she's cradling a butterfly. She's invested so much into it, like charging a magical object, and when Miquel's face doesn't light up with immediate recognition, she's crestfallen.

"It's an inhibitor," she says. "It's stronger than these ones." She wags her eyebrows at the lights. "Fahima Deeb made it. It's been holding back the abilities of someone—" She nearly says *stronger than you,* which sounds hurtful but gets at a truth: she thinks of Miquel's empathy as a disability even when it's fully functional. Where the rest of them had received a blessing, he'd gotten a curse. "The last person to wear it has an overwhelming ability, too," she says. "This held it back for years."

"Why doesn't she need it anymore?" he asks.

Carrie worried about this question. She needed a way to answer that didn't sound judgmental of him or imply that problems with someone's ability were supposed to be overcome. "Fahima had another plan for her," she says.

Cautiously, Miquel takes the shackle. He turns it over in his hands. "It's beautiful," he says.

"It's not jewelry," Carrie says. She's impatient for the reaction she wants: relief, gratitude.

"I know it's not jewelry," he says. "It's nice that it's pretty. A pretty thing to do an ugly job."

"There's nothing ugly about it," she says. "This will fix you."

He looks at her quizzically as if he didn't hear what she said, and Carrie wishes he hadn't.

"I'm not broken, Carrie," he says.

Yes, you are, she wants to tell him. *You can't touch me, and you can't be touched. You live in a basement because otherwise you'll drown in other people's feelings until you're nothing* but *other people's feelings. It is not normal, and it is because you are broken.* She wants to tell him how little he'd lose, how bad the Hive has become, how painful his ability was even when it was working optimally. Instead, she tries to find his hand, meets only the cuff of his sleeve and the edge of his pocket, and gives up. She sets her stance, her posture broadcasting to him that this is not negotiable. Part of her wants him to say no, to make her decision for her. She could walk away knowing she tried. She could leave, and it would be his fault.

"I need you to try it," she says. "I need you back."

Miquel looks at her and without another word clicks the shackle into place around his right wrist. Nothing discernible changes. She could flip the inhibitor lights off and see what happens, but the switch is upstairs and he'd be alone with his ability if the shackle didn't work, even if only for a few seconds. She reaches up and puts both her hands on his cheeks. He flinches, expecting the torrent of her emotions to overwhelm him, but then his face relaxes. The memory of the last time they touched floods into her as she feels his soft stubble, the smoothness of his skin. She pulls him down toward her into a kiss, their first since the end of the war.

ON ARRIVAL

◇

"I don't know whether to be thrilled or sad or terrified," Viola says as the bus pulls out of the mall's parking lot.

"The easiest way to go is all three," Alyssa says, eating a breakfast sandwich one of the kids microwaved for her in the food court before they left. "I like to start out the morning terrified, then sink into sad around lunch. If thrilled happens, great."

"She hasn't been herself for seven years," Emmeline says to Alyssa, a chiding note in her voice. She turns to Viola. "You should be thrilled," she says. "I'm happy to see you again." She hugs Viola, relishing the fresh-from-the-oven heat that comes off her body.

"So I'm clear," Rafa asks, "are we not worried that Hayden disappeared?"

"They didn't disappear," Jerrod shouts over his shoulder from the driver's seat. Daniel sits next to him, his feet in Jerrod's lap. "Pretty Asian Mall Boy said he sent Hayden and what's her name to Chicago to play fuck the police or something."

"You thought he was pretty?" Daniel asks, sounding wounded.

"Oh, don't," Jerrod says, not taking his eyes off the road. There's something game about the way they're acting now, as if Hayden made all their performances real and now they have to work harder at being themselves but have decided to be up for the task. Emmeline likes them more this way, when they're trying to be cool and not succeeding.

"My biggest concern is how we're driving directly toward a giant rift in reality or whatever," says Kristal.

"We're not," Alyssa says. "I mean, it isn't. It never was."

"Can someone explain what happened with Phoenix?" Emmeline asks. They all look at her as if she's committed a massive faux pas, like saying she's never heard of the Velvet Underground, even Jerrod, whose head swivel causes the bus to lurch toward the shoulder before he corrects it. "I was away during the war," Emmeline says. "We didn't always get the news."

When they understand she's serious, they practically trip over one another to tell her the story, a narrative jam session of extended and interrupted solos.

"Phoenix was one of the schools," Rafa says. "And because of what happened to the school in New York, the schools were supposed to be off-limits."

"People were like, yeah, we want a war, but we don't want dead kids on TV," says Newton the sound tech, who's decided that nine in the morning is not too early to have a beer.

"People are bullshit," Jerrod says.

"I was at the school in Chicago, and we weren't hit the whole war except a couple broken windows," says Lana. "Then they put up the black glass and started quartering Faction there because they knew the army wouldn't bust in."

"But that was the thing," says Rafa. He's holding his hands out, fingers splayed, like a magician about to pull off a trick. "Everybody was at the schools, so the army's like, *where do we even shoot?* Meanwhile, our side liberates a different camp or voids out some nukes every week."

"They'd catch our people and put them in a camp," Kristal explains. "Then our people would bust out of the camp. Everybody they caught was someone else they had to guard."

"They must have decided, like, *I guess sending fucking storm troopers to a school is not the worst idea,*" Rafa says.

"They attacked the Phoenix school?" Emmeline asks.

"No, they hit Houston," Jerrod says.

"Yeah, why was it Houston?" Kristal asks.

"It was all acoustics," Rafa says.

"You mean optics," Newton says, punctuating it with a belch.

"Acoustics," Rafa says. "They set up like an echo chamber of inhibitors with the school in the middle. Not regular ones but like, boom, one time, shorts out everybody. Army walked right in. Nobody died."

"I remember seeing it on TV," Lana says. "Some general saying, *Look, no dead kids.* Big stupid grin on his face."

"It was a camp," Viola says. Her voice is entirely flat, and Emmeline wonders, apart from terrible things she might have done, what Viola has seen. "They turned it into another camp. They'd tour news cameras through it like it was a zoo to show how well they were taking care of everybody. All of those kids had boots on their necks."

This was the thing that was challenging in thinking about the Black Rose Faction: how people ended up in it and why they stayed. It was easy to ask now how anyone could commit to something like that, how they could let themselves become something so terrible. But for a time, what they were doing was arguably right. The awful things they did were justified because the other side was worse.

"So this is where it gets fuzzy," Rafa says. "Because what the theory is, is that they found the Gates."

"I've never believed that," Lana says. "At the Chicago school, we all knew the minute anyone came in the front doors, the first thing was you wreck the Gates."

"Except Houston was chaos and shit," Rafa says. "By the time anybody could even *get* to the Gates, they were already in zip ties. So they didn't wreck the Gates, and the army figures out what they're for. They've got back doors into any of the schools."

"Including New York," Jerrod says.

"They *think*," Newton adds.

"I don't think they could've gotten into New York," Kristal says. "Fahima would have figured something out. Like a lock or something."

"So they decide Phoenix," Rafa says, talking over her, eager to get to the end. "It's sprawl and not many students, so they figure they can go in like Navy SEALs and take it out. They fire up the Gate—"

"And Phoenix fucking disappears," Newton says. Everyone on the bus is silent. Rafa glares at him.

"Seriously?" Rafa says. "You make me do all the lead-up and then you jump in on the big finish?"

"Sorry," Newton says without a hint of actual apology.

"Except it didn't," Alyssa says.

"It did," Viola insists. "I saw the reports. I was—for a kid, I was established with the Faction by then. All of us from Bishop who they brought in early, we were lieutenants. We had access to information. The Gate ruptured, and the school collapsed into Hivespace, along with the blocks around it. There were photos."

"Did they come from Fahima Deeb?" Alyssa asks.

"Yes," Viola says.

"They were fake," says Alyssa. "She faked all of it."

"She went on the news," Kristal says.

Rafa nods. "She busted in on every channel," he says. "She was like, *Look what you did. You ripped a fucking hole in the world.*"

"That was her greatest performance," Alyssa says. "And I was around for some Oscar-caliber shit."

By now Phoenix floats at the edge of their vision, refusing to get any larger. Emmeline feels like the bus has been running in place for hours, Arizona 87 and the desert on either side of it cycling beneath them like the mat of a treadmill.

"It's not that Fahima sees everything coming, because she doesn't," Alyssa says. "She has backup plans upon backup plans. She was using the Phoenix school as a lab before the war started. It was where she kept her secrets." She looks at Emmeline. "It's where she built the Chair. The thing you used to make everybody . . . like you."

Something in the way Alyssa looks at her makes Emmeline feel guilty. "Not everybody," she says.

"The minute the war started, the fucking night before, she moved me there to keep me safe," Alyssa says, putting air quotes around the word *safe*. "She needed some place no one knew about. No one from the government and no one from Bishop. When the government took Houston, she moved all the students out of the Phoenix school and placed them in other facilities without anyone noticing. She moved in people she trusted or needed to keep safe."

"And then she blew it up?" Emmeline asks.

"It never blew up," Alyssa says. "It never fell into the sea or the Hive or whatever everyone said. Just because something disappears doesn't mean it's not still there."

As they enter the city, Emmeline sees the shimmering wall of the tear, the membrane between the actual world and Hivespace. It forms a dome high enough to encompass the tops of every building within six downtown blocks, hitting the pavement at a steep angle. The surface of the tear is milky white with iridescent threads running throughout. It reminds Emmeline of the hand soap her mother used to buy for the downstairs bathroom, the one for guests. If you could freeze that soap into a solid but keep the fluidity of its oily refractions intact, it would look like the tear in front of them. Jerrod drives right up to it, parking across the street at an intersection so that it feels as if they have time to turn and avoid it.

"It's shiny," says Emmeline.

"What *is* it?" Lana asks.

Rafa steps forward toward it, extending his hand, then stops. He turns back to Alyssa. "It's not going to kill me if I touch it, is it?"

Alyssa pauses, considering. "It's *mostly* special effects. But it's also a security system. It won't kill *me*," she says. "It knows me. Fahima put a chip in me so the system would recognize me. If I ever came back."

"Your girlfriend put a chip in you?" Kristal says.

"Ex-girlfriend," Alyssa says.

"I see why," Kristal says.

Next to Emmeline, Viola wraps her arms tighter around herself, pressing her right ear to her shoulder.

"It's probably easiest if I go in and let them know we're here," Alyssa says.

"No," says Viola, trembling with anger. "I don't believe any of this. This place was supposed to be lost and they're *fine*? What about Half Moon? What about Houston? Is everyone there secretly okay? Did they get hidden away somewhere too and we couldn't find them? How come no one cared enough to save them?"

Emmeline tries to hold her, and Viola shakes her off, so Emmeline settles for a hand on Viola's shoulder. "Let's knock and see who's home," Emmeline says.

Alyssa puts her hands out in front of her like she's trying to find her way through the dark. Without a pause or a hitch in her step, she walks through the membrane and it seals behind her, no scar or flaw to mark the spot where she entered. The rest of them stand in the intersection, waiting.

"S'hot here," Rafa says after an indeterminate amount of time. Everyone turns toward him like he's committed a sin by breaking the silence. "But, like, a dry heat?"

The membrane ripples, then lifts from the ground like a velvet curtain. An arch opens up, revealing the street behind it. Alyssa is standing there with a pained smile. To one side, there's a boy performing elaborate motions as if he's pushing back the sky with his hands. To her other side, standing close enough to be almost touching, is Fahima Deeb, who Emmeline hasn't seen since before the war. She looks broken, her shoulders slumped, her eyes rimmed in red, hijab askew so one lock of dark hair shows on her forehead.

"Look at all of you," Fahima says. "Get in here so Albert doesn't have to hold the door open." The boy's back arches, the weight of the sky bearing down. "I've got to tell you, this is unexpected. But everything is going according to plan."

Contemplating the paradox of those two sentences, Emmeline steps across the membrane and into a city that by all accounts no longer exists.

EXES

Fahima could not have anticipated Alyssa reentering the story, returning to a place she swore she'd never come back to, and it has her on her heels. *If I'd had more time,* she thinks, but she doesn't have an ending for the thought. They'd end up in bed? She'd call Alyssa out for the way she left? She'd fix everything? Blindsided by Alyssa's return, Fahima can't think of anything to ask from her.

"It all looks the same," Alyssa says once she's showered and dressed. She'd balked at the idea of being naked in their old apartment in any capacity, but Fahima promised to stay in the kitchen so that there was no risk of seeing anything no longer hers to see. Alyssa has found a T-shirt and jeans she'd left behind, which must have taken some digging. Fahima stows the offense at the intrusion away, currency to be used in a later argument.

"I haven't been here much," Fahima says. She looks around the apartment, which is essentially a dorm room. The coffeepot burbles to announce it's done, and Fahima pours Alyssa a cup. "I mean, I'm busy. Been busy. Things in New York and sort of all over."

"How's that going for you?" Alyssa asks, sipping her coffee. She's trying and failing not to sound smug, not to look at the world falling apart as proof she was right about Fahima all along.

"Not great," Fahima admits. "Unmitigated disaster on all fronts."

"How's Sarah?" Alyssa asks. Sarah was the reason Alyssa stayed as long as she had. Fahima was never around, and Alyssa had been Sarah's primary caregiver until the day she left. After that, Fahima had to bring Sarah back to Bishop to keep an eye on her. When Patrick asked where his sister had been, Fahima claimed she'd been in the building the whole time and Patrick hadn't come to see her. That shut him right up. Back then, Patrick had some sense of shame.

"She is exactly the same," Fahima says. "No progress, no regress. It would be sad except Sarah's not mad about it. She knows something's missing, but mostly she's the same." After a sip, Fahima adds sugar to her coffee, which tastes like the sole of an old boot. "You seeing anybody?" she asks.

Alyssa looks at Fahima and busts out laughing. "No, no," she says, trying to get herself under control. "I have this whole thing about not dating while there's a looming apocalypse. A couple hookups here and there, real casual. If they get clingy, I let them know about my policy re: looming apocalypse."

"I've been seeing someone," Fahima says. "Sort of."

"It's funny you become utterly normal in a crisis," Alyssa says.

"I'm trying to communicate," Fahima says. "Honesty and candor and all that stuff you used to complain I was bad at."

"You're still bad at it," Alyssa says. "Let me guess: the person you're seeing is from work."

"I only ever *talk* to people from work," Fahima says.

Alyssa nods. "So technically she works *for* you."

"It's not a control thing," Fahima says.

"It's always a control thing," Alyssa says. She takes a deep breath, about to launch into a list of Fahima's faults, then lets it out. "This coffee's terrible."

"I know," says Fahima. "You want sugar?"

"That would be worse," Alyssa says, taking another sip. "You want to tell me what you have planned for Emmeline?"

"Nothing dangerous," Fahima says. She's fairly sure she's not lying.

"You told me she died at the school that day," Alyssa says.

"I told everyone that," Fahima says. "Everyone needed to think that."

"You needed everyone to think that," Alyssa says, "so you could whip her out as your trump card when the time was right."

"So he couldn't find her," Fahima says. She hates having to explain anything. It's what's beautiful about Omar and Ruth and the people she's surrounded herself with since Alyssa's been gone: none of them ask for explanations. They accept that whatever Fahima says has reasons behind it that they don't need to know. "It was never about me using her as a weapon. It was about keeping her from Patrick." In her head she sees the smiles on the Bloom in her apartment, an expression that was decidedly not Patrick. "Or whoever he is now," she adds.

"You knew something was wrong with him that far back?"

"I didn't *know*," Fahima says. She wonders how much this is true. Hadn't he told her after the riot at the school? *There's something wrong. Keep me good. Tell me when I'm going too far.* She can't pinpoint when was too far, at what point she committed to stopping him.

It was the picture, she thinks. *Lexington Avenue seen from the window of the headmaster's quarters. It wasn't me at all who decided. It was her.*

"I think Emmeline can help," Fahima says.

Alyssa puffs up, haughty. "You're planning on using her."

"Of course!" Fahima shouts. "I used Carrie to get her, and I used Omar to get to Carrie, and I'm using Ruth to get over you. It's what I fucking do. It's how I see all of you: tools. Shitty half-broken tools I have to make do with because you're all I have. But you don't have to worry about it anymore because I have no use for you. You're free to go, Alyssa. Again." Fahima points at the door, but Alyssa doesn't move. "No one asked you to come back."

Alyssa closes her eyes. Fahima's certain she's going to walk out, out of the apartment, out of the building, out of the bubble and into the desert. Alyssa opens her eyes. A tiny smirk plays on her lips. "Her name's Ruth?"

Fahima releases a breath she'd become unaware she was holding. "She's nice," she says. It feels like a belittling way to describe Ruth, but singing her new girlfriend's praises won't help things with her ex right now.

"I'm going to hate her," Alyssa says.

"Probably."

Alyssa hoists herself out of the chair and sits next to Fahima on the couch. It seems like it could be the prelude to a hug. Fahima's not sure her heart could take a hug right now or that she'd be able to let Alyssa go if she held her for even a second. Alyssa puts her hand on Fahima's shoulder, keeps her at arm's length. "It's good to see you," she says. "It's hard but good. It's good you're okay."

Before Fahima can respond, one of the Omars knocks on the door and lets himself in.

"Hey, boss," he says. "Twenty-Two says we've got airborne incoming. It's got to be your girlfriend."

"You could not have timed that worse," Fahima says. Alyssa smiles that smile she gets when Fahima irrevocably fucks up.

———

Provisions are suboptimal, and although the air of the dinner is cautiously celebratory, the fare is piles of red beans and rice out of the box. The scruffy group of young people who arrived with Alyssa and Emmeline dig in as if starving.

"Hot sauce?" Rafa asks, unsure who to address such a request to.

"I think there's Tabasco in the pantry," says Omar Twenty-Eight, who's taken on the role of cook for Phoenix. He starts to stand, but Rafa's already up.

"I'll get it," he says. Twenty-Eight smiles at Fahima as if to say *See, some people can fend for themselves.*

"So what's the situation at Tuning Fork?" Fahima asks Omar Six. Along with a half dozen other Omars, he arrived on the Craft with Ruth, who took one look at Alyssa in the dining room, correctly assessed the situation, and sat down three seats away from Fahima.

"Are you sure we should be talking about this in front of . . ." Omar Six's eyes sweep across the strangers at the table.

"It's cool," Kristal says. "None of us have any idea what's going on."

Omar Six shrugs. "I'm sure things have slowed down without us there," he says. "But they were ready to roll forward with Thao and the Chair in Beta."

"Did Cedric fix the Chair?"

"The casualty rates are the same," Omar Eleven says. "Cedric doesn't care about the casualty rates."

"Neither does Patrick," Fahima says. "I'm not sure he ever did."

"You're so impatient with him," Sarah says. Whenever she speaks, there's an abruptness to it, an interruption in the normal flow of conversation. "Remember that time at school when you . . ." Her hand trails at her side, searching for her dog, once the reservoir for her memories.

"Yeah, Sarah," Fahima says. "I remember." Sarah smiles and returns to her food.

"I think the thing to worry about right now is the Bronx," says Ruth. "I've been watching the Throgs Neck Bridge. They're hauling bodies across by the truckload."

"That's going to have to wait," says Fahima.

"Bodies by the truckload sounds important," Lana says. The rest of the band chimes in with agreement, and Ruth and the Omars avoid making eye contact with any of them. Fahima has forgotten how exhausting the idealism of young people can be.

"I'm not saying it isn't important," Fahima says. She can hear notes of Kevin Bishop's voice ringing in her own, the tone that says *I know you think you understand things but please be assured I understand things far better.* "We have an opportunity to look at things that are big picture, sort of higher up. Those things will fix things on the ground."

"Are you going to send Emmeline back in time and unkill trucks full of dead people?" Alyssa asks with an unkind knife in her voice. The kids from the band turn to Fahima, expecting an answer.

"I can't do that," Emmeline says.

"Tell them about the thing you did," Kristal says. "At the theater when the Faction busted in."

"Tell me, too," Jerrod says. "I wasn't there."

"Because you were fucking Daniel in the mattress store," Kristal says.

"Yeah, but I still want to know what happened," Jerrod says sulkily.

"She knocked the things out of our heads," Viola says. "The little thing that P . . . P . . . that Mr. Davenport put in there. Emmeline killed it."

"I didn't kill it," Emmeline says. "I made it go away."

"She made it go away," Viola says quietly.

"You used the Hive," Fahima says. She tries to phrase it as a question, but it comes out closer to an accusation, and Emmeline's defenses go up.

"I didn't go in there," she says. "Kimani told me never to go in there. But sometimes it's like I can see the whole Hive from outside it."

"It's okay, Emmeline," Fahima says. "You're not in trouble."

"Fahima's trying to figure out how to load you and aim you," Alyssa says. Emmeline winces.

"I'm just glad we're all here and safe," says Ruth. Kristal is staring at her, her mouth full of rice, then breaks out laughing, spraying food back onto her plate. "What?" Ruth asks.

"That is like, the thing you say before everything goes to shit," she says.

"Yeah, nice job," Rafa says. "Now we're all fucked, lady."

ON ABILITY

◇

If Emmeline's being honest, Fahima's new lab is a shithole. She's comparing it with the memories she has of the lab in the basement at Bishop with its controlled chaos, messes of gears and gadgets under the sterility and bright lights of a serious place. Along with that, there's the gloss of memory, the warm soft focus time gives. The current lab looks like the nurse's office at a sleepaway camp for urban survivalists. There's not a single project in progress, weird guts exposed to the world. The top of a gray metal industrial desk, the room's sole furnishing, is buried in papers—charts and schematics marked up with webs of red ink. A bookshelf is built into the wall next to the desk, filled with leather-bound first editions that look unscientific, imported from somewhere else and awkwardly grafted onto this room for staging. In the corner of one shelf, acting as a bookend for the texts that lean against it, there's a Mason jar, which Fahima pulls down and hands to Emmeline. Inside, what looks like a leech writhes in fluid. When Emmeline takes the jar, the leech shoots to the outer edge, away from her hand.

"Interesting," Fahima says.

Without touching it, Emmeline knows what it is. She's seen its brothers and sisters before—its fellow aspects. It's the thing she wiped out of Viola's head, and behind it, beyond and through it, there's the other thing, the bigger thing of which it's a part.

"It doesn't like me," Emmeline says.

"Can you tell me what it is?" Fahima asks. She's trying to make it sound like a pop quiz question, but there's a desperate note in her voice that says she doesn't know the answer.

"It's him," Emmeline says. "It's Patrick. Except it isn't."

"No, it isn't," Fahima says. "It has a lot of Patrick's DNA, but it's something else. Chemically, it looks a lot like—"

"Hivematter," Emmeline says.

"Similar," Fahima says, and Emmeline can tell her purpose here is twofold. She's assessing what the thing in the jar is but also what Emmeline knows about it, what she's managed to glean for herself without the benefit of chemical analysis.

"It's deeper than that," Emmeline says. Fahima nods as if she's affirming something she already knows, but Emmeline sees her lean in, hungry for new information. "It's like what we are, what we can do. This is what it looks like when it's in the real world."

"I've seen it before," Fahima says. "Bishop could—"

"He could pull it through," Emmeline says. "This has been pushed out. Mixed with other things. It's gone bad."

"How do you know all this?" Fahima asks.

"I can hear it," Emmeline says. She hands the jar back to Fahima. "You can't?" There's a jab in the question, an attempt to establish herself as something more than whatever weapon Fahima thinks she is. Emmeline can't shake off her resentment at being brought here like cargo rather than invited.

"Not everyone's as tricky as you," Fahima says. There's a spark of who they used to be to each other, and Emmeline can't help but warm to it. "Let me ask you another," Fahima says as she wedges the jar back onto the shelf. "Your time stuff. Is all that back, too?"

"I haven't tried since I took the shackle off," Emmeline says. "I don't like doing it."

"Because of what happened before," Fahima says.

Emmeline nods. She remembers Viola glitching in their dorm room at Bishop. She remembers the boy in Central Park who asked her to Shake Shack before she froze him and three federal agents in an endless loop she couldn't break.

"I think your ability has matured," Fahima says.

"I haven't practiced," Emmeline says. "I haven't learned anything."

"I understand that," Fahima says. "I think potentially it's grown, the same way your body has. Or your body's grown into it. I think if you—"

"You're lying because you want me to use it," Emmeline says. "You're making it sound science-y to get what you need."

She can see Fahima reach for a denial, then pull back. "Yeah," she says, not sheepish but clearly caught out.

"Don't do that," Emmeline says.

"I might know someone with answers I need," Fahima says. "Except he's dead."

"You should have asked him before," Emmeline says.

"I didn't know the questions then," Fahima says. "I'm not sure I do now."

"You want me to go back and get him?" Emmeline asks. "Bring him here?"

"Can you?"

"I don't think I can," she says. It's something she's wondered about since the minute she took the shackle off. What and when does she have access to? How permanent is anything for her? How dead is dead?

"But you can go back and talk to him," Fahima says. "I'll give you a list of things we need to know."

"Why don't you come with me?" Emmeline asks.

"Can you do that?"

"I have no idea what I can do," Emmeline says. She rubs the spot on her wrist where the shackle used to be. Something small and sad passes over Fahima's face, and Emmeline can see who Fahima has let herself turn into, what parts of herself she's cut off. Preparedness and planning aren't the opposites of hope, but they run at strange angles to it. Maybe if Emmeline had been part of things rather than hidden away, she'd be like Fahima is now, anticipating the worst outcomes. But Emmeline is coming into things new and still has an idiotic willingness to try.

"I'm not sure I can see him again," Fahima says. "I'm not sure I can tell him how badly I fucked everything up."

"I think the number one rule of time travel is that you don't tell people in the past about their future," Emmeline says.

"You're making that up," Fahima says.

"Kimani and I watched a lot of movies," Emmeline says. "The actual number one rule of time travel seems to be that whatever the number one rule is, it gets broken by the end of the story." Fahima smiles. They used to joke like this all the time, an old-timey comedy duo trading one-liners about the fabric of space-time. It's not the most dear of the things Emmeline's lost, but she's glad to have it back.

"How does it work?" Fahima asks. "Do we pick a date and place and set the dial?"

"I think we just find him. Are you ready?" Emmeline doesn't wait for her to answer. She takes Fahima's hand and folds them both up and away.

Emmeline and Kimani spent a lot of time talking about how their abilities work. In Kimani's opinion, Emmeline's ability was the souped-up version of her own. The way she described it was that all Resonants were in touch with this thing that was bigger than they were. She cited Fahima as evidence. *All those things she comes up with,* Kimani said. *They're from somewhere. As in they're already out there and they come to her.* She talked about the Hive, which was transspatial: any place in the Hive is everywhere in the real world all at once. That was already some powerful stuff. Beyond that, there was the Source, which was everywhere and everywhen at once. *I can do some wild things within the Hive,* Kimani said. *When I was young, I folded upward out of the real world and into Hivespace like a bubble blown into glass.* As she spoke, Emmeline could see it, a perfect pearl of space held within a transparent solid, Kimani inside the pearl. *Only like what a bubble is to a circle,* Kimani added, and Emmeline's image of the metaphor burst. Kimani's idea, which jibed with things Fahima used to tell Emmeline, was that Emmeline was folding up one more level than that, going into the Source, and she was doing it without getting stuck the way Kimani was. Kimani could look down at every point in space, pick where she wanted to go, and attach a door to that spot. When Emmeline folded all the way up, she could look down at every point in space *and* time and choose where she wanted to go. *Then you can* go *there,* Kimani said. *No room to carry around. No doorway to stay trapped behind.*

Fahima blacks out when they fold all the way up. There's too much information here; even Emmeline has trouble not being overwhelmed by it. Emmeline sees Headmaster Bishop from the outside, from a direction it's impossible to point to. His whole life is a trail burning across time. She can't say why she picks the moment she does, but she chooses a spot on the line that is him and folds herself and Fahima down toward it.

The world takes shape around them, and they're on a lawn above a beach at night. It's chilly, and Emmeline rubs her arms for warmth. On the grass near them are children's toys: a plastic picnic table, a sand pail and shovel. Emmeline's stomach lurches as she sees a dead cat lying in the grass, its back legs replaced with those of a seagull, its head twisted to stare backward. The small house's door hangs open, the lights on inside. Emmeline can hear a song, a woman singing over the lilt and plunk of a piano.

"There he is," Fahima says, pointing away from the house. At the edge of the tide, Headmaster Bishop sits looking out at the ocean. The moon lights his face in profile. He's younger than when Emmeline knew him, and she has the double-take feeling of seeing pictures of her parents in their teens, the sense that she's aligned herself with youth and put everyone older than her on the other side of that divide, citizens of another country.

"He looks younger than I am," Fahima says. "This must be before he got sick."

"This is before you met him," Emmeline says. She takes the first steps toward Bishop, with Fahima following her down to the water. The sand crunches under their feet, and as they approach, Bishop tenses and turns an ear toward them. His body relaxes, and he looks back out at the water.

"Mr. Bishop?" Emmeline says when they're close enough to be heard. "You don't know us, but we need to talk to you about some things. We have some questions."

"This isn't a particularly good time," Bishop says, not turning.

"We can't come back later. It's complicated," Emmeline says. Bishop turns to face them, and Emmeline hears Fahima draw a sharp breath at the lack of recognition on his face. Emmeline can feel him in her head, skimming the surface of her thoughts. She chooses a terrible memory and focuses on it: an amalgam of the moment she saw the news about Powder Basin and knew her mother was dead and the moment when Kimani told her they found her father's body. It's a clumsy technique, but she doesn't have the energy or focus to follow her white flame training. It's enough to make Bishop pull out of her head.

"I'm sorry," he says. Emmeline can't tell if it's an apology for barging into her thoughts or sympathy for what he saw there. "Come on up to the house. I'll make us some tea. Maybe something stronger." He hauls himself up from the sand, and Fahima steps forward to offer him a hand—the last time she saw him, he was barely able to walk unassisted. He ignores her and wipes his hands off on his khakis. Emmeline turns and starts toward the house where they'd arrived, assuming it's his. Bishop grabs her shoulder, his grip harder, more urgent than seems necessary. "Not that one," he says. He points them toward the gravel road. "Mine's farther up the beach."

There's enough moonlight through the windows that he doesn't turn on any lamps except the fluorescent hood light above the stove. In its harsh blue glow, Emmeline sees the man Bishop was when she met him. The light sinks into every nascent wrinkle of his face and deepens it, making him the ghost of his future self. He fills the kettle and puts it on the stove.

"I was thinking I'd make myself a martini," he says. "I must have some gin here somewhere. Can I interest either of you?"

"I'm okay, thanks," Emmeline says.

In the dim light of the kitchen, she sees tears shimmering in the bottoms of Fahima's eyes. "That'd be nice," Fahima says, her voice half choked. Headmaster Bishop nods. He finds bottles in the cupboard above the sink, one large and transparent and the other small and green. He goes through an elaborate ritual of preparation, a series of exacting measurements. Emmeline sees his lips move, counting as he swirls the liquid in the ice with a long spoon. He takes two martini glasses out of the freezer. They give off wisps of steam and cloud to translucency in the close warm air of the kitchen. He pours the drinks and hands one to Fahima, the liquid vibrating with the quiver of her hand so the surface looks like a pond when a breeze passes over it.

"Steady there," says Headmaster Bishop. He sips his drink. The kettle whistles, and he sets his glass on the counter to search the cupboards again as the kettle continues to whine.

"Young lady," he says. "Do you prefer black tea or one made of flowers?"

Emmeline considers what's ahead of them and momentarily regrets not accepting a martini.

"Black is good," she says.

"Luckily, that's all we have," Bishop says, holding up a half-full box of Earl Grey tea bags. He pours Emmeline a steaming cup. "So, then," he says. "What did the two of you need to ask me?"

"We need to know about Raymond Glover," Fahima says.

"I should have guessed," Headmaster Bishop says. "Is there something specific?"

"Anything you can tell us," she says.

Headmaster Bishop looks at the half-empty gin bottle on the counter. "We'd better take a seat," he says. Fahima and Emmeline sit on the couch, and Bishop takes the armchair, which is so worn he sinks into it like it's about to swallow him. He sighs, and his face goes distant, that of a man who's rehearsed a confession in his head for years. "The first time I met Raymond Glover was on the train from Poughkeepsie to Santa Fe in April of 1940."

CODA

It's hard for Fahima not to sweep him up into the kind of hug he would have suffered stoically while he was alive. She listens to his entire story as he piles martinis on the two of them like weights while Emmeline sips tea that's long gone cold. Fahima keeps up with Bishop drink for drink because she understands that it's necessary for him: the pauses to fix another round like breaths, the alcohol a lubricant to keep his memories from locking in place. Now Fahima understands why he dodged her questions about where he came from. He'd already told her, and the telling was so hard he couldn't bear to do it again. He's as young as he was the day he showed up in the garden at Lakeview when Fahima was fifteen and rescued her from a gray existence in a mental health facility. He revealed what she was and what she could become. As his story winds down, she sees the same burden he carried before he died: the guilt for his mistakes and the things he felt forced to do. She thinks of his hand shooting out to stop Emmeline from going into the other house by the beach and wonders what fresh horror they caught him in the wake of committing.

"The extent of what Raymond had done was amazing," Bishop says. "I read articles about the suicides. I heard about them on NPR and saw them on the news. I understood they'd jumped off the building I'd visited, but I couldn't connect the apparent suicides to Raymond. It would have been a deft bit of craft on anyone, but I . . ." He clears his throat. "I assumed I was stronger than Raymond. Part of that was moral superiority. Raymond wasn't evil, but he wasn't my match when it came to integrity." He cleaves a plump olive with his teeth. "I was so self-righteous I believed everything I did was virtuous, evidenced by the fact *I'd* done it. I expanded that through children's book logic to a belief that I must be stronger than Raymond, whose morals were compromised by personal interest. But I couldn't have done what he did to me. Not out of ethical purity. I didn't have the strength or the skill.

"I'd like to say the spell broke, but it didn't. He couldn't stand the thought of no one knowing what he'd done. After a few days, the media turned their attention to other atrocities. I had an urge to come here to the coast to relax. No doubt Raymond put the idea there. When I arrived, he was sitting on that couch, contemplating that hurricane lamp like he was an antiques appraiser."

Fahima has a flash of memory. One Thanksgiving, she and Sarah and Patrick broke into this house. Patrick knew about a window that was unlocked. She remembers Sarah saying he used to sneak in here when they were kids, to try his ability out, that he had an imaginary friend who told him about it. *I had an imaginary friend who talked to me in my head,* Patrick had confessed, lounging on that couch as if he owned the place. *And I called him Raygun.*

"The first thing I did was kiss him. I can't say if it was because I wanted to or because Raymond wanted me to. We'd arrived at the place where we would be safe together. I imagined that's what this house would be. I was trying to bring him into that dream with me, and here he was.

"In the middle of the kiss, I felt his mouth twist up into a smile against my lips. He undid whatever he'd done to my head. The memory of those men and women plummeting came back to me. Raymond held me in the kiss as it happened. He let me struggle against him a moment before allowing me to pull away. There was a taste like ashes in my mouth as I gripped the counter for balance.

"Raymond told me I was embarrassing myself before I even spoke. He said I knew exactly why he'd done it.

"'I was in so many of their minds,' he told me. 'More than I'd ever tried at one time. And I thought of an experiment. I made them all aware of what I was. I handed them that knowledge in a way that they understood it was undeniably true. And then I told them there was a school full of people like me blocks from where they were standing. That these people, they were children, defenseless, for now.' Every one of them, Kevin. Every one of them imagined coming to your school and burning it down."

Bishop tilts his glass back, but it's empty. Fahima can't tell if he's drunk; exhaustion and alcohol blur into a warm slurry.

"It was the moment I came closest to understanding him," Bishop says. "If I ever shared Raymond's anger, it was then, thinking of those men and women coming for my children, for my school."

Fahima remembers a night toward the end of Bishop's life, a dinner summit with James Lowery and a noted television bigot. There had been a mention of government troops coming for the academy, a prediction of what happened after Bishop died. His flare of mother bear aggression seemed so out of character, but it burned at the core of him, fueling everything he did.

"I collected myself," he says. "Retreated to my proper *thou shalt nots*. I told him he couldn't punish people for their thoughts. He smirked and said, 'Obviously I can. I'll keep doing it until they understand. Or until they're all gone.'"

"What did he want them to understand?" Emmeline asks.

"That they were over," Bishop answers. "That the age of man was at its end. He wanted a war. He said it didn't have to be a war. It could be as simple as blowing out a candle: take them out one by one. 'It's not as if we don't have time,' he said. He didn't think we could die because we weren't getting any older. I had noticed, too. I was too vain not to. I was nearly eighty, and my students still looked at me like an uncle rather than a grandfather. Part of what allowed me to be patient with Raymond, to wait for him, was my increasing sureness that we had infinite time. Time wasn't the issue; Raymond was. Given an eternity, we wouldn't have been together. It was a false future. A silly dream.

"I would like to say I struck Raymond because I saw the threat he'd become, but that wasn't it.

"He broke my heart. He took my dream from me.

"I grabbed hold of his mind and pulled him down into the Hive, like diving off a cliff into a lake. Our Hivebodies manifested as titans, creator gods, returned for a reckoning. I could see others watching us, terrified. The ground of the Hive, a communally agreed upon delusion, cracked and buckled under our struggle. The sky fell, raining down in shards everywhere in the Hive at once. People fled, their Hivebodies blipping out of existence until it was only Raymond and me in the Hive, destroying it in our efforts to destroy each other.

"I found people later, adults who resonated that day, that moment. Unintended consequences. Through the cracks we created, extra light snuck through.

"Raymond fought me, wrestling my mind. I felt him push me

through the surface of the Hive. Not the ground but through what the Hive is, into what's beyond it."

Fahima's hand drifts into the air to indicate her barrage of questions. "I can't fully explain," Bishop says. "It's the place our abilities come from. It's what we resonate *with* when we use them, and we access so little of it, infinitesimal amounts. When we built the bomb, we unlocked a boundless energy contained in the smallest component of matter. What we do with our minds, with the barest effort, is to break open that same potential inside a moment. We channel the energy inside time and allow it to burst into the world. I was drowning in it, every sense flooded with unrealized futures. I was outside of time and history. I looked out at the world, and everything was different. It was like . . ." Bishop trails off, contemplating whatever he'd seen while he was submerged in the Source. In the silence, Fahima hears gulls on the shore, the soft whoosh of tide.

"It was like everything happening at once," Emmeline says. "Everything that ever happened or ever would."

Bishop smiles sadly at her. Fahima used to bring all the strangest new students to Bishop as soon as she could. When a new ability arose, it was her nature to document it, study it, suss out its implications for the way all abilities functioned. Bishop could see what it felt like and what the ability meant to the person who had it. He sees Emmeline that way, assessing the burden her abilities put on her.

"Yes," he says. "It was exactly like that." Emmeline's face is unreadable, but Fahima knows what she's feeling: there's nothing in the world like having Kevin Bishop tell you you're right.

"I came back a second before I'd left," Bishop says. "I don't know how, but there were two of me for a moment: one grappling with Raymond and me, outside him, watching. I knew in a second Raymond would plunge me into the Source. I grabbed him, along with my seconds-ago self, and I pushed. We pushed. We shoved him all the way down into the Source until everything that was him disappeared from the Hive. The other version of myself was gone, and I was alone."

Fahima thinks about how many times Bishop had to kill to protect them, yet this is the murder that haunts him. She wonders how often he's returned to this spot, hoping to be absolved.

"I waited to see if he'd reemerge, but his Hivebody was gone," he continues. "I waited hours before I came back out of the Hive to this room. Raymond's body was on the floor, breathing, eyes open. I have seen too many bodies of people I loved, but his was the worst. Maybe because it was a body I'd known so intimately, every inch. Maybe it was the breath. Breath is a lot like hope. I knelt down, held his nose and mouth shut. He never struggled. His body hitched like a stalling car and stopped."

This crushes one idea Fahima formed while Bishop told his tale: that Raymond Glover was lying in a coma all this time and had woken up at some point. If he was controlling Patrick from a hospital bed, her solution would be as simple as sneaking by the night nurse and snuffing him out with a pillow. But Bishop already had taken care of that.

"What did you to do with the body?" she asks.

"In the morning, I weighted it down with rocks and chartered a small fishing boat. The man who took me out saw the body. I told him what I was doing and that he shouldn't worry about it, so he didn't. We went out several miles, far enough I couldn't see the shore. He helped me haul the body over the rail and into the ocean. When we got back to shore, I gave him a ridiculous amount of money and took away all his memories of the day."

Fahima tries to imagine Raymond Glover walking out of the sea, shoulders strewn with kelp, but it's a *Creature from the Black Lagoon*–inspired nightmare rather than a working theory.

"I keep thinking I see him," Bishop says. "I know his body is dead, but I imagine there's part of him locked away, outside of time."

He straightens up and looks around as if remembering he's been speaking to them and not to himself. "Not too different from you, is it?" he says. "Once you step outside of time, you never entirely come back in. When Raymond held me under, I saw myself on the hill with Raymond and Mona, watching a sun being born. I saw how I'd die, although my mind has been kind and let me forget. Moments in sequence seem alien when you look at them from above. Human beings are like millipedes, trailing segments of themselves behind them in time. It's easier the more you can forget of it."

"They don't look like millipedes," Emmeline says. "They look like trails of light. They're brilliant, all interwoven. It's so beautiful you can hardly bear it."

Fahima has a memory flash of how they got here: something too big to hold in her head is gone without being grasped.

"There's the sun coming up," Bishop says. "Talk about outside of time. Every sunrise is the same sunrise. We only look at it from a different place in space and in time."

He stands up and gathers their glasses and mugs, carrying them to the sink. "That's more or less the entirety of it," he says. He fills a kettle, and the pilot light on the range clicks as the burner comes to life. "Will you stay for coffee?"

"We should go," Emmeline says. Fahima doesn't want to go. She wants to stay here with her friend. She wants to tell him everything she's done wrong so he can absolve her and set them all right. His death was when things fractured. It was when the fighting started in earnest, when she first saw the shadow inside Patrick. *We could bring him back with us,* she thinks. He'd beaten Raymond Glover once; he could come with them and do it again. Emmeline, intuiting what she's thinking, gives an almost imperceptible shake of her head.

"I'm sorry I've kept you up the whole night," he says, spooning instant coffee into a filter. "Probably not the best idea for myself either. I'm meeting two new students this morning. A brother and sister, twins. I knew their parents years ago. They live nearby. I should get myself cleaned up." Fahima imagines little Sarah and little Patrick waiting in the living room of the Davenports' beach house, primly dressed for their prep school audition. She wishes she could stop him, save the two of them from everything that comes afterward, even if it means she'll never meet them. Bishop runs a hand over the stubble on his cheeks. "It was lovely to meet you both. How does it work when I meet you again? Do I tell you about tonight?"

"You didn't," Fahima says. "You never told me."

"What an odd secret to keep," Bishop says. He adjusts his glasses and gives Fahima the sideways smile he often deployed when they were about to try something that was likely to fail in an interesting way. Fahima decides the space-time continuum can get fucked and hugs Bishop as tightly as she can, as if she can squeeze him back to life. He hugs her back politely. He understands there's a bond between them, but he doesn't feel it. It hasn't happened for him yet.

"I need you to do something for me," she whispers, hoping Emmeline doesn't hear, certain she does. "There's a girl in a mental health facility in upstate New York. She's like us, and she needs your help. Will you find her?"

"Of course," he says with a sigh. "That's what I do." She can't tell if the exhaustion in his voice is a result of talking all night or comes from the burden of being the one responsible for finding every lost child and bringing them home.

Emmeline tugs at Fahima's sleeve. Emmeline and Bishop shake

hands, and there's a long pause Fahima recognizes as Bishop communicating with Emmeline psychically. Emmeline nods and whispers *thank you*. The teakettle whistles, and the sound gives them their chance to exit.

"What did he tell you?" Fahima asks as they walk toward the ocean.

"When we first got here, he looked in my head," Emmeline says. "He saw what happened to my parents. He promised to keep them safe."

The two promises—to find Fahima, to protect Emmeline's parents—sit next to each other in Fahima's mind. She knows one will be kept and one will be broken, but her attempts to understand what this means about how time works fail. She looks back at the house one last time.

"Why *couldn't* we bring him with us?" she asks.

"He has so much to do," Emmeline says, taking Fahima's hand. "Did you find out what you needed?"

As Emmeline folds them upward, away and back to where they left from, Fahima can't give a confident answer. She had gotten something she needed. She has no idea if it'll be enough.

ON LIMITS

◇

Emmeline wants to jump over the plan. She wants to be so confident in whatever Fahima decides to do that she can meet herself on the other side. Someone who can move through time might come to think of time as something without value, like a billionaire dropping hundred-dollar bills on the sidewalk, but it's the opposite for Emmeline. She obsesses over time passing, time wasted. She ponders whether she can learn to be rested after sleep she hasn't had, full from meals she has eaten but didn't eat. How much is it possible to cheat, to skip the boring, painful parts and arrive at hard-earned joy without putting in the work?

Waiting suspends agency; it makes Emmeline feel less human, stuck in time solidified like amber, holding her still as she watches the rest of the world in motion. The dull paralytic throb of waiting lends itself to bad ideas. Emmeline wonders if people in full-body casts make terrible plans for themselves, imagine reprehensible crimes they might commit. Emmeline makes terrible plans. She imagines reprehensible crimes.

On the third day with no word from Fahima, Emmeline sits in her bare room at the Phoenix school and folds up out of the world.

It takes effort to find her mother. Not every moment wants to let her in, and this moment is a tricky fucker. It's something Headmaster Bishop said to her once. She remembers it because when she was a kid, swear words contained a special thrill. An aphorism with an embedded f-bomb was a thing worth keeping.

The moment is a tricky fucker.

She knows immediately something is wrong. This moment does not want to let her in. It writhes and snaps as she folds down into it. The world comes into focus around her, and she's standing in the doorway of a bar, a run-down place meant to look like a saloon in a Western. The first thing she notices is that the door stays open rather than swinging shut. There is no sound; sound exists only when time is in motion. The people in the bar are static. Pint glasses tip but don't spill. Hands hover over shoulders, waiting to slap them affectionately. The moment's tricked her: it let her in and holds her trapped.

She sees her mother sitting at the bar, talking to a white boy with a hatchet of a face, slick with adolescent grease and nervous sweat. She's across the room, on the other shore of a sea of bodies, and Emmeline tries to go toward her, but the moment restrains her. The door moves slightly on its outswing from the entrance of the men in front of her, blocking her view of her mother. Time creeps. The boy leans in, saying something to her mother, a look of regret on his face.

Shade by shade, the boy changes. He glows dark—not dark like the black glass; his darkness is a lack, a void. It seeps out of him, mingling with the sweat slicking his skin. It pours from him, devouring the light around him, devouring the *space* around him. Her mother's face registers confusion, then shock, then horror. The void moves toward her, and the moment throws Emmeline out. It pushes her back to her room in Phoenix, sitting on her bed, alone.

She tries again. Again and again. Each time is the same: the doorway, silence, a dark glow. Every time, the moment lets her almost see, then throws her out, as if trying to protect her. She tries until she's exhausted. Each attempt is the same. The doorway. Silence. A dark glow. Out.

The repetition of the failure makes it harder to quit. If she hadn't started, she would have been able to stop. She cycles from now to then, across a divide of seven years. Duration gets fuzzy, but time passes for her body, and eventually she collapses. She's lucky—sleep takes her in her bed and not trapped in the doorway of the bar, watching her mother eaten away into nothing.

When she wakes up, she goes looking for her father. She thinks she might find him on the roadside in Mosul, leg freshly burned away, the wreckage of the jeep that carried him scattered across the desert. Instead, she's in a place she knows, a place she'd been days before. It's Headmaster Bishop's house in Maine, where they stayed up all night talking. The biggest difference is the heat. Like sound, heat needs time to happen—heat and cold are by-products of time. Emmeline stands in one of the rooms off the hallway to the bathroom that looks out on the ocean. The room is bisected by a thick glass wall, with a circle the size of a manhole cover missing. Thrown into the corner like a rag doll is the boy she saw talking to her mother in the bar in Powder Basin. His shirt is covered with blood, and there's a wound above his right eye, a dark angry circle. She can sense the black thing coiled in his head, writhing and twitching in the dead tissue. She hears hitched intakes of breath and looks down. Sitting by her feet is her father, panicked and confused. His right arm has been chomped off at the shoulder, leaving a smooth cauterized cutaway of meat and bone. There's a black coil in his head, too, thrashing and feral, destroying everything in his mind. He looks up at her, and Emmeline knows he doesn't recognize her. There's a blankness that runs all the way down, a pond of clearest water. He's hollowed out, here but gone.

He looks at the scar on Emmeline's arm, and there's a ripple of recognition, motion on the water's surface, but then it disappears.

"Did I hurt you?" he says.

"No, Daddy," says Emmeline. "You didn't hurt me."

"I don't know you," he says. All of him ripples, and Emmeline thinks the moment is throwing her out again, sparing her what's next. It's only tears. Her father looks at the gun in his lap. "Everything's gone," he says. "Can you fix me?"

Emmeline is sure she can. She folds up, intending to come back a minute before this and stop what's happened. She will try until she fixes it even if it kills her. She comes back exactly where she left, her father looking up at her, beseeching. She tries again and again, folding up and down, in and out of time, a moth beating frantic wings against glass. She will save him if it breaks everything. But nothing changes. It's like trying to blink the world away. She opens her eyes, and everything is still there. Her father, hurt, in need. He'd been that way his whole life, and she hadn't been able to see it. The pain of parents is invisible to their kids, which is how it needs to be. Emmeline can see it now and realizes she *can* do one thing. She can be here for him at the end. She runs her hand through his hair. She forgot it had gotten so thin by the end of his life. An island of pale brown curls, pulled away from the rest, adrift in a sea of scalp. She feels him shudder under her hand. *Can you fix me?* he asked a second ago, a heartbeat before, and in that time she tried a hundred times, a thousand, only to end back here.

"I can't," she says. "There are things that happen, and they always happen. There are things I can't fix."

He nods. "You should go," he says. "I have something I need to do. I don't think you should see it."

Emmeline thinks about what Kimani told her, how they found his body in the house on Jarvis Avenue. Her father and Owen Curry, the monster he chased for the last few years he was alive, both dead in a shootout with only one gun. It felt like a curse was lifted off her house, knowing her father hadn't died there, knowing the boy who killed her parents never set foot in their home while he was alive. She looks at Owen Curry's broken body. She spent years wishing he was still alive so she could kill him. She imagined great cataclysms in history she could cast him into: the eruption of Vesuvius, the Chernobyl meltdown. But he was a pawn Raymond Glover moved around the board, a weapon to be aimed and fired, like she is.

"I'll stay here with you, Daddy," she says. She bends down and kisses him above his eyebrow. His skin is fever-hot. She lays her hand against the side of his face the way he used to when he suspected she was sick, when he didn't want to alarm her by checking her forehead. She pulls her hand away, then nods, telling him it's okay.

Her father puts the gun under his chin and shoots himself in the head. The shot rocks his head back, bouncing it off the blood-spattered glass. Emmeline looks away before she sees anything too gory, anything she wouldn't be able to unsee. As the echo of the gunshot fades and the ringing in her ears subsides, there's a stillness disturbed only by the sounds of waves crashing into the shore. The moment lets her stay for all of it, to be with him and bear witness. Then it lets her go. Tricky fucker.

She comes back to the room at the Phoenix school, and someone is knocking on the door. The hem of her nightshirt is wet with her father's blood. Moving with the shocked grace of a sleepwalker, she gets up from the bed and opens the door. Alyssa stands there with a sandwich on a plate.

"I thought you might want—" She stops, arrested by the sight of the blood, and Emmeline can see a switch flip in her head as the doctor part of her comes online. She drops the plate, and it shatters on the cement floor, the shards skittering away from one another. "Where are you hurt?" she asks. Her eyes expertly scan Emmeline's body, looking for tears in her clothes, patterns in the way the blood is distributed.

"It's not my blood," Emmeline says. She folds back a few seconds, retrieves the unsullied sandwich and the unshattered plate.

"That is in no way comforting," Alyssa says. She notices the plate in Emmeline's hands and the shards of the same plate on the floor. "How does that work?"

Emmeline shrugs. "It doesn't work," she says. "I can fix little useless things. Anything that matters is fucked." Emmeline sets the sandwich down on her bed, pulls off her nightshirt, and throws it into the corner. She fishes another out of her backpack and puts it on; the fact that Alyssa is a doctor erases any shame about undressing.

"What happened?" Alyssa asks, down on her hands and knees picking up pieces of the broken plate.

"I tried to save them," Emmeline says. "Either one of them. I tried, and it didn't work. What are my abilities even for if I can't save them?"

"This stuff gives me a headache," Alyssa says. She collapses onto Emmeline's bed, cradling the pieces of the broken plate. "It's like every undergraduate metaphysics class I ever slept through has come back to haunt me. Maybe everything has happened and you can only go back and be part of it the way it was. A witness."

"I don't want to be part of things if that's how it works," Emmeline says.

"It's also possible I'm wrong," Alyssa says. "I have a plate and you have a plate, and I think they're the same plate. So seriously, I would not listen to me about any of this. But you need to eat."

"I will," says Emmeline.

Alyssa leaves, shutting the door softly behind her. Even though she feels like her insides are made of broken glass, Emmeline tries again. She folds up out of everything until she can see her entire life as if it's separate from her. At the same time she feels the blazing line of it pass through her. She's observing it but also part of it.

She's surprised when she folds down into her old room in the house on Jarvis Avenue and finds it occupied by someone else. The boy is a few years younger than her, the same age as the kids in the Flagstaff mall, but he looks healthier. This boy has been cared for all his life; he has the relaxed smile of someone who has never doubted that he's loved. He's sitting on Emmeline's old bed, studying a Polaroid. He looks up at Emmeline and smiles. "Hey."

"Hey," she replies, thrown off by his calm.

He tucks the photo into his back pocket. "I wasn't sure if you were gonna come the first night we got here or what," he says. "I've been hanging out up here after dinner every night. I tell my dads I've got homework."

"You knew I was coming?" Emmeline asks.

"You told me when we met," he says.

"When was that?"

He shrugs. "A month ago?" Pieces come together in Emmeline's head. She thinks about how Kimani made her play three games of chess at once, how she felt as if she could see the three boards layered on one another. By the time she left Kimani's room, she could feint on one board to set up moves on another. They were clumsy attempts and Kimani caught her before the trap sprung, but Emmeline imagined the possibilities in a wider field of contest.

"I wish you'd told me what was going to happen," the boy says.

"I know you said it was all going to be okay, but honestly it's been shitty."

Emmeline pauses before she responds. She doesn't know this boy's name, much less what's happened to him, only that he's met her before and she hasn't met him yet. *There are things that happen and they always happen,* she thinks. *Maybe everything has happened and I can only go back and be part of it.*

"There are rules," she says as much to herself as to him.

"I know all about special people and their rules," he says bitterly. "This is what you meant when you said it would be all right?"

"I guess so," Emmeline says. She looks around the room, which feels familiar and strange at once. "I mean, you are okay. I used to live here. I thought something bad happened here and the house was cursed. But it's not. It's a good place; it's only haunted. You stay in a place and you fill it up with memories, and they're like ghosts."

"Is that what you are?" he asks. "A ghost?"

"What do you think I am?"

"I thought I was going crazy and you were like my imaginary friend, only a hallucination," he says.

Emmeline thinks of the ghost who came to her when she burned herself with the pot off the stove. She thinks of the woman who visited her in this room before her abilities manifested. *I can't,* she thinks. *There's nothing I can do to help that girl. I don't know any more than she does.*

But I did help her.

"I was sure you weren't real until I showed my friends the picture," the boy says. "Once I knew they could see you, I knew I hadn't made you up." He looks down at his shirt, pinching it between his thumb and forefinger. "It's today." He takes the Polaroid out of his back pocket and shows it to Emmeline. "See, we're wearing the same stuff."

It's a photo of Emmeline and the boy sitting on her old bed. They're wearing the clothes they currently have on, and the Polaroid is from the camera in Emmeline's backpack in Phoenix.

"It must be today," she says. She folds back to where she started and fishes the camera out of her backpack before returning to the house on Jarvis Avenue. Something goes slightly wrong, and she folds into her father's office in the attic in the spot where Kimani's door first appeared and took her to the Bishop Academy. There's a man sitting at her father's desk, and although she can tell by the color of his skin and the breadth of his shoulders it's not her dad, she thinks for a second she's landed farther back, when he was still alive. She takes a step toward him. The floorboards creak underfoot, and the man spins the desk chair around. Emmeline folds away before he sees her, and she's back in her old room, next to the boy, who blinks quickly as if he's seen some amazing magic trick.

"Ready?" She holds the camera out as far as she can, thinking how stupid it is to have a camera you can't see yourself in. She presses the shutter button, and the camera makes the loud click that comes before the mechanical whir as it spits out the picture. She pulls it out of the camera and stares at the milky surface, hoping an answer will appear like the die rising out of the blue murk of a Magic 8-Ball.

"Should I see it?" the boy asks. "Maybe I shouldn't look at it yet. I know what it looks like, but still. And is it in my pocket and also right there?" Emmeline thinks about the plate: broken and intact. "This shit is really weird. You must be used to it."

She looks at the picture as it resolves. "I don't think I'll ever get used to it."

"Shit, I wasn't thinking," he says. He's using more swear words around her the longer they're together, and she can't tell if it's because he's getting more relaxed or if he's trying to show off. "Do you even know my name?"

"I—I don't," says Emmeline.

"It's Rai," he says.

"It's good to meet you," she says. "I'm Emmeline."

"I know," Rai says. She catches him trying to peek at the photo and pulls it back.

"I gave this to you a month ago?" she asks.

Rai nods. "You told me it was proof everything would be all right," he says.

Emmeline looks at the picture. It's two kids smiling like idiots at the camera. Looking at them, it's hard not to feel like maybe everything *will* be all right.

"I should go deliver this, then," she says. The photo feels as if it's buzzing, humming in sync with the other iteration of itself tucked in Rai's pocket. If there can be two of a thing, maybe time and the world aren't as static as Emmeline fears.

"Will I see you again?" Rai asks.

"Yeah, but before," Emmeline says, still parsing what all this means.

"What about *again*?" Rai asks. "Like, the normal *again*."

"I don't know," she says. "Nothing after this has happened yet."

Rai nods like she's said something deeply meaningful, and Emmeline thinks of Rafa and smiles. Thinking the smile is for him, Rai returns it. He looks like he's about to hug her when Emmeline, suddenly uncomfortable, folds herself back up and then down into the room, before.

There's a girl lying on her belly on the floor, her legs kicking back and forth, intent on the piece of paper in front of her. She's wearing shorts and a T-shirt, which she does only when she's alone. She's shy about the scars on her arm even around her parents, because one of the kids at school saw them and called her Swirly Skin. Emmeline listens. She can hear talking downstairs. There's a vent that connects this room to the kitchen, and sound carries clear through it. The girl's father is saying it's a one-month embed in Mosul. He says they're not even fighting there anymore. *Fine,* the girl's mother says. *Fine.*

"Hey there," Emmeline says to the girl. "What are you drawing?"

The girl looks up, unsurprised. *She's seen me before this,* Emmeline thinks. The girl smiles coyly and turns back to her drawing. "Me, but I'm a grown-up," she says.

"What are you going to be when you grow up?" Emmeline asks.

"An artist," says the girl, as if it's the most obvious thing. Emmeline hunkers down next to her.

"I knew a girl like you," Emmeline says. "She grew up and had amazing adventures."

"Tell me," says the girl.

And because if there are rules, Emmeline doesn't know them, and because you can't be punished for breaking a rule no one told you about, Emmeline does. She folds back into the room night after night and tells the girl about every amazing person she's met. People who can fly, people who can disappear. A man who can grow as big as a house but is the nicest person and a girl who's as warm as bread that's right out of the oven.

Each time she folds back into the room in Phoenix, it's as if no time has passed. The night there goes on forever, leaving room for a thousand stories.

Until she folds into the house on Jarvis Avenue and knows exactly what day it is. Something about the cool evening air means it's October. More than that, there's something about the girl. She gives off the same buzz the photo of Emmeline and Rai did when it was in the same room as another iteration of itself. It's also an insistent call to Emmeline from the Hive, the *come find me* murmur that calls Resonants to one another.

"Tomorrow's a big day," Emmeline tells the girl as she works on a pencil drawing of a boy with skin like tree bark whom she won't meet for months. "Things will start with your dad, but everything is going to change."

"Is it going to be okay?" the girl asks her. Emmeline is looking at the back of the girl's head, the mess of corkscrew curls. She watches the fast-twitch movements of the girl's right arm as she draws, the only time she entirely forgets about her burn scars. Emmeline wants to snatch her up and carry her to the far shore, but she doesn't know where or when that is. It's as if being alive means never feeling safe.

"I don't know," Emmeline says. "It isn't over yet. But I guess the fact it's still going means it's okay."

HYDE PARK

◇

It's hard to imagine that "how do you play basketball?" would become an issue of deep import. The reconceptualization of a game so intrinsic to Clay's upbringing as to feel genetic is an unlikely bearer of serious political implications. Clay sits in the bleachers of the Unity School, Dom's hand gripped anxiously in his lap, watching an attempted answer to this newly crucial question play out on the court.

It's an intramural game, and the first problem came down to the selection of teams. According to Rai, some kids, most of them baseliners, argued the game should be baseliners versus Resonants, to prove a point. Bryce stepped in to nix this. So mixed teams were created, names picked at random to avoid the mythologized relic of the adolescent emotional trauma of someone being picked last. Bryce told Clay he'd put his thumb on the scale of randomness a bit to ensure an even distribution of kids with and without abilities on each team.

As it often did, the question of the use of abilities came up.

Some kids said it was insulting to ask anyone to play at less than their best, so the use of any ability should be allowed. This was quickly knocked down, but then what constituted an ability? This Resonant could fly, but that baseliner was taller by a head, so who's to say which is fair? Rai said it was a good talk. "I know Bryce planned it that way; I'm not dumb," he said. "But it was one of those 'we're all special in our own special way' kinda things, and it made me feel better about stuff." As he pointed out, "Reading minds isn't going to help you sink a free throw," a statement that turned out to be directed at one kid who was preternaturally strong on defense despite the promise not to "anticipate" anyone's moves but useless at the line.

It was good to see Rai lost in something big enough to eclipse everything else going on. He had become passionate about basketball, although it had never been more than a hobby before. Clay suspects it's that it's something Rai can own, something his dads can look in on without being part of. Clay has downplayed his interest in and understanding of the game to preserve this as Rai's territory; if Clay did something as stupid as offering to assistant coach, Rai's interest would wither.

"He's good," Dom says, giving Clay's hand a squeeze.

"He's got to learn to go left," Clay says quietly, as if Rai might hear. "Point guard's no good if he can't go left."

"I don't even know what that means," Dom says. Clay pulls his eyes away from the game and looks at his husband.

"We're doing okay, aren't we?" It's more of an affirmation than a question, but Dom answers anyway.

"Not as good as we were, but we're going to get there," he says. "I don't know that I would've said that two weeks ago." He looks down at their intertwined hands. "We've been through worse."

"That other thing wasn't worse than this," Clay says. They've never come up with a nickname for Dom's cheating. It would be useful to have one, a way to refer to it without giving it too much conversational weight, but then they'd need to title each of their domestic disputes. The Dishwasher Incident. That Thing at Your Mother's. It sounded like a list of B movies playing at a second-run theater.

"I thought that was the end of us," Dom says.

"That was you and me, and it wasn't him," Clay says, pointing his chin at Rai as Rai steals the ball from the free throw–impaired psychic. Clay stands up to clap for his son while Dom cheers from his seat. Rai misses an easy layup and falls back to set up the defense. Clay sits down. "I mean we're easier to fix," he says. "We could've done couples therapy, we could've—"

"We didn't, though," says Dom.

"We would've found some way to fix it," Clay says. "This? We can't talk this out. We can't word it away. I think of the stuff I'd be willing to do, and it's either impossible or wouldn't do any good."

"You mean to make him like us?"

"Rai *is* like us," Clay says. "He's charming like you, but he plays his cards close like me. He's as kind as his father was, and he's as trusting as his mother. He's like all of us."

"I didn't mean that."

"I know, Dom," says Clay. Sometimes Dominic's defensiveness can be exhausting, an offense all its own. "I'm saying, for what little we could do from where we were at, with what we were given, I think we're getting to be all right."

Rai throws up a shot that's off to the left, and Clay's sure the girl who grabs the rebound extended her arm farther than an arm ought to reach. "Watch nine, ref, watch nine!" he shouts, and the girl looks directly at him, clearly guilty, before passing the ball up court.

"Are we going to Bryce's thing after this?" Dom asks.

Clay shakes his head. "It's a high school reunion," he says. "All the kids that went to their gifted and talented school going on about their glory days. You want to tell them about being a teenager without anything special about you?" Dom chuckles. "Besides, Rai doesn't need to be around that. Or in that bar."

"It's sort of a dive," Dom whispers.

"You ever go to a gay bar when you were a baby?" Clay asks. Dom shakes his head, slightly embarrassed. He was barely out when they met and had never put in the hours on the dating scene. "They were all dives, done up with tinsel and a lighting rig. When you build a place to feel safe, all you need's the space and a decent sound system." Rai ducks by the psychic kid with a solid pump fake, pulls up, and takes a shot from the top of the key that swishes soundlessly through the net. Dom and Clay are both on their feet. When they sit back on the bleachers, Clay finishes his thought. "That bar must have been like that for them when they were kids. Places like that feel used up to us because you and I don't need them anymore."

THE NEXT FIVE YEARS TRYING TO BE WITH YOUR FRIENDS AGAIN

◇

The sun goes down and comes up and droops again, and they do not leave their apartment or their bed. They're supposed to meet everyone at Vibration at nine, but Carrie refuses to go anywhere until they are starving, every calorie in them depleted.

"We should go," Miquel says. He sits at the foot of the bed, watching the sky turn purple.

"We can tell them we got lost," Carrie says, pulling on her jeans. "You haven't been out of the basement in years. I'll say you led me astray." Carrie sees the soft bruises of hickeys forming at the base of his neck and flowering on his ribs. She reaches over and touches one of them, the thrill of being able to touch his skin again still not abated.

"I think they're going to suspect the truth," he says. It's an adolescent thing to leave her mark on him, but they never got to be lovers as teenagers. It's appropriate for them to act like teenagers now—or forgivable at least.

Eventually, they make their way out into the city. Miquel is amazed by everything, as if he's seeing Chicago for the first time. They're already late, but he stops to chat with everyone on North Avenue, slowing them down. He hasn't seen any of them in so long, and they are so happy to see him. Carrie feels the way she used to when she walked around with him in Topaz Lake: as if she's the wife of the mayor, basking in the secondhand sunlight his loving constituents direct at him. Even with all the time that's passed, he knows everyone's name, remembers tiny personal details that cause their faces to light up when recalled.

At Vibration, it's exactly what Carrie asked Waylon not to do: a surprise party. It's manageably small so as not to overwhelm him, but Carrie can't help but worry. Waylon and Bryce are here. Travis and Diane and Edith, who were at their wedding in Topaz, and Thought Bubble, an old bar regular whose thoughts materialize in pink puffy letters over his head and who Carrie now remembers is named Leonard. Jonathan is here, sporting a black eye and a scabbed lip. She heard he got into a scuffle with some Faction agents in Pilsen the other day. They came for one of his neighbors and Jonathan tried to help. He was lucky to get off with the shiner and split lip. His expression says everything between him and Carrie is forgiven and forgotten. That was the appeal of Jonathan to begin with, her sense he'd be willing to set the counter back to zero when she decided to end it. She loves him for not needing an explanation.

On Waylon's cue, the DJ starts in on a nostalgia-heavy set, leaning into the stuff they listened to in their first days living on North Avenue, along with mixtape fodder from Bishop. It all sounds dated, like transmissions from another planet. When she and Miquel make their way to the dance floor, it's as if they're acting in a play about the people they used to be, trying to invoke some spirit that's gone.

Hayden shows up late and already drunk. They kiss Carrie

chastely on the cheek, then hold Miquel out at arm's length, appraising him. Carrie knows Hayden sees the toll his ability has taken on him and wonders if they clock the hickey on his neck. Hayden pulls Miquel in and holds him.

"The minute Carrie turns her back, I'm stealing you from her," they say, winking at Carrie over Miquel's shoulder. They're trying to be playful, but they have the same look of hurt they had both times they walked out of Carrie's apartment.

If the booze doesn't improve their impersonations of their past selves, it makes them less inclined to judge themselves on their quality. This won't be a perfect night; the magic of perfect nights is that they just happen. There's an effortless element required, and all of this is trying hard, striving toward perfection. But it's a good night, and it's difficult to remember the last time she had one of those. After a while, things even feel comfortable with Hayden again, as if they've gone back to the place where their friendship was only that, anything beyond it unspoken and unconsidered.

In an inversion of the way things used to be, the tipping point where a night would wobble into chaos becomes the apex of the party, from which everything recedes. The DJ, younger than all of them by ten years, keeps throwing out jams, but the dance floor clears as they settle into small groups to finish drinks they don't necessarily need and shout stories about other nights over the noise. Eventually the DJ reads the room and drops things down a register, but by the time that happens, the party has the feeling of a wake or, worse, a reunion. Everything points backward; nothing is new. It's everything Carrie was afraid she'd become back then, before the world gave her bigger and better things to be afraid of.

She orders what she tells herself will be her last beer and finds Waylon, who's assumed his usual position slightly outside it all. His preference has always been to orchestrate, whether it's smuggling networks or webs of information or social gatherings like this. He is the one who cooks the dinner, who makes the arrangements, and his pleasure doesn't come from involvement so much as seeing everything play out.

"What are you hearing?" she asks him.

"I don't know; is this Depeche Mode?" he asks. "You have a better ear for this stuff than I do. You should DJ sometime. Drinks are free."

"My drinks are always free," Carrie says. "And that's not what I'm asking."

"It's a party, Carrie," he says, the hint of a whine sneaking into his voice.

"A friend out west told me the Faction was gearing up for an evacuation," she says. "Does that track with what you're hearing?"

"There's a lot of activity around Willis Tower," he says. "They're moving people in, but not at the levels they'd need to evacuate the city. The Faction is committed in the Bronx right now."

"Evacuation?"

Waylon shakes his head. "That's how they're playing it to the press. We have someone who came from there, and he says it's a bloodbath."

"Evacs were ugly," Carrie says.

"He says it was a culling."

From across the room, she hears Miquel's laugh piercing through the music. He and Bryce are cracking up over something. She's gotten conspiratorial giggles out of him in bed, but she can't remember the last time she heard his full barking laugh. She feels like it's a disappearing sound, one she's already moving away from. She runs some loose numbers in her head. After the Armistice, the evacuations were kept as bloodless as possible partly because the world was watching. If the Faction had escalated to a massacre in the Bronx, they must feel as if no one's looking or as if no one who's looking cares.

"What do you know about the efforts to create the Pulse abroad?" she asks Waylon.

"Funny you should ask," he says. "The guy I mentioned who got out of the Bronx? He was working with Project Tuning Fork."

"Are they close to making it happen?"

"He said they could do it tomorrow but the fatality rate would be off the charts," Waylon says.

"That's only an issue if people care about the costs," Carrie says.

"A week ago Fahima Deeb was heading the project," Waylon says. "She wasn't about to let a bunch of people die. But she's out. Disappeared."

Carrie sips her beer. Whatever Fahima has going, whatever she wanted Emmeline for, must be moving into its endgame. She wants to take comfort in this, imagining Fahima as a chess master thinking ten moves ahead, but something tells her Fahima's as much in the dark as she is.

"Who's running it now?" Carrie asks.

"Cedric Joyner," Waylon says. "You remember a couple years ago, he—"

"I know him," Carrie says. The final piece clicks into place. The reason the Faction isn't worried that *they* are watching is that soon there won't be a *they. Soon everyone is going to be us. Or dead.*

The room tilts and spins, and she's grateful to have Miquel to hold on to. "Sleep," he says. She doesn't, but it's nice to have him here to say it. She's sure she stays quiet and still long enough for him to believe she's fallen asleep in his arms when he asks, "What did you talk to Waylon about?" He's quiet enough that it wouldn't have woken her if she'd been asleep.

"Local work," she says.

"You were different after," he says.

"It wasn't anything."

"I still know when you're lying," he says. "I don't need magic powers to—"

"You've never known when I was lying," she says. "I used to wonder why you didn't know how I felt about you when we were kids. I was a blind spot in your ability. And then when we were together and I started running drugs for Waylon and you thought I was temping at a dentist office. And the war. And this last year when I've—"

"I knew," he says. "I didn't say anything because I thought you didn't want me to."

"I *wanted* you to," she says. "Every time. I wanted you to so bad. You left me alone with it when we could have been together. We could have fixed things, and you left me to make them even worse."

"You didn't," he says. "You didn't make it worse. You tried your best."

She rolls over to face him, although it's pitch-black and she can see his face only as vague shapes. "How much do you know about what I was?" she asks. "The things I did after Topaz Lake?"

"It felt like an invasion," he says.

"It was your job," Carrie says. She's holding her voice low, as quiet as she can, but she can feel the alcohol trying to pull the lid off, to let this seething thing explode into an all-ending argument. "You went into people's heads and you fixed their horrible shit, but you didn't do that for me."

"It was too much," he says. "I couldn't help you. You were so strong to get through the day with everything you carried, and I couldn't help."

She knows he's telling the truth; she's always known he would have helped her if he could. But it makes no difference. She resents that he didn't try. She rolls away, facing the wall.

"It's going to start again," she says. She's thinking of what Waylon told her but also of the dynamic between her and Miquel, the way they cycled close and distant in permanent elliptical orbits.

"You don't have to be part of it," Miquel says.

"They're going to kill people."

"There are other people who will stop them," he says. He puts a hand lightly on her shoulder but with enough pressure for her to register it. It feels less like pulling her close than like holding her back. "You can be done. You can rest."

"I don't think I can," she says. His hand on her shoulder goes slack.

"You can choose me instead of the whole world this time," he says. With his hand barely touching her, she feels as if maybe it's true, that she does have the space to choose. "Sometimes I think that's all I wanted from you, was for you to pick me rather than everything else." She closes her eyes. She can remember Miquel's face every time she's walked away from him, his heart breaking each time.

Every time you leave me for a minute, it's like goodbye. I like to believe it means you can't live without me, she thinks. She can't remember if it's something he said or a snippet of dialogue from one of his movies. That's the problem with Miquel: she can't tell where the borders of him are, what's him and what's everything around him.

INFILTRATION

◇

When she was with Alyssa, it never occurred to Fahima that the body is a set of inputs and processes that can be manipulated to achieve certain outcomes. She has approached things with Ruth from this mindset, and the results have been overwhelmingly positive. There's a cost: Fahima misses sex as something to get lost in, a space ruled by nonlogic. In return, she gets to experience sex as something to be good at, with obvious indicators of success. There's been so little Fahima feels good at lately, so few obvious indicators of success. As Ruth collapses against the headboard, breathless and spent, Fahima's brain floods with a different kind of pleasure: the dopamine rush of a job well done. She rolls over, resting her head on Ruth's thigh.

"The problem is that basically we're trying to kill a god," Fahima says, staring up at the drop ceiling.

Ruth shimmies herself up to a proper seat. "You don't get how pillow talk works, do you?"

"I'm sorry," Fahima says. "There's this moment after sex when my head feels clear, and Alyssa used to let me—"

"Okay, you can hold up there," Ruth says. "Postcoital mentions of the ex—who, by the way, is sleeping down the hall—are a definite no."

"I used to talk through problems after," Fahima says. "That's all."

"Is this something I need to be here for, or am I like the dudes in a Plato dialogue?" Ruth asks. She puts on a low, stuffy voice with a badly executed British accent: *"Oh, Miss Deeb, what a fascinating observation. Can you please further enlighten me on this point due to your obvious wisdom?"*

Fahima gently slaps her leg, then rolls over and searches the floor for her clothes. "I'm going to go to the lab for a bit."

"No, by all means, go ahead," Ruth says. "Mentally jerk off in front of me. Not weird at all."

Fahima kisses her and promises to be back soon. She fixes her hijab and gently shuts the door, alone in the halls of the Phoenix school. It's silly to call it a school: nothing's been taught here for years. She stopped referring to Bishop as an academy the day the war started even if she thinks of her apartment there as the headmaster's quarters. Phoenix has been her oubliette, the place she puts things to forget them in the hope the rest of the world would forget them, too. Now it's a foxhole. It's hard to imagine any of them getting out of here. The curtain drawn over it was gauzy at best, and all the machines and fail-safes she's built to protect them amount to nothing more than warding spells and a circle of salt. When the Faction comes sniffing, they'll find Fahima and the people she's stowed away and either kill them or press-gang them. For herself, Fahima would prefer the former.

Before that happens, she needs to see the gears of what Glover is doing. One thing is clear: the thing living in Patrick Davenport's head is still thinking in terms of linear time. Either it's no longer trapped in some atemporal Source, or keeping one foot in the real world is limiting it. If Raymond Glover wised up, he could hit them at every moment in their history. He could make an enemies list and snuff them all in their cribs. So far he hasn't, which means his presence here has him locked into the linear flow of time. It's also clear Glover doesn't have complete control over Patrick. Maybe he's doing a good impression of her friend, but there's a glimmer of Patrick Davenport that suggests that Raymond is only influencing him or operating him by remote.

If that's the case, Glover is peeking out into the real world from the Source. However he's doing it, it got worse after the Pulse, which was Fahima's attempt to break the bottleneck of the Hive. Its success meant expanding the conduit between the Source and the real world—creating millions of new Resonants was a side effect.

"I fucking helped him," she mutters. "I let this asshole out of the bottle."

It explained why he was pressing so hard on Project Tuning Fork. The Pulse created more connections between the Source and the real world, but it affected only two-thirds of 5 percent of the global population. A global Pulse would—

"—blow the doors off," Fahima says as she arrives at her lab. She's surprised to see the lights are on. She opens the door, and Sarah is squatting on the floor in a T-shirt and sweatpants. "Hey," Fahima says, trying not to sound alarmed. "What are you doing up?"

"Walking around," Sarah says. Her voice is singsong, a child's cadence. "I feel like I forgot something."

It's hard to imagine a sentence that better sums up the tragedy of Sarah's current state. It's not only that she forgets, it's that she forgets she's forgotten. There are strings of days when she understands her condition, but mostly she exists with the permanent sense she might have left an unidentified object in another room. Fahima's not sure which days are worse.

Sarah stands up. She wipes her hand on her white nightgown, leaving a red streak across her belly. Fahima steps to her and takes the hand, which is sliced deeply across the base of the thumb, tracing Sarah's lifeline.

"What happened?" Fahima asks, scanning her desk for a towel, something to soak up the blood.

"Something fell," Sarah says. She looks at her hand like it's a foreign object. "I cut myself," she says, not explaining but realizing it now, again.

Fahima notices a puddle and broken glass on the floor. The lid of a sample jar lies faceup, a ring of jagged glass jutting up from it like a crown. She looks at the spot on the shelf desk where Yorick's jar ought to be, but it's gone, the books it supported slouching to one side. She checks places where the jar has never been, hoping she's wrong, that she put it somewhere else while she was talking with Emmeline or after they got back from meeting Bishop. Except she's ritualistic about placing it *right there:* third shelf, right-hand corner. She looks on the floor to see if the little black leech is trying to squiggle under a filing cabinet to hide. "Sarah, where is it?"

"It just crawled into my hand," Sarah says, holding out her bloodied palm. The look on her face is pure innocence, but it's oversold—the baby-doll come-on, the *who me?* look of someone who wants you to know they're getting away with something.

"Sarah?"

"No," Sarah says. "Not really."

Someone else smiles at Fahima with Sarah Davenport's face.

Fahima bolts for the door. No Dampers in here. Stupid, lazy Fahima. She slams the door shut behind her, and Sarah's body crashes into it. Fahima feels Sarah's mind slip into her own, hissing, *open it for me, Fahima. Let me out let me out.*

My mind is a white flame, Fahima thinks, using techniques Sarah taught her, the trick they'd practiced for hours and hours when they were kids. Fahima used to joke that Sarah had some trick she wouldn't teach Fahima and Patrick to defend against. *I am a white flame*, Fahima thinks, her back pressed to the door, hoping it will be enough. She locks the door from the outside and sprints down the hall. Certain Sarah is right behind her, she trips and stumbles down the stairs, righting herself with the railing. She finds Emmeline's room and throws the door open, casting light onto the sleeping girl. The sight triggers a memory of retrieving Emmeline from her grief over her parents to start all this, to create the Pulse. Sarah's mind peeks out at her from behind the memory. *I'm sending everyone, Fahima,* she says, the words burning in Fahima's head like the afterimage of flashbulbs. *A hundred black flowers are going to bloom in the desert.*

My mind is a white flame.

"Emmeline, go!" Fahima shouts. Emmeline sits up too slowly, props herself up on an arm, and looks at Fahima. "Go, get out of here."

"Wait," Emmeline says. Her eyes close, and her body goes limp. Fahima rushes to catch her before she falls. Fahima can hear Emmeline screaming in the Hive, calling out for Kimani. It's a piercing cry, and Fahima realizes with horror that every Resonant on the planet can hear it.

Emmeline isn't a blip, Bishop had told Emmeline's father when they first met. *She's more like a flare.* Now she's a shout, the sonic blast of a girl come into her full power but desperate for help. Fahima's last best secret is revealed for all to see: the martyred girl returned, the second coming of Emmeline Hirsch.

Emmeline's body becomes animated again. "It's okay," she says. "She'll be here any minute."

That's perfect, Fahima, says the flashbulb voice in Fahima's head. *Hold her right there. I'm on my way.*

"You have to go!" Fahima shouts.

"Where?" Emmeline asks.

Fahima looks at her, wishing there was somewhere safe she could name. "Just go," she says.

Emmeline folds away into nothing. Fahima's arms swing together around the newly created absence as if she's hugging herself. The door appears on the wall of Emmeline's room. Kimani opens it, and Fahima wonders why there's never time to tell people how much you've missed them.

"Where's Emmeline?" Kimani asks frantically.

Where is she, Fahima? says the voice in Fahima's head.

Kimani grips her forehead, her face contorting in pain. "Who the fuck is in my head?" she says. "It sounds like—"

"He's in Sarah," Fahima says. She sees Kimani thinking the same thing she is: *It's over. We lost Emmeline and Sarah. Who's left?* Then Kimani's face sets into the resolve Fahima needs and should have but can't muster.

"Where is she?" Kimani asks.

"In my lab."

Kimani pulls Fahima into the room and closes the door. "When I open this, grab her," she says. "When I open it again, throw her out."

Kimani opens the door, overlapping the locked door to Fahima's lab, which Sarah has been pounding against. There's no need to grab her; Sarah tumbles into Kimani's room. Her mind is huge in Fahima's head, a shout, a scream. *Give me Emmeline now.* Fahima picks Sarah's body up by her bony shoulders as Kimani slams the door, then reopens it. Fahima sees enough of what's beyond to recognize Central Park at night, the Bishop Academy looming over it. *Take me back and give me the girl,* the voice in her head seethes. Fahima shoves her outside, and Kimani slams the door shut again. They're both still, listening for thoughts that aren't their own, but there's only the sound of their breathing.

"We have to go back and get everyone out of Phoenix," Fahima says. "He's going to send Faction, as many as he can. We need to evacuate."

Kimani pauses. She looks around her room like a person locking up a deceased parent's house. She opens the door back into Fahima's lab and gently shoves Fahima out.

"Step back," she says. Kimani stands in the threshold of the door. Trying to understand what's happening, Fahima notices the toes of Kimani's shoes resting on the concrete of the lab floor outside Kimani's room.

Once, drunk, Fahima asked what would happen to Kimani if she stepped across the threshold of her room and back into the world outside. *I can't,* Kimani said, sounding as if she was explaining an impossibility to an insistent child. Fahima thought she understood what Kimani meant. They all had limits on their abilities, thankfully. Some of those limits were hurdles to be overcome, which was half the reason Kevin Bishop started the academy. Others were absolute. Kimani's doorway was, as Fahima understood it, one of the latter.

Kimani braces herself against the door frame, arms extended, hands pushing out. Her eyes focus past Fahima, past the lab. She makes a sound like she's being torn in half, a birthing sound of pain and force and release.

Fahima feels it before she understands it. A rush like warm

water passes over her, and in its wake a change in the air. There's a brittle quality to the air in Phoenix, dry and crispy like something baked too long, but now it's softened. It feels more familiar, more like home.

Kimani drops to one knee, stumbling forward through the door and into the lab. She catches herself on her fingertips, poised like a sprinter before the gun. Through the open doorway, Fahima can see that Kimani's room is gone. The door goes through the wall of the lab and out into the hallway. An ordinary door. Kimani looks back at it.

"Never seen it from this side," she says, still out of breath. "Does it always look like that?"

"You came out," Fahima says. "You came out of your room. I thought you couldn't—"

"I didn't come out," Kimani says. She's distracted, running her fingers along the dark wood molding that surrounds the door. "I brought you all in."

FIVE

IMAGINING DEFEAT

He stared at ruin. Ruin stared straight back.
He thought they was old friends.

—JOHN BERRYMAN,
"Dream Song 45"

EVACUATION

◇

The bank of monitors makes Fahima feel like a supervillain. Her first design routed the signals into her optic nerve, but the results made her dizzy and nauseous. This has a theatricality she appreciates. Ruth and Alyssa are in the room Omar Six nicknamed "Control." In a rare show of unity, all the Omars insist on calling it that. Twenty-Four is operating the communications with teen Omars on the ground while single-digit Omars rescued from the Ruse stew in the hall.

Ruth and Alyssa have reached the worst détente, forged out of in-jokes and observations of Fahima's hang-ups, although this wears on Ruth. If Fahima is the shared topic of discourse, Alyssa can't help but pass herself off as the ultimate expert, and her air of *I will always know her better than you do* raises Ruth's hackles. They're all playing professional, except the Omars, who have turned the operation into a slapstick routine. Since they're the boots on the ground, they can treat it however the fuck they want.

Their options were severely limited after Emmeline disappeared. The first priority had been to find her. Fahima had tracking equipment, but the best stuff was at the Ruse or in the basement of the Bishop Academy. Kimani hadn't been able to open a door into Bishop in years—as if the Hive were warped and twisted around the school—and opening one into someplace as heavily monitored as the Ruse long enough to load equipment would give their location away, giving the Faction the means to track them.

"Would it be worth it?" Kimani asked. Fahima took a long time before saying no.

As devices probed for Emmeline's energy signature, skilled Hive users braved Hivespace to look for her. They came back damaged. They weren't infected with anything—no little Yoricks nestled in their heads—but they were shaken and unwilling to go back in. After a week of fruitless search, Emmeline was given up as lost. Fahima tore up diagrams and schematics in front of Alyssa, who had been the only one to ask, "What the fuck *was* the plan anyway?" Fahima shouted that it didn't matter now, crumpled up another indecipherable drawing, and crammed it into a wastebasket.

Two paths had to be pursued simultaneously. The first was to get people out of the Bronx before they got killed. The other was to stop Project Tuning Fork from moving forward, which looked more difficult. The culling in the Bronx was being carried out with bureaucratic diligence: two Blooms crossed the bridge in the morning, killed off whoever they found for a couple hours, and clocked out. Project Tuning Fork had the Faction guarding the global sites where the Chairs were being constructed and kept their primary operator, Thao Bui, under constant guard. Tuning Fork was the highest priority in Bloom deployment, confirming Fahima's theory that setting off another Pulse was a get out of jail card for Raymond Glover.

Yesterday, Omars Thirteen through Nineteen landed in the Bronx. Kimani opened a door in Kansas, and Ruth ferried them into the borough before zipping off to an extraction point in northern Canada. Their job was to spread the word about an evacuation with a boat big enough for everyone. Fahima was confident the Omars could publicize the mission: the ones who went in could split into dozens, knocking on doors and enlisting known influencers to get their people to the site. The Kindred Network was an advantage in spreading information: whether or not cells in the Bronx tapped into a national organization, they talked among themselves. The problem wasn't publicity; it was trust. For people in the Bronx, Fahima and her ilk were no different from the Faction Blooms sent in to kill them. *Gather here at this time* sounded like a shepherd ordering the lambs to organize themselves for slaughter.

"Control, this is Seventeen, headed to the site," says Omar Seventeen.

"Seventeen, you have to say over, over," says Omar Thirteen, the whiniest rule follower of the bunch. "Control, tell him he has to say over, over."

"Right there you said over before you were done," Seventeen says. "You don't even know what you're saying over for."

"Over," says Omar Nineteen, busting out in giggles.

"This is like D-Day with idiots," Fahima says.

"Control, I didn't copy that, over," says Omar Thirteen. "Tennine, Control."

"He means repeat," Omar Twenty-Four says. "Ten-nine is—"

"No more talking until you're at the site," Fahima shouts. Ruth and Alyssa laugh into their hands. "Where's Kimani? Someone go wake up—"

"I'm right here," Kimani says, walking into Control with a

steaming cup of coffee. She sleeps twelve hours a day since she swallowed the Phoenix school, and this mission falls within a rest period for her. She's in pajamas she deems suitable for public viewing, fresh flannel with duck prints that make Fahima wish she could be done with this and crawl back into bed.

"We have numbers?" Kimani asks.

"I'm hoping a hundred," says Fahima. "Probably less."

"How much time are we talking?"

"As quick as possible, Kimani," Fahima says. "The longer we've got a door open, the better chance they can track you and—"

"Do you ever say *I don't know*?" Kimani asks.

"No," Alyssa and Ruth say simultaneously.

"Make it fast," Fahima says.

"I'm ready when your boys are ready," says Kimani, sipping her coffee.

The monitors show a dimly lit theater at the Concourse Plaza Multiplex near Yankee Stadium. Its plastic and faux-velvet seats are empty, and Omar Twenty-One, whose eyes they're watching through, constantly checks the exits, the entrances, and the ceiling above him, which is a web of shadows, girders, and ventilation pipes. Two other screens show East 161st coming up past the stadium, where Omars Fourteen and Sixteen move their people down the center of the street at a slow jog. Fahima wants to tell them to hurry the fuck up, but she can't see who's in the crowd. There could be kids or people with physical disabilities. She told the Omars not to leave behind anyone who wanted in; now she's reconsidering. She should have said *save who you can* and left it to their discretion. They could lose the whole pack for the sake of one old lady with a walker.

Other Omars are already in the mall, heading for the multiplex. They pass abandoned food courts, fountains that sit stagnant.

Flashlight beams check the corners and the hallways. The Omars have split into two philosophical camps: One believes the fact they've made it this far without encountering any Faction means they're getting away with it. The other thinks they've been too lucky already and the shit will hit any second.

"Control, we have our first group in," says Omar Twenty-One. "You want to open the doors for us?"

"That's a negative, Twenty-One," Fahima says, cursing herself as soon as she hears it.

"Negatory there, good buddy, over," says Omar Eighteen. He's striving to keep things light, but he's out of breath. Fahima checks his feed: he's in the parking lot at the far end of the mall.

"We get everybody in the room and then we open the door," Fahima says.

"You have to say over, over," Omar Thirteen insists.

"Hurry the fuck up," Fahima says. "Over."

On the main feed, people file into the theater and, on instinct, take their seats. "Keep their asses standing," Fahima hisses at Twenty-One.

"Everybody up, everybody up," says Omar Twenty-One. People grumble but oblige. A third group arrives with Omars Fourteen and Sixteen, larger than expected. All the rows are filled with people, and the aisles are brimming.

"Call in if you're still on your way," Fahima says.

"Waiting outside the theater," Omar Thirteen says. "Does that count? Over."

"Down the hall, be there in two," says Omar Seventeen.

"We're looking for an unlocked door," Omar Eighteen says. "But we'll be there in a couple."

"Thirteen, how many people you have?"

"Thirty-some," he says.

"Eighteen?"

"I got maybe a dozen," says Omar Eighteen. "I'm going to bust us through the glass; we'll be right there."

"You guys suck at this game," Omar Seventeen says. "I've got a hundred people waiting to get in. You can line up behind my ass."

"Fuck," says Fahima.

"What's that put the total at?" Kimani asks.

Fahima doesn't answer.

"There're three hundred seats in the theater, so there's more than that in the room," says Alyssa. "If Seventeen's not lying, we're talking about five hundred."

"This would be the first time we talked about five hundred," says Kimani. She sounds unhappy.

"No one's seen any Faction," says Ruth. "We've got time."

"We don't know that," says Alyssa, too sharply.

"It's not a matter of time," Kimani says. "It's a matter of space. I'm not set up to accommodate another five hundred people."

"We'll figure it out," Fahima says.

"*I'll* figure it out, you mean," says Kimani.

"Yes, I mean you'll figure it out."

"Saving your ass the second time this week," she says. She smiles, but it's a tired one that reminds Fahima of Bishop on days when he couldn't keep up his flawless front. "Do I get a headset?"

Ruth and Alyssa both offer theirs, and Kimani takes Ruth's. "Mr. Twenty-One, do you hear me?"

"I read you, Control," says Omar Twenty-One.

"Please can the walkie-talkie bullshit for the next five minutes," Kimani says. "In a minute I'm going to open a door at the base of the stage there, right in the middle. I need you to line people up four by four. That's as wide as I can get it, and we want to move them in fast. Can you start doing that for me?"

"Of course, Miss Moore," he says.

"Thank you, Mr. Twenty-One," Kimani says. She closes her eyes and takes a deep breath like a gymnast about to start a routine. On the screen, people in the left-hand aisle get in formation. Others in the rows complain that they were here first and Omar Twenty-One makes it clear they can listen to him or fuck right off.

Kimani takes one more breath and exhales. What appears to be an elaborate garage door appears exactly where she said and pulls open inward. On one of the lower monitors, they can see the open doorway from the inside of a basement room the crowd will be evacuated into.

"Okay, march them in," Kimani says.

The line starts into the doorway, and as they disappear from Omar Twenty-One's feed in the theater, they reappear on the feeds of Twenty-Six and Twenty-Seven, who wait for them in the basement with water and blankets. The rows empty into the left aisle, and the aisle drains before Seventeen's group enters and fills it. People in the right-hand aisle protest, and Omar Twenty-One picks an arbitrary point at which they'll switch the aisle from which they're feeding.

"Everybody's coming aboard," Fahima says. "Eighteen, where are you?"

"Control, I have a problem," says Omar Eighteen. "I think we've been followed."

"What?"

"I'm trying not to be heard by my people here, but I'm seeing ghosts," he says.

Fahima finds Twenty-One's feed on the monitors. His movements are quick and jittery, but she doesn't see anything suspicious.

He only has a dozen, she thinks. *Cut him loose. Close the door.*

"Twenty-One, I need you to double-time people in, now," she says.

Twenty-One's feed jumps up and down as he nods. "Move them to the back," he shouts through the doorway. "Make some room." His hand pinwheels as he hurries people through.

Fahima covers the mic of her headset. "Isolate Eighteen," she tells Omar Twenty-Four. He types a quick sequence, and the banter and trash talk of the other Omars cuts out of her headset. "Eighteen, can you tell me what you see?"

"I'm saying a ghost," he says. "A face popping out of the walls, running alongside us. And I'm . . . Control, I'm not sure those doors were locked. I think there's someone in my head."

A transphasic and a psychic, Fahima notes. She tries to imagine the other three-fifths of the Bloom. Ji Yeon had a gift for putting together pentads that combined to something larger than the sum of their parts. *Voltron that shit,* she told Fahima. Fahima could never get her head around Ji Yeon's system, much less duplicate it. Eighteen's feed flicks upward, and Fahima sees what he sees: someone moving above them, visible through the tinted skylight.

"Flier," Eighteen says. "They're tracking us in. I'm going to lead them off. Close the door."

"How much longer do we need?" Fahima asks Twenty-Four, covering her mic.

"I don't know, two minutes? Five?"

"Can you get there in five?" she asks Eighteen.

"It's not a matter of how fast we get there," Eighteen says. "It's who we're bringing with—fuck!"

The glass above him shatters, and Eighteen screams for his group to run from the raining shards. Through the feed, Fahima watches as a girl appears out of a pillar, snatches a teenage boy out of Eighteen's group, and phases him halfway into the wall, his eyes and mouth immediately welling with blood. The flier swoops low, scattering the group in a panic. They run toward open storefronts, looking for shelter as a second flier swoops in with someone dangling from each arm. One of them Fahima doesn't recognize; the other she does. Sarah Davenport still wears her nightgown from the Phoenix school. It billows around her legs as the flier lowers her down by the fountain.

They're fucked, Fahima thinks.

"Everyone in the theater is in," Omar Twenty-Four says. "Hold the door?"

The panicked evacuees suddenly stop and walk calmly toward the fountain, piloted.

"Sarah was never that strong," Kimani says. "She could puppet somebody, but not more than one at a time."

"She's got help," Fahima says, remembering the malice and glee in Sarah's face the last time she saw it. The first evacuee, a middle-aged woman, reaches the fountain, and the Faction agent Fahima doesn't recognize places his hand on her forehead as if giving her a blessing. With a bright flash and a scream, the woman's head is gone and the rest of her body falls.

"Oh, fuck," says Omar Eighteen.

"Eighteen, you cannot let them catch you," Fahima says quietly.

"Fahima, do I shut the door?" asks Kimani.

"She's in my head," Eighteen says.

Another evacuee meets his burning end at the edge of the frame.

"Eighteen, I'm so sorry," Fahima says.

"It's okay, boss," Omar Eighteen says. "It's okay." His feed slowly pans down, looking across his stomach to the gun holstered on his hip. He takes it out, but his attention focuses on Sarah. He takes another step toward her, and Fahima's sure he's lost. The Omars are a complex structure, and without explaining to Fahima how they share information, they've made it clear to Fahima that no Omar can ever be captured. Eighteen takes another lurch forward.

"Eighteen, please," Fahima says. The feed moves up and down

slowly: a nod. The sound of the gunshot comes through the audio as the feed goes black.

"That's it," Alyssa says, throwing her headset on the floor. "I am done. Drop me anywhere. I don't care. I'm done."

"Kimani," says Fahima. "Shut the door."

ROGERS PARK/WICKER PARK

◇

They've been taking turns driving Rai to school since the announcement a week before. Nothing feels as if it's changed, but after the fighting started at the Bishop Academy, there were days of eerie calm when the news felt like dreams. Going to work in Manhattan and seeing tanks blocking off Lexington Avenue registered as if someone were shooting a movie.

Clay drives by Faction agents standing on corners like beat cops, but he doesn't know what, if anything, is supposed to happen next. When nothing does, they continue with their days as if all this were normal. Every night, after Rai goes to bed, Clay and Dom stay up talking about whether it's time to leave. Every night, they decide *not yet*.

Today is Clay's day to drive, but Dom's helping a student committee plan the winter formal they're holding at Vibration, so he's taking Rai in.

"I might swing the kids by the venue afterward so they can get a sense of the space," Dom says. He bustles around the kitchen while Clay pores over a printout of one of Avi Hirsch's unpublished articles, a story about a Resonant woman outside Riyadh who liberated all the women in her village and teleported them to the United States, only to have them sent back and killed.

"Uh-huh," Clay says.

"Then I'll run Rai back out to the school for basketball practice, so it'll be you and me for dinner."

"Yeah, sure," Clay says.

Dom stops, gently closing the fridge. "You are not listening at all, are you?"

Clay looks up, caught. "Downtown after school," he says. "Basketball. You and me for dinner. You want that Thai place?"

"The one in the Ukrainian Village?" Dom asks. He kisses Clay on the cheek and rubs his shoulders. "No, baby, I want *decent* Thai food, but I will settle for the place in the Ukrainian Village."

"Like you settled for me?" Clay asks, wrapping his arm around Dom's waist.

"Never," Dom says as he kisses Clay.

Rai bounds down the stairs and into the kitchen. He opens the fridge and stares blankly into it. He glances over his shoulder at his dads.

"Stop being gross," he says.

"Hey, at practice today, don't forget to follow your shot," Clay says.

"Okay, Dad," Rai says, continuing to scan the fridge.

"Nobody on that team crashes the boards," Clay says, unclear who he's explaining this to. "There's a real opportunity to—"

Rai looks at him, confused by this sudden deployment of basketball jargon.

"I mean, hustle, right?" Clay says. He turns his attention back to the article. "It's all about hustle."

Rai kisses him on the cheek. "Bye, Dad."

He spends his days in the attic, especially since "the shout." Everyone heard it, and everyone knew who it was. No one will say Emmeline Hirsch's name out loud. As with the Faction's announcement, the fact that nothing came afterward caused doubt. If Emmeline Hirsch was back, why wasn't she working miracles: writing messages in the sky or appearing in somebody's soup? Why wasn't Project Tuning Fork revising its plans to include the original operator, the only Resonant to work a Chair successfully?

Clay doesn't doubt it was Emmeline Hirsch who screamed a woman's name across the psyche of every Resonant there is, but he isn't sure what it means. In the absence of a path forward, he moves back, digging into whatever archive of the Hirsch family remains in the house on Jarvis Avenue. What strikes Clay is that they were like any other family. On Avi Hirsch's hard drive, there are photos of him and his wife and daughter huddled together in front of a church, bundled in winter coats; of Emmeline at the kitchen counter drawing; of Hirsch and his wife at an office party, he uncomfortable in a suit and she easily elegant in a black sheath dress. The pictures date back five years before the war started, after which there's nothing. It's part of the myth of Emmeline Hirsch: the whole family wiped out in the span of a week. But for the last five years of his life Avi Hirsch didn't take a single photo he felt was worth saving.

Clay scrolls backward, falling deeper into the family's past, when a shout spikes through his brain. There were times all Faction agents would get an ice pick of a headache in the center of their skulls. They understood it was the thing that had been put in them, although Clay's ability shorted out whatever it was. As the pain subsides, he's ready for the garbled message that used to follow the piercing sensation, as if he were back in the war. With the pain at a distance, he can distinguish it from the past. It's reminiscent of the two recent broadcasts through the Hive from the Faction and, later that night, from Emmeline Hirsch. This is different, a signal on another wavelength.

Clay, can you hear me? says a voice in his head.

"Who is this?" Clay says out loud to the empty room

It's Waylon. Where are you?

"I'm at home," Clay says. His voice echoes in the small space of the attic.

You need to get down here, Waylon says. *It's the Faction. They've got the kids.*

Clay feels Waylon's presence slip out of his mind. He looks around the office as if he might find a weapon, something he can use. He checks the drawers of the desk, although he's gone through them before and knows there's nothing but notes. He looks at the locked bottom drawer. The first time he came up here, he decided to respect the drawer. He gives a tug, enough to assess the weakness of the lock. One hard yank and it comes free. Inside, there's the paperwork for a divorce, signed only by Kay Hirsch. The papers are arched, resting on something. When Clay removes them, he finds a .22 and two boxes of bullets. It wouldn't be his gun of choice—too delicate—but it's at hand. He loads it and stuffs it into the back of his belt, then pockets the extra ammunition and leaves.

ALL WE'VE WON WITH
THE SABER AND THE GUN

◇

The assemblage of Resonant and baseliner parents at Vibration looks more like a PTA meeting than a military council. Carrie isn't sure what she hoped to find when she answered Waylon's shout and rushed here, but it isn't encouraging. She wonders how many people here saw any combat on either side. Even if they had, that was a long time ago, plenty of time to get soft and comfortable.

She finds Waylon sitting in a booth with Hayden, their hand resting on his shoulder while Waylon has his eyes closed and his head back, a pained expression on his face. Hayden holds up their other hand for Carrie to wait.

"He's in touch with Bryce inside the school," Hayden says. "We're waiting for a full report. Where's Miquel?"

"He left," Carrie says. Her tone makes it clear she doesn't want to discuss it any further.

Waylon's head snaps forward, and his eyes open, falling immediately on Carrie. "No one's been hurt," he announces. People immediately clamor for answers, throwing the names of their children at Waylon as if he can check an attendance sheet. A man muscles his way through the crowd until he's standing next to Carrie.

"Are Rai and Dom in there?" he asks. "Can Bryce see them?"

Carrie turns to look at the man, and recognition and action come in the same moment: before Carrie can articulate who he is, she's got the knife out of her belt loop and at his throat.

"Carrie, what the fuck?" Hayden screams. Everyone who'd crowded forward pushes back, and Carrie feels the barrel of a gun press against her stomach, under her ribs.

"He's with them," Carrie says. "He's Faction."

Hayden is about to try to calm Carrie down but backs off when they see the gun. Carrie feels Waylon in her head and burns him out with the white flame.

"I can handle a gut shot better than you can handle a slit throat," she hisses at Clay.

"I'm not gonna take that bet, kid," Clay says.

"Is it still in your head?" she asks, tapping the point of the knife twice against Clay's temple before putting it back to his throat.

"Mine doesn't work, especially after Houston," he says. "I could hear it squawking sometimes, but it was garbled. And they couldn't hear me."

"Ever?" Clay shakes his head, a slight movement to avoid a slice. "But the shit we—"

"I was doing what had to be done," Clay says.

"I thought you died in Houston," she says.

"Thought you did, too."

"Did anyone else make it out?" she asks. "Nicole? Maaya and Koyo?" He doesn't move, and that's her answer. They hold their pose, she with the knife pressed against his neck and he with the gun aimed into her guts.

"I found Rai," he says. "Maaya and Koyo's kid. My husband and I, we adopted him."

Carrie's eyes fill up with tears. "Little Rai?" Her knife pulls away from Clay's throat, hovering below her hip to indicate the height Rai was when Koyo would project an image of him running around their encampments. Clay takes her hand in his empty hand and lifts the blade back up, past his neck to the level of his chin.

"Not so little anymore," he says.

"Oh, fuck," says Carrie. She falls against him, sobbing. "Clay, it got so bad. It was so bad for so long. I could shut it out, but it was like this bad voice in my head all the time. All the time."

"Is it still in there?"

Carrie shakes her head. "There's a girl I was traveling with," she says. "She did something and knocked it dead. In me and a couple other Faction people."

"Emmeline Hirsch," Clay says.

"You know her?" Hayden asks.

"Where I used to work, she's sort of a legend," Clay says. "I heard her call out the other night."

"We all did," says Hayden.

"Any chance she's on her way down here?" Clay asks.

"I left her with somebody else," Carrie says. "The name she said in the Hive—she was only supposed to do that in an emergency."

"I don't mean to interrupt," Waylon says, "but can we focus on *this* emergency?"

"What's the situation?" Carrie asks after taking a deep sniff to regain her composure.

"Don't you army types say sitrep or whatever?" Hayden asks. They fold their arms and glare at Carrie.

"I wanted to speak civilian so you could follow," Carrie says.

Hayden smiles, but it isn't particularly warm. Clay offers them his hand. "Clay Weaver," he says. "My kid's a big fan."

"Your kid?" Hayden says.

"I love the first album," he says sheepishly. "Carrie used to play it when we were—"

"What were you two exactly?" Hayden asks.

"Here, let me link us all in," Waylon says, playing peacemaker. Carrie staggers and finds a seat as her head floods with voices: Clay, Hayden, Waylon, and Bryce, word-salad monologues of thoughts and emotions. Like the levels being adjusted on a stereo, they drop and Waylon's voice, clear and considered, emerges.

Baby, I've got some people here, he says. *You want to fill everyone in on where things are at?*

Carrie feels like her entire personality is being surveyed. It's Bryce, checking to see who's sharing his headspace. *Hey,* he says, addressed to everyone but individuated so that Carrie hears something closer to *Hey, kid.*

You okay? she asks.

Had better days, says Bryce.

"Walk us through what happened," Clay says, his voice booming in the bar and through the psychic link.

They showed up this morning, Bryce says. *Walked right in the front door. One Bloom.*

Fuck, Hayden says.

That's not so bad, says Carrie.

Depends on who it is, Clay says. Carrie chuckles and feels Hayden's attention focus on her, trying to prize out some secret. *You ought to know better,* Carrie thinks at Hayden. *My mind is a cool white flame.*

They've got us locked down, Bryce says. *Resonants in the cafeteria, baseliners in the gym. They say they're going to load up the baseline kids and take them to a secure facility out west. They say they'll be reunited with their parents once the full evacuation's finished.*

You don't believe them? Waylon asks.

There's no vehicles out front, Bryce says. *I think they're waiting for the green light to kill the kids.*

Can you find Rai and Dom? Clay asks. Carrie hasn't spent much time on these kinds of psychic conference calls: Waylon tried to hold team meetings this way back in his drug-dealing days, but everyone hated it. Words come through bearing not their literal meanings but their emotional connotations. It's how she knows without being told that Dom is Clay's husband, the person he talked about in guarded terms when they were in the Faction.

There's a long pause, and it's not because Bryce is looking for them—he would have located them immediately, obeying a gut instinct to prioritize family.

They have them in the other room.

DIPLOMACY

◇

As much as she hates it, Fahima gets a thrill seeing one of her machines fully realized in the world. It's shot through with a vein of disappointment: the machines in her dreams are impossibly beautiful but end up bent and twisted when they descend into dull matter. At the implementation stage, she opts for a steampunk aesthetic, leaning hard into the clunky but necessary mechanics. If nothing will have the sleek, otherworldly beauty of her dreams, let them find a strangeness that speaks to the constraints of being a thing in the world.

Her excitement at seeing one of her ideas come to life maps directly onto its size. Smaller devices can be marvels of intricacy, but nothing matches the exhilaration of a building-size project come to life: human-scaled so she can take it in all at once but big enough that she has to step back to do so. The MTA revisions are her biggest project, but she can't *behold* it, so it returns to the realm of abstraction.

Although it's her most unwanted child—she's in Berlin solely for the purpose of its destruction—Fahima's heart flutters when she sees the Beta Chair fully constructed on the Alexanderplatz. It's a massive crèche with thick cables snaking around the television tower, awaiting its user. It's not the way she would have done it—Cedric has encased it in sleek black surfaces like something designed by Apple. It's hers even if Cedric's grubby prints are all over it.

There's a crowd on the Platz, and the translation nanites she injected herself with—not designed for text—struggle to render their picket signs into English. She tries reading the signs out loud under her breath, hoping the nanites will translate her own speech, but her pronunciation is choppy and it doesn't work. From what she can hear of the chants coming off the Platz, the crowd is split. Half is the crowd Fahima's used to: they shout *abomination* and *monster*, like a song she hasn't heard in years.

The other half clamors for change. *Turn it over now,* they say. *Resonance today. Make us like you.*

Five Blooms patrol the fence around the machine, assuming there aren't others Fahima doesn't see. If Fahima needs evidence that this is the highest priority, she gets it when she sees Ji Yeon Kim, the top cog in the Faction machinery, calling out orders from atop a chair sculpted out of bronze, the unoccupied one of a quartet on which the likenesses of Edward Snowden, Julian Assange, and Chelsea Manning stand. The thing that breaks Fahima's heart about what Ji Yeon became was that she used to speak truth to power and hold people to account. The Ji Yeon she met behind the barricades in Revere should have helped them shape the America that came after the war into something good. Patrick or Raymond Glover or whatever got put into her head took that away from her, and it makes Fahima that much more determined to stop him.

Fahima blinks her eyes rapidly. The contacts she designed show her a web of sonic shielding forming a dome over the device.

"So is there a plug I can pull?" Omar Six asks. "Or do I stick a wrench in it somewhere?"

"He blackboxed it," Fahima says. "It'll be tough to get into its guts."

"Have we considered throwing a very large Molotov cocktail at it?"

"I *have* considered that," Fahima says. "But I need a better sense of their security. Keep at a wide spread and don't get caught."

"Do I get extra points if I blow it up?" he asks.

"Only if you can do it without blowing yourself up, too." As soon as she says it, she thinks of Omar Eighteen shooting himself in the head to avoid capture. Omar Six is thinking of him, too, and Fahima wonders how the loss of a duplicate registers for the Omars.

"What are you going to do?" he asks

"I'm going to lob some charm bombs at it."

"So we're fucked, then," says Omar Six. He flips up his collar and walks onto the Platz. With a shimmer of air, he doubles, then doubles again. The four Omars disperse, blending into the crowd. Fahima watches until she can't track any of them, then turns to go.

She's never been happy with the image inducers she invented: the low-res results don't hold up to close scrutiny. She wants sci-fi-movie perfection in which the mask isn't apparent until it's taken off for the big reveal. In the movies, when they switch out the actress and the computer-generated imagery it is in play for only a heartbeat. Fahima's best efforts make the wearer look like an early Pixar animation of a human being, a walking uncanny valley.

Luckily for Fahima, she has access to one of the most compelling disguises in existence. To become someone else, she need only remove her hijab. Any official working with Project Tuning Fork would recognize Fahima Deeb and hand her to Cedric. But Leisl Hoffstrader, an undersecretary from the Federal Ministry for the

Environment, Nature Conservation, Building, and Nuclear Safety with pristinely forged identification and dark hair carefully styled into an asymmetrical bob by Ruth before they flew out, can sit in the waiting room outside of Niklas Babisch's office in the Bundestag looking at the pictures in *Der Spiegel* with no one the wiser.

Two minutes before her appointment, a crew-cut young man right off a Nazi propaganda poster steps out of Babisch's office and, nodding briskly at Fahima and muttering "*Guten tag,*" strides out of the room. The door closes softly behind him. As the minute hand clicks up to twelve, the door opens again and Niklas Babisch's head pops out. "Miss Hoffstrader," he says. "Please." Fahima stands, gathers up the manila folder full of blank papers that completes her costume, and steps into his office. Babisch has already landed comfortably in his desk chair, fingers tented, as if he's been waiting for her. He smiles patiently as the door shuts, then reaches under the edge of his desk. There's a click and then a hiss of white noise that registers in Fahima's mind rather than her ears.

"Our people call it psychic chaff," he says. "It is to mind readers what the old running water trick was to Stasi bugs. I assume you want privacy, Dr. Deeb."

"You knew it was me?" Fahima asks, sitting down.

"There is no overlap between my ministry and whatever long list of fiefdoms 'Leisl Hoffstrader' oversees," he says. "I've been following what Cedric tells us is going on with you. Mysterious disappearances make old Germans uneasy. When I saw an obviously fake appointment on my schedule, I assumed it was either you or someone coming to kill me." He pauses. "I'm happy it's you."

"The Chair isn't safe," Fahima says.

Babisch smiles. "I've missed your straightforwardness," he says. "Will you tell me what about it is unsafe?"

"The original Pulse actualized two-thirds of the people within range and left the rest unchanged," Fahima says. She wishes she'd brought charts. Babisch seems like a man who enjoys a good chart. "This Pulse will actualize or kill. I don't know the casualty rate, but anyone who doesn't resonate will die."

"Your Mr. Joyner has assured me—"

"He's lying," Fahima says. "There's a mandate to get this done regardless of collateral damage. Joyner was brought in to replace me because he has no qualms about following orders."

Babisch smirks. "Americans assume they say 'following orders' to a German and Hannah Arendt sings arias in our heads. Do you have any proof that Joyner is lying to me other than he has the weak will and mild malignancy of an Eichmann?"

"I know what the numbers looked like before I left," she says. "Joyner isn't smarter than me, and if he's made improvements, they're minor. And I'd have to be either very stupid or very sincere to walk into your office given the number of Faction agents in Berlin. I'm asking for your trust."

Babisch nods, taking all this in. She's read him wrong: he's not a man of charts. He trusts people and his ability to read them. It's why she's here rather than in Mumbai or Tokyo. He's the only one who might trust her enough to do something.

"I could not stop what will happen tomorrow," he says. "It has passed above my station and out of my hands. If I did believe you, and I am not saying I don't, I'm not certain I'd stop the test."

"We're talking about millions dead," says Fahima. *Hannah Arendt might not mean shit, but millions dead has got to hit him somewhere,* she thinks.

"You told me when I was in New York the master-slave politics that came after your war would not happen here once we accepted your gift," he says. "I think your optimism was misguided. We've had increases in every form of racial and sectarian violence in the weeks since construction on the device began. In some cases, it's last punches in before the tables turn. But I see a prelude. We are handing shiny new boots to people who will put them on their brothers' necks. You tell me those who don't become gods will die, and I wonder if they will not be better off. Give me superpowers or give me death."

"We don't say superpowers."

The phone on Babisch's desk buzzes, and he raises his finger, putting millions of deaths on hold while he takes the call.

The tiny genius machines in Fahima's blood are wearing down. She should have taken a booster shot before the meeting. Their translation is crackly. "That is unacceptable. They have no right to take a prisoner on our . . . Of course you brought that up. Did they explicitly say— Yes, that is unambiguous. If he were German, I would push, but no. I'm afraid they keep their man. Thank you for informing me."

He hangs up the phone and tucks it into his pocket. He tents his fingers again, and Fahima can't help feeling she's in Bishop's office, being reprimanded for reducing a teacher to tears with her incessant questions. "I should have liked it if you had come to me before pursuing other avenues," Babisch says. "The Faction have your doubling man." Fahima's mind races. She curses Omar Six for letting himself get captured and thinks of all the things she should have done. A cyanide capsule in the tooth. Basic spy tricks she forgot.

Except she didn't forget. She refused to allow the possibility of another Omar dying on her watch, and that refusal has netted her something worse. "Our authorities have made the appropriate noises about lawful extradition, but the response was a threat to take their ball and go home. You understand I cannot take risks at this time."

"I understand," Fahima says. She gets up to go, leaving the dummy folder on his desk. "You have family here, right?"

"Two sons and my wife," Babisch says.

"Get them out," Fahima says. "Fly them to South America tonight. Get them away from that thing."

"And then what?" he asks. "Bring them back to Berlin with no magical powers? Move them around the board, avoiding each activation until they are the only humans left? No. Tomorrow we will eat breakfast together. Our flat is on the Platz; we have watched this thing being built since it started. My boys speculate on what their abilities will be." He smiles. "Friedrich is sure he will be able to fly." He nods his head, affirming something Fahima doesn't understand. "We will go to the window and hold hands, and we will see together what fate has in store for us."

"I'm sorry," Fahima says.

"That is the first thing you have said to me that I have entirely believed."

Before she's out the door, he calls for her to stop. "Will it hurt?" he asks. "For the ones who don't change?"

She remembers the one live test: the abattoir in the Bronx they dragged Cedric Joyner out of years ago. The bodies were twisted and broken as if the people had tried to crawl out of their skins. Some gouged out their eyes to claw away the pain at the center of their skulls as the parahippocampal gyrus thrashed and grew, destroying the precious gray matter around it.

"No," she says. "It'll be as if they've been shut off."

"That is good," Babisch says. "That is a good death in the face of all this. Thank you, Dr. Deeb, for your work and your warning. I hope to meet you again one day as an equal."

HYDE PARK

◇

It's terrifying to feel those muscles flex again. It's a relapse; the cigarette in his hand he doesn't recall lighting. Clay is glad he remembers what it's like to fight a war. Other than he and Carrie, there aren't veterans to take up arms against the Faction. The little worm Patrick Davenport put in their heads as a signing bonus meant that those who fought for the Faction were permanently "on call." After the Armistice, veteran support groups sprang up in New York, and at Dom's insistence, Clay went to meetings. Everyone had a blankness that wasn't attributable to PTSD. Clay knew the thing they put in his head didn't work. He'd felt it squirming around as it went in, heard the voice like a shadow under his own thoughts, but every time he used his ability, it got quieter like a radio signal fading as you turn the dial. He didn't talk about it with the others in his Bloom—trust was important, but paranoia was a survival skill—but by the time they got to the Houston school, Clay wasn't hearing orders anymore.

Having Waylon psychically network him with the others feels

like what he wanted the Hive to be and what he wished being in the Faction had been. The little voice in his head never made him feel connected. It told him he was valued and loved, but Clay knew praise was a carrot delivered by someone who preferred to use the stick. As for the Hive, there was something performative about it, like social media sites where you covered up depression and boredom with shiny manufactured representations of yourself. After an initial shyness, the sense of his thoughts standing naked in a crowded room, Clay feels comfortable being mutually exposed.

From the inside, Bryce gives them a list of assets among the students. It doesn't amount to much. The Unity School attracted oddballs and outcasts. Kids with more practical abilities gravitated toward schools more in line with the Bishop model or the training academies of the Black Rose Faction. Among the kids held in the auditorium, one can mimic and project any sound or voice and another has an extraneous arm. There's a kid with "hot fingers," three untrained psychics, and an energy projector whose accuracy Bryce rates as "buckshot." Even the teachers are less than awe-inspiring: a healer, a universal translator, a math teacher with infrared perception, and an empath the kids call Mama Bear.

"Have you seen the Faction use their abilities?" Clay asks. He talks out loud even though they're communicating with their thoughts, unable to break the habit.

They have an obsidianist, Bryce says. *He sealed us in the auditorium with black glass, and he carries some sort of knives. I'm not sure about the rest.*

So we're going in blind, Carrie says.

"Not quite," Clay says. "Waylon, can you link us to the math teacher?"

Ms. Beasley? Bryce asks.

Waylon obliges, and the voice of an obviously flustered older woman joins them in their heads.

"Can you look around the building and tell me where every-one is?" Clay asks.

An image of the whole school appears in his head. There are two clumps of glowing dots: the Resonant students in the auditorium and the baseliner kids in the gym. He focuses on the second set, wishing he could tell which ones are Dom and Rai. He scans the rest of the image. There are dots outside the gym and the auditorium; two more move about the halls.

"Where's the fifth?" Clay asks.

Roof? Above? Carrie suggests. *I'd want a flier for surveillance.*

"So we assume?"

We never assume.

Oh my God, you two are insufferable, Hayden says. *Bryce, did you get a good look at any of them?*

The obsidianist, yeah, Bryce says.

Show me.

An image forms in their heads of a man who looks as if he's cosplaying a pirate. He has a bandolier of obsidian knives across his chest, a week's worth of stubble, and a face so lopsided it looks like someone smudged half of it with a wet thumb.

Fuck, I hate being ugly, Hayden says. Their pop star features go soft and doughy, dark prickles of beard rising through the skin of their chin, their blond hair withering into dirty brown curls as their gut expands and their shirt folds on itself to mimic the bandolier.

You want the gym, right? Carrie asks Clay. He nods. *Waylon, give me as many of the kids as you can hook us up with.* Clay's head is filled with the panicked chatter of two dozen kids, and despite the fact they're less individuated voices than a dull collective roar, he searches for Rai's voice among them, with no luck. *Everybody here?* Carrie asks. There is a general murmur of assent. *Okay, this is what we're doing.*

They approach the Unity School's front door underneath the blanket of Carrie's ability. The world takes on an opalescent quality like the way it appears to Clay when he's looking out of his bubble. At the door, Carrie takes a knee to jimmy the lock. Clay asked once where she picked up some of her less legal skills. *Is that the shit they taught you at Bishop?*

Misspent youth, she replied.

When the lock pops, Clay speeds them through the door so it's open less than a second, then slows time so the door closes soundlessly. Wearing the face Bryce showed them, Hayden heads toward the auditorium while Carrie and Clay move toward the gym.

"Hey," Hayden calls before turning the corner. Their voice is comedically gruff. Carrie turns back. "Don't die."

"Got it," says Carrie.

As they pass the cafeteria, Clay hears someone whisper "over here" from down one hallway, then from another. He knows it isn't real, that there's a kid sitting in the auditorium planting noises all over the school, but it shakes him. The fear isn't real either—it's the woman the kids call Mama Bear, using the flip side of her ability to project a low thrum of paranoia throughout the school like Muzak. Turns out he can know there's nothing to be afraid of and be scared shitless at the same time, as any kid could have told him.

"You have a plan from here?" he asks Carrie.

Stab people, Carrie says through the psychic link. *Hope they don't have impenetrable skin or something.*

Through their connection, they see Hayden approaching the door of the auditorium. Hayden's plan hinges on the Faction agent guarding the door not being the one whose face they're wearing, and they're relieved it's a girl in her late teens whose body from the waist down consists of eight spidery legs in constant motion, dancing to inaudible music. She gives Hayden a what's-up nod as they approach.

"They want you over by the gym," Hayden says in the thick, gruff voice they imagined the Faction agent might sound like.

"For what?" asks the spider girl.

"How the fuck should I know?" Hayden barks. The spider girl holds her hands up defensively and scurries down the hall.

Headed your way, Hayden says.

Thanks loads, Carrie says.

Clay and Carrie see the doors to the gym. There are two Faction agents there, one covered in luminous boils and the other with a ring of eyes all the way around his head.

"You hear that, Hank?" says the one with the boils.

Hank cocks a half dozen eyebrows skeptically at his partner. "It's nothing," he says. "Quit trying to creep me out."

"I heard something. Go look."

"Why do I have to—" Hank begins, but stops himself. The guy with multiple eyes must be used to getting stuck with lookout duty. He rolls an odd number of eyes and starts down the hall toward Carrie and Clay.

"Can he see us?" Clay whispers.

I don't know, maybe, says Carrie. *Do the thing.*

"Which thing?"

The put them to sleep *thing you used to do,* Carrie says. Clay waits until Hank rounds the corner and then creates a bubble of slow time in his carotid artery. All of Hank's eyes roll back to the whites as he slumps against the lockers. Carrie picks the lock on one, and they cram Hank into it like they're high school bullies.

Clay pulls the gun out of his pocket, and Carrie presses it back down with her hand. *Stay behind me,* she says. They walk up to the remaining guard, and Carrie draws the knife from the back of her belt. She stands directly in front of the guard, invisible to him, and delicately presses the point of the knife against his throat.

"I don't particularly want to kill you," she says quietly. "But I'm also running low on fucks to give. You open that door and my friend will help you sleep through what happens next."

The man's face quivers in fear, each boil sweating nacreous liquid. He takes a step toward the door, then stops. His face twists into a grin Clay swears he's seen in his head before, back when the little black worm still worked.

"It's nice, the two of you coming back to the fold," the agent says in the soured honey voice that once whispered and buzzed in Clay's ear. "There's nothing for you in here. They're all dead."

"Clay," Carrie shouts.

Shaking himself out of a trance, Clay reaches into the agent's brain and slows the blood flow through the carotid. The grin holds, but his eyes roll back and he collapses in a heap. It's possible Clay held it too long, did permanent damage, but as Carrie had said, they're short of fucks to give.

Carrie searches the man for the keys, checking the pockets of his pants and shirt but coming up empty. The whispers continue to echo through the halls, and Clay is having trouble not firing at each sound when a voice shouts "Hey, what the fuck?" Clay looks to his left and sees the pirate guy running toward them with an ebony knife raised.

"Shit, what if it's Hayden?" he says, the piped-in fear overriding his judgment.

"Why the fuck would Hayden come running at us with a knife?" Carrie asks. She's trying to pick the lock, but her hands are shaking. Clay is comforted knowing she's experiencing the same baseless fear he is. He turns toward the Faction agent, steadies his trembling right arm with his left, and fires three shots: one high on the shoulder, one under the ribs, and the third snapping the agent's head back, dropping him. The door swings open, and Clay turns toward it, searching the gym for Rai and Dom, forgetting he's brandishing a pistol. The kids shriek; the room is wired with a combination of secondhand and actual fear. Carrie gently takes the gun out of Clay's hand, and the burden of it, removed, is massive. His son collides with him, almost knocking him over, but Dom is there to hold him up.

"Are you all right?" he asks them both.

"We're fine," Rai says. "Dad pretended to be normal and came with me. He kept me safe."

Dom is about to amend this gently to something like *both your dads kept you safe* when Clay hears the rapid approach of scuttling legs. He tells himself it's more imaginary sounds until the spider girl appears in the doorway of the gym, her face grinning like the other agent's, a smile that stretches her face painfully until it looks as if the skin of her lips will split at the corners. She skids to a halt, changing her vector, but before she can move toward the kids, Clay slows time to a crawl around her legs and speeds it around her torso so that the girl cleaves neatly in half, her upper body landing on the hardwood floor in a rapidly spreading pool of blood.

With one hand, she presses herself up slightly so that she can look at Carrie and Clay.

"You should come back to me," she says, her voice deep and not her own. "I'm the only place you'll ever belong."

THAT WAS YOUR MOTHER,
THAT WAS YOUR FATHER

◇

Parents wait outside the Unity School to gather their children and rush them away. The kids make a point of thanking their rescuers, especially the ones saved by Hayden. Carrie and Clay don't get the same level of gush, but then Hayden had managed to get their roomful of kids out bloodlessly. The thanks Carrie receives are muttered, whispered, delivered with eyes averted. Even with the body count, it's good to save people rather than attack them, although they're past the point where she can do one without the other. *Remember when all the camps were empty and you still had to fight?* she thinks. *That day's coming back around soon enough.*

She hears the voice in her head, a memory now rather than a live broadcast: *I'm the only place you'll ever belong.*

"That's the end," Bryce says, scratching at the patch of leaves that top his scalp. "None of them will come back. The baseliners will go west, and the Resonant kids will sign up for some other school. Even if they stay, what's the point?"

"You have things to teach them," Carrie says. "Whether or not—"

"They learned the last lesson this place is going to teach," he says. "Thank you for getting them out. I know you don't do this shit anymore."

"I keep saying that, and then I'm out here doing this shit again," says Carrie. Bryce hugs her tightly, then goes to check on a couple of kids whose parents haven't shown up yet.

Carrie sees Clay being comforted by his husband on the school steps. She had time to adjust to being back in the middle of this shit, but it's new to him and hitting him hard. She stands there watching them, thinking about Miquel and about Hayden, who's signing autographs on notebooks, textbooks, whatever the kids have at hand. She notices the boy sitting on the ground near her feet, his attention fixed on Clay and his husband.

"Hey," she says. "You're Rai."

"Do I know you?" he asks. Carrie hunkers down and sits next to him on the pavement.

"I knew your folks."

"My dads?" he asks, pointing his chin at Clay and Dom.

"Your one dad," says Carrie. "But I knew Maaya and Koyo too."

His attention perks up, but he covers it with a veneer of adolescent scorn. "When you were all Nazis in the war or whatever?"

"We were the good guys," Carrie says. She considers this, thinking about the voice, the wolf's grin that surfaced on the agents' faces, the little black worm that used to live in her head. "We thought we were."

"Nazis probably thought they were the good guys too."

"Your dad talk to you about any of that?" she asks.

"He said he was in communications."

Carrie takes a sharp breath in. Once she asked Koyo what he'd tell Rai when it was all over. *I'd never tell him I wasn't in it*, Koyo said. *But I won't tell him what I did. I'll say I was in communications. Something bloodless.*

"Your dad and your folks?" Carrie says. "They were heroes. I fought with them for months. There was this one time—"

"Lady, I don't know you," Rai says. "I don't say this to make you feel bad. But the army you and my parents and my dad used to be in tried to kill me today. So I don't care how badass all of you were back in the day. Great fucking job; you won. How's it all working out?"

Carrie thinks about the day before she left to go looking for Emmeline, when Bryce invited her to the Unity School to offer her a job. By trying to avoid being around kids, she's damned herself to some steaming helpings of teenage contempt the last couple weeks.

"It's fucked, huh?" she says.

"Not for you," Rai says. "You've got special powers, and you rule the world. Sounds nice."

"When I was your age—"

Rai rolls his eyes so epically Carrie's sure she can *hear* it. "That is the off switch for my caring about what you're going to say."

She smiles and pushes forward. "When I was your age," she says, "I hated everybody older than me." She clicks off classes of adults on her fingers. "Hated my parents because they didn't understand me. Hated my teachers because they told me to hide who and what I was. It's how it works. Old people fuck up; young people have to fix it. Then they get old and fuck it up again."

"So where are you and where am I in all this?" Rai asks.

"You're young people," Carrie says. "I'm somewhere in between. I've fucked up plenty of things. So I'm trying to fix them, which makes me like a young person."

"That is a very old person thing to say," Rai says.

"You sound like a friend of mine," Carrie says, thinking of Emmeline and her attack on Carrie's middle-age taste in music. Rai watches his dads, then looks at the school. He knows the same thing Bryce did: the Unity School is over. Carrie imagines what a comfort a school like this must have been to him, the way Bishop had been to her.

"So are you going to tell me how my parents were badasses?" Rai asks.

Carrie shakes her head. "Wouldn't matter, right? What would that tell you about them? I can tell you they loved you a lot. They never shut up about you. Your dad used to ..." She struggles to find the word for Koyo's ability. *Hologram* feels too cheesy: there was a solidity to what he could do. "He could make these three-dimensional light projections. Did you know that? He made one of you all the time. He said it was the closest he could get to having you there."

For Carrie, it had been no different from having an actual child with them. When they were attacked in camp outside an army depot in Boise, she scrabbled through the tents looking for a boy who wasn't there. "Your mom hated it," she says. "She never said anything because it made your dad happy, but I think it made it worse for her, being away from you and seeing this image of you she couldn't hold on to. She'd sleep with her arms wrapped around herself, and I remember thinking she was imagining you and hugging you as tight as she could." Carrie felt jealous when she'd see Maaya sleeping that way, an emotion she could never map. It wasn't longing for her own mother or a childish wish that Maaya, only a few years older than Carrie, could be her mother. It was wishing she'd had a mother who missed her when she was away rather than forgetting her while she was in the room. "Maaya was funny," Carrie says. "She had whole books of jokes that she memorized. Like, anything someone said would remind her of a joke."

"Were they good?" Rai asks.

"Oh, no, they were terrible," Carrie says. "Bad puns. Dad jokes."

Rai nods as if this confirms his belief in the unfunniness of all adults. "Do you remember any of them?"

Carrie's head floods with punch lines out of context, setups that don't land. What she remembers more than the content is the rush of warm feeling that wasn't laughter but something akin to it that came whenever Maaya told a joke. The dark thing in her head went silent in those moments. "I can't do them as well as she did," she says. "I liked them when she told them. Without her they sound dumb."

"Can you tell me *one*?" he asks.

Carrie rifles through all the mismatched fragments in her head, looking for two that go together. When she assembles a pair, she wishes it were something more relevant, symbolic of Maaya and her love for her son or representative of who she'd been. Carrie clears her throat, trying to hear Maaya's delivery in her head.

"Why couldn't the pirate learn the alphabet?" she says.

Maybe wishing the same thing, treating it like a riddle, Rai spends time considering. After a minute, he gives up. "Something something arrgh?"

"Because he got lost at *c*."

Rai stares at her blankly, then stifles a laugh, a contagious little one. "That's terrible," he says.

"Yeah."

"Thanks, lady," Rai says.

"Sure, kid," Carrie says, patting him fraternally on the back.

"Rai," he says, holding out his hand and introducing himself.

"Carrie," she says, happy to start again with him at the beginning.

INHERITANCE

◇

The Craft touches down on lush grass that's never seen the blade of a mower. Droplets of dew crush against its belly as it lands. When Ruth pulls the construct back into herself, she shivers as if the cool drops have run down the back of her neck. Below, in the foothills of the Alps, the city of Innsbruck expands with a march-like rhythm, its buildings not identical but similar enough to give that impression; the variations in color aren't a simple red-yellow-blue repetition but suggest a pattern that would reveal itself under deeper analysis. It looks untouched by time, which was the original appeal.

"I saw pictures of it in a book," Fahima's father told her. "It's as if it's never seen a hint of war. If I had to go anywhere, I'd go there."

He was wrong, not that Fahima could ever tell her father he was wrong. The city was razed by Allied bombers in World War II and, like many German cities, rebuilt itself as its own prewar replica. All the things her father perceived about it from books and magazines—"It has authenticity," he said—were false, except that it was beautiful. The sunlight has a quality as if sunlight every-where else passes through gauze and only here touches the earth in true form, and the air, which her father had no way of anticipating, is charged with the smell of incipient snow.

Her mother had shrugged. "There must be a gas stove," she said. "I'm never cooking on one of those coils again. And separate bathrooms."

This was an encapsulation of her mother, so hardened against hardships that she thought of her second forced emigration in terms of amenities. In the early days of the war, Fahima hid her parents at the Phoenix school—not that anyone was looking for them, but Fahima had so little sense of what shape the conflict might take, the only place she considered any baseliner safe was in her pocket. When it was over, their appreciation at being kept safe turned to discontent, not as sharply as Alyssa's had but with a creeping increase of disapproval Fahima remembered from child-hood, when a behavior would be smiled at indulgently one day, tsk-tsk-ed the next, and abruptly punished, the course among the three a rising curve Fahima could never plot correctly. As they were clearly unhappy, she offered to put her parents anywhere on the planet. Anywhere other than America.

"You could go home," she offered. "Back to Lebanon."

"There is no home there," her father said. That shut down the first attempt at conversation, and it was a week before she could coax other options out of them, each one dismissed for reasons that seemed minor to Fahima but were deal breakers for one or both of her parents.

Her father raised the possibility of Innsbruck, musing about it one evening when Fahima slipped through the Gate in her apart-ment to have dinner with them in what her mother called their "shabby little dorm room." Nothing was decided that night, but at the next dinner conversation turned to Innsbruck again, and her mother gave her a short list of conditions. Fahima bought them a house, and Ruth carried out her first big favor for Fahima: the trans-Pacific expatriation of Khalil and Rima Deeb from the Phoenix desert to the Austrian Tyrol.

"We should move fast," Ruth says. "I don't completely understand what we're dealing with, but I don't want to be racing it."

"Sure," says Fahima, overwhelmed by the beauty of the place she's standing. Her father chose well: this is a good place. She's a terrible daughter for coming to steal them away from it.

They hike down into the city, neither one sure-footed on the hills and the dew-slick grass. On the street they're greeted with nods, smiles, and hat tips befitting a possessed town in a horror movie, made all the more unsettling by being genuine. Each cheery utterance of *schön dich zu sehen* confirms that yes, it is nice to see them, too, and nice to be seen. The prevailing *niceness* of Innsbruck is over and over restated, reaffirmed until it is an overwhelming fact about the place, the day, and extends into Fahima and Ruth themselves.

The quaint edifice of her parents' house belies its cost. Purchasing it was the first time Fahima realized the Bishop Foundation's accounts were limitless—the price tag that seemed ridiculous to Fahima was barely a blip on the Bishop ledgers, disappeared under the "Additional Facilities Expenses" line in the budget. Fahima lets the brass knocker strike its plate three times before she hears the bustle of her mother within, arguing with her father before the door's open. There is no chain, no sound of a dead bolt retracting: Who would lock their doors in a place where everyone is so *nice*?

"Habibat," her mother says with more of a sense of relief than excitement. She thinks of Fahima as constantly at risk, in some perpetual war zone. Every call and visit is greeted with a sound like a held breath released. "Khalil," she calls back into the house. "Fahima is here."

"No warning," her father shouts from the other room. "Never any warning with this one."

"We've just had breakfast," her mother says by way of explanation.

"Bring her in; I'll put the kettle on," says her father.

Her mother sucks her teeth. "The kettle will wait. Come kiss your daughter."

Her father's glacial speed and gray hair are the only signs of his age. His skin is taut and healthy looking and his eyes bright, all things Fahima attributes to the Alpine air rather than the antioxidant nanites she peppered his food with while he was in Phoenix. When they left, she gave a bottle of pills packed with them to her mother. "For his blood pressure," Fahima said, knowing her father would accept Fahima's medications as long as there was plausible deniability but her mother would insist she was fine with her own unguents and elixirs, suspiciously eyeing anything Fahima tried to feed her. It's hard to argue with her: Rima Deeb looks nowhere near her seventy-five years, and it seems possible she'll outlive her husband, whose blood teems with machines designed by his daughter to defy old age.

He kisses her on both cheeks, then turns to Ruth, who, on closer inspection, he realizes he doesn't recognize.

"This is Ruth," Fahima says. Her father extends his hand, looking formal with a hint of regality.

"A white girl," her mother says in Arabic.

"Alyssa was a white girl, and you loved her," Fahima responds in Arabic.

"Alyssa was a *doctor*," says her mother. "Is this one a doctor?"

"A pilot," Ruth says, smiling uncomfortably. She turns sheepishly to Fahima. "The translator bots I took are still working."

Fahima's father claps his hands as he barks out a single laugh.

"We said there was no breakfast, and now there's egg on your mother's face," he says. His laughter fades into fake coughs and throat clearing as her mother glares at him and walks back to the kitchen to put water on for tea.

"We should go," Ruth says.

"Now you must stay or my wife will stare daggers at me for the rest of the day," says Fahima's father. "I'm afraid we've damned each other to tea. Come."

Ruth holds Fahima in the doorway by her arm. "I wasn't joking," she says. "We're going to be in a blind sprint in the direction of *away* with no real idea of the range. I need as much of a head start as I can get."

"She's making tea," Fahima says. "It's rude to refuse." It's a trick she used to use on Alyssa, claiming traditional mores that could not be violated. She's thinking of what Babisch said about sitting with his family and watching the Pulse come, going all in together on this final bet. She's thinking of her mother's staunch refusal of "unnatural" assistance, how much her father loves this place, and the fact she has nowhere else to take them, not anywhere this beautiful. Her parents have lived into their seventies. They've survived evacuation from two countries they called home. They deserve not to have to run anymore.

She threads her hand into Ruth's and pulls her into the parlor. The kettle takes forever to come to a boil, and with each second Ruth's grip torques incrementally tighter. Fahima's father describes a recent mushroom hunt he went on with some of the locals, detailing the ugly ones that had turned out the most delectable, the beauties that stank of unclean feet when sautéed in butter, and the biggest tease of all, a majestic angel he nearly added to his basket before his friend warned him it would leave him shitting himself to death. Fahima smells the sweetness of sesame seeds toasting and knows her mother has hastily thrown together lavash, which will take even longer to bake. *We couldn't escape it now at a full gallop,* Fahima thinks. As if reading her mind, Ruth leans over, whispering in the middle of Fahima's father's monologue. "We can call Kimani," she says. "Open a door and be gone."

"We're not going," Fahima says. "The tea will be ready soon, and there's bread." Her eyes well up with tears. *All this time and where was my skin in the game?* she thinks. *Tucking my dearest ones away and pretending I understood the stakes. Here,* she thinks, addressing herself to the absence left behind when the religious faith of her childhood faded. *Here's my bet on the table. Here's me. I'm all in.*

It comes as Fahima's mother is bringing in the tray, which is so broad she has to turn to the side to come through the kitchen door. Ruth feels it first, and it slams her back into her chair, the opalescent envelope of the Craft emerging from the center of her chest without warning and hanging suspended in the air over the coffee table. For Fahima, it's a rolling tide that douses her with solutions to problems that have dogged her for years. She wants to grab one of the books from her father's shelves and begin writing things down—if even a third of the things in her head in that moment could be translated into actual inventions, the lives she saved would be countless—but she steadies herself, watching her parents, imagining the ball on a roulette wheel bouncing the last time before coming to rest.

Fahima's mother glows—it starts in the center of her chest, and she doesn't notice it until it reaches her forearms, at which point she drops the tray onto the carpet, the teapot spilling its contents onto the fresh bread. She holds her hands up in front of her face for a moment, wondering at their luminescence, then drops to her knees to pick up the mess.

Fahima's father's eyes go entirely white, the irises and pupils drowned in a milky sea. "Karima," he says, an endearment he hasn't used since the FBI took him away from her when she was ten. "I can see your bones. I can see the skull beneath your skin."

"I know, Aba," says Fahima, her voice hitched with a joy that sears and burns. "It's going to be all right."

IF ONLY TONIGHT WE COULD SLEEP

◇

Clay invites Carrie and Hayden back to "the house," and Carrie wonders if he knows how badly she dreads returning to her apartment since Miquel left. It makes no sense—she lived there without him for years, much longer than they'd lived there together—but now for the first time it feels empty.

Rogers Park is so far out of the city it might as well be Deerfield, and as they arrive on Jarvis Avenue, Carrie feels like she's somewhere familiar, a variation on the theme of the American suburb. The house plays many of the same notes as the one she grew up in, and its sense of being lived in, a home rather than simply a house, makes it hard to believe Clay and his family have been there only a couple of weeks.

Dinner conversation is awkward as they talk around what happened. Carrie and Clay reminisce, careful not to give any of the gorier details of who they used to be. Rai conducts an amateur interview of Hayden, as if he's profiling them for a magazine piece. Dom busies himself in a way that reminds Carrie of how her father became a servant at family gatherings, trying to avoid conversation with constant motion. Dom gives her looks as if she's the other woman, here to steal his man away.

The family goes to bed before the sun has fully disappeared, and Carrie wonders if this is normal or if they're trying to put distance between themselves and today. Dom suggests it, saying they could all use some rest. Rai sulks, then acquiesces. She thinks Clay might stay up to discuss strategy, but his eyes drift toward the stairs and the quiet that awaits him up there.

"There's beer in the fridge," he says. "The couch pulls out, and there's a love seat up in the attic if you don't mind a mess."

"Thanks," Hayden says.

"Let's let all this be over for the night," Clay says. Carrie nods, all three of them knowing that it's barely started.

"You want the foldout?" Hayden asks.

"I want a beer," Carrie says. She doesn't need one, but she deserves one, and having it will put off discussions of who sleeps where. Hayden goes to the kitchen and comes back with two open beers, leading Carrie to the couch.

"You want to tell me about the bug in your head?" Hayden asks. Carrie knew this talk was coming, but she'd hoped it would wait until tomorrow.

"You knew I went out again after Topaz Lake," Carrie says.

"I didn't know you joined up with the Hitler Youth," Hayden says.

"They came and found me," Carrie says. "Patrick from Bishop and Ji Yeon Kim. They came and told me they needed me. They told me I was good. I was having dreams. I was seeing what I did to Warden Pitt when I thought Miquel was dead. Miquel was falling apart, and it was because of me. It meant so much for someone to tell me I was good."

"I would have told you that you were good," Hayden says, moving closer.

"You and Waylon and Bryce were building things," Carrie says. "I didn't want you to have to baby-sit."

"You were gone for months, and none of us saw it," Hayden says. "How did we miss that?"

"It's what I do," Carrie says. "I disappear."

"I should have found you," Hayden says. They touch Carrie's face, and she is too tired to know what she wants. She wants to dream of Hayden kissing her. She wants it to happen. She wants it to stop. None of the thoughts hold; nothing in her head will sit still. Hayden doesn't come in for a kiss. They take Carrie's beer and set it on the coffee table next to their own. They hold her and lay her down, curl up next to her on the couch that barely has room for one of them. They rest their head on Carrie's shoulder, drape their arm over her. She can feel Hayden's heart beating against her arm, and although she knows there's no message encoded in its rhythm, she ascribes language to it. *You're good,* it says. *You're good.*

"There's something I want to show you," Carrie says. She reaches into her back pocket, into the space between the two of them, and retrieves the Polaroid she found on the fridge the night before she left to find Emmeline. She holds it so Hayden can see it over her shoulder.

"Who are those kids?" Hayden asks. "What happened to your face?"

"I don't know," Carrie says. "I've had it for a while. I have some ideas about where it came from, but . . . I think they're our kids."

Hayden's body shifts away from her. "I know this isn't something we've talked about, but I can't—"

"Look at the girl," Carrie says. "Her eyes." She hands Hayden the photo, and Hayden rolls onto their back, nearly knocking Carrie off the couch.

"She's Miquel's," Hayden says.

Carrie nods. "You can see little things about him in their faces."

Hayden sighs but doesn't hand the photo back. "We fooled around with it being all of us, and it didn't work," they say.

"Miquel and I are done," Carrie says. "I see that now. I've known for a while."

"Then I'm not sure what you're suggesting," Hayden says.

Carrie takes the photo and holds it where she and Hayden can see it. "I keep pulling it out of my pocket and wondering what it means," she says. "I pull it out of my pocket and think of it as the place I want to go. When this is all over, this is where I'll be. Before Emmeline took the thing out of my head, I'd look at this picture and I knew that *that* Carrie didn't have it in her anymore. She found something I haven't."

"So is that this?" Hayden says. Their arm tightens around Carrie for a moment and then releases, unsure. "I keep thinking you're going to stay with me while we're fighting and then run off once we win."

"Do they look like they won?" Carrie asks, moving the picture closer to Hayden. Carrie hasn't decided. Maybe it's possible to live that way: to be okay and never stop. "I'm not running off," she says. She rolls over and presses herself against Hayden, exhausted but completely awake, feeling like she's in the air but on the ground for the first time she can remember.

ON RETURNING

◇

When Emmeline comes back into the world, she's in the dark with nothing for her senses to attend to but the panicked sound of her own breathing and the measured sleeping breath of someone else. The space feels familiar, the way her body sometimes wakes confident of where it is.

The light next to the bed clicks on. Rai sits up in Emmeline's old bed, staring at her with the same lack of surprise he showed the first time she met him, the second time he'd met her.

"You came back," he says.

"How long has it been for you?" Emmeline asks.

"Two weeks," he says.

Emmeline nods. "A year," she says. They absorb the strangeness of this: that their meetings begin with these conversations.

"Hayden Cohen is sleeping on our couch," Rai blurts out. "Their girlfriend knows my dad." Emmeline's puzzled about why he's bursting to tell her this rather than ask her where she disappeared to until she realizes she isn't the focus of Rai's story, only an occasional guest. Having a pop star on his couch *is* his biggest news.

"There was an attack today at your school." Emmeline says. It isn't a question. She's looking for confirmation of something she already knows.

Rai nods. "They were going to kill us." He puts on his brave face, more resolved than the last time he tried it. "My dads kept me safe."

"I need to talk to Hayden's girlfriend," Emmeline says. "You and I will talk again soon."

"Cool," Rai says as he turns off the light. He's banged up from shock and has decided his best option is to accept all this. There's a power in simply saying yes.

Emmeline quietly opens the door and goes downstairs, careful to avoid steps she remembers creaking when she was little. She was a talented sneak back then, not as good as Carrie but good enough to spy on her parents countless times. She finds Carrie asleep on the couch, wrapped in Hayden's arms. *How many things start today?* she wonders. Everything is always beginning—Carrie and Hayden started years ago, before Emmeline knew them. It makes sense until she tries to break it down into moments and points. Everything is moving and fluid, and although there's something beautiful about that, it's terrifying at the same time.

Emmeline reaches out and touches Carrie's shoulder. She shakes her gently, trying to wake her without waking Hayden. Carrie's eyes flutter open.

"Hey," Emmeline says. "Sorry to wake you. Can you—" She mimes parting clothes in a closet, but Carrie understands and extricates herself from under Hayden's arm. Hayden mumbles something, then rolls over to face the back of the couch.

"Come on," Emmeline says, gesturing toward the kitchen. Carrie follows and takes a seat at the counter. Emmeline turns on the light over the stove.

"What are you doing here?" Carrie asks.

"This is my house," Emmeline says. "It's where I grew up before I came to Bishop."

"Are you serious?" Carrie asks. She looks around as if she might find a picture of Emmeline somewhere she hadn't noticed, then turns back to Emmeline. "Wait, but why are you here? You're supposed to be in Phoenix."

"I've been away," Emmeline says.

"Did Fahima send you to help?"

"I haven't gone to see Fahima," Emmeline says. "She doesn't know I'm back."

"Emmeline, I don't understand what you're saying," Carrie says. "Where are you back from?"

Emmeline wants to tell her that *where* is the wrong word, but she also feels the need to speed everything up, to get them all where they're going faster.

"Do you have the picture?" she asks. "The one you showed me before you left?"

Carrie takes the picture out of her wallet and holds it out, not like the last time, when it was an accusation. "You said you didn't know what it was."

"I didn't," Emmeline says. She takes the picture and lets her fingers drift over it. "Their names are Lynette and Shane. They're nine, and they're the sweetest kids I've ever met. I am so glad I got to meet them. Out of all of this, it's the best thing that's happened. The last few months, with them."

"I don't understand," Carrie says.

"They're yours," Emmeline says. "I took that picture yesterday. It was the last thing I did before I left. It won't happen for you for ten more years. I think I understand now how it fits together. I think I know how we win."

SIX

A MURMURATION
OF STARLINGS

and there are children in the tower
and the tower has been crooked for so long
—EVE L. EWING,
"Sightseers"

PILLS

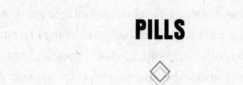

When Fahima gave the government inhibitor tech, she told them that she built in a back door they'd never find, to access the tech if they used it in ways she didn't like.

The trouble was, inhibitors were as technologically complex as a tanning bed crossed with a transistor radio. Exploits become easier to build as complexity increases—software and electronics offer thousands of hiding holes, but hacking a lawn mower by remote is next to impossible even for Fahima. There was no back door on the inhibitors. They were weaponized, used to keep thousands of her people in camps, and there was fuck all Fahima could do about it.

She likes to think she's a person who makes one kind of mistake only once. She finds unique ways to fuck up, but she's not much for repeats. Everything she's invented since the inhibitor has a peephole she can peer through, including systems at Project Tuning Fork and the Ruse.

During the war, she learned about spycraft and skullduggery.

People think they're smart and accept evidence that confirms that without examination. To hide an exploit in tech handed off to someone suspicious, tuck it behind a dummy exploit that's easier to find. Within the Ruse's systems, Fahima built a series of back doors that were increasingly well hidden.

The first is a command-line sequence that can be used onsite. It's what Fahima used to fudge the Tuning Fork data, keying in from the lab bays and moving numbers around. The second is a data leak to a server farm in Alaska that sent the data to random ISP addresses at irregular intervals. Cedric dispatched agents to the server farm two weeks ago, and they've been tracking down the ISPs, accosting confused Resonants about why their phones and laptops downloaded gigs of secured data.

She hoped after finding that one, Cedric would laugh at how he outsmarted the great Fahima Deeb and call it a day. Unfortunately, like any man who lands a job by luck rather than skill, Cedric was paranoid and kept digging until he found her third: a fully remote back door into all the Ruse's systems. It was a labyrinth through the architecture, winding its way toward the middle before pulling all data paths into one straight shot. It would let Fahima commandeer all systems at the Ruse, wiping data and fucking up electrical grids to short out the Chairs. It would have been beautiful, and she was heartbroken when pieces were sniffed out and deleted.

Convinced of his cleverness, Cedric stopped looking. A full remote back door with fragments tucked away across all systems was such a massive undertaking, it had to be her big play.

He never found the fourth door.

It's read-only access to data associated with Project Tuning Fork. It lacks the scope of the third, but by being so small, it's virtually untraceable. It's how she knew the Berlin Pulse was expected to result in a 30 percent casualty rate and how she examined the data stating that other than a handful of accidental deaths caused by the onset of new abilities—comparable to what happened after the first Pulse—there were no fatalities.

It's also how she knows where to find Thao Bui, the operator who caused the Berlin Pulse, now Project Tuning Fork's most valuable asset. He's moved every two days while assembly is completed on six other Chairs. His biometrics are monitored, and his every whim catered to. Catering turns out to be Fahima's fifth and final back door into Project Tuning Fork.

The Omars handled or subcontracted food service needs for the Ruse. When Fahima ran, no one bothered to weed through contracts looking for sympathizers. Phone calls from Omar to friends and former lovers get Fahima a room service shift at the James Hotel on Thompson and Grand, the safe house for Thao Bui before he flies out to Tokyo. Thao survives on well-done steaks and french fries, and Fahima, sans hijab, is delivering his dinner.

She flashes credentials at the Faction agent guarding the door. She considered the risk that Glover might be looking out of the eyes of the agent on the door, but Kimani convinced her it was unlikely. *He can't pay attention everywhere at once,* she said. *Unless he can, in which case we're all fucked.* The agent glances at the pass and opens the door to let Fahima and her cart through. The room brings back a visceral memory of the day she helped capture a murderous kid named Owen Curry in a shitty motel outside Chicago. The air has the same meaty fug to it, the stale masculine smell of someone who's given up on hygiene, and the room is littered with empty bottles of beer and vitamin water, clothes strewn everywhere, bed unmade. She hears Thao pissing in the bathroom, and when she glances over, she gets a quick glimpse of his ass through the open door.

"Sir, room service," she calls, jumping her voice up half an octave.

"Cool, leave it," Thao shouts from the bathroom.

"I need you to sign for it," Fahima says. The sound of his pissing peters out.

"The guy out front does that," he says.

"He said you'd do it."

After a moment that notably does not include flushing, Thao emerges from the bathroom in boxers and a ketchup-stained T-shirt. "I don't tip or anything," he says. "My shit is all comped."

"I need to talk to you," Fahima says in her normal voice, hoping he might recognize it from the handful of times they've talked. He doesn't. "It's Fahima Deeb," she says.

"Holy shit," Thao says. "Where's your—" He swirls his finger over the top of his head to indicate her missing hijab.

"Doesn't matter," she says. "I need to know how you did it."

Thao crosses his arms petulantly. "I just *did* it," he says. "You didn't think I could. Cedric said you were fucking up my numbers to make it look like—"

"I made your numbers worse, but they were bad," Fahima says. "Berlin was zero casualties. You topped out at a 30 percent fatality rate. How did it happen?"

Thao eyes her warily, and Fahima wishes she'd taken the time to make friends with him when he worked for her, or at least conceal her dislike of his bro-dawg approach to the project. "I could knock on that door and the dude would come in and arrest you," he says.

If she challenges him, he'll do it. She hears Ruth asking her what the escape plan will be. *There are no escape plans,* Fahima told her. *Not anymore.* Fahima has nothing left but all-in attempts. She's relying on the commitment that comes when she doesn't leave herself a way out.

"You fly to Tokyo tomorrow to get strapped into another

Chair," she says. "Maybe you'd like to know how come you didn't kill a couple million people the first time so you don't kill a couple million people this time. I'm not saying I'm going to know. But I'm the last person you have who's willing to try."

Thao's lack of self-reflectiveness made him the most effective operator she had at Tuning Fork. He wasn't burdened by doubts about his ability. It also formed the upper limit of what he could do. Operators like Roxane and Clay assessed and adjusted the way they used their abilities with the Chairs; Thao stepped into Lab Bay Beta every day and did the same thing he'd done before but harder. She bets that when Cedric told him they were going ahead despite the risks, Thao was thrilled. Now everything rides on her hope that in the moment before he activated the Chair, he was horrified at what he was about to do.

"There was a girl," he says. "A teenager, black girl. I even thought it was—"

"Emmeline Hirsch," Fahima says. It's impossible but very much like Emmeline to disappear and show up again at the last possible moment. Emmeline and her impossible possibility.

"It was like she came out of nowhere," Thao says. "We were a minute from go. I was about to tell them we needed to abort, but there was this voice." He taps his temple, a gesture Fahima is too used to seeing. "He put something in my head. He said it was a tracker, but it wasn't. I could feel it all the time. I wanted to stop, but it wasn't going to let me. Then she was there, and I couldn't hear it anymore. She took my seat, and she . . ." Thao's face quivers with a mix of fear and rapture, the look of someone saved by a miracle. "It wasn't me; it was her. If it was me, all those people would have died. And now I have to do it tomorrow, and if she doesn't show up, I don't know what I'm going to do."

"It's okay," Fahima says. She reaches into her pocket and takes out a bottle of pills. She's about to hand it to Thao when there's a knock on the door. Startled, Fahima drops the bottle onto the carpet, the soft rattle of the pills like a klaxon in her head.

"Everything okay in there?" calls the Faction agent.

Fahima looks at Thao, sure he's about to give her up. "We're good," he shouts.

Fahima kneels and retrieves the pill bottle from the floor. From a posture of genuflection, she offers it up to him. "I've been looking over your data," she says. "It's why I went away. All the other shit they had me working on, I couldn't see the numbers anymore. I knew *you* were going to be the one to crack this." Thao doesn't smile, but he's buying what she's selling. "I needed time to figure out what I was missing. Patrick took it the wrong way. He thought I was moving away from the project, but I was *finishing* it." She gives the bottle a suggestive shake. "These will modulate your ability enough to prevent fatality. The problem is, you're too strong. You're blowing people's minds, and the Chair can't compensate without wiping out the benefits. This will help you meet it in the middle. All your power in a shape the Chair can handle."

Thao reaches for the bottle, and Fahima hesitates, pulling it back. The pills are a mix of sodium thiopental, pancuronium bromide, and potassium chloride, the latter two coated in time-release gel. It's the cocktail used for lethal injection. The sodium thiopental knocks him out, the pancuronium bromide paralyzes his lungs, and the potassium chloride stops his heart. It won't be painless, but it's what she could throw together, and it prevents millions from dying screaming, clearing her schedule to deal with whatever horror is next.

Her wrist tips forward, offering the pill bottle, but Thao sees her hesitation and the bottle hangs between them, unclaimed. A hand closes over Fahima's. Her gaze follows the fingers up to the hand, the smooth skin of the forearm, the bare shoulders, and finally the haunted eyes of Emmeline Hirsch.

"Not like this," Emmeline says quietly. Fahima feels herself tugged out of the world as Emmeline folds them upward.

They fold back down into Fahima's office in Phoenix, startling Ruth, who's sipping coffee on the small couch. On the wall, there are sketches of a machine, one more ridiculous Rube Goldberg device Fahima might chuck at the universe in the hope of changing its course. Like several before it, this diagram has a single upper-case letter at its center:

E.

"I thought we were picking you up at the—" She stops as she registers Emmeline's presence. "Hi."

"Hi, Ruth," Emmeline says. "It's nice to see you."

"I need to talk to Emmeline privately," Fahima says, speaking to the room rather than directly to Ruth, who speeds out.

"Where in the name of fuck have you been?" Fahima says, rounding on Emmeline.

"I don't think I should tell you," Emmeline says.

"You're back two minutes and I already have a headache from this shit." Fahima goes around her desk and takes two bottles out of the bottom drawer: one clear, one green. She brings out a metal flask that's wide at the base with a thin neck. The silvery metal surface moves like oil on water. Fahima starts pouring gin into the metal flask, and Emmeline interrupts her. "Can you make me one of those?" she asks. "They always look good, like the idea of cold."

"They look better than they taste," Fahima says. She pours another helping into the flask, then finds two less than clean glasses on a bookshelf. She sets them on the desk and fills them until they're brimming.

"How do you not spill it?" Emmeline asks.

"Bishop said the key was not to look at it," Fahima says. "But I'm sure he used telekinesis or some shit." She leans over and slurps from the surface of one of the glasses like a bird drinking from a pool. Emmeline follows suit. She winces and shivers.

"So you're not going to tell me anything," Fahima says.

Emmeline smiles at her. "You have a plan," she says, pointing to the diagram on the wall. "You modeled it on the gun assembly bomb."

"Little Boy," Fahima says.

"You were going to shoot me at Raymond Glover and hope something exploded."

"It is a shitty plan," Fahima says.

"The bomb I saw when I started the first Pulse, it wasn't a gun assembly bomb."

"You saw the Gadget," Fahima says. Emmeline doesn't remember much about what happened when she created the Pulse, but Fahima, ever the data collector, recorded everything Emmeline said that day. *There's a candle in the desert,* she'd said. *Mr. Bishop is watching it from a hill.* Emmeline reached out her finger after she said that, toward a light only she could see, more than a half century away. She changed something. "If you saw the Trinity test with Bishop and Glover, the one Bishop told us about, what you saw was an implosion bomb."

Emmeline makes her right hand into a fist. "Take a core of subcritical material," she says. She hovers her left hand, open, over her fist. "Surround it, then compress it all at once." She grips her fist with her hand. "It happens in an instant."

"There's more to it than that, but basically," Fahima says. "There's also something embedded in the center of the core called a neutron initiator. It's two elements that get pressed together by the compression wave."

Emmeline nods. "That's the plan."

"That's not a plan; it's a description," Fahima says. "We can't go up against him with a Wikipedia entry on the Trinity bomb."

"External compression from all possible angles," Emmeline says. "Two elements, embedded in the center, combined at the exact moment. The bomb can be a metaphor, but a metaphor can also be a bomb."

Fahima looks at her like Emmeline's stopped speaking English.

"How sick is Kimani?" Emmeline asks. She sips her drink in a way that ought to look sophisticated but results in a loud, childish slurp.

"She's not sick," Fahima says. "She's exhausted. She's holding this whole building in her head."

"We have to save her, and we have to stop him," Emmeline says. "We need everybody, all at once."

Something in the phrase *all at once* opens up the divide between them. All this time, Fahima has thought in terms of inputs and outputs—causality, whether as a chain or a web. Emmeline is thinking in terms of simultaneity, and Emmeline might be the one who's right.

ON PREPARATION

◇

Everyone Emmeline visits, she tells the same thing: *It's going to happen very fast.* She says it to communicate across two systems of thinking. From her point of view, it's taking forever. When she was little, her dad took her to see a domino run at the Chicago Children's Museum. He was stressed because the Red Line was slow and they were running late. *We have to be there* at *three o'clock,* he said, tugging her arm as he wove through people on East Grand. They got there in time for Emmeline to take in the whole setup from a spot on the balcony. The museum had cleared all the exhibits on the ground floor, covering it in dominoes along with a collection of bits and bobs: a Hot Wheels loop-the-loop, a xylophone, a miniature Ferris wheel, an oversized pachinko board. With her father short of breath, a scoreboard clock counted down from ten, the crowd counting along. The first domino tipped, and within a minute the whole thing was over.

On the way home, her father was disappointed by her lack of amazement. *You have to think about the time that went into it,* he said. *All those hours setting them up, positioning them. It's impressive.*

She *didn't* have to think about the time—the results were all that mattered, and the results hadn't amounted to much—but she tried it his way. It changed her reaction from underwhelmed to sad. She felt bad for the people who had spent hours on their knees, placing thousands of dominoes to amuse a room full of kids who'd rather be somewhere else. She felt like she'd failed those people and her father by not being forever changed by the sight. The only thing that made her happy was that it had worked: each domino in the sequence dropped as it was supposed to. She could imagine the embarrassment she'd feel on their behalf if the chain had been broken, the collective gasp as one misplaced domino failed to fall.

If this fails, I'll be a lot worse than embarrassed, she thinks.

The kids at the Flagstaff mall are confused when she appears from nowhere, but Tuan is happy to see her. They seem older, as if adulthood came and took something from them while she was away. They throw a party to celebrate her return, although Emmeline suspects they're using her as an excuse to throw a party. Some of the kids have been making wine out of the grapes grown in the makeshift greenhouse, and, reasoning that it can't taste worse than gin, Emmeline tries some. It does, in fact, taste worse than gin.

Emmeline asks about kids she remembers from the last time, and Tuan shrugs. "Bunch of people coupled off and split," he says as he sips out of crystal stemware in the center concourse. Rain patters on the glass dome of the atrium, and one of Hayden's albums plays over the mall's main speakers. Designed for piping in Muzak, they make Hayden's voice sound tinny. These aren't songs to dance to, but people make a go of it, swaying like sea grass in rhythm with the rain as much as to the beat of the music. "Estella and Percy decided to head east and apply for repatriation or whatever. Like they're going to show up and everyone's going to be like *Oh, you have zero dollars, yes, let's get you set up in an apartment and shit*." He hiccups and slurps his wine.

"New York has universal housing," Emmeline says. "With all the people who left, they have space."

"Who says a couple is the best thing?" he says. "Who thinks they need to get back to nuclear family shit? Families break. They mess you up. Kids want to fall in love and move out to the suburbs? Who taught them that?"

"It's in movies," Emmeline says. "It's in books. They remember something good about it. It's familiar, which feels like being safe."

"The older kids pair up and move out. The younger ones look at me like, *Get out of the way, Dad*." He turns to look at her, and it's a movie moment: the dimmed light of the mall concourse, music playing, reunited after time apart, across distance. "Maybe they're right," he says as he leans toward her. Emmeline hears the hiss of the mall speakers, the buzz of the fluorescents. She sees the blue stains on his teeth and the glassy haze in his eyes, tastes the ugly tang of the wine in her mouth. She turns her head so Tuan's nose brushes her cheek. "Sorry," he says. "I didn't mean—like, we could just—"

She puts her hand on top of his, flips his palm up, and holds it. "It's okay," she says.

"I didn't mean to weird you out," Tuan says. "Like you said, it's in the movies and everything. If you love something and it comes back or whatever. But it's bullshit."

"I don't think it is," Emmeline says. "I'm not sure that's going to happen for me."

"You bought into the other line of bullshit," he says. "About how you're a weapon."

"Will you sit here with me?" Emmeline asks. "You can think

it's whatever you want it to be, and I can be here. I'm barreling forward as fast as I can, but also I'm trying to stop and breathe and collect moments with people. It's funny, but there isn't much time."

"Why's that funny?" he says, draping his arm around her, letting her head rest on his shoulder. "I told you that before."

She smiles a smile he can't see. On the rim of the fountain, a couple gives up waiting for the music to speed up and starts dancing on their own to a song playing in their heads, shared. When Emmeline left here, Tuan told her there would be no time for any of them to grow up. Youth is untenable in the long term. There are things she wants to get rid of, limits on the things she's able and allowed to do. Then there are things she worries she'll lose. Emmeline wonders if there are ways she'll stop being able to feel as she gets older, like not being able to taste salt or see certain shades of green. She imagines giving up this over time for that. She wants to build a self that's the best of both: wiser and more powerful but with the same size heart. Tuan meant that nothing was coming, that an ending would intercede between them and those future selves, but it's the opposite. Everything is on its way, and it will sever them from the adults they thought they'd be. Those selves will be outdated and obsolete.

She wishes she wanted him to kiss her. His kiss might wake something, the way her ability came back after years away. Fairy tales hint at the act creating the desire, the kiss waking not just the lover but love. A kiss won't change her, but it isn't a handicap or a lack even if she can describe it only in those terms. Her heart isn't broken. She snakes her arm behind Tuan's waist, hooks her thumb through his belt loop.

"You understand belonging to something bigger," Emmeline says. "What you built here, you built by understanding that."

"Otherwise you're alone," he says.

"Do you wonder if you're thinking big enough?" Emmeline asks. "Alone isn't enough. A couple isn't enough. Are you sure *this* is enough?" She gestures toward the rest of the kids at their revels.

"There could always be more," he says.

"Do you think you could belong to everyone?" Emmeline asks. She thinks about what people look like from outside time. When she came looking for Tuan, she cheated and looked ahead. His life spirals together with someone else's. She catches the girls glaring at her. *One of you is for him,* she thinks. Each person Emmeline recruits, she's taking something from, stealing who they would be. She wishes it was clear who she needs. She wants enough and nothing more. Worse than wasting people's futures would be to end up short and waste everything for nothing. If a single domino is missing, the chain breaks. She crafts apologies in her head and sends them to each girl who watches her as if she's a thief come to steal Tuan. *You're right,* she thinks. *I have come for him and for the thing you would have had, because I need it, and I am so sorry.*

After she first resonated but before her mother found out, Emmeline snuck onto the stairs late Christmas Eve and watched her mother set the stage for the next morning, putting the gifts and the stockings just so, taking careful bites out of the cookies and carrots she'd had Emmeline leave out for Santa and his reindeer. Her father sat on the couch drinking wine, looking mildly annoyed the way he did when her mother insisted on any tradition with Christian roots. Even though Emmeline no longer believed in Santa Claus, it was as wondrous as coming down to see a magical stranger in a red suit putting boxes under a tree. How much did you have to love someone to do this for them secretly, to do it and work to cover it up? Emmeline isn't sure she has that kind of love in her, but she needs to summon something like it.

She folds into Carrie's empty apartment weeks ago and places the Polaroid of Carrie and Hayden and the twins on the fridge. This is a thing that always happens: she does it because she knows she must have done it. It isn't worth it to worry over the paradox of how the origin of the idea disappears into the loop.

She folds into the headmaster's quarters on the thirteenth floor of the Bishop Academy. As she emerges, she has the feeling of something stirring, like a sleeping dog that twitches at a noise but doesn't wake. *The building knows I'm here,* she thinks, and the thought is both irrational and true. She feels it watching her from above, all those stories clad in black glass aware of her, not recognizing her but registering her presence. She goes to the big window and places her palm against the cool of the glass. It trembles at her touch. Dawn breaks in the window. On the street below, a film crew sets up lighting rigs. Fahima will need a reason to start, a sign it's about to begin. Emmeline takes the camera out of her bag. She stands as close as she can to the window to minimize the glare and takes a shot of the street below. She finds a Sharpie in Fahima's desk and writes in the white space under the image: 5:45 A.M. WEDNESDAY JUNE 8TH. She goes to tape it to the window, thinking about what the photo will say to Fahima. What if she decides that it means someone's broken in, taken the photo, and left it for her? Emmeline folds back a week earlier. She tapes the picture that won't happen for days to the window—the impossible thing Fahima will need to get her off her ass. As Emmeline turns to go, she sees a woman sitting in the armchair, staring blankly forward, her hand absently stroking the air above the floor at her side.

"Hi, Sarah," Emmeline says.

"Hello," says Sarah Davenport with no recognition on her face.

Emmeline comes close so she can whisper and be heard by only Sarah, not Fahima, not the building. "Don't tell Fahima I was here," she says.

"Fahima is here?" Sarah asks.

Emmeline tries to read through Sarah's eyes and determine what remains in her head. She looks as if she's a complete blank.

"Sarah," Emmeline says, taking both of Sarah's hands in her own. She wants to create as many paths to this moment in Sarah's mind as she can—sound, sight, touch. "I need you to remember your brother. Whatever else happens, I need you to remember him."

Sarah smiles. Her smile is dazzling in its purity and a little scary—it contains not even a hint of pain.

"I remember Patrick," Sarah says brightly. "How could I forget him?"

The apartment looks like the aftermath of a wild party, but closer inspection shows the malice with which it's been disarrayed. Nurse novels have been cleared off the shelves but also torn down the spine, DVDs removed from their cases so they could be snapped in half. Most telling, the brass statuette of Ganesh has been melting into a pile of slag on the rug. Unobserved in a doorway, Emmeline watches Alyssa move through the ruins deftly, already used to this new geography. She wonders if Alyssa made one decision not to clean when she came back and found it this way or if she makes that decision over and over, confronting what's happened and retreating.

Emmeline clears her throat, and Alyssa jumps. When she sees it's Emmeline, her expression twists. "You came back," she says. Emmeline is unable to read the statement, whether it's relief or annoyance.

"I thought you'd still be with them," Emmeline says. "I was surprised you were gone."

"That must have been new for you, being surprised," Alyssa

says. Self-conscious, she begins picking up broken things from the floor.

"Let me help," Emmeline says, squatting down.

"Don't," says Alyssa. "Is there something you're here for? I told Fahima I wanted out. I was hoping she'd send a memo to the rest of you."

Emmeline holds the head of a Precious Moments figurine, a cherub face obscured by a doctor's face mask. The ceramic is all jagged edges around the neck. There was a part to play for Alyssa in what was coming, and although someone else could do it, Emmeline had hoped to avoid that. If she asks, Alyssa will do it. There are people whose nature is to protest until they're needed, at which point they set their feelings aside. But whether Alyssa will or won't, she shouldn't have to. Emmeline thinks about her parents and how if they'd allowed themselves to step out of the story, they might have lived.

"I came to say goodbye," Emmeline says. "I didn't get to before. And thank you. You didn't have to do any of this."

"I think I signed on a long time ago," Alyssa says, sitting on the arm of the couch, cradling the rest of the doctor figurine in her upturned palms. "You were little, and you needed help, and I jumped in with both feet. I didn't know how big it would be. But now I can't anymore. It's time for me to stop."

EVERYTHING THEY SAY
WE ARE, WE ARE

◇

The first time Carrie saw Hayden play live, she had to sneak out of Bishop to a club in Brooklyn. The show was supposed to be a secret, but it was listed in the *Voice,* along with *Time Out, Brooklyn-Vegan, Under the Radar,* and a dozen other music sites. Carrie called Hayden out on it, but Hayden texted that they were ALL ON THE LIST and it was IMPORTANT that she be there.

She can't remember the name of the venue. The room was so full, it seemed impossible that the people on the line outside would fit. Everyone looked like they belonged here. Carrie lived in New York for years without becoming a New Yorker, staying within the confines of Bishop. Even after Resonants went public and were free to move around the city without hiding who they were, New York made her feel like a kid from the suburbs who should be home listening to records rather than hanging among the hip and beautiful.

There was a red velvet curtain, dense and dark. The lights in the bar went down, and people cheered for the darkness. They faced the curtain the way crowds make choices that are their own and everyone's. For the second before the curtain crept up, Carrie thought she could live in that moment forever, waiting for an event in which she had total faith.

She feels the same way sitting on an old rug in the attic of the house on Jarvis Avenue, knowing that staring at a wall isn't special but actually is. Hayden sits next to her, fingers intertwined with hers. Clay and his whole family are there, along with Waylon and Bryce. Carrie thinks of the speech at the beginning of Prince's "Let's Go Crazy" in which he tells the listener they are gathered together to get through this thing called life. Why else does anyone gather together ever? Why flirt and kiss and meet up for coffee and send thank-you notes and fuck and fight? Carrie knows what it's like to fail at getting through alone. She's remembering what it might be like to succeed at getting through together.

"If she can time travel, why isn't she here already?" Waylon asks.

"Making an entrance is important," says Hayden.

On cue, a door made of dark wood appears on the wall beneath the octagonal porthole. It doesn't open for a second, then swings inward, with Kimani holding it open for them. She looks tired; the seed of heartbreak Carrie saw on her face when Carrie came to take Emmeline away has bloomed through her whole body.

"Hurry," Kimani says. "She set something up to get them looking the other way, but they'll see us if we're here too long."

They file in until it's Rai's turn. He pauses at the threshold.

"Can I go through?" he asks. "Even though I'm not—"

"You can come in, honey," Kimani says. "We take all kinds. She's been asking about you." Rai smiles and might even blush as he steps through.

They enter into a room that feels like it's the basement of somewhere. Kimani shuts the door, and everything lurches. Carrie feels as if all natural sense of direction has been stripped from her. Her feet are below her, but she isn't sure she could point at them and say they are *down*. The sensation doesn't last as her brain accepts a new set of cues to orient itself, but the disorientation means they're in Hivespace, detached from the world.

"Come on; she's upstairs in Fahima's office," Kimani says. "She said there'd be more of you, but she said a couple people might not join in until tomorrow."

"Where are we exactly?" Waylon asks.

"You could say we're nowhere or everywhere," Kimani says. "I've been hanging out with Emmeline long enough I'm talking nonsense. Fahima says we're in Hivespace, and that doesn't mean anything. Or she says we're in Phoenix, but that's not true anymore. I think of it as my room even though it's bigger than that. Some folks here have started calling it Haven."

They fall into single file without being asked, and Kimani leads them up a stairwell like an elementary school teacher being followed by her class. They walk into a room whose walls are studded with thumbtacks and pushpins, none holding anything up. Carrie thinks of the day she moved out of the Bishop dorms, stripping posters from the walls and leaving torn corners and stray tacks for someone else to deal with. Emmeline sits on a desk in front of a blank whiteboard, talking with Fahima, who clutches a dry erase marker, ready to elucidate a point. A woman Carrie doesn't know stands close enough to Fahima to signal they're involved. Emmeline smiles broadly as they enter, and Carrie recognizes the look of feigned confidence, a fake-it-till-you-make-it boldness that's easy to spot if you rely on it to get through every high-pressure situation. Carrie's not bad at it, but Hayden *owns* that look and calls Emmeline's bluff before they're through the door.

"Oh, shit," Hayden says. "One of you has a plan."

"All her," says Fahima. She gestures at the blank walls.

Rai squares up in front of Emmeline as if they're about to play rock-paper-scissors. "Two days," he says. "You?"

Emmeline sighs. "It's complicated."

"You two know each other?" Clay asks.

"She's my imaginary friend," Rai says, grinning.

"I'm glad you're here," Emmeline says to Rai. She turns to Carrie and pulls her into a hug. "It's not too late to stop," she whispers.

"Feels too late to stop," Carrie says. "Are you sure whatever you came up with is going to work?"

"Pieces won't fall into place unless it works," she says. "It's tough to see. But kind of exciting."

"I'm about done with excitement," Carrie says.

Emmeline laughs, a tiny huff that brushes Carrie's neck. "You'll never be done with excitement, Carrie," she says. Carrie laughs, too. As much as she doesn't want to admit it, it's true.

Rafa, Jerrod, and Kristal cram in, along with the rest of the crew from the bus. It's disorienting to see them again, and it forces Carrie to realize that while she's thinking she's in Chicago and they're in Phoenix, neither of those things is true. She's spent too much time covering distances, and now distance doesn't mean anything. Time might not either.

"Tell me you two are at least fucking," Rafa says to Hayden and Carrie. Bryce's head swivels toward Carrie, waiting for the answer.

"That's no one's business," Hayden says.

"It's *band* business!" Rafa wails. "I have told you all about every fuck I've had since we've been in this band."

"Not that we ever asked," Jerrod says.

"The point remains," Rafa says.

"Rafa, let it go," says Kristal. Carrie is grateful for the intervention.

"Is this everyone?" Fahima asks Emmeline.

"For this part."

"What about your assistant?" Hayden asks Fahima. "If we're going to war, it'd be good to have a guy who can be a whole platoon."

It's the first time anyone's said *war* aloud, and the word changes the atmosphere. Once it's spoken, there's no more space for reunions, gossip, or jokes.

"Omar is . . ." Fahima struggles to find the next word. The plump, pretty blonde puts her hand on Fahima's shoulder.

"The Omars are compromised," she says. "Anything he hears, they might hear."

"We already had a war," Emmeline says. "It didn't work. This is going to be something else."

NORTH AVENUE

◇

Reading Avi Hirsch's notes and articles, Clay constructs a narrative that begins with a boy walking into a church. There's a video on Avi's computer of Owen Curry strolling into a black church in the Chicago suburbs as if it belonged to him. Nothing in Avi's notes suggests a reason Curry targeted that church. If anything comes across in reading Avi's notes, it's how little he understood Curry and how desperately he wanted to. Without a motive, there's only a boy walking into a church and using his ability to wipe it out of existence.

Whatever his reasons, Owen Curry set events in motion. His actions convinced Kevin Bishop to bring his people out of hiding. Having a name hung on them made Resonants an issue people had to decide about, and, against what Bishop hoped, those decisions came from a place of fear. They built cages and put Resonants in them. Smarter and more cynical, Fahima Deeb saw what was coming and made ready. When war was inevitable, she changed the world so her side could win. She changed Clay and Dom, ripping them out of their average lives and putting them at the center of a story that's brought Clay to the front steps of another church.

Opened days after the Pulse, Chicago's first Bishop school is housed in a megachurch on North Avenue. It's not like the church Owen Curry destroyed, whose first stones were laid by freed slaves who came north thinking things would be better and found them too much the same. This church was built with money obtained by squeezing the poor and faithful, persuading people to give *because* it hurt. The megachurch operated as a house of God for a few years before the nexus of faith and money came apart and the men who ran it bagged up what they could carry and split. It was vacant when the Bishop Foundation bought it, too unwieldy for practical use. The building was called into service to be a place of faith in something no less nebulous than an omnipotent god: a belief in the future and the moral arc of history. The idea that things would get better and could be made better, that their abilities combined would be enough to build a stronger world.

Clay wishes he could have been a student at the Bishop schools when they were trying to instill that belief. His ability has always been tied to conflict and war, which makes him wonder if that ability is tainted. There was a sigh of relief in the tiny office in Haven when Fahima explained that there was a monster who made things this way, but though it was comforting to have someone to blame, Clay didn't buy it. It was bullshit the way the moral arc was bullshit—it was negative faith. It's one thing to say the bad man made things bad. It's a bigger jump to assume that absent that, things would be good.

After this, there'll be things we need to prove, he thinks. *We told ourselves that after the war we'd be better.*

This school is now a training facility for the Black Rose Faction, a shift so pronounced that Fahima Deeb ordered Bishop's name removed from the building, which no one got around to doing. The sign out front says it's the Kevin Bishop School for Resonant Education. It was built as a church and dressed up as a school, and now it's a fortress.

A boy walks into a church, Clay thinks. *Maybe.*

They're in an apartment kitty-corner from the church. The couple who live here are letting them use it; their abilities are artistic, creative, and beautiful but for today only quaint. They reason that this is the best way they can help. Waylon's trying to get an estimate on the power levels and training status of the junior Faction members inside. He hoped a line of sight on the building would help, but he's getting nothing. Whatever the specifics, the general situation is not good. "There're more of them than there are of us," he says. "I can't figure out how many are students and how many are real threats."

"A college team's not the NBA, but a college team will beat your ass," Clay says.

"I think we go the same way we did at Unity," Hayden says. "It's not like we can go full frontal. However many are in there, it's more than we can handle."

"It doesn't do us any good to sneak in," Carrie says. "We need to take the Gate. Getting one of us to it won't help."

"So what's your idea?" Clay asks.

"Full front," Carrie says.

"We'll get our asses handed to us," Clay says.

"Emmeline says it will work." This hangs in the air as if all of them are trying to find a way to break bad news to her.

"You trust her," Clay says.

"I believe her," says Carrie. "Is that enough?"

"She's a kid, and she's bullshitting her way through," Hayden says. "You can see it." They grin at Carrie the stupid way people look at one another when they've realized they're in love. "But it's not like we have other options." That dumb look comes back every now and then, flaring up like an old injury. Clay has looked at Dom that way even after they've been together years and still looks at Rai like that, struck into idiocy by the wonder of having these men in his life. Seeing that look exchanged between Carrie and Hayden reminds Clay that he has other options. He can take his boys and run. Run or fight, whichever he chooses now, he has to do it until everything ends or everything changes.

This started with a boy walking into a church.

"Come up with a plan," he says, getting up to go. "But it's got to be airtight."

Carlton, the chef at Vibration, assures Dom all the beef is organic and grass-fed and a list of adjectives that Dom is concerned about, leaving aside the fact they're feeding Rai a hamburger the size of a Frisbee. It's Dom's way of taking control of something, caring for Rai in a situation in which he can do nothing to keep the boy safe. Clay wishes he could think of it as sweet, but it feels like a reprimand, as if Clay's responsible for where they are. It's not Dom's intent, but it's hard not to take everything personally and reflect it back onto himself. It's important now not to do that. There's more here than Clay, and he needs to break out of himself and enjoy this in case it's the last time.

"I feel like I'm in a Western," Dom says. "People keep peering out their windows like there's going to be a showdown."

"Might be a showdown," Clay says. "Carrie's working on a plan."

"I thought Emmeline had a plan," Rai says through a mouthful of burger.

"She told us what to do, not how to do it," says Clay. "How to do it's the hard part."

"Your father is very good at how to do it," Dom says, wagging his eyebrows.

"Gross," says Rai.

"Carrie's better at putting together ops than I am," Clay says. "Honestly, I prefer being told what to do. That's why I married your father." Dom snorts out a tiny laugh.

"Stop it, I'm eating," Rai says.

Dom squeezes Clay's hand, sending a signal that says *Are we going to be okay?* Clay squeezes back, signaling that they will. If Dom asked him out loud, he wouldn't know how to respond in a way that was honest but affirmative.

"A school seems like an easy fight," Rai says, mawing down fries by the fistful. "What happens after?"

Clay doesn't know, but he suspects it's nothing good. If they take the Gate, they head someplace worse.

"Worry about after after," he says.

"I know you're going to, but I don't want you to go," Rai says. There's a bitter edge in his voice; the sentiment is resigned, but he wants it clear this is a live argument.

"Rai," Dom says. "That doesn't help."

"Why should I want to help him get himself killed?"

"Don't say that," says Dom.

"It's okay for him to say it," Clay says. "I don't want to go either. But I don't have it in me to sit back and let things get worse."

"If they win and you die, things'll be worse for me," Rai says. He stares at his plate, hands fixed on the edges of the table, elbows rigid. "Does that factor in?"

Clay reaches over and puts his hand on the side of Rai's face. His thumb rests along the boy's cheekbone, fingers curled around the back of his neck. He feels the tension in Rai's jaw and wants to pull him in, upend the table full of greasy food and hold his boy. Instead, he grips him gently but strongly. It's how he wants Rai to think of him if he's gone.

"You are the biggest factor in every decision I make. If there were something I could give up that meant you would never experience a moment of pain, I would give that thing up so fast. You are my heart beating outside of my body, and I know how hard this is to understand. I know this looks like part of something bigger, but Rai, this is all about you."

Clay has seen Carrie choreograph the movements of a dozen Blooms against Army Ranger units, and now he finds himself angry at the idiotic simplicity of what she's come up with.

"What do you even call this?" he asks.

"A leap of faith," Hayden says. Contained in saying it is Hayden's own leap. Carrie is choosing to believe in Emmeline; Hayden chooses to believe in Carrie.

Clay asks for another walk-through, trying to look at it a different way. With those words, *leap of faith,* he can see the plan as confident. It relies on everything working out in the best possible way and has no contingencies, allows for no mistakes. It's a plan made by a true believer, and it works if everyone buys in all the way. It's Emmeline's larger plan writ small.

"When?" he asks.

"By ten the students will be in their dorms or in the common rooms," Carrie says. "There's less chance of running into anyone on the lower floors. We can barricade them in and take the Gate."

"You're assuming it's like our school was," Hayden says. "This is the Hitler Youth training camp. Maybe they don't spend their evenings smoking and fucking."

"Not all of us spent school nights fucking," Carrie says.

"No, some of us were getting high and listening to sad songs while pining away for—" They cut themselves off, but the joking mood has fled the room. Clay wonders what Hayden was about to say. He wishes he had time to sit down and hear the whole story of the two of them, celebrity gossip and catching up with an old friend. On the other side, there'll be time. Carrie goes to find Waylon so he can relay the plan to everyone else on the street, leaving Hayden and Clay alone.

"You finally get what you want, and then you have to go off and fight an atemporal shitbag and probably die," Hayden says. "This is why we can't have nice things."

"She seems happy," Clay says. "I don't know if it's you or all of this. But she seems like she's okay."

"Was she not okay when you knew her?" Hayden asks.

"I always got the feeling she was about to float away," he says. "Like fighting was the only thing that kept her grounded."

"She used to worry she'd disappear," Hayden says. "She thought it was the end point of her ability: she'd get stronger and stronger until she was gone."

"If everything works—"

"When," Hayden says.

"*When* everything works," Clay says. "When it's all done, she's going to be tough to live with."

"Tougher to live without," Hayden says. Clay smiles because it's the only reason he knows to commit yourself to anyone.

Waylon blares a message into their heads. *Change of plans,* he says. *There are five Blooms in the school in addition to staff. One of them's headed up by Ji Yeon Kim.*

"Then we're fucked," says Clay. Carrie says the same thing in his head. They had a chance against junior Faction and a handful of teachers, but Ji Yeon's Bloom will hand them their asses. Clay was lucky to get away alive the last time he saw her.

Her psychic contacted me, Waylon says. *Says they want to talk. She'll be waiting on the front steps.*

"Talk to who?" Clay asks.

They asked for the deserters, Waylon says.

They expect us to come in alone? Carrie asks.

They said you couldn't be that stupid, Waylon says. *They said go ahead and bring everybody, but they're only going to talk to you.*

Each war decides how it will be fought, but it comes down to ground. Bodies are fungible; ground is real. Trench warfare is the most brutal iteration of this truth, but it's evident in every form of war. There are two basic versions: one group holds ground and the other tries to take it, or a piece of ground stands open and contested and two groups rush in to build a bridge of bodies to its other side. The latter is prelude to the former, a subset. Weapons and methods change, but at its heart, war is about taking ground and holding it.

The contested ground is a block of North Avenue and the church that claims to be a school. Clumsy and ragtag, the imitation army they've assembled marches up the center of the street. They're not soldiers. They're postal workers and baristas and students. There isn't anyone on their side who wouldn't rather be home in bed except maybe Carrie. The Faction is always spoiling for a fight. You don't train people to kill and keep them idle. A sword's blade hungers for blood.

About to get it, Clay thinks.

Five Blooms stand in the parking lot in front of the Bishop School in a wedge formation. They're outnumbered but not outgunned. If they take out the small collection of fight-ready folks Waylon dug up, they'll roll over the rest regardless of numbers. The two groups look at each other across an expanse of asphalt and concrete, the Midwestern sky full of stars.

"Fliers ready, lithics to the front," Clay calls. Waylon and the other psychics relay the message to everyone on their side.

"Someone's seen *Lord of the Rings*," Hayden says.

"Do you walk over there and meet them?" Bryce asks.

"I guess we do," Clay says. He looks at Carrie, who nods. They step forward, and the impulse to take her hand is so strange and so strong that he does. She squeezes his hand in hers, and for a second he feels her faith that all this is going to work out. It drains away at the sound of Ji Yeon's voice, commanding and full of the confidence that comes with the backing of trained killers.

"You gave me a motherfucker of a headache back in the Bronx," she says as they approach.

"Imagine the headache I'm about to give you."

Ji Yeon smirks. "Maybe one of us will have a change of heart."

"Seems unlikely," Clay says.

She steps close to him, close enough to whisper. "The kid's back there, isn't he? Maaya and Koyo's boy."

"Don't talk about—"

Before he can say Rai's name, a piece of macadam the size of a Buick sails overhead and crashes against the building, disintegrating against the reinforced concrete. The first shot fired, and it's come from their side.

"Fuck," says Ji Yeon. "I thought we had a minute." The wedge of Faction agents behind her take battle stances while the men and women behind Clay stare in wonder at the asphalt chunks raining onto the highway.

One of our lithics jumped off early, Waylon says in their heads. *What do you want us to do?*

"Hold," Clay says out loud.

A burly, bearded Faction agent snarls at him. "You don't give us orders."

"No," says Ji Yeon, turning to face her troops. She produces small glowing spikes in her hand and, with a snap of her wrists, flings them into the foreheads of two men in the back of her group. Nine more agents, her Bloom and another, pivot, attacking the other agents in the wedge with wind and telekinesis, with blasts of energy so quick that the assailed are taken out without a chance to retaliate. No one speaks: there's only the labored breath of the attackers, taxed by the intense if brief exertion, and the clomp of Hayden's boots sprinting across the street. Hayden skids to a stop, out of breath, and takes in the scene.

"Did you fucking kill them?" Hayden asks.

Ji Yeon looks at Hayden and at the agents behind her. Half are on the ground, with the other half standing over them. "Probably not, pop star," she says. "But they're going to know tomorrow they were in a fight."

"What the fuck is happening?" Clay asks.

"Change of heart," says Ji Yeon. "Or change of head." She taps her temple, a signal everyone inducted into the Faction knows. "We were stationed in Berlin, guarding the Chair. That asshole with the eye patch told us there would be bodies to clean up afterward. Fucking grinned while he said it. Makes me sick now, but at the time it didn't bother me. Fuck, I probably grinned back."

She puts her fingers to her cheek, pressing into the skin, checking if feeling has returned. "Sometimes I can tell he's using my face, not just looking out my eyes. The Chair went off, and it was like . . . it was like the Pulse again." She turns to Carrie. "Do you remember what it felt like? Like your ability was flowing through you? It felt so pure. It was over, and the thing in my head was dead. Was for all of us who were there." She waves her hand at the fallen agents. "These ones they sent me from Buffalo or whatever. We were supposed to take you all out and go make sure the Pulses go off as scheduled. But I'm done." The others nod emphatically. "Turns out I've been fucked with for a long time. I'm ready to do something about it."

The volunteer army creeps forward, scared but too curious to stop. Rai breaks from the pack and runs toward them, stopping before coming too close. He looks warily at Ji Yeon, who has one glowing javelin in her hand. She stares at Rai, eyes blinking as she realizes who he is, and the javelin retracts, leaving only her open palm.

CHAIR

The Craft lands in a playground in Astoria between a slide spotted with rust and a swing set from which the swings have been removed. The ground is covered in wood chips spongy from the previous night's rain. There was a ferry from here down the East River that dropped passengers on Roosevelt Island before stopping in Queens and Kips Bay. It's Fahima's opinion that ferries are slow and terrible, as are all boats. With better train lines orbiting Roosevelt Island, there was no need to keep the boats running. The decommissioned ferries sit in Kips Bay, too worn and rusted to be worth salvaging. From here, she can see the Roosevelt Island Lighthouse across the East River.

"Is there a signal or anything?" Ruth asks. "Are they going to flash the light at us?"

"We have to trust they'll be there," Fahima says.

"They'll be there," Emmeline says.

Fahima clicks on a flashlight, and they walk down to the edge of the river, a quick drop and a short cliff. Ruth extends the Craft back out of her stomach in its usual shape, then wrinkles her brow. A straight fissure appears on one side and arcs up and over like a canopy opening. The simple shape of a boat rests in the water, transparent, pressing down the river.

"Will it be fast?" Fahima asks Ruth.

"Do you want it to be fast?"

"I don't like boats."

"Would you like fast boats less?"

"I would dislike them more but for a shorter amount of time," Fahima says.

"Let's be fast," Emmeline says. She checks the sky as if she can tell time by the stars. There are things she's not telling, which bothers the shit out of Fahima, but not as much as getting onto a boat. It reels as she places her foot into it, and Fahima says "woah there" as if she's trying to calm a horse. Emmeline smirks and Ruth giggles. Fahima glares at both of them, although neither sees it in the dark.

"Sorry," Ruth says. "I'll hold it steady. I wanted to give you the full boat experience."

"I don't want the full boat experience," Fahima says. "I want the 'I have gotten to the place I need to be undetected and can now forget my means of conveyance' experience."

"And fast," Emmeline adds. Ruth nods, and Fahima regrets slipping into the employer-employee aspect of their relationship. Alyssa was right that there's a power dynamic between them that benefits Fahima, but wrong that it's inherently toxic and dooms them to failure. Those parts are true only if Fahima doesn't stop being a shit about it.

"It's going to be great," Fahima says, giving a weak thumbs-up. "Full boat experience."

It's not as bad as she feared and takes only a few minutes, barely long enough for her to worry about what's waiting on the other side. She felt confident about her inside people when she contacted them but keeps remembering the worm in Thao Bui's head. Why wouldn't Glover implant everyone on the Ruse? Maybe there's a limit to how many he can spread around, but when she considers all the Faction agents who carry bits of him in their heads, a few dozen more doesn't seem difficult. If the people they're supposed to meet have been suborned, this is going to end quickly.

The Craft pulls onto the shore and shoves forward onto the sand. It's the first moment Fahima considers propulsion, the fact that Ruth is not only creating the vessel but moving it. They get out, and Ruth sucks the Craft back into her guts.

"If this works, you'll be able to fly out of here," Emmeline says.

"I don't love it when you say 'if,'" Fahima says. Two figures are coming down the beach. Fahima tries to read into their body language and the speed of their approach, but there's no way to tell until they arrive if they're who she's expecting or if they've brought passengers.

"You made it!" Roxane calls. "We thought you were dead. Everything is so strange right now."

"Thao's missing," Marlon says. "He was supposed to be at the Tokyo Chair this morning, and he never showed up."

"Did they call it off?" Fahima asks.

"They pushed it back to tonight," Roxane says.

"Who are they calling up?"

Marlon and Roxane look at each other as if they haven't considered this. Fahima wonders if they know about the thing Glover put in Thao's head when he was picked. One of them is next, and like Thao, neither of them can operate a Chair without a massive casualty rate. Cedric makes his pick, and one of these two becomes another cell in the organism that is Raymond Glover.

"We got a golf cart," Marlon says. "Where do you need to—"

"Are you Emmeline Hirsch?" Roxane asks. She has the star-struck look people get around Hayden. Fahima feels a ping of envy: despite everything she's done, people never look at her that way.

"It's nice to meet you," Emmeline says. She extends her hand, and for a second Fahima thinks Roxane is going to kiss it rather than shake it.

"My job for five years has been to try to *be* you," Roxane says. "When I heard you in the Hive a couple days ago, calling that name, I felt like all this wasn't for nothing. I felt like you were going to come and fix it all."

"I'm not," Emmeline says. "But if this works, we'll get to a place where we can start to fix things."

Like with the back doors into the computer systems, Fahima worried someone would find the door in the janitor's closet that leads to a basement that's nowhere on any of the Ruse's floor plans. A lithic might notice the void in the building's structure; a telemetric might brush up against a mop that noticed Fahima's late-night coming and going.

"No one's been in the lab bays since they decided to activate the project," Marlon explains. "There are folks on diagnostics and data, but nobody checks in on the other Chairs."

She leads them down the stairs and is relieved to click on the lights and see that nothing's been touched. The original Chair sits in the middle of the space, wired to devices that siphon off the massive amount of energy it's designed to handle. It hasn't been turned on since the day Emmeline used it to generate the Pulse, but Fahima comes down to visit it, to remind herself that she did one thing right, once.

"It's sort of ugly," Ruth says.

"Every machine that works is beautiful," says Fahima, running her hand along the armrest.

"Is she going to undo it?" Marlon asks Fahima, eyeing Emmeline. "Take away everybody's abilities?"

"Some of us came by our shit naturally, Pulser," says Roxane.

"*She* is not going to undo it," Emmeline says, climbing up into the Chair. The first time Emmeline sat in it, she looked tiny, like a kid usurping a mall Santa's empty throne. Now it fits her. When Emmeline stayed Fahima's hand and kept her from poisoning Thao and as she laid out a plan that was nebulous but better than anything Fahima came up with, Fahima told herself that Emmeline was an adult now. This is the first moment she sees it's true.

"*She* is going to do something else," Emmeline says.

STEP INTO THIS HOUSE

◇

Ji Yeon throws the front doors open onto the narthex of the megachurch. Young people crowd balconies and lurk in doorways. This doesn't negate Carrie's theory that most of them would have been in their rooms this time of night. A true thing about schools is that when something *new* happens, everyone knows and tries to press closer to it, as if novelty gives off heat. These kids heard their teachers moving out and caught the rumor that Ji Yeon Kim, the fucking founder of the Black Rose Faction, had shown up—they must have run down there en masse.

"Hang back and let me talk to them," Ji Yeon says. She hasn't explained enough about what's going on, but Carrie's trying to accept more things on faith. Maybe Emmeline knew this was going to happen. Maybe for Emmeline it already had.

"Whoever teaches covert surveillance is getting fired, because I can see every damn one of you," Ji Yeon shouts as she swaggers into the center of the room. The kids laugh nervously. *They know her,*

Carrie thinks. *She shows up and gives the commencement speech every year or passes through on inspection. She's their Kevin Bishop.*

"Who can tell me the function of the Black Rose Faction?" Ji Yeon asks. A boy with a stripe of dark purple over one glowing green eye raises his hand, and Ji Yeon points at him.

"To protect Resonants," he says.

"Good, good," says Ji Yeon. "Protect Resonants against what?"

Everyone is silent for a moment, and a low murmur passes around the room. They know there's an answer—the question is too obvious and important not to have one—but scouring their memories, or in some cases the memories of others, they can't find it.

"It's not your fault you don't know," she says. "We never made it clear. We needed enemies to fight, and we made them. Or we became them. The Faction has done terrible things for terrible reasons, but it doesn't have to be that way. When you leave here, be better. Be good."

The students murmur among themselves. Carrie wonders how many hear what Ji Yeon's saying and how many care. When she was with the Faction, she worked closely with nine people across two Blooms. Four were good people in bad circumstances, and Viola had the worm put in her head so young she hadn't "set" as a person yet. Left alone, she might have grown up to be kind, but at that age it was possible to get knocked off course. Sweet kids turn into angry teenagers, and sometimes that sweetness never comes back. That left three people Carrie never had a read on. It was possible that even without a voice squawking in their ear, they'd be willing to do terrible things. What are the percentages in a school for kids who volunteer to join an army during peacetime? What are the odds they hear weakness rather than strength in Ji Yeon's words and fall on her like crows on carrion? Carrie looks to Ji Yeon's hands, where the bud of a glowing spear shines in each palm, ready.

"Back to your quarters," she shouts. Her voice trembles slightly, and Carrie is sure the kids hear it. "Classes are canceled tomorrow, but I hope you'll all use the day to ... to ..." Carrie holds her breath. She's seen substitute teachers lose a room to stutters and slips no worse than this. Once they lose it, they're dead; teenagers don't offer second chances. "Whatever," Ji Yeon says. "Jerk off and get high, I don't care. It's your time."

This kills across the room. Going for the laugh is a high-risk move that fails more often than it succeeds, but Ji Yeon pulls it off, rescuing herself.

"Nobody can jerk off all day," one of the kids jeers.

"Pendelton can," shouts another.

"Fuck you, Krueger," yells someone Carrie presumes is Pendelton.

"To quarters, all of you," Ji Yeon shouts, quieting the rising din. "I'll report anyone below third floor in five minutes. Nobody taught you to hide; show me they at least taught you how to retreat."

The kids scurry off and disappear, leaving Carrie, Ji Yeon, and Clay in the silence that adheres to large empty rooms. Ji Yeon's shoulders slump; she's exhausted from the effort of pretending to be someone she no longer is. "I wish I could tuck them in bed until it's over," she says. "You think there's any way to keep them from getting hurt?"

"Win fast," Clay says. He doesn't trust Ji Yeon, but Carrie's inclined to. The Bishop student inside her heard Ji Yeon's speech as it was intended. It echoed off something Kevin Bishop put there a long time ago, an idea that's the opposite of what the Faction put in her head and a vaccine against it.

"Gate's in the offices behind the apse," Ji Yeon says. They walk through the narthex and into the nave of the church, which the school uses for assemblies. Ji Yeon's boots clack on the hardwood, and the sound reverberates, amplified by the sacred acoustics of the room.

"I want to play a show in here," Hayden whispers in Carrie's ear.

Carrie imagines Hayden's voice filling this room like that of a full choir.

"Victory party," she says, wrapping her arm around Hayden's waist. "Everybody who lives gets on the list."

ON GATHERING

◇

Emmeline talked briefly with Clay and Thao about what it felt like to use the Chair, and it makes her sad that their experiences were confrontational. Thao said something about "punching against it," and Clay said it was like coaxing an animal out of hiding. For Emmeline, it's a feeling of intense relief. Some people's abilities are intuitive—Carrie has to work against hers to stay visible—but Emmeline's takes enormous effort to use. When the Chair turns on, she feels as if someone else is doing the lifting for her, as if her ability is fluid and light and she has only to direct it. With the Chair contributing, her ability is limited only by what she can imagine herself doing.

Creating this Pulse isn't as easy as the first time. It's easier than the second—the Chair in Berlin wasn't built for her, and it had taken work to shape her ability into something the Chair could feed off—but it's difficult this time to find the sense of connection. The problem is she's trying to do it the same way she did the first time and expecting different results.

She thinks back to the moment in the movie theater at the mall. She remembers what it felt like to see the bits of darkness in Viola and Carrie and flush them out. It's not the same as inducing Resonance, which is like ringing a gong so loudly in the living room the glassware in the kitchen shakes. This is like striking thousands of tiny bells delicately and all at once to produce something that passes as a unified sound. As the Chair hums to life, Fahima and Ruth fade out and Emmeline makes herself manifold. She is everywhere in New York and also here; she is in the Hive and in the real world and beyond both for a moment so small it could slip into the crack between two seconds. A half of a half of a heartbeat and it's done.

"What the fuck was that?" Fahima asks. "The readings are . . ."

"It was something different," Emmeline says. "I did it once before but smaller. This was big. This was all of New York." She climbs down from the Chair, and her legs buckle under her. Fahima and Ruth rush to her, each slipping herself under one arm. She's exhausted, and they've barely started, and all she can think is that she can't tell anyone she isn't sure she can make it to the end. She needs everyone operating with irrational confidence, and Emmeline's the only one who can carry it off.

"Head rush," she says, although the truth is the exact opposite.

"Your nose," Ruth says. Her hand moves toward Emmeline's face but stops. Emmeline dabs her nostril with her fingers. The substance that's trickled out is viscous, the consistency of honey. It's pearlescent white with threads of deep red, and it makes her fingertips go numb.

"Is this the first time that's happened?" Fahima asks. Emmeline nods. It isn't a lie if you don't say anything out loud. Fahima wipes her nose clean with the corner of her hijab. "Bishop got nosebleeds like that before he died. He said this was—"

"It's everything," Emmeline says. "It's the black glass and its opposite."

Fahima looks at her like Emmeline's stopped speaking English, which, from Fahima's point of view, maybe she has. Emmeline struggles more and more with language. The way she looks at things, the way she's planning, can't be expressed in the linear march of one word after another. She wishes she could talk to Fahima in a language of maps, a lexicon of schematics. Maybe then they'd have common ground, but even that wouldn't be exactly right.

"Are you dying?" Fahima asks.

"No," Emmeline says. "I don't think so."

"We need to trust her," Ruth says. She touches Fahima's cheek. "We did things your way, and now we do it a different way. It's all right. You don't have to carry everything yourself."

Emmeline sees Fahima struggling with this, and she can imagine Fahima digging in her heels here so hard that nothing will go according to plan.

"What do we do?" Fahima asks.

"You can still backdoor into the systems now that you're on-site?" Fahima nods. "When I give you the signal, activate all the Chairs. It'll take a while to get them ready, so you should hurry."

"We can't activate them; there's no one in them," Fahima says.

"I'll be in them," Emmeline says. *Or I won't,* she thinks. "Be ready," she says. "Think about the implosion model. It's all about timing."

"It's also about shit blowing up," Fahima says.

"We'll have that, too," says Emmeline. She sits on the edge of the Chair, resting her elbows on her knees, head in her hands, as she slips into the Hive. Something stirs, and she thinks how Kimani told her some predators see their prey only when it moves. She's dancing in front of Raymond Glover because there's no more point in hiding. The last time she was in the Hive, it flooded her with memories of when she first resonated and the Hive itself had reached out to grab her. She panicked and screamed for Kimani. This time she speaks Kimani's name calmly and quietly. Emmeline's eyes flutter open as a door appears on the wall of the basement lab.

"My ride," Emmeline says. She kisses Fahima on the cheek. She feels the tension in Fahima's body, her resistance to all this manifesting in her jaw. Ruth hugs Emmeline as if they've known each other forever. "Take care of her," she says to Ruth.

"No one touches her but me," Ruth says. Emmeline smiles at them as she opens Kimani's door. They are nothing alike and have nothing in common, but by some magic they work. Two elements smashing together can change the whole world.

It's strange to find Kimani in a room that isn't the one they shared for so many years. She lies on a shabby couch in what was once a storage closet, staring at static on a television. The room has none of the grace notes Kimani loves: no art on the walls, no eye for design. Emmeline can see the wear and strain of bearing this much weight. It's possible Emmeline is doing all of this to ward off what might happen to Kimani. *Maybe none of this is about the world,* she thinks. *Maybe it comes down to saving at least one of my parents.*

"It's grim in here," Emmeline says.

"I asked Fahima to put me somewhere with no windows," Kimani says. "It creeps me out, looking out into it. I know what's out there, but there's something unsettling about looking."

"You made me get posters and tape them up," Emmeline says. "When we lived in Paris, you sent me to tourist shops, looking for posters of the Eiffel Tower and Notre Dame. We hung them

around the apartment and framed them like they were windows."
When they left Paris, Emmeline took down the posters and left
the frames, but that made it worse. Kimani made approximations
of the moon and the sun that alternated space in the sky outside
holes carved through the walls of her room. Emmeline considered
what this felt like, how it might be like cutting out chunks of her
own skin. *Sometimes people hurt you because they love you, and
sometimes they hurt themselves,* she thinks. She remembers her father when he died and her sense that he'd paid in pieces of himself
to keep her safe as best he could.

Emmeline reaches out and touches the static on the screen as
if she could push her hand through it, into something behind.
Snow, Kimani used to call it. Emmeline pulls out the Polaroid
camera that was left in her room here in Phoenix when she jumped
away.

"Can I take your picture?" she says. "I tried to draw you once
while Carrie and I were together. There was something I couldn't
get."

Kimani sits up slightly and offers a weak smile. In the flashbulb
light, the circles under her eyes are more pronounced, the concentration lines on her forehead deeper. When the picture comes out,
Emmeline tucks it behind her back before it develops.

"I can't keep my mind on anything," Kimani says. "I try to
watch movies, but I get headaches. It's hard holding all this together. I feel like I'm at my limit."

"It's amazing," Emmeline says. "It's like our home was."

Kimani smiles. "You never used to call it that," she says. "You
called it 'our place.'"

"It was home," Emmeline says. "I know that now."

"I'm glad," Kimani says, holding Emmeline's hand.

"You're almost done," Emmeline says. "You can set it down
soon."

Kimani laughs. "It's a ten-story building, not a helicopter, Em," she says. "I can't land it in the middle of Manhattan."

"Of course you can," Emmeline says. And because Kimani can't exactly see the world the way Emmeline does but doesn't think like Fahima and because it will at least get a laugh out of her, she tells Kimani her whole plan.

Pikwitonei, Manitoba, is too small to be called a town. It's got fewer than a hundred people, the rail station Miquel got off at, and the bar Emmeline finds him in, which doubles as a general store. The Drink & Feed is a repurposed trailer with a wooden sign out front. Inside, the wall is stocked with dusty liquor bottles on one side and canned goods on the other. The bar is a slab of wood on sawhorses long enough to accommodate three. Miquel sits alone while the bartender busies herself checking the inventory on the grocery side. She turns to Emmeline as she enters.

"You better have about ten forms of ID if you expect a drink, kid," she says.

"I'm not here to drink," she says. "I'm here for him." She points to Miquel.

"You can have whatever's left of him if you pay his tab," the bartender says.

"I can pay my own tab," Miquel says. His voice is raspy, more breath than sound. The shining bronze edge of the shackle peeks out from the cuff of his parka.

"I know you can, honey," says the bartender, giving him a sad mothering look. "I'm giving you grief."

"All stocked on grief," he says.

She runs her finger down the sheet on her clipboard. "Yep, looks like our morbid drunk shipment came in on time."

Emmeline approaches Miquel and sits down on the barstool next to him, which wobbles so much she's afraid it will pitch her off. "We haven't met," she says. "I'm Emmeline. I'm a friend of Carrie's."

"That is not going to make me more inclined to talk to you," Miquel says.

Emmeline taps the edge of the shackle on his wrist. "This used to be mine," she says.

"You want it back?"

Emmeline is surprised to find she pauses before shaking her head. "I wore it long enough."

"She gave it to me as a gift," he says. "Who does that? Who cuts part of you off and calls it a gift?" She wants to tell him about the first shackle, a brutalist chunk of metal that chafed her arm, and how Fahima worked with jewelers to make it into something beautiful. She wants to tell him both of those were gifts.

"You have to care very much," Emmeline says. "It's not a pretty kind of love."

Miquel considers this, sips his drink, then nods. "I don't want it," he says. "But maybe I need it." Emmeline doesn't know if he's talking about the gift or Carrie's feeling behind it.

"The things we can do can feel like a weight," Emmeline says.

"Mine feels like a fissure," he says. "A crack in everything."

"That's how the light gets in," says Emmeline.

Miquel laughs. "Carrie loves that song," he says. "She loves all that depressing shit." He means it as an accusation, but it comes off wistful.

"I need you to come with me," Emmeline says. "I can bring you back here after, and you can shut back off and run away." She taps the shackle with her fingernail. "I need you to take that off and come with me."

Miquel looks into his glass as if he can see through it into every drink that will come afterward. He sets it down on the bar unfinished. "Yeah, all right."

In Emmeline's old room, Rai listens to records on the turntable from her father's office. When she was little, they had two turntables in the house. There was the nice one downstairs her mother bought as a Father's Day gift, slick and black and shaped like a pill. The first time Emmeline saw black glass up close, she thought of the way her father took that turntable out of the box, unsure what it was. Her mother's face soured when her father failed to be as excited as she'd hoped, and he got it together a moment too late and said how amazing it was. Emmeline remembers him saying it had a warm sound as he laid the needle down on a brand-new copy of the *Purple Rain* soundtrack, a record Emmeline knew he had upstairs in the office, and she tried to hear the warmth he was talking about as they sat around the living room listening, watching the record spin.

Then there was this one, older than her, older probably than her father had been. It was dinged and dented, a mix of brushed metal and faux wood. Its built-in speakers produced a sound like an old-time radio underwater. It was the one he used to play records for her when she was little, setting the needle in and watching her bop around to the Ramones on chunky legs or precariously pirouette to Queen ballads.

Seeing Rai with it doesn't evoke possessiveness so much as joy and relief at its being used again. He's focused on the music and doesn't register the stir in the air when Kimani's door opens. It's a David Bowie song, the last one on her father's favorite album. Bowie sings about the clock waiting on your song. Bowie tells them they're not alone, and Emmeline remembers her father singing along. *Oh, no, love. Not alone.*

"Rai," she says quietly as the last violin chord dies. It's the first time she's shown up out of nowhere and managed to startle him. There's something she likes about that.

"I thought you were off fighting a war," he says.

"I keep telling people it's not a war," Emmeline says. She sits on the bed next to him. "My dad said the only thing that sounded good after the end of this album was the beginning of this album." She reaches across him and flips the record, setting the needle on the platter. A bass drum and a high-hat stumble across the room.

"How long?" Rai asks.

"This morning," she says. "What's that, ten hours?"

"Me too," says Rai.

"I know how long it's been for you," Emmeline says.

"I'm superboring, huh?"

"Today we were both boring," Emmeline says. "Walking through the world one second at a time, in the order they come."

"It had to be normal once, I guess," Rai says. He can't know what a charged word that is. At Bishop, *normal* had been a profanity. He watches the label on the record as it revolves.

"I got you something," she says. She hands him the Polaroid Sun 600 camera she "borrowed" from Carrie's bag in Boulder. "There're only a couple shots left, but you can probably find more film."

"It's old," Rai says, hefting it in his hand to assess its bulk.

"Doesn't make it bad," says Emmeline. "It's been fun to have, but I think I'm done with it."

"Thanks," he says as he places it on the nightstand.

"Rai, I need you to come with me."

"Why? I can't do anything," he says. He holds up his hands and turns the palms to her as if to show there's no power, no strength in them. "I'm not part of this."

"Everyone is," Emmeline says. "Especially you. You're critical." She smiles again, thinking how Fahima would have gotten this little joke. She has the punch-drunk feeling of having stayed up into the hours when everything is too funny or too sad. Exhaustion amplifies her emotions, and outsized feelings contribute to her exhaustion. Everything is circling, spiraling, coming together at once.

I ACHE IN THE PLACES I USED TO PLAY

◇

The jet engine roar of the Gate means that they communicate in gestures and mouthed words. Ji Yeon is prepared for this, having worked out a complex if idiosyncratic set of signals in her time as head of the Faction. Carrie feels a swell of relief that in being "cured" of the dark voice in their heads, they haven't lost everything. She imagines the worm in her head as a thread with jagged hooks, yanking out every memory in its proximity as it's removed. Thankfully, that hadn't happened. They were allowed to take what was best from that time and carry it forward as long as they remembered the worst alongside it.

She steps through the Gate into a room where she'd spent her first months at the Bishop Academy. Fahima Deeb's basement lab was one of two places in the school where students were admitted only by invitation; the other was the headmaster's quarters on the thirteenth floor, which was seen only by Kevin Bishop's favorites. The lab hosted the misfits and freaks, people like Carrie whose abilities threatened to harm themselves or others. Fahima worked one on one with Carrie because when Carrie first resonated, she was invisible by default. Fahima compared it to a muscle always tensing. *Those are the knots they knead out of you in a massage,* she said. *We've got to figure out how you can let go and not disappear.* She helped Carrie so she no longer disappeared when she slept or when she forgot to concentrate on being *there.* Carrie's feelings about this room are mixed. She got attention here when she was a kid, something she'd struggled to get from her own parents, but her sessions had been intense and full of failure. Sometimes she had wondered if disappearing wouldn't be better.

She turns back and looks through the Gate. The others hesitate before coming through. She wants to explain the way Emmeline is staging this moment. She wants to tell them about the chessboards in the room in Boulder and how Emmeline made it look as if she were losing on two boards while she rushed to victory on a third. She wants them to understand that the schools linked by the Gates are one school. By stepping across, they aren't leaving the school in Chicago but moving to another room in a massive, multifaceted structure. The mechanism of the Gate is too loud to tell them anything but the simplest sentiments, and so Carrie plants her feet and points to the ground. "We fight here," she shouts, overemphasizing each word so they'll be able to read her lips.

Hayden comes through first, followed by Clay. Confident that the rest will follow, Carrie turns toward the elevator. Clay, Hayden, and Ji Yeon step in with her.

"I've got the clearance codes for the upper floors," Ji Yeon says as the doors shut. She steps over to enter a key code, but Carrie holds her off.

"They'll be sending agents from all over," Carrie says. "We need a rear guard."

"What, the kids?" Hayden asks.

"We were kids when we fought," Carrie says.

"I've seen these kids," Ji Yeon says. "They're not ready for this."

"Nobody's ever ready." Carrie presses the button for the first floor and is thrown off when the elevator shoots upward. "They fixed it," she says to Hayden. "Remember how slow it used to be?"

"Slow enough Doug Collins once got to second with me on the way up to the tenth-floor dorms," Hayden says.

Carrie makes a face like she's swallowed a snail. "Lame Doug?"

"I was on so much ecstasy," Hayden says, rolling their eyes.

"How were we even friends?" Carrie asks.

"Because you loved me," Hayden says, flipping their hair glamorously. Carrie wonders if she loved Hayden like that back then and decides she didn't. It's silly to think that love is an eternal, static thing you find and keep like a treasure. It's something you build, something you maintain.

The doors open on the lobby, and Shen stands in a wrestler's ready stance, puffed up so the top of his head scrapes the ceiling tiles. Behind him are four Faction agents, equally at the ready. A glowing spear lights up in Ji Yeon's hand.

"Faction, stand down," she says. "That's an order."

"We're done taking orders," one of them says. Carrie recognizes him as Nolan Emerson, one of the kids they graduated from Bishop with. "We know what you put in our heads. Now that it's gone, we're—"

"He did it to me, too," says Ji Yeon.

Carrie taps her temple. "He's not in here," she says.

"I never joined your Junior Fascist League to begin with," Hayden says.

Shen sighs, and as he does, he diminishes to his normal size, still fairly huge. "I'm sorry," he says. "It's wonderful to see you, but you picked a real bad time."

"You remember us?" Carrie asks.

"I remember all my students," he says. He blushes and scuffs his shoe like a gigantic child. "I'm a big fan of your records, Hayden. I tell everyone, 'I knew them when they were a kid.' "

"Thanks, big man," Hayden says.

"What's the status here?" Ji Yeon asks Nolan.

"Confused," he says. "Something happened, like a wave. There was a surge, and then the voice in my head was gone."

"Emmeline," Carrie says. It feels like faith rewarded even if it only means the first trick has been pulled off.

"Where's your fifth?" Ji Yeon asks. Nolan points to the fountain in the center of the lobby. A man's body is slumped over the edge, facedown in the water.

"Whatever happened to us didn't happen to him," Nolan says. "He came at us rabid, thrashing. Florence overpowered him. She didn't mean to kill him. He wouldn't stop."

"It's okay," says Ji Yeon.

"I'm remembering things I did," Nolan says. "We were in the Bronx yesterday. We were—"

"That wasn't you," Carrie says, but there's no conviction in her words. She wants to exonerate herself from everything she's done, but when she remembers things, it's not as if she was manipulated like a puppet but goaded, cartoon devils on each shoulder affirming dark, cruel thoughts that were ultimately her own.

THE BISHOP LOBBY

◇

Clay remembers days of nothing but fighting, hours dragging on in a slurry of pain and hate. It's strange to be back with Carrie; he'd counted her among his dead. He hadn't made time to mourn her after Houston, and by the time the war was over, grief was too big to attach to any one lost person. Clay remembers how she became the leader of their Bloom despite being the youngest of the five. She saw the whole field. She moved with sureness and the grace of a dancer. People followed her without being asked, without realizing they were being led. Ji Yeon barks orders like she's in a World War II movie, but Carrie's the one they listen to. When she told the civilians in Chicago to march through the Gate, leaving the ground they had secured to join a fight elsewhere, no one questioned her. When she tells a Bloom of Faction agents to hold the door of the Bishop lobby, they obey.

"You think there's incoming?" Ji Yeon asks.

"What would you do if you saw a Gate breach in this building?" Carrie asks.

"Send everyone," Ji Yeon admits.

"Four out of these five got their heads clear," Carrie says, pointing to Nolan and his Bloom. "It's only luck all four jumped sides when they got the choice. Half the Faction agents in New York are going to be fighting the other half to get here."

"It's going to be war again," says Shen.

"I don't think it will," Carrie says.

"You weren't here," he says. "Our students—*my* students—died in the lobby. I made myself as big as I could until my bones strained under their own weight, and I couldn't save them all."

"Can you send the kids to their rooms?" Ji Yeon asks. "Put them on lockdown or something?"

"We tell them what's coming," Carrie says. "If they want to hide, they hide. If they want to fight, they fight."

"They're children," Shen says. "It's my job to keep them safe."

"Nowhere's safe today," Clay says. He thinks about Rai and Dom. He sent them back to the house before he went into the megachurch, but the Faction agents in Chicago there haven't had their heads cleared. They're still puppets.

Shen walks slowly to his desk and picks up the phone. He dials three numbers, and speakers in the upper corners of the lobby hum to life. "Attention, students," he says. His voice booms through the public address system but sounds broken and small. He takes a deep breath, but it's evident he can't go on. Carrie puts her hand over his and takes the phone.

"Students," she says. "My name is Carrie Norris. I'm a graduate of the Bishop Academy, a long time ago. The school is under attack. The Black Rose Faction has been compromised. Some of them intend to hurt you, and they are on their way here. We can't keep you safe. That sucks, but it's true. You can lock your doors and hope for the best, or you can join us and fight. All we can give you now is a choice."

Carrie closes her eyes and hangs up the phone.

"Okay," she says. "Let's go up."

"I'm staying here," Clay says. "My ability's more practical for holding ground than taking it."

"I was planning on having you with me," Carrie says.

"You know I'm right," Clay says.

"Of course you're right," she says. "I wish you were coming up, too."

She puts her hand out, and, rolling his eyes, Clay drags her into a hug. He extends his ability around them so this second stretches out.

"I don't understand what we're doing here," he says. "I can't see the win."

"We live through it; that's the win," Carrie says. "We get to go back to our people and stop doing this shit all the time."

"You see you've got people to get back to now," he says.

"I've got a whole future I'm thinking about," Carrie says.

"Starts tomorrow," he says. He brings time back up to speed, and Carrie, Ji Yeon, and Hayden take off toward the stairs. When they open the utility door, a flood of students spills out.

"What can we do?" asks a girl who must be younger than Rai. Luminescent energy swirls around her hands.

"Ask him," Carrie says as she squeezes by them into the stairwell.

Clay looks around, hoping she's talking about someone else, but everyone is looking at him.

"Okay," he says. "We're holding the door."

As Clay assigns them positions and jobs according to ability and skill, he thinks about what Nolan said, how the fifth agent in their Bloom hadn't been affected the way they were, how he went rabid when he realized they were no longer all on the same page. They'll need to be ready for an army of Faction agents foaming at the mouth. If Glover is not just influencing but controlling all of them, he might push everyone's rage buttons and point them at the school rather than coordinate and pilot hundreds of bodies. Clay stations fliers at the high windows of the room and rows of kids behind him on the revolving door, with Shen standing in front of them, big enough to block them all. If a wave of Faction decides to take down the whole wall, there's nothing any of them can do.

It's a relief when he sees them show up on Lexington, moving normally, not shambling like a zombie horde. The first few look like they've come from a fight. *Somebody got shots in before they were taken out,* Clay thinks. *Sometimes that's the best option you get.*

"I've got visual," he shouts. "Four I can see, but that doesn't mean there aren't more. Everybody ready?"

His answer is silence. These kids are scared shitless. Their brave moment was walking out of their dorms when Carrie gave the call; everything past that is a consequence of that choice.

An agent spots him through the door, and the other three turn as one. Clay steps into a quadrant of the revolving door as the agents make a rush for the building. With a wider view of the street, he sees ten, eleven more approaching. The first agent crams his body into the quadrant opposite Clay, and Clay slams on the brakes, bringing time inside this circle to a halt. The fire of anger on the agent's face goes out—he looks confused, a sleepwalker awakened.

"Listen to me," Clay says. "I can only hold us here for a while, and as soon as time speeds up again, he's going to be back in your head. Do you understand me?"

"Please help me," the agent says. "I don't want to do this. The voice got so loud. He made me hurt my friends."

"I know," Clay says. "And in a minute he's going to try to make you hurt me. Probably one of us is going to die. But we can hang out in this moment and be ourselves. My name's Clay. What's yours?"

The agent panics, unable to remember his own name. "Vince," he says suddenly. He gasps for air. "My name's Vince."

"That's good, Vince," says Clay. "Let me ask you: you have kids?"

Vince shakes his head. "They don't like us to have kids," he says. "It's not forbidden, but I don't know anybody who does."

"Well, now you know me, and I've got a son who's fourteen," Clay says. Behind Vince, the other agents approach, moving as if through a clear and viscous liquid. "If I hadn't been in the Faction, I wouldn't have him. That's weird, right?"

Vince doesn't seem to know how to respond to this. "Yeah?" he says after a pause. He sounds like Rai when he isn't sure whether Clay's asking him an actual question or a rhetorical one. Distracted by the memory, Clay's ability slips and time within the revolving door comes closer to the pace of time around it. In that moment Clay sees all of Lexington Avenue fall into shadow, as if a dense cloud is passing over. The agents look up, and their faces show horror. Vince spins around, and, distorted by the slowing of time like a record with a thumb rested on its edge, the sounds of their screaming enter the revolving door.

Clay lets his grip on time go, ready for Vince to come at him as soon as he does, but Vince and Clay are transfixed as a ten-story building drops out of the sky and onto the hotel across the street. The building teeters like a drunk, then falls toward the Bishop Academy. Clay wants to warn the others in the lobby, but there's no time. He braces himself in the doorway as the top of the building slams into the middle of the Bishop building like one domino falling against another.

Out in the street, it rains shards of black glass.

LET ME TAKE MY CHANCES
ON THE WALL OF DEATH

◇

The stairwell shudders like a shivering spine as Carrie leads Hayden, Ji Yeon, and an indeterminate number of Bishop students up to the thirteenth floor.

"What the fuck was that?" Hayden asks.

"Something hit the building," Ji Yeon says. "Sounded close."

Carrie realizes the error she's made. She was trained to fight normal people who came at her with two feet on the ground. She asked Clay to hold the front door, but why would she assume anyone would use the door?

"Wait here," she calls down, knowing from the clamor of the kids that none of them are going to listen. They're caught up in the field trip quality of all this. They've picked up more recruits on every floor, kids coming out of their dorms ready to storm the castle. Carrie considers the possibility that she's leading them to their deaths.

Carrie throws her ability over Hayden and Ji Yeon. The throng of kids holds in the stairwell, but they won't wait long. Carrie and the others climb the rest of this flight of stairs, then step through the utility door on the thirteenth floor into the short hallway between the elevator and the entrance to the headmaster's quarters.

"You ever get to come up here?" Hayden asks her.

"Headmaster Bishop couldn't stand me," she says. She tries the doorknob and, seeing it's locked, drops to one knee, pulls out her wallet, and extracts a set of thin metal shims. "He said I was his worst headache since Fahima Deeb," she continues as she picks the lock. "Anytime I saw him in the hallway I accosted him about going public."

"Look how well that turned out," Hayden says. The lock gives, and the door pops open. They enter a nice apartment that's been blown up recently. Because Carrie is familiar with bombs and their effects, the first thing she notices is that the damage is blown in rather than out. As she looks for the source, her attention is drawn outside the massive hole in the building's western wall. The view of the street is blocked by another building leaning against the Bishop Academy, its roof smashed into the black glass of the floor above them. Shards of obsidian scatter across the wound in the building's side, and more rain toward the street. The hole in the Bishop building aligns with shattered windows in what Carrie recognizes as the Phoenix school.

Emmeline's face pops into one of the windows on the opposite side of a ten-foot gap. "Some help?" she asks.

A telekinetic student who joined as they passed the tenth-floor dorms volunteers his aid, floating Emmeline across the gap and landing her on the debris-strewn carpet of the headmaster's living room.

"You dropped a building on us?" Hayden asks.

Stepping carefully through the broken glass and bent metal, Emmeline shrugs. "Kimani had to put it down somewhere," she says. "And I can't fold in higher than here while the building's covered in black glass. He doesn't want to let me in. This seemed like the best solution."

"So you huffed and you puffed," Carrie says.

"It's a little dramatic," says Hayden.

"I thought you'd like it," Emmeline says.

"Now can you get us up to the top floor?" Ji Yeon asks.

Emmeline shakes her head. "The glass is cracked, but everything above is still his," she says. "I won't be much use until the top. I need you to get me up there."

"What happens when we get you to the top?" asks Carrie.

"Everything comes together," Emmeline says. Carrie looks over Emmeline's shoulder at the Phoenix building and sees Rai through the window, bracing himself against a door, watching them.

On each of the office floors above the thirteenth, Faction agents fight one another, a snake with two heads, each snapping at the other. Carrie makes quick assessments. If it seems like the bad side's winning, she has Viola weld the edges of the door shut. If the good guys have a chance, she dispatches students to their aid. It's terrifying how easily the kids follow her orders. Every flight they go up, she's leaving the place she knows. Since she stepped into the building, the thing in her head she thought Emmeline killed has itched. It's not moving or whispering to her, but it tingles unpleasantly. She wishes she could pop her head open and claw it out.

With Emmeline in the lead, they step out at the top floor. There's a door made of black glass, bigger than it needs to be, slightly ajar. Emmeline takes both of Viola's hands in her own.

"Seal it up behind us," Emmeline says. "No one else comes in."

"What about me?" Viola asks.

"You don't need to see what's in there," Emmeline says. "Seal the door and head downstairs."

Viola nods, then shakes her head. "I'll wait here to let you out," she says. "After you win." Emmeline hugs her tightly, then pushes the door open. Carrie, Hayden, and Ji Yeon follow her inside.

The room feels like a church with its cathedral ceiling and its vast space, but the moment Viola seals the door, it becomes claustrophobic. The carpet is damp and spongy underfoot, and the entire room is wallpapered in an unpleasant peach, including the vaulted ceiling. Carrie tries to pinpoint what's making her uncomfortable, but all she can think is that the walls are breathing.

In the corner of the room, a thin wisp of a woman with matted blond hair stands with her back to them. She looks like the ghost of Sarah Davenport come back to haunt the school. She's talking with someone tied to a chair. Carrie recognizes him as one of the Omars, his eyes staring vacantly at the ceiling, his mouth agape.

A stalagmite of flesh rises out of the floor in front of them and shapes itself into something vaguely human. Legs separate from each other, arms drip from a torso, and a head inflates on the stump of a neck like a soap bubble blown through a straw. Its features resolve into the pinched patrician face of Patrick Davenport with his sweep of blond bangs. The flesh around the body darkens to give the impression of clothes or at least a sense of modesty.

"Emmeline, it's so good to see you," he says. "I was gone most of the time you were here at Bishop, but I knew your—"

"Stop that," Emmeline says. Emmeline is trying to sound commanding, but she sounds like a scared teenager. Patrick grins, and the grin widens into a painful rictus before it bisects his entire face. The top half of his head hinges back like some horrific toy as his body melts back into the floor. Tendrils wind through the air and twine together in the vacated space. The same process of resolution takes place, but it begins with a suit, perfectly tailored like something out of an old movie. Hands emerge from the cuffs, and a head, fully formed, rises from the collar, a man with classically handsome features, dark hair, and deep-set eyes. He gives Emmeline a tired smirk.

"You're too late," says Raymond Glover. Carrie recognizes his voice: she heard it in her head for years. "Also too late to interfere. I understand how you thought this was going to go, but let me show you what's going to happen."

Carrie feels it first on her ankle, then snaking up her leg. Dark tentacles of flesh wrap around Ji Yeon's waist, Hayden's neck. Carrie's leg itches along the calf. She pulls the knife out of the back of her belt and stabs it into the tentacle, which lashes out, slashing across her cheekbone and brow, leaving a deep cut that narrowly misses her eye. She drops the knife and puts her hand to her bloodied face as another tentacle bats the knife out of her reach. She looks down to find it and sees that the tendril isn't moving. It's encased in the shimmering sheath of Clay's deployed ability. She's never seen him use it so precisely, wrapping a bubble of slow time around the winding tentacle, around each of the tentacles that have moved to grip their friends.

"Lobby's secure," he says. "The kid out front let me in." His teeth are clenched, and his eyes are deep hollows.

"No," says Emmeline, as if someone ruined her tea party. "You were supposed to stay downstairs."

"I thought you could use the help," Clay says. Carrie extracts her leg from Glover's grasp, and the others extricate themselves as well.

"You've improved, Clay," Glover says. "I bet given time you could have gotten the Chair to work for you. But how long do you think you can fight me?"

"He's not the one who's going to fight you," Emmeline says. She takes Hayden's hand and walks across the floor of flesh that writhes and snaps at their ankles. Clay is in agony trying to hold Glover down while Carrie struggles to stay in place. Her part now is to let

Hayden go. Sarah Davenport raises her head as Hayden and Emmeline approach. Hayden grows taller and thinner. Their features shift until they are a better, truer replica of Patrick Davenport than the poor puppet Glover assembled.

"Sarah," Emmeline says softly. "I brought someone to see you."

"Patrick," says Sarah. "I thought you were gone."

"I'm here," Hayden says, their voice deep.

"Get away from her," Glover snaps. A wave of flesh surges toward the three of them, but Clay slows it.

"I'm trying to take control, but I can't remember myself," Hayden said to Sarah. "If I had some piece of myself to hold on to, I could fight."

"I remember you," Sarah says. She places her hand against the wall, and Raymond Glover screams. The body he assembled out of Patrick's flesh quivers and loses its edges, reduced to a thrashing mass.

"There you are," Sarah says. Her eyes drift closed. "You're hurting so much."

"I tried to be stronger than him, but I couldn't," says Patrick's voice, wheezing out of nowhere. It's raspy, barely a whisper, but Carrie recognizes it from her time at Bishop. She remembers Patrick doling out barbed reprimands and occasional praise when she managed to best one of the lunkhead physical kids who populated his classes. He and his sister were so different but so similar in withholding compliments until students got off on them like a drug fix. She should have known it wasn't Patrick who came to recruit her after Topaz Lake. He was effusive in his compliments. Patrick Davenport was never like that.

"Sarah can you see it?" he says. "He found me when I was little. The first time I went in the Hive. The only time I went in without you. He was a little light that spoke to me before any of the others could see me. He said his name was Raygun."

"Your friend," Sarah says. "You said he was your friend. I remember. I kept everything I could. I tried to keep everything about you in my head. I tried to hold on to you."

"Sarah, I—"

"Let me give it all back," she says.

The flesh that coats the walls and floors shudders like a sail filling with air. A pool of it collects and swirls near Sarah's feet, and Patrick's body, naked but solid, its edges clearly defined, rises up from it. Sarah grabs him and pulls him to her.

"I did so many bad things," he says. "And he's not done. I can still hear him. I can't win, Sarah. I'm not strong enough."

She puts a finger to his lips, and he quiets. "Do you remember the thing I taught you?"

"I don't know where he starts and I end," Patrick says. "I tried to think of the flame like you said, but—"

"Patrick, I kept a secret," Sarah whispers. "I taught them about the flame, but I made them think it was only a little light. It's much bigger than that. Patrick, do you want to see how it burns? It burns everything away until it's clean."

"Please, Sarah," Patrick says.

"You and me, then," she says. She pulls him in, and although he's taller, she rests his head on her shoulder. The room shudders, trying to tear itself apart. Carrie feels Sarah's ability radiating out, a heat that is almost like love. It grows stronger until it's unbearable, the all-obliterating love Carrie felt as a teenager, and she knows she's experiencing the edge of it, a contact high. She can't imagine what it must be like on the inside, the positive feedback loop between Sarah and Patrick Davenport as they restore each other, each bringing the other back enough so that finally they can both let go.

The room holds its breath, then releases it one last time. Sarah's empty body falls to the floor, and Patrick collapses in a heap.

Hayden, wearing their own face again, looks around the room before turning to Emmeline. "Was that it?"

"No," Emmeline says. "The next part is worse." She calls to Carrie. "Can you hold me up?" Carrie rushes over and takes her arm at the elbow. "This will only take a second." Emmeline's body goes limp, and Carrie thinks she's gone, like Sarah and Patrick. She tries shaking Emmeline awake when she feels the floor underfoot shift.

"Did you—" Hayden says, but before they can finish their thought, a tendril emerges from the wall and flails at Ji Yeon, batting her across the room.

"Emmeline," Carrie yells into the girl's face. "What do we do?" Then she hears Emmeline's voice, through the Hive, whisper: *now*.

SIN EATER

◇

An ability is like any other talent: it needs to be developed and practiced. One thing Fahima finds impressive about Ruth is not the Craft that emerges from her body but her skill in using it: the Craft is her ability, and flight is her skill.

Fahima's ability is twofold: she can imagine mechanics, dream impossible machines, but she also *hears* machines expressing themselves in strange emotional aggregates. It's the part of her ability that overwhelmed her and landed her in the mental institution where Bishop found her. It's the part she never bothered to practice or develop. Sitting at the terminal for Lab Bay Theta, she wishes she'd practiced more. The back door works fine, but a better version of Fahima could communicate with the system and get it to do what she needs it to do without intermediary coding.

"You should probably do that faster," Ruth says. She keeps watch at the farthest point in the arc of the hallway where she can see Fahima.

"I hadn't thought of that," Fahima calls back. "Thanks so fucking much."

"I don't want to die here," Ruth says, "and the longer we're here, the more likely that seems."

"Then go," Fahima snaps. "Fly far away and come back when it's over."

Ruth looks at her, hurt.

"I'm serious," Fahima says. "Go. Get safe. There's no point in the two of us getting killed."

"How would you get out?"

"I wouldn't," says Fahima. "Which is the way it ought to go. All of this is my fault."

"It's not."

Fahima wishes she had time to lay out for Ruth all the fuckups that led them to this and point out how each is marked with her initials. She can't spare the mental effort—it's more important to persuade the system to fire all the Chairs simultaneously.

"I'm not going," says Ruth.

"I know," Fahima says. "Thank you."

"Just, faster maybe," Ruth mutters.

The Chair in La Paz is being particularly difficult. Cedric delegated more than Fahima, which was smart in terms of speed, but produced incompatible protocols. In most circumstances, it wouldn't matter—the Chairs were independent and didn't need to communicate—but it makes Fahima's task difficult. She hears the system pointing her toward a hack, when the entrance to the project's wing hisses open and a bullet whines by her head, shattering the glass of the lab bay. Ruth runs from the other direction and skids to a stop behind Fahima.

"Did you think I wouldn't see you scurrying around in our system?" Cedric says. "Did you think you were that much smarter that you could take control and I wouldn't know?"

"If you were smarter than me, you would've shut me out instead of blundering in here with your shitty aim," Fahima says. "But you're not smart, Cedric. You're a vicious little shit who stole every idea he's ever had."

"Seven years and you couldn't create another Pulse," he says. "It took me weeks."

"All you had was a willingness to let people die," Fahima says.

"I had *courage*," he says. "I had *balls*."

"If you had balls, you'd shoot me instead of shouting."

"I'm not going to kill you," Cedric says. "Not until I take all those original ideas out of your head." The gun shakes at his hip as he steps toward Fahima. He reaches out his empty hand like he's about to pat her on the head.

"Don't touch her," Ruth shouts. Cedric turns the gun on her and takes another step toward Fahima. He puts his hand on Fahima's forehead, and she feels him scrabbling in her brain like a rat looking for meat. She tries to summon up the white flame meditation Sarah taught her, but the scrape of his mind against her thoughts makes it impossible. She remembers the other way to get someone the fuck out of your head. *Clumsy*, according to Sarah. *Dirty pool*, Bishop used to say. *But sometimes the best tool is the one at hand*. Fahima takes the burning feeling of every mistake she's made, the names of everyone who died on her watch or by her hand, and shoves it all at Cedric, pushing it to the front of her brain where he's foraging for precious things. In his idiot hunger, he gobbles it up, taking it from her in one massive gulp. She feels his attention shift to other bits of her, things that matter, things she loves. She threw everything awful in her at him, and it wasn't enough. Now it's gone.

"I said don't touch her," Ruth shouts. The Craft emerges from her midsection as an amorphous and transparent blob and takes on a clamshell shape as he fires a shot at her. The bullet glances off and embeds itself in the metal of one of the other terminals. With a twitch of her head, Ruth sends the Craft flying at him. Its transparency allows them both to see the look of shock on Cedric's face as he's borne backward, speeding across the room and smashing against the wall with a wet crunch.

Ruth calls the Craft back. With hitched breaths, she pulls it into herself, sloughing off blood and viscera as it goes, leaving them to spatter on the floor in front of her.

"Holy fuck," Fahima says, transfixed by the sight of Cedric's broken body. Ruth grabs her by her chin, turning Fahima's face toward her own.

"Fahima, it's me, Ruth." She looks into Fahima's eyes as if she's trying to read something off the back of her skull. "Do you remember me? Please tell me he didn't take us."

Fahima smiles. "The things he took . . . I think they were bad. I think they were things I didn't want."

"Oh, thank God," Ruth says. She kisses Fahima on the lips, on the cheeks, over and over like a too-affectionate auntie, but Fahima basks in it for as long as she can before she remembers what she has to do.

"I need to finish," Fahima says.

"I need to sit over here and have a heart attack," Ruth says. She slumps into a chair, her head hanging back, eyes toward the ceiling, and lets out a long sigh.

As Fahima sits back at the console, she hears rumblings from the system more clearly. It's not that they've gotten louder, but a filter in her head has been removed, as if she's taken out earplugs and hears the whole of the world for the first time.

"There it is," she says. The hack shows itself, tying all the Chairs together, tethering them to the keyboard in front of her. *One but-*

ton to rule them all, she thinks. Before she has a chance to tell Ruth she's done it, she feels a violent tug down, into the Hive.

Now, says Emmeline's voice before Fahima bounces back up into her body.

"Okay," Fahima says. She rests her middle finger on the Y key. "Now."

THIRTY-FIRST FLOOR

◇

Clay is losing his grip. The thing he's holding at bay writhes and seethes against the membrane of his ability; it pushes at him from a thousand directions and grows new arms to grab at him. Something warm like skin brushes his belly under his shirt, and he wraps it in a bubble of slow time and spins his body away.

The wave of flesh he'd held back crashes onto Emmeline and Hayden, enveloping them, and Carrie screams as she leaps onto the mound, hacking at it with her knife, calling Hayden's name. A blue light streaks across the room as a yard-long spike pierces the flesh, and the room shrieks as a hole opens up, with Hayden and Emmeline emerging from it, gasping for air.

Ji Yeon launches two more spikes into shapes extending from the wall, and Clay casts bubbles of slow time into the mass of the thing, hoping to find a nerve center. The thing thrashes and convulses. It doesn't seem like a result of anything Clay or Ji Yeon has done, but the entire room is spasming. Faces appear on the wall and sink back into it, screaming masks pressed through flesh-colored latex. The membrane tears, a sound Clay remembers from the war, the sound of skin being sundered. Each hole, each tear, is a mouth, screaming.

"The body's dying," Emmeline says. "He needed Patrick to hold it together, and Patrick's gone."

"He beat you, asshole," Hayden yells at the ceiling. "Crawl back into your fucking hole and die."

"Glover's not dead," Emmeline says. "There's one more place you can go, isn't there, Raymond?"

As the face disappears and reappears, the tears are left behind, multiplying until every wall is covered in wounds, the surfaces stabbed again and again from somewhere, rent but refusing to bleed. Swaths and hunks fall from the ceiling and land with wet thuds. Sheets of flesh peel off the walls. It is almost over before Clay can comprehend what he's seeing: it's Raymond Glover vacating Patrick's body. One last scream and the curtain of flesh that covers the wall of windows rips down its middle, parting like the Red Sea and sloughing into the corners of the room. The sickly light of evening in Manhattan illuminates a bloodless abattoir: piles of flesh shudder like gelatin as Glover gives them up. The stench of putrescence, spoiled but sweet, fills the room.

A wave of nausea passes through Clay, a gag reflex that has nothing to do with the smell. The feeling isn't based in his stomach. He can feel it at the center of his skull.

"There's something in my head," he says. He can tell from Carrie's face and Ji Yeon's that they feel it, too. But Hayden has the same look, and they were never Faction.

"It's something else," Carrie says. "Oh, God, it's my whole head."

"My mind is a clean white flame," Hayden screams. "Carrie, do it! My mind is a clean white flame." Hayden repeats the mantra, but by the third time it's the babble of a child, empty syllables without meaning.

"I'm sorry," Emmeline says.

Clay feels it expanding out from the place where his ability resides, the beautiful bit. It's not the same as when they put the thing in his head. This is radiating outward, a tone that becomes deeper and higher at the same time. Clay thinks of Rai's concert, the choral voices blending into something beautiful. This is the opposite, one tone becoming many, discordant. Rai and the chorus filled him up, but this empties him out, vibrating everything in him the way you shake a sieve, only everything in him is falling through itself. Rai and Dom and everything he cares about fade behind an all-encompassing dissonance.

ON OPPOSITION

◇

Emmeline knew she'd reach this point and that from here she'd be unable to look back. It wasn't clear that she'd be walking away from her friends as they screamed for help. With the sound of their pain vibrating in her heart, Emmeline draws herself up. She wipes away the trickle from her nostrils, streaking her sleeve salmon pink with the mixture of blood and whatever powers her ability, the way the Source looks when she pulls too much power into the real world. Emmeline falls into the Hive, leaving her body unsure if it'll be viable when and if she tries to come back.

She's relieved that the first part of the plan worked, although the results are terrifying. As Pulses fire all over the world, the Hive is riddled with routes to the Source in which Glover was trapped. With no body to inhabit and all those paths of egress, he achieved what he had been trying to do since the idea of him crawled into Patrick Davenport's head. Raymond Glover *is* the Hive. He animates every bit of its strange matter. From here, taking over the minds of every Resonant in the real world is a slow process of infil-tration. He's seeping through into them, his consciousness mani-fold, an end point of the omnipathic abilities he and Kevin Bishop had been imbued with in their genesis moment. When he was alive, with his ability radiating out from the tiny sea horse–shaped structure in his brain that resonated with the Source, Glover could control anyone, a few at a time. Inhabiting Patrick's malleable body, he could infect hundreds, transmitting into their heads and tak-ing control when he chose. Bodiless, rooted in the Hive, Raymond Glover can *be* everyone.

Everyone except Emmeline.

As her Hivebody touches the ground, black vines pull back, creating a clear circle for her to land on. She's never been comfort-able here—memories of her first time are of terror and constraint, a hand holding her against her will, keeping her trapped—but she has power in the Hive. She looks at the circle around her feet. She sees it at first as clear, but it's her Hivebody extending and fusing with the space, pushing *him* back. Not all of the Hive is Raymond Glover. This tiny patch, the width of a spotlight's span, is Emme-line. She pushes it outward, making the Hive more her, less him. The entire place rumbles as if it's chuckling, amused by her ef-forts. Something pricks at the edges of who she is, pressing against her. She shoves it back, and the bright circle expands.

"You're more than I expected," says Raymond Glover's voice, booming from everywhere at once. "I thought of you as a tool rather than an opponent."

"I'm not your opponent, and I'm not a tool," Emmeline says. "I'm something else."

"You gave up the game creating so many more of us," he says. "I'm broadcasting myself into all of them like a signal. A bit of me in everyone."

"Is that what this has been about?"

"This is about saving *us* from *them,*" Glover hisses. "Where I was, I could see every possible future. In every one, they kill us. They keep killing us until there are none of them left. I've been there forever, watching the world end. I'm going to stop it. I'm going to save everything."

"You were so scared," Emmeline says. "You saw everything you were afraid of reflected back at you, and you thought it was the world. It was you in the mirror the whole time, and you almost made it happen. The Source is pure potential. The possibility of everything. You imagined a bad ending, and because you were there, soaking in that potential, it happened."

"I stopped it," he says. "There's so few of them now. I only have to hold on a while longer. I'll clean up the ones who are left, and then I'll let go."

"You won't let go," Emmeline says. "I've seen what happens. You grip tighter and tighter until you squeeze out everything that matters. I can't let you."

She pushes again, and the circle of herself expands. Cracks and fissures shoot through the obsidian ground, and Raymond wails in pain. She knows she can't win this way—she's surrounded and so small—but he doesn't know that. She can play off the paranoia of a man who's had nothing to do but think of every way things can end badly.

"I've been watching you this whole time," he says. "I can see you every time you use your ability. You light up everything. A flare, Kevin said. I see how you laid out your pieces across time. Without Patrick's body holding me back, I don't have to fight you here and now, do I?" The Hive rumbles again, bemused. "Emmeline, do you remember the first time you met me?"

"No!" Emmeline screams. She's no actor, but she needs him

to see her as scared and to think he's about to win. She wants him to think he's figured out the one way to beat her and end this.

The Hive goes silent, the thrum of Raymond Glover's presence noticeable by its absence. Emmeline knows where he's gone: right now, years ago, a little girl resonates for the first time. She sees the Hive, a sprawling, shimmering place out of a fantasy novel, and falls toward it slowly, Alice tumbling down the rabbit hole. Something dark, solid where everything else is ephemeral, reaches up and plucks the girl out of the air. It encases her, keeping her from seeing the new world she's found or returning to the world she knows. It tries to push in and crush her. On instinct, she pushes back, holding it at bay, but she isn't strong enough to break out. She won't be for years.

But help is coming.

Emmeline is thinking of time as a canvas spread out in front of her and as a resource slipping away. *Maybe I've lost,* she thinks. *Maybe I changed things and now everyone goes to hell.*

A bright circle appears in front of her. Through it, she sees Kimani's room the way it looked the first time she saw it, when she stepped through a door that wasn't there and toppled out of her normal life into this one. Miquel steps through the portal, followed by Rai and Tuan. Behind them, Emmeline sees Kimani, her face lined with worry. It was a long shot, a theoretical leap she had to hide from Fahima because it would have driven her nuts, but from inside Kimani's room, embedded in Hivespace, Tuan was able to open a physical portal into the Hive and bring Rai in. Tuan and Miquel look pained: being here exposes them directly to Glover's influence, but Miquel connects them to Rai, uninfluenced by Raymond Glover. What Rai thought of as his lack is their asset: it holds them together for the moment.

"Tuan, go," Emmeline says softly. "Go far and don't come back."

"It's going to get worse, isn't it?" he says, tapping his temple. "It's going to hurt."

"It is," she says. "But hopefully not for long."

Tuan steps through the portal and stands next to Kimani, who blows Emmeline a kiss before he seals the portal like a zipper.

"He won't be gone long," Emmeline says. "We need to be ready when he gets back."

She isn't sure she has the strength to finish this. So much of her is elsewhere that there may not be enough of her here. Raymond could see everything she's done, so she had to count on herself to do the final part afterward. Iterations of her exhausted from activating Pulses across the world turn their attention backward. They fold out of the world and arrive at the moment they always come to. They find a little girl trapped in a box of black bone, and they come together to save her. Emmeline isn't there yet, but she will be. She has so much left to do.

She feels a surge of confidence, passed through Miquel and doubled back. It's enough. She expands herself, taking up as much ground as possible. She wants to give Glover less to come back to, although she can't say for certain that it matters. This isn't the battleground; it's the space between. What matters about the Hive is that it isn't here or there.

The ground around them comes alive as Raymond Glover returns, howling, wounded. The entire Hive attends to her again, which is good, which is what she needs. Shielded behind Rai's mind, Miquel is invisible to Raymond. She needs to keep it this way one more moment.

"You think I can't do that?" Glover bellows. "You're teaching me how to beat you. I'm going to catch my breath, and then I'm going to rain down on every moment of your life at once."

Emmeline smiles. Raymond has been thrown out of the Hive in the past, beaten back by a host of future Emmelines, along with

Fahima and Sarah and Patrick and Kevin Bishop. It means Emmeline gets through this. Raymond's already lost but doesn't know it yet.

"You forgot what it is to be a person in the world," Emmeline says. Her voice is small and sad. "What a lack of imagination it takes to be everything when you could be something. Everyone rather than someone."

The Hive around her rears up like a black wave. Before he can move to strike, Miquel grabs hold of her mind and Raymond Glover's all at once. Like pinning a cloud to the ground, he connects them to every Resonant on earth. All their emotions rush through Miquel and into them, and as they do, the Hive becomes not Emmeline and Glover battling for ground but everyone, connected, the way it should have been from the start.

You can't build something like this for *people,* she thinks. *You have to build it* with *them. It has to be theirs.* She feels Raymond Glover's consciousness gripping at the Hive, trying to keep it for himself. Emmeline turns her attention to the Source, the energy that passes from nowhere to somewhere through the Hive. The Pulses have poked millions of new holes in the Hive, each one shining with promise, letting more of the Source through. Buoyed by everyone, drowning in their emotions, she tears the Hive apart. An ocean crashes into an ocean, the Source and the real world swirling into each other. For a second all futures are real. Everything that can happen does. In the face of that, Raymond Glover's nightmares, the apocalypses that held him together, are infinitesimal. There's a piece of him in everyone, but the consciousness those pieces answered to is wiped out in a flood of possibility.

Too big, too abstract, Emmeline is lost. It's the threat of universal connection, the weapon she used against Glover turned back on itself. She loses herself. Glover had his paranoia to cling to, but as Emmeline sublimates into everything, she wonders what she has to tether her thoughts to the world. The Hive comes apart, and infinite lights rise up. Some she knows. Some she loves. Emmeline remembers she has things to do. She has no interest in being everything. She falls back down into herself, into time and the world, waking to what it has become.

AFTERMATH

The Craft speeds them across the East River toward Midtown, and Fahima looks through its transparent bottom onto Manhattan as black glass grafted onto its skyscrapers and towers degrades into ash and drifts down toward the streets like dark snow. She remembers a statue Bishop made a few days before he died, pulling a white opalescent substance he claimed was a physical iteration of where they got their abilities from into the world. He said it would make them all stronger, and it had. When she saw it after he died, it was Swiss-cheesed with holes, like a rotted tooth. If the black glass was the equal and opposite of that substance, an amplifier for what Raymond Glover had become, the fact it's dissolving in front of her means two things. The first is that they've won. The second is that Fahima has so much work to do. For the first time since she started working to improve the city, Fahima feels ready to give it time and space, let it decide what it wants to be. She's thought of the city and the country as mechanisms, but they're organisms, too. Some things you can't build. Some you have to allow to grow.

When the Bishop building comes into view, she doesn't recognize it. Her mind has adapted to seeing it topped with the extra floors, sheathed in black glass, and now she's looking at the bare bones underneath: structural supports, wires and plumbing, the guts of the upper floors' walls. The top of the building, once a jet-black pyramid, is gone, and the top floor, the massive room that housed the nightmare Patrick turned into, is fully exposed to the night air.

As the Craft touches down at one corner, a door made of dark wood appears, freestanding, in the middle of the room, its shape casting a long shadow over piles of what look like sheets of wet leather. The door opens, and Miquel, Rai, and Tuan emerge. Kimani stands in the doorway, taking in the scene. Ruth retracts the Craft into herself and walks with Fahima toward the door.

"Our girl did it," Kimani calls. "I don't know how, but she did."

"Where is she?" Carrie asks. Her face is smeared with blood, and there's a furious line of red across her forehead and cheekbone.

"Honey, come here and let me see that," Hayden says, but Carrie keeps coming toward Fahima.

"Where's Emmeline?" she shouts.

"I don't know," says Fahima.

"We just got here," Ruth says.

Carrie calls for Emmeline into the open air, and seeing she's distracted, Miquel sneaks out of the opening that was once a massive obsidian door. He steps over the body of Viola Wilkerson, crushed between the door and a flood of bodies whose owners now mill in the entryway, dazed, or wander through the opening into the larger room, hoping for answers. Miquel has to press through a throng of students coming up the stairs, and the open space that was Raymond Glover's penthouse fills with curious kids.

At the edge that looks over onto Lexington Avenue, Emmeline Hirsch appears from nowhere. She looks out at the sky, examining it as if something about it might be different. It's off-putting when huge events leave no trace. It seems wrong, as if someone forgot to press a final button. Fahima sees the bodies of Sarah and Omar Six and knows they're not asleep. There are ways bodies can lie sleeping and ways they can't, positions and shapes they can't assume. Losing all interest in Fahima, Carrie joins Emmeline at the edge, with Hayden following. Clay, gripping his skull, sees Rai for the first time and tries to form words.

"Hey, Dad," Rai says. He goes to the edge too. Fahima stands next to him and looks down onto the street. From there she can see the ruin of the Phoenix school propped against the side of the Bishop Academy. Below it, people emerge from the front doors of Bishop, moving through the wreckage of black glass that juts up from the street like teeth. They look up the same way Emmeline searched the sky for a discernible change. Some are bloodied; some wear the armbands of the Black Rose Faction but make idle motions to tear them off, like picking at a scab. They haven't reached the decision yet, but the seed of it is there.

"You broke the Hive," Fahima says.

"It was ours," she says, not turning, speaking with a sureness Fahima has only ever pretended to possess. "It was ours, and I gave it all back."

Fahima looks around her at Patrick's distended, ruined body. "Is he dead?" she asks. "Glover. Is he out there somewhere?"

"He was dead a long time ago," Emmeline says. "But yes, he's gone now."

Fahima closes her eyes. She kneels and lays her hand on the ground, which is still warm. "O Allah, forgive Patrick Davenport," she says. "And elevate his station among those who are guided.

Send him along the path of those who came before and forgive us and him, O Lord of the Worlds. Enlarge for him his grave and shed light upon him in it."

"What's that?" Emmeline asks.

"Dua," Fahima says. "Prayer for the dead."

"It's pretty," says Emmeline.

"Then are we still—" Carrie says. Before Emmeline can answer, Carrie flickers out of visibility and back.

"Everyone is, if they want," she says. "There are no limits now, or at least not any someone else sets."

Next to Emmeline, Rai gasps as his feet leave the ground, his body drifting upward. It isn't possible. Fahima had examined the problem from every angle. There were people who resonated and people who could potentially, but there were also those who couldn't and never would. But here is a boy who couldn't and never would, flying. Emmeline gives Fahima the canny look she's had since she came to the Bishop Academy as a little girl.

"No more us and them," she says. "All us."

EPILOGUE

ON ENDINGS

Everything in nature is perfectly real
including consciousness, there's absolutely
nothing to worry about. Not only have the
chains of the Law been broken, they never
existed; demons never guarded the stars,
the Empire never got started, Eros never
grew a beard.

—HAKIM BEY,
The Temporary Autonomous Zone

For the year after, Emmeline travels. It seems like a thing people do at her age: gap years and backpacking trips through Europe, journeys of reality avoidance passed off as self-discovery. There are ways to stall the onset of responsibility and adulthood in the hope that when she gets to it, it won't be as terrifying.

She goes to Europe and the Great Wall of China. She goes to Tunis and the ruins at Carthage. Kimani told her about Hannibal and the elephants, all the kingdoms of Africa swallowed up by history. She could sit under a spruce tree in the Italian Alps and watch Hannibal lead his elephants up a mountain path. Someday she might.

She finds her friends as they die. It's simple. She spots the moment their Resonance disappears and goes to the time before that, like turning a record a half turn backward to catch the silence between the songs. She's there with each of them at the end as she was for her father, as she couldn't manage to be for her mother.

She's with Miquel, who returns to Manitoba, existing there

alone for three years. He meets a young woman at the little bar in town. She tells him about the child she lost and how her entire life feels haunted in the wake. She tells him how hard she's trying to get *away,* but there is no away. Miquel excuses himself to use the men's room, an outhouse attached to the trailer bar with a couple of bolts, lit up by a work lamp hanging off an extension cord. He slips the shackle off his wrist and places it on the edge of the grimy sink.

When he reenters the bar, he gasps as if he's dived into freezing water even though the bar is warmer than the air outside. Miquel holds his breath as he walks back over to the woman, trying to keep her pain out of him a few more seconds. He sits down, lets the held breath go, and places his hand over hers. Her pain comes at him, an unimaginable wave, and he lets it pour out of her and into him. She looks dazed—there is no way to understand this deep, irrational giving by means of taking. Without another word, Miquel leaves the bar and walks home lit by a waning half-moon. He finds a bottle of pills he stole from a pharmacy in Winnipeg. He swallows them in two handfuls, pausing to smoke a joint to ease the nausea. He lies down on his couch, and Emmeline is there to take his hand and hold it as he falls asleep.

She misses Ruth, lost in a crash over the Urals, moving at her all-time top speed. Emmeline imagines her joyful in her last seconds.

She nearly misses Waylon—he goes so fast, shot in a robbery in the last year of money—but she's with him as he bleeds out on the North Avenue sidewalk. Bryce stays in Chicago but eventually goes north, following Miquel's route and then continuing. Emmeline likes to think of him completing Miquel's journey, finding the north of fables and stories and planting himself there. If he has an end, she never sees it. There are ways to stop without dying.

She's there when Alyssa is unplugged. Having lost Ruth, Fahima refuses to let Alyssa die, and each piece of her body that gives out is replaced with a loving replica until Alyssa tells Fahima she feels like an old car with none of its original parts. Fahima looks into eyes she built for Alyssa, which glisten with saline pumped through artificial ducts. She kisses her and reaches into her chest cavity, where a plastic heart flutters. Fahima can't bring herself to do it. Her finger rests on the switch, her cheek against Alyssa's skinlike cheek. It's Emmeline who presses down on the switch, like turning off a light. Alyssa sees her and whispers *thank you* into Fahima's ear and is gone.

The things Fahima invents to keep Alyssa alive advance medical science a hundred years. Fahima being Fahima, she refuses to give herself the credit she deserves. Emmeline goes to tell her. She smiles at Emmeline when she sees her.

"You look so fucking young," she says.

"I am," Emmeline says. She remembers when she was a student at Bishop, terrified of what she might become. She remembers being in awe of a woman who could imagine anything.

"Miss Deeb?" she says.

"You haven't called me that since you were a kid."

"Fahima," she says. "I want to tell you about the future."

Fahima starts in about paradoxes and continua, and Emmeline grins. It's a song she almost forgot. Fahima exhausts herself with protests, and Emmeline says, "Let me tell you what you've done."

Fahima looks genuinely afraid. Emmeline smiles. "Let me tell you how many you've saved."

Emmeline tells her the numbers, statistics compiled and brought like flowers gathered from a field. By the time she's a century ahead, Fahima understands what it means that Emmeline is telling her these things. She knows the conditions under which Emmeline would risk the paradoxes Fahima warned her about. Emmeline asks if Fahima wants her to stay.

"No," Fahima says. "I've got some things I want to finish up."

Emmeline finds Fahima later, slumped at her desk, a drawing half finished. She looks like she's fallen asleep during a lecture, worn out from a study session the night before. Emmeline whispers the words Fahima said, the ones for Patrick and Sarah and countless others: *O Allah, forgive Fahima Deeb. And elevate her station among those who are guided. Send her along the path of those who came before and forgive us and her, O Lord of the Worlds. Enlarge for her her grave and shed light upon her in it.*

Emmeline visits Kimani often. It's so quiet there.

She finds Dom and Rai with Rai's wife and kids by Clay's bedside. His ability aged him faster each time he used it, so by the time Dom approaches sixty, Clay has seen a century of life. He hangs on to meet his granddaughter. Rai names her Emma. He says a big name like Emmeline is too much for such a small thing to bear. Clay's talked them through everything; they've been ready for this day for years. The baby rests on Rai's shoulder, her big brown eyes fixed on Emmeline, as her grandfather slips away.

She has to go far to find Hayden. They live another hundred years. When she finds them, they're so tired. They founded a school for the arts, had it snaked out from under them by a duplicitous board of directors, and stole it back. They had buried the twins, Lynette and Shane, who will always be the nine-year-olds in the Polaroid, and the twin's children—five of them in all. For all that, they don't look a day past thirty. On tour across Europe and Africa, playing a show near the ruins of Carthage on a makeshift stage, with a full band who they keep calling by the names of old bandmates—Rafa and Kristal and Jerrod long gone—Hayden plays their last show. An electrical surge feeds 440 volts back into their mic during the second encore. Emmeline is there before the roadies.

"So fucking short," Hayden says, lips trembling as their body loses the race to repair itself.

"People talk about this show for a hundred years," Emmeline says. "It'll be mythic." It's true. Emmeline has checked.

"So fucking short," Hayden repeats.

Emmeline looks everywhere to find Carrie's end and never does. She sees Carrie later and later, older and older. She lasts decades after losing Hayden. She goes back to fighting with the weariness of someone returning to a gift they never cared for and the abandon of someone who doesn't care about dying. She isn't always on the right side, but she tries to be. Emmeline looks a hundred, two hundred years to find the moment Carrie's Resonance goes silent, and she can't find it. Finally she gives up. The only thing she can assume is that Carrie never dies.

Emmeline folds back, rejoining the world a year after she left. She takes a train from New York to Chicago. She wants to move on a fixed path through time and space, through the interstitial zones where people are figuring out what the world will be like now. Progress radiates out from the cities, but changes are starting everywhere. People move back into homes they were forced out of, and as the train stops in small towns and villages, there's life there again, if only early stirrings. It's like watching dead leaves in spring twitch with the growth teeming beneath them.

She takes a cab to the house on Jarvis Avenue. It doesn't fly but chugs along Lake Shore Drive, spewing exhaust. People are coming back to Rogers Park and Jarvis Avenue, although she doesn't recognize any of them. The house looks better than the last time she saw it. Her father was never any good at taking care of things and let the place fall apart even before it was abandoned, but Clay and Dom have built it back up. The lawn is trimmed and the stucco scraped away, replaced with bright blue siding that makes the house look like a carved-out piece of the sky. Clay told her she was always welcome, even gave her a new key, but she hadn't come back. She waits across the street, tucked behind a tree, to be sure none of them are home, then unlocks the door and enters. She has the feeling of being inside a museum exhibit dedicated to her own life. She goes upstairs to her old room, where Rai has decorated one wall with flocks of Polaroids arranged in a galaxy swirl: a year's documentation of his life, his friends, his dads, his school. In the center is the picture of the two of them, sitting on this bed, grinning as if everything was wonderful. The camera, passed now from Carrie to Emmeline to Rai, sits on the bedside table next to a stack of spent film.

The other wall is covered in Emmeline's childhood drawings, rescued from the attic. They're illustrations for stories she used to tell herself at night, thinly veiled warnings about what was coming. A tour bus speeding across the desert. The tower seen from Central Park. Teenagers flying over a field while a little girl chases after them. A magical door perched on the top of a hill. Emmeline thinks about the pictures she took with the old Polaroid. The band and the tour bus in the desert. Carrie and Hayden and their beautiful kids. Kimani lying on a couch holding a whole building in her mind. It all turned out so much better and so much worse than she had imagined it or than she'd been able to communicate to herself. Pictures and drawings didn't capture the heart of any of it; they only point her back to the place in her memory where she holds on to the true thing.

She sits on the edge of the bed and folds backward. She isn't sure when she's going to land, but as soon as she gets there, she knows which night she's chosen. The girl stirs in her bed, covers tucked in tight around her. Her mother sealed her up like that on nights she put Emmeline to bed, as if her daughter would float away.

"I was hoping you'd come," the girl says.

"Bad night?" Emmeline asks.

The girl shakes her head. Emmeline hears her curls rustling in the dark.

"Indian food, right?" Emmeline says.

"I had chicken makhani," says the girl.

"You should try the tikka," Emmeline says. "It's spicier."

"I'm not big on spicy."

"Maybe someday." She puts a hand on the bed somewhere short of the girl's shin. It's remarkable how little space she occupies, how tiny she is, like a seed. "A good night, then?" Emmeline asks.

"They were getting along," says the girl. "It felt like the last time they're going to."

Emmeline thinks about the night she played a shepherd in the Christmas pageant at her grandmother's church. She knew how bad things were by then and heard them fighting when they got home. They could act like they were okay, but this night—when they ate takeout on the living room floor and read comic books out loud, and Emmeline went to bed early—this was the last night it had been real.

"Why did we go to bed early?" Emmeline asks. "Why not stay and soak it up?"

The girl takes a deep breath. "Last year Daddy took me to see birds of prey at the library," she says. "There was a youth group from one of the high schools that trained owls and falcons. He thought I might be interested."

"Raptor Club," Emmeline says. The girl always acts as if she doesn't know who Emmeline is. She treats her like a fairy godmother, which makes Emmeline think how in the story, maybe the fairy godmother is Cinderella coming back to save herself. She remembers when her father took her to see the birds but lets the girl tell it.

"There was a girl with a kestrel perched on her wrist," the girl says. "She had thick leather gloves that looked furry. The bird was tiny compared to the others. There were eagles and owls as big as fire hydrants. The girl looked so proud. It must have been the first time she got to show everyone her bird. Her teacher came over and said it was time to put the bird back in the carrier, but the girl didn't listen. The kestrel fidgeted, and I remember looking at its tether and thinking it was long enough to keep it from getting to me. There was danger, but I was safe from it. The girl beamed, looking at everyone but the bird. She held her arm out straight at the shoulder, crooked at the elbow, but it sagged. Her arm dropped, and this little bird flew right across and nipped a bite off her cheek. I saw it in its beak, fresh and bloody. It looked like—"

"A ripe strawberry," Emmeline says. She never told anyone that. The whole summer after, she felt sick whenever she saw a bowl of strawberries, thinking of the hole in that girl's cheek, the hunk of flesh in the kestrel's beak.

"Anything good can bite you if you wait too long," the girl says. It's a strange moral to learn from the incident and not what Emmeline remembers as her takeaway. Her hand finds the girl's ankle under the sheets.

"Maybe it means little things can be dangerous if no one's looking," she says. The girl lays her head back down and pulls the covers up to her neck.

"It's going to get bad soon," she says. She puts it out as a statement in the hope Emmeline will deny it.

"Soon," Emmeline says. "Then good again, then bad again. Same as ever."

"But you'll be there," she says in the same tone, stronger, surer.

"One more time," Emmeline says. "There'll be others to help you. Wonderful people, Emmeline. You're going to care for them so much."

Emmeline stands up and walks to the head of the bed. She holds back her curls with one hand, pushes back the girl's with the other, and bends down to kiss her on the forehead, then on her cheek, which is wet with tears.

"Where are you going?" the girl asks.

Emmeline considers this. She's been to the end, and now she's come to the beginning. It's time for her to go back, to find a way to move through the world. There's only one thing she needs to do first. "Downstairs," Emmeline says. "For a minute."

"Be careful," says the girl. "The fourth step from the top creaks."

"Don't worry," Emmeline says. "They'll never know I'm there." Emmeline hears her parents voices from downstairs, her father laughing at something her mother said. As she opens the door, light from the hallway comes into the room. She can see the girl's face, bound up in the idea of what's possible, the limits of what she's able to do. If there were more time, Emmeline could tell her none of that is true. There aren't rules or limits. There are no impossibilities except the ones they put on themselves.

"See you soon," Emmeline says as she closes the door.

ACKNOWLEDGMENTS

This book is less a sequel to *The Nobody People* and more like its second half. In fact, the scene that originally ended *that* book ended up at around page 183 of this book. It was always one long story in my head, so if these acknowledgments look similar to the ones at the end of the first book, that's the likely reason.

Thank you to my agent, Seth Fishman, for encouraging me to not just dip a toe into science fiction writing but to dive in face-first, and to everyone at the Gernert Company for their advocacy and support.

Thank you to my editor, Sarah Peed at Del Rey, who kept this book from sprawling out endlessly. Especially as we came down the home stretch, she helped the book maintain its grounding in the emotional lives of the characters, even when I was showing more interest in, say, detailing at length how resource economies might work in a post-capitalist America. Thank you to all the folks at Del Rey who made every edition of both these books super good looking and helped get them out into the world

Relatedly: thank you booksellers for putting this book in the hands of readers. I'm wrapping this book up at an extremely weird time, and I hope by the time these particular words are in print, you'll be back at it connecting books and readers.

Thank you to my reading group, Melanie Conroy-Goldman and Jennifer Savran Kelly, for helping see this book through rewrites large and small, even when doing so required charts and spreadsheets and who all knows what.

Finally, thank you to my wife and partner, Heather Furnas, who has put up with me keeping a couple hundred extra people in my head for the last four years. The good news is I'm letting them all go. The bad news is, new folks are moving in, and they might be worse.

BOB PROEHL is the author of *The Nobody People* and *A Hundred Thousand Worlds*, a *Booklist* Best Book of the Year. He has worked as a bookseller and programming director for Buffalo Street Books in Ithaca, New York, a DJ, a record-store owner, and a bartender. He was a New York Foundation for the Arts Fellow in Fiction and a resident at the Saltonstall Arts Colony. His work has appeared in *Salon,* as part of the 33⅓ book series, and in *American Short Fiction.*

Twitter: @bobproehl

ABOUT THE TYPE

This book was set in Garamond, a typeface originally designed by the Parisian type cutter Claude Garamond (c. 1500–61). This version of Garamond was modeled on a 1592 specimen sheet from the Egenolff-Berner foundry, which was produced from types assumed to have been brought to Frankfurt by the punch cutter Jacques Sabon (c. 1520–80).

Claude Garamond's distinguished romans and italics first appeared in *Opera Ciceronis* in 1543–44. The Garamond types are clear, open, and elegant.